Jenna Kernan has penned over two dozen novels and has received two RITA® Award nominations. Jenna is every bit as adventurous as her heroines. Her hobbies include recreational gold prospecting, scuba diving and gem hunting. Jenna grew up in the Catskills and currently lives in the Hudson Valley of New York State with her husband. Follow Jenna on Twitter, @jennakernan, on Facebook or at www.jennakernan.com.

For Jim, always.

HUNTER MOON

BY
JENNA KERNAN

MILLS & BOON

First Published in Great Britain 2016
By Mills & Boon, an imprint of HarperCollins*Publishers*
1 London Bridge Street, London, SE1 9GF

© 2016 Jeannette H. Monaco

ISBN: 978-0-263-91893-9

46-0116

Chapter One

Black Mountain Apache Reservation

Izzie Nosie lay low over the mare's neck hoping to make herself less of a target for whoever was shooting at her.

Damn, this was her land.

What was going on?

Her legs flapped as she kicked her chestnut quarter horse, Biscuit, to greater speeds. Who was up there shooting at her?

She leaned to the right, touching the leather bridle to her horse's strong neck. The signal was received, and Biscuit darted between two pines, jumping the downed log that blocked escape. She knew her pursuers were not on horseback, so she did her best to take the route hardest to maneuver on foot. Still, she couldn't outrun a bullet. The next shot hit the tree to her left, sending shards of bark and splintered wood flying out against her cheek, barely missing her eye. She ignored the sting, focusing on flight.

Just a little farther and she'd be below range. She knew the terrain as well as she knew the layout of her barn. Fifty feet more and she could cut down a sharp hill and be clear. It'd take them a few minutes to reach the embankment for another shot, and she meant to be long gone by then. She

broke from the woods and right into the path of another
gunman. This one was mounted on a tall buckskin.

She drew up short, causing poor Biscuit to rear back
as her mare tried to go from a gallop to a stop and nearly
made it. The rider was Indian, big, lean and aiming a rifle.
She used a trick of her ancestors, throwing her near leg
over the pommel and falling until she lay pressed to Biscuit's opposite side. Her fingers gripped the coarse hair of
her mare's neck, and she squeezed the pommel with her
upper knee to keep from tumbling to the ground.

"Izzie. It's me. Clay Cosen."

She felt her already galloping heart pound painfully
as emotion bled through her. What was Clay doing here?
Was he one of them?

No. Never. But the doubt lifted its head like a rattle-
snake in a bed of bluebonnets. Her mother's words echoed
in her mind.

He's a convicted criminal.

"This way," he called. "I've got a truck."

She hesitated just long enough to cause him to look
back. She saw his face go hard. Somehow he knew at a
glance that she no longer trusted him. His tight, guarded
expression filled her with regrets. So many regrets.

"You coming?"

Emotion paralyzed her, and she lost her balance, slipping from her saddle and tumbling along the ground. The
jolt of pain made her suck wind between her teeth. She
fell, rolling to her feet. Clay was there, rifle gripped in one
hand and the other extended out to her, as he guided his
horse with only the pressure of his legs. She knew the man
could ride. His rodeo titles proved that, and he was a sight
to see approaching at a full gallop. She didn't think. She
just acted, grasping his gloved hand as he charged by and
leaped into the air as he pulled. He swung her up behind

him. His horse never broke stride as he continued on, down the embankment. Behind them one more shot sounded.

Then they were racing over her pasture and down the steep incline. She could not see past his slate-gray cowboy hat and broad shoulders sheathed in a navy blue gingham check. He wore a battered leather vest the color of his horse, work gloves and faded denim jeans over cowboy boots that had seen better days.

Izzie wrapped her arms about his narrow waist and glanced behind them. There came Biscuit, galloping after her mistress. Izzie looked beyond but saw no one step from the cover of the aspen and pines and heard no more gunshots.

Her ears buzzed, and she trembled as the adrenaline ebbed. Izzie gave herself permission to hold him again and pressed a cheek to Clay's back. The horse's breath sounded like a great bellows as they charged on and on through the tall, yellowing grass. She held tight, feeling the taut muscles of his abdomen beneath her splayed fingers. Their bodies moved together with the horse, rocking, and Izzie closed her eyes and savored this moment, because, regardless of the reason, it had brought Clay back into her arms again.

It wasn't until his mount began to slow and Clay's posture became more erect that her mind reengaged.

Why was Clay Cosen here in her pasture? How could she know that he was not with them? But instead of thinking, she had just jumped right into his arms like the damn fool she always was every time she got around this particular man.

Poison, that's what her mother, Carol Nosie, called him. The kind of man to ruin a girl and not just her reputation. Look what Clay's father had done to his poor mother. A cautionary tale of the consequences that came of choosing the wrong kind of man. This one would take everything, her position in the community, her self-respect, her obligations to her family and, most importantly, her heart.

So why did holding him again feel so right?

Izzie's hands slipped from his middle, paused for one instant on his hips and then let go.

Clay twisted and glanced back at her.

"You okay?"

What kind of a question was that? She'd been shot at, lost her seat and then her horse and now sat tucked against his body as if she belonged to him.

"Hell, no, I'm not all right."

Clay made a sound that might have been a laugh. Then he turned the horse, so they could see the way they had come. Biscuit was trailing her at a trot.

"I don't see any sign of them." He glanced back at her, giving her an enticing view of his strong jawline and the slight stubble that already grew there. His russet skin was so beautiful, taut and tanned. Izzie lifted her hand and had it halfway to his cheek when she realized what she was doing and forced it back down.

"Who were they?" asked Clay.

"No idea. I noticed I was missing cattle and thought they got up into the woods. There's another small pasture up in that draw. But the next thing I know, I see someone on foot, and when I called out, the idiot started shooting at me."

"I'd say at least two idiots from the sound of the shots. One was using a semiautomatic weapon."

Her body went cold at that news.

He scowled at her, and still he was a welcome sight. His expression was a mix of concern and aggravation, as if she had intentionally put herself in danger.

Clay had been born a month earlier to the day, but at

twenty-four, she no longer needed him shepherding her, did she?

"You're bleeding," he said and leaned in her direction. She held still as he removed one glove and swiped a thumb gently over the crest of her cheek. She felt the sting of pain, and his fingers came away bloody. He held her chin and tilted her head as if she were a child. Well, they weren't thirteen anymore, and he was not hers. So why was it so hard to draw back?

"It's fine."

Clay motioned with his head. "Let's go."

They rode at a canter across the pasture, and she noted her herd had moved far down field. Good, she thought. Farther away from the bullets. That's all she needed— dead cows. It was hard enough to make ends meet with the water restrictions.

"Why are you here, Cosen?" she asked, refusing herself the intimacy of his first name.

He pointed to a truck parked along her fence line. "Collecting strays."

Clay worked for Dale Donner, the general livestock coordinator. One of their jobs was gathering strays from all reservation highways, which included this out-of-the-way road snaking along her grazing land. But she kept her fences in good repair, mostly because she could not afford to lose any cattle. Yet he was here, working. Her mouth went dry.

"Strays?" she repeated.

Her cattle were the only ones up here, and she was missing more than a few. Izzie had a sick feeling in her stomach.

"You catch any?"

His expression was serious. "Some."

"How many?"

"Izzie, someone just shot at you. I'd feel a whole lot better if we had this conversation out of range and behind cover. I've got room in my trailer for Biscuit."

He remembered the name of her favorite horse. What else did he remember? Their first kiss? The night she let him go a little too far? Or the day she told him she could not see him anymore?

They rode through her downed fence, the wire lying on the ground. She didn't see any cattle on the road, but she swung down to lift the wire.

"It's been cut," she said.

He dismounted, too, glancing back toward the woods, his rifle still out and ready.

"Get behind the trailer."

"The fence," she said.

"The hell with the fence."

"Did you do this?" she asked.

In answer, his color rose and his jaw set. Then he grabbed her with more force than necessary and hustled her over to the horse trailer.

Clay opened the gate and lowered the ramp. She loaded Biscuit and exited the trailer to find his mount tied to the ring on the side of the trailer. She watched him disconnect the trailer hitch.

He jerked his head toward the truck. "Get in, Bella."

He hadn't called her that since her sophomore year in high school on the night she told him she must stop seeing him.

Why, Bella? Why?

Clay rounded the trailer, and she heard the gate shut with a resounding clang.

"I can't leave Biscuit."

Clay took hold of her arm and muscled her along. He was much bigger and stronger than she recalled. He had to release her or the gun to get the door open, and he chose her. He motioned to the interior, and she slipped into the cab. Then he jogged around the front of the grille and slid the rifle into place on the rack behind them.

She caught the movement and shouted.

"There!" she said, pointing.

Someone moved on the top of the tree line. Clay leaped into his seat and started the truck, accelerating into the U-turn and narrowly missing the opposite ditch.

They traveled a half mile down the hill before he lifted the radio from his hip.

"My brothers are coming. Don't want them riding into gunfire."

She nodded her agreement to that. He must mean Gabe and Kino. Gabe was the new chief, and Kino was now a police officer for the tribal police. Izzie had heard that Clay's little brother was about to be married.

Clay called his office, relayed the details and clipped the radio to his belt. He glanced in the side mirror and then back to the road. "Who are they?"

She shook her head. "I don't know. I didn't get a good look." She dabbed at her cheek and winced. The blood was already drying on her face. "Why would men with automatic rifles be sneaking around in those woods?"

"A good question," he said. "What's up there?"

"Just another pasture. Oh, and a road. The tribe just improved it. It's gravel now. They did a really nice job."

"Why would the tribe improve a road going to pastureland?"

Izzie wrinkled her brow as she thought about that. "I don't know."

"It's just an open field?" he asked.

"Well, there's some dry fill up beyond the pasture, some

digging. The tribe uses the dirt to fill holes. Maybe that's why they need the road. To bring in bigger equipment?"

"Maybe."

But he didn't sound convinced, and his tone made her realize she should know what was happening on the land she leased. Izzie needed to get some answers.

Chapter Two

Clay had sworn he'd never be back here.

But here he was, sitting in the police station interview room. The room that he had hoped to never see the inside of again. The very same room where he had been brought in handcuffs. Had it really been eight years? Seemed like yesterday.

Clay felt the sheen of cold sweat cover him, and he tried to tell himself that this was different.

Was it? Or was he in that kind of trouble all over again?

They had met the authorities at the bottom of the pasture. After the tribal police had cleared the scene and found no sign of the gunmen, one of Gabe's officers had taken Clay's rifle, and they had told Izzie that fifty-one of her cows had been impounded for trespass on tribal lands by a representative of the General Livestock Coordinator— in other words, by Clay. After hearing that news, Izzie hadn't spoken to him once on the long drive to the station, and he expected that she'd never speak to him again. That realization was more disturbing than sitting in this damned room again.

But he hadn't done anything wrong. Unless he had. You didn't have to know it to have done it. He'd learned that lesson well enough. Maybe this was just like the last time, only it was Izzie setting him up. Letting the cows out, calling the manager's number, drawing him into a gunfight.

No, that was just crazy, his stupid paranoid fears rearing up like a horse in the shoot at a rodeo. Tighten the cinch. Open the gate. Watch it buck. Eight seconds and all you could do was hold on. Clay held on now. He'd tried to make the right decisions. Tried to think before he acted. Tried not to take everything at face value, not be so gullible. But when he'd seen Izzie running for her life, he hadn't thought about the consequences. He had just ridden full speed into gunfire.

Clay rested his head in his hands and drew a deep breath. He still felt sick to his stomach.

He'd asked Gabe to call his boss and tell him where he was. Clay knew that if there was even a whiff of misdeeds, Donner would fire him. He'd do anything to keep this job. Anything.

He'd been lucky to get hired in the first place—with unemployment so high on the Rez and so many men searching for honest work, men without his priors.

His younger brother, Kino, came in to speak to him. Kino had been on the force about a year, acting as a patrolman. It was something Clay could never be. They didn't take men with criminal records into the police or the FBI, where his uncle Luke Forrest worked. Kino had been surprised that they had let Clay work with the Shadow Wolves on Immigration and Customs Enforcement. But Clay was a special case because he was Native American, which was a requirement, a very good tracker and his conviction was not a felony. Though it nearly had been.

"So, busy day?" asked Kino, taking a seat and opening his laptop.

Clay didn't laugh. The last time he was here, Kino had been thirteen years old.

What was his boss going to say? He'd sent him to clear strays and he'd ended up in jail, again.

"Where's Izzie?"

Kino thumbed over his shoulder. "Captain's office."

"You mean Gabe's office."

"I call him captain here. We only have one interrogation room."

Clay knew that.

"She says you had no right to impound her cattle."

"They were on the road."

"She's claiming that they were released."

"Upper fences were cut," said Clay.

"Yeah, I heard that."

"I *saw* that. Don't know about the lower pasture. I didn't see anything, but I wasn't looking."

"We'll check. You didn't cut them, did you?"

Clay blinked in astonishment, expecting Kino to laugh or smile or say this was some joke. He didn't. He just sat there, waiting.

"No."

"I think all our guys are up in the woods," said Kino. "I'll ask them to run the fence lines."

"They're going to ruin the scene."

"You and I are not the only ones who know how to track, brother."

Clay nodded.

"So you want to do this, or would you prefer one of the other guys handled it?"

"No. Go on."

His kid brother asked the questions, and Clay answered. He'd picked up four truckloads of cattle with Roger Tolino. They'd gotten a second call about cattle on the upper road. He'd sent Roger back with the cattle truck. Clay had found the cut fence after Roger left.

"Clean cut. All three lines, right by the post." Clay had searched the ground. "One man was wearing boots, weight about two-fifty, judging from the depth of the tracks and recovery of the grass inside the tread." He had seen the strays and thought it easier to just steer them back into the pasture. He was just repairing the fences when he'd heard the first shots. "I couldn't call it in because there's no cell service up there." So he'd used his radio. Called Veronica in the office and asked her to call Gabe.

Getting his statement took a while because Kino had to type his replies. Clay waited as Kino pecked away on the laptop, feeling like a damned fool. Eventually, Kino closed the computer and regarded Clay.

"You didn't do anything wrong," said Kino.

"That's what I thought the last time."

Kino nodded. "You really didn't know what they were doing?"

Clay stared at his kid brother in astonishment and then realized they had never spoken of the crime.

"Who?" asked Clay, making sure he wasn't talking about today.

"Martin and Rubin."

"Martin said he wanted some pop. I stopped. They went in. I waited. They came out, and I drove away."

"Just like that. Didn't you see the blood on Martin's shirt?"

Kino stared. Clay knew what he was thinking. His older brother was guilty or he was a fool. Clay never liked the choice. He lowered his head. "Are we finished?"

Kino stood. "Yeah. Sure. So, I'll see you Saturday?"

Clay rose. "Saturday?"

Kino's voice held impatience. "The wedding?"

Clay's mouth dropped open as he realized he'd forgotten. His kid brother was getting married and then honeymooning in the Badlands of South Dakota, so he could pick up the trail of their missing little sister.

"Yeah, of course. Sorry. My mind is just… Like you said, long day."

Kino walked him out.

"Want to go for a beer after work?" asked Clay.

Kino rubbed his neck. "Sorry. Can't. Wedding stuff."

"Oh, right. Well, see you Saturday."

"Don't forget the barbecue. Thursday night. Rehearsal and dinner at Salt River on Friday."

Clay nodded and left the station, shedding the stale heated atmosphere for the crisp air of a perfect September day. Relief poured down on him with the sunshine. He looked to the west, to Black Mountain. Emerald-green Ponderosa pines that were broken by patches of brilliant yellow aspen ringed the base. Nearer the top, forest gave way to the browning grass. The crown looked as if someone had scraped away all vegetation. This was where the reservation got its name, from the dark of the tallest mountain in Arizona. Eleven thousand two hundred and twenty feet. On this cool day, the crown looked black against the bright blue sky, but soon the snow would cover it again. He'd been to the windy peak. All Apache boys climbed it. There, on the top the Crown Spirits lived. *The Gaan*, as his people call them, had been sent by the Creator to teach them to live in harmony.

When Clay told outsiders he was Black Mountain Apache, they assumed he lived in the desert and wore a red head scarf and a long belted shirt. The truth was that he did wear a red kerchief, but about his neck, and his reservation was mountainous with a ski resort in addition to a casino. They had plenty of lakes and some of the best trout fishing and elk hunting anywhere. But mostly what they had was the grassland, and much of it had been broken into permitted grazing areas. Raising cattle was still big business here. Some pastures had been in certain families for generations. Like Isabella Nosie's grazing rights. It had been her grandfather's and her father's—William's—and now it was hers for as long as she kept filling out the application.

Some folks thought that system unfair. That they should have a lottery. Clay had no cattle, so he stayed out of the debate.

He took one final look back at the station. Was she still in there?

Clay had missed Isabella more than he'd ever admit. She came to him in dreams sometimes, and on a good day he might see her in town. He'd caught her looking back at him once, but she never spoke to him. He didn't blame her. Lots of folks looked right through him now. Or they hurried the other way as if he was contagious.

Clay recovered the truck he drove for his job, headed back to the offices and checked in with Dale Donner. Besides managing the communal cattle and horse herds, Donner's offices collected fines, cared for impounded livestock and sold unclaimed stock at auction. That meant showing up in tribal court and dealing with the tribe's various livestock associations over disputes. Donner was also on the tribe's general livestock board, along with Boone Pizzaro, Franklin Soto and two members of the tribal council. Boone Pizarro was the general livestock coordinator, in charge of managing the tribe's cattle holdings including all grazing permits issued to ranchers on the reservation. Franklin Soto oversaw the health of the herds on the Rez and made sure all Black Mountain cattle complied with regulations with the state's livestock sanitary board.

Clay drove the two blocks, parked and entered Donner's office. He felt as if he had been away for a week.

Donner did not glance up as Clay came to a stop before the battered wooden desk littered with piles of paper. His boss was a barrel-chested Apache with dark braided hair that framed a face deeply lined and aged by the sun to the color of a well-oiled saddle. He seemed perpetually impatient with the stupidity of both his cattle and his men. Behind him, various clipboards hung on nails beside a calendar featuring a large longhorn steer's photo. On the lower half of the calendar, Donner had crossed off all the days in the month up to and including today, Monday, September 7.

His boss glanced up, and his flint eyes fixed on Clay.

"We registered fifty-one cows with Nosie's brand," said Donner.

"There were four more, but I shooed them back into their pasture. Mr. Donner, those fences on the upper pasture were cut."

Donner lowered the clipboard. "What do you mean cut?"

"I mean with a wire cutter. Someone came in from the road, parked, cut the fences and left."

"What about the lower pasture?"

"I didn't see anything, but I was pretty busy rounding up cattle."

"Well, heck. We got to call your brother about that."

"Didn't he call you?" Had Gabe forgotten to alert his boss?

"Yup. Said you'd been delayed."

Clay realized Donner didn't know about what happened with Izzie and the shooters. It took several minutes to relate the story, and his boss's mouth hung open for most of it. Clay didn't think he'd ever talked so much in his life. Except that day in court. When he finished, his shoulders sagged.

"Well, a heck of a day." Donner sat back and scratched his head, sending one of his long graying braids wiggling. "I'll call Pizzaro and Bustros. Update them and have them take a look at the fences and the cattle."

Victor Bustros was not technically on the general livestock board, but worked under Pizarro, the livestock coordinator. Bustros's title was livestock brand inspector. Because of the record keeping of individual brands, Bustros had a clerk who helped him keep up with the paperwork. Bustros's job also including overseeing the weekly cattle auctions.

Cattle were still the tribe's main source of income, though tourism was catching up. These four men—Bustros, Pizzaro, Soto and his boss, Donner—held positions of importance in this enterprise overseeing the care, business and health of the tribe's holdings. Clay felt lucky to work with them. Now Clay hoped that his actions today had not jeopardized that.

"Sir, would you like me to have a look at Nosie's lower pasture?"

"Leave that to your brothers. If what you say is true, that might be a crime scene."

If it were true? Clay felt his face heat. Even after six-and-a-half spotless years of work, his boss did not take his word at face value.

If the impounded stock hadn't belonged to Izzie, then Clay would have let it go. But instead, he opened his mouth again.

"Sir, I could…"

Donner's gaze snapped to his, and he gave a slow shake of his head. It was a gesture Clay recognized as a warning. Clay closed his mouth.

"You've done enough."

Clay accepted the long, hard look Donner gave him.

"Finish your paperwork before you leave."

Knowing he'd been dismissed, Clay returned to his desk in the outer office to wake up his ancient computer. An hour later he had his hat back on his head and was leaving for the day.

Clyne and Gabe, his older brothers, still lived in their grandmother Glendora's place. But he and Kino had a small house outside of Black River, one of four towns on the reservation and the one that housed the tribal headquarters. Since Kino and Lea Altaha would like their own place, Clay planned to move back to his grandmother's while they waited for placement. It could take over a year for the newlyweds to get their house through the tribe's housing organization, and Clay recognized that they needed privacy.

Clay climbed into his own truck, which was older, smaller and dustier than the one he used for tribe business. He drove by his grandmother's house, knowing he was always welcome for dinner. But the prospect of telling his story one more time did not appeal, and so he skipped the chance at the best fry bread in Black Mountain in favor of frozen pizza and privacy. Since Kino would be out, there might still be one last beer in the frig.

When he pulled in the driveway, he realized he wasn't getting that pizza or that beer or any peace, because Izzie Nosie stood, leaning against her pickup with her arms folded beneath her beautiful bosom. She looked ready for battle.

She lifted her chin as he stepped out of his truck. Was it only a few hours ago that she had clung to him while they raced together across the wide stretch of open pasture?

"Izzie, what are you doing here?"

"I want to know who let my cows out."

"I'll bet."

"You are the best tracker on this reservation. So I want to hire you, Cosen."

Clay could only imagine how hard it was for her to ask the likes of him for help.

"You might be better to ask Kino or Gabe. They're the investigators."

"And they *are* investigating. But I want someone who is looking out for my interests. That's you."

"That's a conflict of interest, Izzie. Or did you forget that I work for the livestock manager?"

Her eyebrows rose. "Still?"

That stung. "You think he fired me? For what, doing my job?"

She held on to her scowl, but her cheeks flushed a becoming rose. Then she pressed a finger into his chest. "You should have told me that my cows were on the highway, Cosen."

"They pay me to collect them. Not to contact the owners."

"Do you know how much it will cost me to get them out?" She ticked off the amounts on her fingers. "Gathering fee, five dollars a head. That's two-hundred and sixty dollars, and that's only if I can sell some cows and get that money to them in twenty-four hours, which I can't. Then it's two dollars a day per cow for every day you have them. That's a hundred and four dollars more."

"Izzie, your strays were scattered all over the highway."

"Cosen, my fences are good. I need you to help me prove that, so I can appeal."

He leaned against his truck, trying to think, but his eyes kept dipping to her lovely face and those soft lips. Izzie's hair was dark brown, and she often wore it pulled back to reveal her small, perfectly shaped ears and long, slender neck. She knew he liked her hair loose; it was loose now and had been recently combed. She wore pink lip gloss that made her full mouth look ripe and tempting.

Clay frowned.

She lifted her pointed chin, and her fine brows rose. She rested a hand on his chest. His heartbeat accelerated and his skin tingled. He had to force himself not to reach out and gather her in his arms.

He stared down at her hand, fingers splayed across his chest, the left ring finger still somehow bare. Then he followed the slim line of her arm to her narrow shoulders. Her soft hair brushed her collarbone, and she wore no jewelry except the gold crucifix about her neck, the one her father had given her at her first communion. Her face was heart-shaped and her upper lip more full than the bottom, giving the impression that she was forever freshly kissed. Her skin was soft brown, and her eyes sloped downward at the corners. He stared a moment at the light brown eyes that were flecked with gold, but it was like looking at the sun—dangerous and alluring all at once.

He knew what she wanted, and it wasn't him. But his body still remembered her touch. And the memories of her threatened to make him do something stupid, like risk his job for this woman.

"You haven't spoken to me in seven years," he said. "Now you're asking for my help?"

A STAB OF guilt spiked inside Izzie, and she couldn't hold his gaze. He was right. She'd avoided him and the scorn she knew would come by association. This was a small community. A person's place in the tribe depended on many things—character, family and who you chose to love. Loving Clay had cost too much. So she had let him go. Now she wanted a favor. She thought of her two little brothers and stiffened her spine. Then she met the accusation in his gaze.

"I'm asking," she said.

He exhaled loudly through his nose. "Izzie, I need this job. I won't do anything to jeopardize it."

"And I'm not asking you to. Just take a look at the tracks."

He was staring at her again, debating. She saw it now. The anger in his stance and the unwillingness.

"Call Gabe. He's the chief of police."

"I want someone who is working for me—not the tribe. Plus he made it very clear that I'm a suspect in whatever is going on up there."

"You?" He laughed right in her face. The sound was hard. "Isabella Nosie? The girl with all As in high school. The good girl, sings in the choir, took over for her dad, helps raise her brothers and has never made a mistake in her life?"

That was just one step too far. She planted a fist on her hip.

"I made *one*."

His laughter died and their eyes met. She read the hurt in his expression as her words hit their target. They both knew the mistake she meant. She had loved him.

Clay sagged back against the truck bed as if she'd slapped him. Izzie felt terrible.

"I'm sorry, Clay. I didn't mean it." Actually, going out with Clay had been the best thing that ever happened to her. Until she'd let her parents run him off. Why hadn't she stood up for herself?

Because she'd been sixteen with dreams of college and a career, and, after his mom had been killed by that drunk driver, Clay was so angry and reckless, she barely recognized him. Then her father got sick and she'd made that promise. The next thing she knew, she had become responsible for her brothers and mother, and now she might lose it all.

"Will you help me?" she asked.

"No."

"Fine. Then I'll just do it myself."

She turned to go, and he captured her wrist. She paused and he released her.

Clay removed his hat and struck it against his leg. His face went bright, with two streaks of color across his prominent cheekbones. Did that mean he did care what happened to her? Her heart fluttered at the possibility, and she cursed herself for a fool.

Clay regrouped, releasing her as he looked down his broad straight nose at her. He was scowling now and his nostrils flared. He'd never looked more handsome.

Clay didn't wear his hair long, like his brothers Kino and Clyne. Neither did he wear it buzzed short like Gabe. Clay chose a length that was neither fashionable, functional nor traditional. His black hair ended bluntly at his strong jawline with bangs that he either swept back or let fall over his piercing eyes. His brow was prominent and his eyebrows thick. His black lashes were long and framed his deep brown eyes. She'd always wondered why he didn't recognize his model good looks, but Clay seemed unaware of how he turned heads.

She met his hard stare, gnawing on her lower lip.

"If you are involved with anything illegal up there, you best tell me right now."

She gaped as the shock hit her like a slap. He couldn't really think she had anything to do with this. Could he?

He looked serious enough. "Because I will not be dragged into another mess."

"I'm not involved with anything illegal."

He continued to stare, lips pressed thin and colorless.

She threw up her hands in disgust. "Okay! I swear! I'm not involved in anything, and all I know is someone cut my fences, half my herd is gone, I'm missing cattle and now I owe a fine."

"What is it you want me to do, exactly?" he asked.

"Check the fields for tracks. Tell me everything you can. Maybe poke around in the upper pasture."

"The crime scene, you mean."

"Yes."

"How much?"

"Fifty bucks?"

He shook his head. "I want a cow for my sister's Sunrise Ceremony."

"Your sister?" Some of the fight drained out of her, replaced by shock. Izzie touched the gold crucifix, rubbing it between her thumb and index finger before letting it drop. "I thought Jovanna was..."

"So did we. She's not. Just missing. We are going to find her."

Izzie absorbed that bit of news. It was really none of her business, but she remembered the bright and happy little girl who left with her mother for her first contest and never came back. If they could find her, they'd need every bit of that cow to feed all the company and relatives who would attend. A homecoming and a Sunrise Ceremony. Goodness, there would be hundreds of people.

"She's been gone a long time," said Izzie.

Clay said nothing to that.

"All right, then."

He replaced his hat. They were close to a deal. Once she'd known him intimately. But then he had been a boy. This man before her had become a stranger.

He made a sound of frustration in his throat.

When he met her gaze, she braced, knowing he had reached a decision. And also knowing that once Clay Cosen settled on a course it was nearly impossible to change his mind.

Chapter Three

When he finally spoke, his voice was tight, clipped and frosty as the snow off Black Mountain.

"All right. One cow. My pick."

It took a moment for Izzie to realize that she had won. She blinked up at Clay, recovered herself and nodded.

"My pick," he repeated. "And if you are lying to me or dragging me into something illegal, I will turn you over to Gabe so fast, little brothers or no little brothers."

It was a threat that hit home, for while her mother still ran the household, Izzie owned the cattle. It was a sticking point between her and her mother, for her father had left the entire herd to his eldest daughter instead of his wife. Her mother, a righteous woman with a knack for scripture, also had a habit of spending more than her husband could make. And though her father had had trouble telling his wife no, Izzie did not. Which was why she had increased the herd by forty head and also why her mother was equally furious and proud of her. Izzie planned to keep her promise and pass her father's legacy to her brothers. Up until today she had done well. Up until today when she had lost fifty-one head. Her shoulders slumped a little, but she managed to keep her chin up.

"That's a deal." She stuck out her hand and pushed down the hope that he would take it.

He stared at her hand and then back to her and then back to her hand. Finally he clasped it. The contact was brief. But her reaction was not. She felt the tingle of his palm pressing to hers clear up to her jaw. Why, oh why did she have to have a thing for this man?

Clay broke the contact, leaving Izzie with her hand sticking out like a fool. Clay rubbed his palm on his thigh as if anxious to be rid of all traces of their touch. She scowled, recalling a time when things were different.

"When do we start?" she asked.

"Sooner is better. Tracks don't improve with time."

"Let's go, then. We can take my truck."

He hesitated, glancing to his vehicle. She followed his gaze, noticing he did not have a gun rack.

"You want to bring your rifle?"

"Don't carry one."

She frowned, thinking she had not heard him correctly. Clay hunted. He fished. Surely he had a rifle. It was part of life here. Shooting at coyotes and gophers and rattlesnakes, though she usually took a shovel to the snakes. Everyone she knew carried a firearm. But everyone she knew had not been charged with a crime.

He was allowed to carry one. His rescue earlier today proved that. Was it because he now knew the difference between robbery and armed robbery?

"What did you use earlier?"

"Belongs to the office."

She eyed him critically. He didn't just look different. He *was* different in ways she could only guess at.

"You don't hunt anymore?"

"Sometimes with my brothers. I mostly fish." He glanced away, and his hands slid into his back pockets as he rocked nervously from toe to heel, heel to toe.

Finally he looked up. She met Clay's gaze, and his expression gave nothing away.

"Still want my help?" he asked.

Izzie nodded.

He glanced toward his house, and she realized that he must not have eaten yet, since she'd caught him before he even made it to his front door.

"I'll buy you a burger after," she promised.

His mouth quirked. "Okay."

He strode past his battered pickup toward her newer-model Ram with the double wheels front and back and the trailer hitch behind. Oh, how her mother hated this truck, even though it was a used model.

Izzie watched Clay pass. His easy gait and graceful stride mesmerized her until she realized he was headed toward the driver's side. For a minute she thought he meant to drive. Izzie still had two years' worth of payments on her truck, and nobody drove it but her. But instead of taking the wheel, Clay opened her door for her and stepped back.

She felt her mouth drop open but managed to hold on as she nodded her thanks and swept inside the cab. He waited a moment and then closed the door before rounding the hood and removing his hat. Then he slid in beside her, hat in his lap. He fiddled with the seat controls, sending his seat as far back as it would go, and still his knees were flexed past ninety degrees. Then he sat motionless as she headed home.

"Who do you think cut your fences?" he asked as they rolled down the narrow mountain road from his place and toward hers out past Pinyon Lake. Here the forest lined both sides of the road with the pavement creating a narrow gap in the walls of pines.

"I have no idea."

"Anyone threatening you or trying to buy you out?"

"Buy me out, no." She remembered something, and she squeezed the wheel. "But my neighbor did ask me out a few times."

"Who?"

"Floyd."

Clay straightened. "Floyd Patch? He must be close to forty."

She and Clay were both twenty-four. He was born in February and she was born on the same day in March. There was a time she had joked that she liked older men. But that didn't seem funny right now.

"He's only thirty-six."

Clay rolled his eyes and brushed the crown of his felt hat, but said nothing. He considered the ceiling of the cab for a long moment. His usual posture, Izzie recalled, when he was thinking.

She smiled at the familiarity. It seemed that so much about him was the same. But not everything. Izzie steered them onto the main road, deciding to take the long way back to keep from the possibility of encountering her mother on the road. Izzie glanced at the clock, realizing her mother would likely be home because the boys should be climbing off the school's late bus about now. Clay's voice dragged her back to the present.

"Clyne said he was on the agenda a while back. I saw him talking to my boss a time ago about the tribe's communal pastures."

Who was he talking about?

"Which ones to close for renourishment."

Patch, she realized. Her neighbor.

"I heard Donner say that Patch was asking the council to impose a lottery for grazing permits again."

Izzie clenched the wheel. "But that doesn't make any

sense. Lotteries mean ranchers might get grazing land clean on the other side of the reservation."

Clay shrugged. He had no horse in this particular race.

"You think Floyd wants my permits?"

"Don't know. But if he can't get the council to change the way permits are distributed, he could get them by marrying you."

Izzie let out a sound of frustration. "Those permits and the cattle don't belong to me. They are my brothers'."

"Whose name is on the permits?"

Izzie said nothing because they both knew that a minor could not own permits. Of course you had to be of age and Apache to even apply. As long as she didn't miss the October first application date, which she never did, then the permits were hers until her brother Will was old enough to apply in her place. That was the way it had always been. She hadn't come up with the system, but now she was starting to wonder if Floyd was indeed interested in her permits.

She turned on the cutoff that took her up the mountain, and Clay cast her a glance, wondering, no doubt, about her choice of routes. This way wasn't faster.

"Daylight is burning," he said.

"I know." She increased her speed and leaned forward, as if that would make them climb the hill quicker.

"Did you go out with him?"

She had to think for a minute about who he meant.

"No. No, of course not."

"He's got twice your herd."

"But not enough land to graze them. He'll have to sell some or apply for another permit."

"Or add them to the communal herd."

She and Clay shared a concerned look.

"Can you tell if he is the one who cut the fences?"

"Maybe." He toyed with his hat. "Let's start on the lower pasture?"

"Sure." She'd have to drive by the upper area where the shooting had been. Would the police still be there? "Then I want you to see the road and the place where the tribe is taking fill. They've leveled a wide area, for their trucks, I guess."

"To get at the hillside?"

"All they told me was that pasture permits didn't keep them from timbering the forest or exercising mineral rights. But this isn't timbering. Well, some is."

"What do you mean?"

"They aren't choosing which trees to take to thin the forest or clear the brush or whatever. They clear-cut a patch in the middle of the forest about fifty-by-fifty feet."

Clay frowned and rubbed the brim of his hat with his thumb and index finger, deep in thought.

Both she and Clay stretched their necks as they passed the new gravel road leading into the forest, but she saw nothing remarkable and no evidence of police activity. Whoever had shot at them was long gone. They passed the spot where his truck had been parked and arrived a few minutes later at the lower pasture, where most of her remaining cows milled close to the fence.

Izzie wished she had risked the shorter ride, as the sun was already descending toward sunset. It had been hard to give up the long days of August, but the air was already cool up here at the higher elevations, and so she shrugged into her denim coat, then realized Clay did not have one.

Clay pointed at her rifle, hooked neatly to her gun rack behind the seats.

"Take that," he said.

She did. He had told her to take one of her rifles but left

the second firearm in place. Was that because he knew she was a better shot or for some other reason?

"You had a gun earlier," she said checking the load and adding a box of cartridges to her coat pocket for good measure.

"Have to. Part of my job." He tried to step past her. She blocked his path. He stopped and faced her.

"Why don't you own a gun, Clay?"

"No one wants to see an ex-con with a rifle in his hands."

"But you weren't charged with a felony. You are allowed to own one, right?"

"Right."

He raked his fingers past his temples and lowered his hat over his glossy black hair that brushed the collar of his shirt.

"Can we get started?"

She extended an arm in invitation. He continued, walking the highway, scanning the ground.

"Do you think the police are done investigating up there?" she asked, indicating the site of the shooting. "I didn't see any activity."

"For the day, maybe. But I'm not poking around in their crime scene."

Clay already had his eyes on the ground; she kept hers on the trees far above them, perhaps two miles away. For a shot you would need a scope and some luck to make the target. But still she held her rifle ready as she searched for more gunmen.

She followed behind him as he walked the highway. No one drove past. This road was too far from anything or anyone and was rarely used, except for today, of course.

Clay headed toward the pasture, and all the curious

cows that had crowded the fence line fled in the opposite direction. She resisted the urge to count them.

He had already stepped through the fencing and stood lifting the upper strand of barbed wire to make her passage less difficult. Then he continued on, following some trail clear only to himself. She could see the routes the cows took along the fence line. She followed until he stopped and then glanced past him at the knee-high yellowing grass. The parallel tracks of a small vehicle were clear even to her.

"What the heck is that?" she said.

"ATV. Came from up there where the fence was cut. Saw the tracks this morning, but with the shooting, it slipped my mind until you showed up in my driveway. He rode down this way, in a circle, gathering your herd. Cattle tracked that way." He pointed.

"He?" she said.

"Could be a she. Won't know unless they get out of the vehicle."

They walked a bit farther on. The grass was flat by the fence. She could imagine her cattle pressed up against the barbed wire.

"Stopped here and then headed that way." He pointed back the way the vehicle had come.

"What was it doing on my land?" She had a sick feeling in her stomach as she looked at the grass flattened on both sides of the fence line. They'd exited there. But how?

Clay advanced to the fence and touched one of the wires. It fell, snagging the one below it and bringing that down, as well. Clay pointed to the splice, where someone had reconnected the cut line exactly beside one of the barbs using thin pieces of wire.

"You've been rustled," said Clay.

"But they didn't steal them."

"No. Just drove them to the road and called the livestock manager so we'd come scoop up your cows."

"Who made the call?"

"Don't know. But you best ask and take a few photos of this. You got a phone that does that?"

She shook her head. Clay withdrew an older model smartphone and began photographing the line and the break and the one remaining patch. Then he photographed the pasture and, for good measure, took a short movie.

"That should do it."

"I'm calling the cops again," she muttered.

"Let's check up top first."

She nodded glumly. Then realized something and stopped.

"I can get my cows back. If someone cut the fences and drove them out, I shouldn't have to pay the fine."

"If you can prove it."

"You just did."

Now he looked glum.

"What's wrong?"

"Nothing," he said, continuing back the way they came, exiting through the broken fence and replacing the small bits of wire.

"Why didn't they fix the upper one?" she asked pausing as Clay took more photos.

Clay tucked away his camera. "Don't know. Maybe they ran out of time or someone saw them. Where were you this morning?"

Chapter Four

Izzie stilled at Clay's accusation as heat flooded her face. Indignation rose with the pitch of her voice.

"You think I did this?"

"What? No! I just asked where you were."

Now her face flamed with embarrassment.

"I don't accuse folks of things, Izzie. That's Gabe's job."

She touched his arm and felt his bicep flex beneath the worn cotton. "I'm sorry."

He nodded his acceptance.

"I was with the ferrier. Biscuit and the other horses were getting their feet trimmed and teeth filed."

"So the ferrier was here. I wonder who else knew you'd be with him."

She started to compile a list in her mind. When she got to ten people she sighed and gave up. Clay trailed back out on to the road. Izzie went to her truck to grab some wire to fix the gaping hole.

"I wouldn't do that until after they have a look. The police, I mean."

Izzie wasn't leaving a hole between two posts, so Clay helped her rig a temporary closure.

When they got back to the truck Clay got her door again. After she climbed up into the cab, he hesitated before closing the door.

"Somebody is after your herd, Izzie. You need to watch your back."

Izzie met the concern in his gaze and tried to look brave. But inside her fears gobbled her up. Keeping the herd was hard. Keeping them while under attack...

She reached out and Clay took her hand. He gave a squeeze.

"Thank you for helping me."

He flushed and released her, stepping back, closing the door. She watched him round the front of her truck.

She started the engine and waited as he climbed in. She was so darn lucky that he was a big enough man to put aside her snub and help her when she really needed him. Would she have done the same?

Izzie swallowed her uncertainty as these questions made her shift with discomfort.

The motor idled, and Clay glanced her way, his hat in his hands and brows raised in an unspoken question.

"I don't know what I would have done if you didn't agree to help me."

His voice was quiet. Intimate. "I'll always help you, Izzie."

"Maybe we can be friends again."

His brows lifted higher. "Is that what we are?"

Was he thinking of what she had been? How could you ever be friends after you loved someone? Was it even possible to mend the fences cut between them?

"We could be," she whispered.

Clay faced forward and said nothing as she drove them up the hill.

"There is cell service at the top of the mountain here. I can call the police from up there." She hoped the gunmen and the police were gone. Really, she wanted nothing more than to wake up and find this day was all a nightmare. But then she looked at Clay sitting beside her again and wondered if it was all worth it just for these few minutes together.

At the top of the pasture, she turned onto the improved road. The sun shone through the tall pines to the west in flashing bands of brilliance, but it was starting to go down now. Clay directed her where to park and then exited the truck. Izzie followed, just as she always had. What would he do if he knew the reason she'd dated Martin? Would he be flattered or angry?

It had been a stupid, childish idea, and it had blown up in her face.

The entire episode was embarrassing. Funny that Martin had charmed her mother into believing he was a good guy. A good Christian boy, Carol Nosie had called him. He'd fooled a lot of folks with his manners. But she'd known what he was, and she'd still agreed to go out with him, for a while.

She could see nothing on the gravel that Clay studied, so she watched him, enjoying the way the light gilded his skin and the stretch of denim and cotton as he stooped and rose.

On the gravel road the rocks crunched beneath his feet. He walked slowly, his eyes scanning back and forth. At last they reached the wide bulldozed stretch that had been muddy the last time she'd been up here but now was packed earth. Clay made a sound in his throat, and Izzie wanted to ask him what he saw, but she cultivated patience. He walked back and forth, ventured into the woods, knelt a few times, lifted a stone, and examined a branch. The only thing Izzie saw for sure were the prints of her cattle that had made it up this far. She tried to count the number of cows, but they circled back on themselves, so she gave up.

"Look," she said, finding an interesting track at the edge of a drying puddle. "Dog."

"Coyote," he said from some forty feet off.

She gripped her rifle tight as she squatted to examine the print. Why hadn't she learned to track?

"This way," Clay said, and she followed him past the cut of dirt, up the steep incline sprinkled with quaking aspen. She glanced up at sunlight shining its last rays on the golden leaves and smiled at the beauty. With her focus elsewhere, she did not see Clay stop and nearly ran right into him. He stood with hands on hips, staring down. She heard the buzz of many flies before her attention snapped to the three cows all lying motionless in the tall grass. Her cows.

Izzie gave a little cry and tried to rush past him. But he halted her with one hand, effortlessly bringing her back to his side.

"That your brand?" he asked.

She glanced at the flank of the closest cow and recognized the two interlocking circles.

"Yes. Are they dead?"

The question was answered by their absolute stillness. It was two heifers and one yearling. Their legs stuck out straight as if they had been stuffed and then toppled, and their eyes were a ghostly white. Izzie calculated her herd. One hundred and eleven in all, minus one to Clay, minus three to death was a hundred and eight. But that included the fifty-one now impounded. She glanced around, searching for more dead cows. This was a disaster.

She threw up her hands in frustration. "What are they doing way up here?"

"You got a fence between this and the upper pasture?"

"Too much ground to cover. They mostly just stay together in the pasture."

Clay pointed at the grass. "Coyotes chased them."

Izzie fumed and lifted her rifle to her shoulder, searching for the coyotes. Then her brain reengaged, and she realized coyotes couldn't take down two heifers. They'd been after the yearling.

Clay rested a hand on her shoulder and gave a squeeze before releasing her. She turned from her dead cattle to glance up at him.

"Coyotes didn't do that! There's not a mark on them."

He nodded his head and glanced back at the carcasses. Flies buzzed and landed in their nostrils and on their filmy white eyes. She looked at the lolling tongues and noted the saliva was a neon-green color. She'd never seen anything like it before.

"What's that?" she asked, her voice a whisper.

He shook his head. "Not sure. Sick?"

The very thought of that caused a surge of terror to crash through her like a wave, the impact rocking her on her feet. Clay steadied her with a gentle clasping of her elbow. She shook him off, looking for a fight.

"My cows aren't sick!" she said, more to herself than to him. She could think of no greater catastrophe than sick cows. But her eyes locked on the green sputum. Oh, Lord help her if they had something contagious. The tribe would order them slaughtered. She'd be left with nothing. And without the cattle, she couldn't maintain the permits. She gripped the rifle tight and tried to think.

Clay withdrew his phone from his front pocket.

She clasped his wrist, feeling the cool skin and the roping tendons beneath.

"Wait a minute."

He did, but his face was granite.

"Give me a second." She glanced around as if someone would come to her rescue. But no one ever did that. She stared up at Clay. "Someone chased my herd onto the road. Now they are trying to make it look like my cattle are sick. It's another setup."

"Maybe. Need a vet to know for sure."

She gripped the forearm of the hand that held the phone. "Don't call them," she begged.

His eyes widened, and his mouth gaped. Then his look went cold and his posture still. Her cheeks burned with shame. Had she just asked him to break the law?

He lifted his arm, and she let her numb fingers slip from his sleeve as the shame burned her up with the last of the sunlight.

Clay drew up a number and pressed the call button. A moment later she heard a familiar voice. "Gabe? It's Clay. I've got a problem."

Chapter Five

Clay and Kino had gone over the tracks using floodlights. Kino agreed with what Clay saw. Gabe was busy directing the investigation, but he took a look at some of the more important signs. All the Cosen boys had learned to read sign from both their father and from their maternal grandfather. Reading sign was a part of their inheritance and the skill that had made their ancestors so valuable to the US Cavalry. And Clay's ancestors had found Geronimo. It was why their tribe was still on their ancestral land, an anomaly for most Native peoples.

Some things never changed because now Apache trackers were in demand with Border Patrol, Immigration and Customs and, lately, the US military. Clyne had spent six months as a special instructor in Afghanistan teaching elite military units how to track terrorists in the desert. And Clay and Kino had only just returned from the Sonora Desert, where they had tracked drug traffickers entering over the Mexican border.

Clay was cold, hungry and surly by the time Gabe got the go-ahead to call the Office of the State Veterinarian, from tribal officer Arnold Tessay. Clearly, Izzie had forgotten her offer to buy him dinner. Right now, he could eat that frozen pizza cold.

Both Tessay and Clyne arrived well past dark. The

tribe's president was in Washington testifying before the House of Representatives on Indian Affairs. Gabe also had called Donner, since he managed the tribal livestock and needed to be made aware that there might be some new illness killing cows on the Rez. Gabe told Clay that Donner was calling both Pizarro, who covered the tribe's cattle business, and Soto, who oversaw livestock health. Donner and Pizarro arrived together. Clay knew from his boss's angry stride that he was pissed. He was a big man, nearly as tall as Clay, though twenty years and forty pounds separated them. His face was fleshy and had been pulled by time and gravity. Behind him came Boone Pizarro. By contrast, Pizarro's skin stretched tight as a drumhead over his angular face, and his body was thin with ropy muscles. Clay heard that his wife preferred the casinos to cooking, but whatever the reason, Pizarro had a perpetual hungry look. Both men stopped before him, expressions stern.

"I don't remember sending you over here again," Donner said to Clay.

"No, sir. Ms. Nosie asked me to check for sign. Her herd didn't break loose. The fences were cut."

Pizarro's mouth went thin. "Cutting is a serious charge."

Thankfully Gabe stepped up at that moment. "They were cut, all right."

"And you didn't see this earlier?" said Donner.

Izzie interjected now. "Maybe it was the bullets that distracted him, or being pulled in for questioning."

Donner cast her a sour look. While Pizarro laughed, Clay gave her a slow shake of his head. He didn't need that kind of help. His boss was angry enough. Plus sarcasm might not be the best option against a man who had the authority to quarantine her entire herd. Beside him, Izzie fumed but said no more.

"You got any suspects?" Pizarro asked Gabe.

Tessay moved closer to Clyne, making Izzie the lone woman in a circle of men. She always had been, he realized, as a rancher and before that with her two brothers and father. But Clay noticed they'd closed Izzie out. He stepped back, and she wedged in beside him.

"Nope," said Gabe, his posture relaxed. "Just starting the investigation."

If he was stressed by the late hour or the presence of his superiors from the tribal council, he gave no sign and instead only radiated confidence and authority. Clay admired that. Gabe was a keen observer of everything, and he was very good at noticing inconsistencies. Perhaps that was why he went into law enforcement. Or it could have been to make up for their father. That was a tough legacy.

Gabe hitched a thumb in his utility belt, as comfortable with his sidearm as Clay was uncomfortable with one.

"We got shots fired, cut fences, repaired fences intended, I believe, to give the illusion of an intact fence. We've also got three dead cows with no sign of predation."

"Disease?" asked Tessay.

"Vets will tell us that. They're en route."

Pizarro and Donner exchanged looks.

"Where's Soto?" asked Pizarro. "He should be here."

"On his way," said Gabe, failing to be sidetracked. "Either of you have any idea why this area has been improved?" Gabe directed his attention to his brother Clyne and Arnold Tessay. As tribal leaders, they were the logical ones to ask.

"Not me," said Clyne.

Tessay hesitated and then shook his head. "Don't know."

"Looks like a pretty nice level area. Not sure why it's here," said Gabe.

His comment went without reply from any of those gathered, but Izzie was shifting from side to side. Did she know more than she had told him? Clay watched Gabe's attention flick to Izzie, and Clay resisted the urge to still her nervous motion.

"We need to quarantine Nosie's herd," said Pizarro.

"I don't want to get folks all in a tizzy over nothing," said Tessay.

"We don't know what killed those cows, yet," said Gabe. "But better safe than sorry."

Donner looked to Clay. "Pick them up in the morning. I've got no budget for overtime."

"You can't just take my cows," said Izzie, but her voice lacked confidence, for she surely knew that they could and would do just that. Keeping all cattle certified and disease free was essential to their survival.

Clyne rested a hand on Izzie's shoulder. It was a fatherly gesture, and still it raised the hackles on Clay's neck. He had to resist the urge to shove his brother as if they were still kids. Not that he'd ever won a fight against his eldest brother. Clyne was eight years his senior. Clay thought he might just be able to take him now. Instead he reined himself in.

"Izzie, we'll expedite this. I promise. If possible, we'll get your cows a clean bill of health and get the ones that were impounded returned to you as soon as we can. But you have to help us here."

"Councilman," said Izzie, "my family depends on our herd."

"She's no different than the rest of us in that," said Tessay, whom Clay recalled had a cow or two pastured in the tribe's communal herd.

"She is different," argued Clay, wondering when he'd suddenly decided to pursue a career in public speaking. "Because she has more cattle than most of the other members of the tribe and because her family has been herding on this land since before they built Pinyon Fort."

Gabe was rubbing the back of his neck in discomfort. Clay wondered if he were the one causing that pain. He glanced to Clyne to find him grinning at him like a fool. Izzie gaped at him as if he had just sprouted a crown like one of the mountain spirits.

Donner grasped Clay's arm. "Will you excuse us for a minute?"

Clay had a sinking feeling he was about to get fired as his boss led him out of earshot. Donner stopped them a short distance from the others.

"That's my boss you're dressing down," he said.

Clay stared at the ground. Outside of the circle of the headlights, there wasn't much to see.

"I'm sorry, sir."

"What's gotten into you? I mean, what does it matter to you, anyway?"

"Nothing," Clay admitted. "Izzie is an old friend."

Donner snorted. "Friend, huh?"

Izzie had stopped being his concern long ago. She'd made it very clear that she didn't want any part of him... until today, or was it yesterday? He glanced at the sky, glittering with stars, and decided from the angle of Orion that it was past midnight. He stretched his shoulders.

"You working for her?"

"No. Well, she asked me to read sign."

His boss flapped his arms. "It's called moonlighting, and I can fire you for it. You can't work for someone else while you're working for me."

"I—I didn't know," Clay said.

Donner made a face. "I believe you, son. But this isn't just about what's right and wrong. It's about the appearance of right and wrong. Appearance is the same as reality."

Clay scratched the stubble on his chin. "I'm interested in the truth."

"Son, an inspector working for a rancher is a conflict of interest. That didn't occur to you?"

It had. In fact he'd warned Izzie that he would not be a part of anything illegal.

"I just read the signs."

"Okay. You read the signs. It's done. I'm giving you a warning and telling you to stay out of it. She needs help, she can hire your kid brother to track. Anyone on the Rez but you."

"Yes, sir."

"You know I went to school with your father?"

Clay did know because his uncle Luke had told him when he'd spoken to Donner about hiring Clay. His uncle Luke Forrest was his father's half brother and so was not a Cosen.

"And your uncle put in a word for you. So do us both a favor. Keep out of politics. When Tessay or Clyne are talking, you hush up unless you need to say, 'Yes, sir.' You got that?"

"Yes, sir." He said it without sarcasm but still gleaned a long, hard stare.

His boss left him standing there and returned to the circle. Clay swiped his hand at the long grass in frustration. Izzie needed his help. But he sure needed this job. Kino found him first.

"They're wrapping it up for tonight. Can't see anything, anyway."

"The vet here?"

"Yeah. And Soto finally made it. They're gonna set up tents and do the necropsy right here. Damn, that green puss is something. Ever seen anything like it?"

Clay gave his head a slow shake. "How long for results?"

"Couple days, at least." Kino rested his hands on his hips, tucking his thumbs under the utility belt and staring out at the investigation, winding down as men headed for their vehicles.

"What?" said Clay. He knew his brother well enough to know that he wasn't done talking.

Kino shrugged. "Clyne is worried about you and Izzie."

"What about us?"

"None of my business. His, either. I told him that. But you took it pretty hard the last time is all."

When she'd dumped him. Great, now his brothers where discussing his love life. Add it to the long list of his failures. Must make a nice change from gossiping about his other shortcomings.

"She hired me to read sign."

"Okay. Just be careful."

Did Kino mean because of the shooting or because he'd been a complete train wreck when Izzie had broken it off?

"Yeah. I'll tell her to ask you if she needs any more help reading sign." He called himself a liar even as he uttered the words. "Told her all I could. That should be that." But he hoped it wasn't. He wanted to see her again, was already plotting how he could make that happen. She owed him dinner.

"Good, because Gabe told me to remind you to leave the police work to us." He kept his head down now as he delivered his message.

Clay tore off his hat and raked his fingers through his hair.

"Sorry," muttered Kino.

Clay turned his back on Kino and headed toward the group of men. He noted that Izzie's truck was already gone. What had he expected, a good-night kiss?

Clay glanced down out of habit, scanning the ground,

and saw something he hadn't before. A track—a big one,
one that did not belong up here in the middle of nowhere.

Clay lifted his head. He had to find Gabe.

Chapter Six

Izzie did not sleep well or much. Her wake-up call the next morning was Gabe Cosen serving her with notice that the remainder of her cows would be seized and quarantined. Her mother returned from running errands and confronted her about seeing "that Cosen boy again." Her mother loved gossip, unless she or her family were the subject of talk. Izzie wondered if her mother ever tired of being above reproach.

"Of all the people in this tribe to call. Really, Isabella. What were you thinking? What about that nice Mr. Patch? He certainly has made his interest known. And he has all that cattle."

Izzie cringed, and her mother's hands went to her hips.

"What's wrong with him? I mean, we could certainly use some help around here."

"We're doing fine." At least they had been yesterday. Now she felt as if the ground beneath her was sliding away.

"I mean, Clay Cosen, do you honestly want our name and his linked? Your father certainly didn't."

The below-the-belt blow hit home. Izzie flinched. It had been her father's opposition that had finally gotten her to break it off with Clay. She'd been so sure her parents would change their minds about Clay, and then he had been arrested. Case closed. Her mother had basked in smug satisfaction at being right again while her father had offered comfort. How she missed her father, still, every single day.

"I don't want that man on my land again," she said to Izzie.

Izzie wanted to tell her mother that the land did not belong to them, but to the tribe. They had use of it by permit only. She wanted to tell her mother that she was a grown woman who could see who she liked, and she wanted to tell her mother that running the ranch was not her business because her husband had left that job to Izzie. Instead she said, "I've got chores."

"But wait. I want to hear what is going on up there."

Izzie kept going, knowing that her mother didn't want anything badly enough to walk into a pasture dotted with cow pies and buzzing with flies. Izzie changed direction and headed for her pickup, deciding that would be faster than riding Biscuit.

"He's trouble," her mother called after her.

Izzie swung up behind the wheel. "Mom, I've got bigger trouble right now than Clay Cosen." So why was she thinking of him instead of how to get back her cows? "I just got notice. They're taking the rest of the herd, Mom."

Carol pressed a hand to her chest. "But why?"

"Quarantined."

"But…you… They… Isabella Nosie, you have to get them back."

Finally, something on which they agreed.

"Working on it." She pulled the truck door closed and started the engine, using the wipers to move the dust that blanketed her windshield.

Izzie headed up to the area where Clay had found the dead cows and now saw that a large white tent had been erected over the spot. Several pickups were parked beside the police cars in the gravel pad. Only one was familiar. It belonged to her neighbor Floyd Patch.

Izzie groaned as Floyd headed straight toward her. His gait was rushed, almost a jog. His skinny legs carried his round body along, reminding Izzie of a running ostrich. He was short, prematurely gray, with bulging eyes and skin that shone as if it had been recently waxed. His usual smile had been replaced by a look that hovered between stormy and category-five tornado.

She didn't even have the driver's-side door shut when he was on her like a hungry flea on a hound. He hitched his fists against his narrow hips and drew himself up, making his shirt draw tight across his paunch. It was hard for Izzie to recall that she'd initially found his attentions flattering. Now she greeted his occasional appearances with the reluctant resignation of an oncoming headache.

"I don't appreciate you sending the police to my door," said Floyd, his voice higher than usual.

"I did no such thing."

"Asking me where I was yesterday and checking the tires of my truck, as if I'm some kind of criminal. They ought to check Clay Cosen's tires. I heard he was up here yesterday. What did you tell them, that I poisoned your cattle?"

"No, I never—"

"And I have to find out from the police that you've got cows dying up here."

"Floyd, it only just happened."

"Yesterday. And you didn't think I might want to know? I've got my own herd to protect." He pointed in the direction of his pastures, across the road and down the hill. His pasture was rocky and more wooded, because her ancestors had invested more sweat in clearing the land.

"There's been no contact between your cattle and mine,

and you haven't been on my property in two weeks or more. Your herd is in no danger."

Floyd's gaze flicked away, and he pursed his lips. *Had he been on her land?*

His gaze swung back to hers. "If there is no danger, then why did they quarantine your herd?"

"A precaution."

"I understand that one of your dead cows had green stuff in its mouth. That's not normal."

If Floyd knew that, then everyone else did. "Who told you that?"

He didn't answer, just continued on. "What if it gets in the water? What if it's airborne? Three cows don't just drop. Something killed them."

"Floyd, I have to go," she said.

The day just got worse from there. Izzie spent the afternoon waiting for information outside the necropsy tent of the State Office of Veterinarian Services. By day's end, she knew only that the cows had showed renal and liver damage, mucus in the lungs and swelling in their brains. Cause of death was ruled as sudden cardiac arrest in all three. As to why, well, that was the question. What was it, and was it contagious?

The best answer she received was that more tests were needed. On the way back to her truck, Izzie found Chief Gabe Cosen speaking to Clay, who was sweat-stained, saddle-worn and sexy as hell. Clay noticed her approach and gave her a sad smile.

"Didn't think you'd be back up here," she said to Clay. "After your boss warned you off."

Chief Gabe Cosen quirked his brow at her. Clay's brother was handsome with classic good looks and that distinctive angular jaw shared by all the Cosen brothers. But it was only Clay who made her heart pound.

"I was just telling Clay that I'd served you notice to collect the rest of your herd. I'm sorry, Izzie."

She pressed her lips together to resist the temptation of tears.

"And he told me that you hired him to have a look around yesterday."

Of course Clay told his brother. Did she really expect him to pick her needs over his brother's investigation?

"I'm looking into who cut your fences. Sorry for your troubles." Gabe tipped his hat, the gray Stetson the tribal police wore in the cold season. He turned to Clay. "Well, I've got to verify what you found." With that the chief of police made a hasty retreat.

"What did you find?"

"I wanted to tell you yesterday, but you'd gone when I got back here, and I didn't think you wanted me knocking on your front door."

That made her flush.

"Was I wrong about that?"

Izzie thought of her mother's earlier tizzy and shook her head. She let her shoulders slump. She lived for the day that her brothers were old enough to take over, and she could live her own life. But from the way it looked now, there would be nothing to pass along to them. Izzie rallied. She could not let that happen. No one and nothing would stop her from retrieving every last cow.

"I've got to get them back," she said.

Clay motioned to her truck and lowered the back gate. Then he offered her a hand up. They sat side by side amid the comings and goings of inspectors, livestock managers, tribal council. More than one cast them a cursory glance, and she wondered which ones would be reporting to their wives, who would report to her mother later on. Her mother had connections like the roots of an ancient pinyon pine. They were branched and deep.

"It looks like the rodeo," Izzie muttered.

"Yeah." Clay surveyed their surroundings and then focused on her. "Izzie, you hired me to give you a report."

"I can't pay you now." She lowered her head, fighting against the burning in her throat. Crying in front of Clay was too humiliating, so she cleared her throat and gritted her teeth until the constriction eased.

Clay placed a hand on her shoulder and squeezed. She glanced up, eyes somehow still dry.

"Izzie, you had a heck of a big truck up here. Only left yesterday."

"You mean the earth-moving machinery, bulldozer and dump trucks?"

"No, I mean an eighteen-wheeler, actually, two of them."

"Eighteen-wheelers? Yesterday. Eighteen-wheelers can't haul dirt."

"That's right. But they were here. And they were loading and unloading the trucks. Moving contents from one to another. Five guys."

"What were they doing up here?"

"Not certain."

She knew that look. He had suspicions.

"What, Clay?"

"Moonshining, maybe, or drugs."

"You mean stashing drugs here?" She glanced around, half expecting to see a pile of boxes. She'd heard about the Mexican cartels using Rez land for holding their illegal merchandise, guns, drugs and people because treaty restrictions prevented federal authorities from entering sacred lands and from conducting investigations without obtaining permission first.

"But that wouldn't kill my cows."

"It might. If they were cooking up here."

"Cooking what?"

"Crystal meth."

Izzie rocked backward as confusion wrinkled her brow.
"I don't understand."

"There are fumes, by-products. They are poisonous."

"Poisonous?"

"Gabe is checking for residue."

Izzie straightened as a ray of light broke through the
clouds. If Clay was right, then there was nothing wrong
with her herd. She could get them back. She could still
keep her promise to her father.

"They're not sick!" Izzie threw herself into Clay's arms.
"Oh, thank you!"

He stiffened for just a moment, and then he wrapped his
arms around her. She didn't know how it happened. She
was pressed against him as relief flooded through her, replaced a moment later with blinding white heat. Her body
tingled. She tipped her head back, offering Clay her mouth.
He did not hesitate but swooped down, angling his head
as he kissed her greedily. Her fingers raked his back as
she hovered between the sweetness of the contact of their
mouths and the need for so much more.

"Isabella Mary Nosie!"

Izzie recognized her mother's sharp admonition and
pushed off Clay's chest at the same moment he released
her. The result was that she rocked dangerously on the tailgate, and only Clay's quick reflexes kept her from toppling
to the ground. He freed her arm the moment she regained
her equilibrium and slid to his feet.

Izzie faced her mother, who stood with eyes blazing
with fury as she glared at her eldest daughter. Izzie tried
to keep her head up, but she found herself shrinking under

her mother's censure and the curious stares of the men she had forgotten were even there.

"What do you think you are doing?" asked her mother.

Clay looked to her, but all she could do was stammer, so he answered instead.

"Izzie asked me to help her figure out what happened to her cows."

Her mother shot her a look, and Izzie nodded.

"Well, that's a fine how-do-you-do." She turned to Izzie. "He's a felon. You don't ask felons to do police work."

Izzie found her tongue. "He's not a felon."

Her mother laughed. "Criminal, then. A skunk can't change his stripe, and this one is just like his father. Now you come along home with me this instant. If word of this gets out, I'll die of shame."

Izzie straightened her spine. "No, Mom. I can't. I've got work to do."

Her mother gasped and then glared, but Izzie held her ground, drawing a gentle strength from Clay, who stood silent by her side.

"Work? Is that what you call it? You said you were up here to get our cattle back. Instead I find you fiddling with this…trash."

Beside her, Clay showed no sign that the insult had landed. He remained still and relaxed, propped against the back of her truck.

"Go home, Mom."

"I don't like it," she said at last and wheeled away in the direction she had come.

Izzie sagged against the tailgate, feeling suddenly like a kite that had lost the buoyant wind.

"What did I just do?" she whispered.

Clay's mouth quirked. "You stood up to your mother."

Chapter Seven

Despite Clay's theory about the possibility of illegal drug activity, Clay's boss had received orders from Franklin Soto to collect and quarantine Izzie's herd until such time as they were shown to be disease-free. So late Wednesday morning Clay rode beside Mr. Donner in the big cattle truck toward Izzie's place, followed by a pickup with two more cowboys pulling a four-horse trailer. His boss had an ATV for herding, which was now in the back of the pickup.

Donner had called Izzie before their arrival to inform her that her herd would be collected today. They were working with the tribal livestock coordinator, who currently rode behind them in his pickup with the tribal council member Arnold Tessay. Mr. Pizarro managed grazing permits for the tribe and wanted a look at the area that was causing all the fuss in full daylight, so Tessay had agreed to ride him up there.

Back in Black Mountain, Franklin Soto, the tribe's livestock inspector, was waiting to take custody of her herd.

Clay fiddled with his lariat, dreading the task of rounding up the rest of Izzie's cattle.

"You remember me telling you that reality is less important than perception," said Donner.

"Yes, sir."

"Well, you kissing Isabella Nosie before God and everyone has put me in a tight spot."

"I'm sorry, sir."

"You stay away from that gal or folks will assume that her special favors to you are getting her special treatment from us."

Clay's jaw clenched as he considered the gossip he might have started by kissing Izzie. It had all happened so fast, and he hadn't thought. He needed to think. Not thinking, taking things as they came. It had all gotten him into trouble. He didn't want that again.

"…ruin her reputation and call into question every blasted decision that I make all in one… You hearing me, son?"

Clay collected his wandering thoughts and nodded as his fist tightened on the stiff coils of rope. He never meant to hurt Izzie, but his boss saying that kissing him would ruin her reputation didn't sit well, even if it were true. So he said nothing, because he needed this job and wasn't likely to get another.

His boss knew his way around cows and also politics. Donner had kept his job by staying neutral in contentious issues and staying out of controversial decisions. But if you asked him, he'd only say that he didn't set tribal policy, he just enforced it.

"Did you know that your uncle Luke and I were teammates?"

Played basketball together, Clay knew.

Donner continued. "He assured me that you'd do the job and not cause me a lick of trouble." Donner glanced at him for a long moment before returning his attention to the road. "You've caused me more than a lick already."

Clay stilled, waiting to hear that he'd be fired.

"I'm real sorry, sir. It won't happen again."

"Your actions reflect on you and your family, Clay. Now they also reflect on me. You should know that by now."

He sure did. Clyne was a tribal council member. Gabe was chief of police. Even his younger brother was a patrolman. While Clay's claim to fame was spending eighteen months in a juvenile detention center and six months looking for work before his uncle intervened. Why had Donner said yes?

Donner had accepted his uncle Luke's request to hire Clay when no one else would. Now Clay wondered if his boss had acted to help an old friend or to curry favor from an up-and-coming FBI officer and war hero.

Clay's uncle was everything Clay was not. He had a clean record, no skeletons in his closet. He'd distinguished himself in Afghanistan and was recruited into the FBI. He had prestige, position, influence, power and the respect of everyone on the Rez.

Clay wondered again if it was possible to regain what he had lost that night on Highway 4.

He'd made a mistake. But would he be forever marked by that error like a cow after contact with a hot branding iron?

Clay thought it might be different after he'd come back from the Shadow Wolves. Being a member of that elite tracking unit of Immigration and Customs Enforcement carried some serious distinction. But not for Clay. Things here were the same as always, and folks just assumed that Clyne or Uncle Luke or Gabe had asked someone else to throw Clay a bone.

He watched the pastures roll along. This was Floyd Patch's grazing area. Rocky with clumps of woods and farther from the stream that cut through Izzie's property. Floyd had to dig a well for water.

"One more thing, son."

He turned his attention back to Donner.

"If you are right about the activity up top, well, Izzie might be involved."

He blinked in stunned surprise. When he found his voice it was to issue a denial. "She's not."

"How do you know?"

He didn't of course. But he did know Izzie. "She's never been involved with that sort of thing. Never."

"Well, here's something to chew on—her mother once had a gambling problem, which is why her dad left her."

Clay didn't know Izzie's dad had ever left her mom.

"Then she found God and blah, blah, they got it worked out. But he left the herd to Izzie. Too much for one little gal, my opinion, but that's not my business. Word is that her mom's got some unpaid debts. People with financial trouble can make some bad choices."

Clay sank back into the seat. Was it possible? Was Izzie's mom still a gambler? Did Izzie have unpaid debts? Clay didn't want to believe it, but he'd learned from hard experience that things were not always what they seemed.

"Don't hitch your wagon to that horse, son. Right now, Izzie is in trouble, and she *is* trouble. Best keep your distance."

When a friend was in trouble, wasn't that when they needed you? Clay remembered when everyone he counted on had left him. But not his family. They had stuck.

A tribal police car passed them, pulling in front of their truck and leading them the rest of the way to the Nosie place.

Donner turned the wheel with a grunt, and they headed up Izzie's drive. They passed a police unit parked by the fence. Pizarro pulled beside it, and Donner stopped in the drive.

Izzie stood before the gate. She had all the cattle in the

lower pasture and waited by the fence, her face stoic and her posture erect. Clay's heart hitched at the sight of her, alone with only one hired hand, Max Reyes, to help her. Must have taken them all morning to round them up.

"Any results on the blood work on her cows?" asked Clay.

"That's between your brother, Gabe and the state. We just do as we're told."

"Yes, sir."

"Come on. Jeez, I hate this part."

He'd expected to see Gabe there, but it was Kino waiting in the squad car. He stepped out as Donner descended. Clay hung back with Kino as Donner and Izzie exchanged a few words. Donner handed over the order of collection.

He and the other two boys got to work. They didn't need the horses or ATV. Just used their lariats to shoo the herd to the truck. Clay drove the first load in with his coworker, Roger Tolino, riding shotgun. Once they had them in the tribal quarantine area, they returned for the second load.

Izzie clutched the order of removal in her hand like a stress ball, watching in silence as they gathered her remaining cows. Beside her, her mother smoked a cigarette and focused her attention on Clay and the distance he kept from Izzie.

Clay had never seen Izzie look more downcast, not even after Martin's death. Then, at least, she had wept. Now she stared like a woman in shock. He wanted to go to her, comfort her. The urge to do so was strong and unrelenting.

But he couldn't.

Still his eyes found her often. Izzie did not look at him. She had her attention only on her disappearing herd.

Gabe arrived, and he and Kino spoke by the fence. His brothers did not help or speak to him as he did his job and they did theirs. Clay and the others went to work loading up the remaining eighteen-odd cows. But before Clay climbed back in the cab, Gabe pulled him aside.

"Grandma is worried about you," he said.

"I'm all right." But he wasn't. His heart hurt for Izzie, and he felt as he had after the trial when the records were sealed because of his age. It would be better, they all said. But it wasn't. In the vacuum of knowledge, folks had just made up their own stories, theories, speculation. Most were worse than what had actually happened. At least in the versions he had heard, he didn't come out looking like a damned fool.

Which was worse—to look a criminal or a fool?

They'd be doing the same to Izzie soon. Her name would be linked either to drug activity on her land or bovine sickness. Which was worse?

The girl with the sterling reputation was about to take her first trip through the mud.

Clay should find some satisfaction in that. His reputation was the reason she'd cited for breaking them up. But Martin had had her parents snowed. They'd believed he was a gentleman. He hadn't been. Still, you didn't speak badly about the dead.

Gabe cleared his throat, and Clay returned his attention to his brother.

"Grandma says she wants you to come to supper tonight."

"All right."

Gabe turned to go, and Clay reached out, clasping his elbow, drawing him back.

"Any results from the state?"

Gabe glanced around as if seeing who might overhear. Then he walked away without a word.

But Kino lingered, then spoke. "Asphyxiation," Kino said. "No blood work yet."

"Mechanical or...?"

"Clay, it's an ongoing investigation. Okay?"

Kino gave him a pained look as Gabe, now Kino's boss, retraced his steps, coming to a stop beside Kino.

"Her cows aren't sick, are they?" asked Clay.

Gabe adjusted his felt hat so the brim shaded his eyes that now glittered like a hawk's. "Stay out of it, Clay," said Gabe. "It's bad business."

Chapter Eight

Izzie waited in her pickup outside the offices of the tribal livestock manager because Clay had called. Left a message. Said it was important.

Finally Clay appeared, carrying a saddle over his shoulder as if it weighed nothing. She straightened and stared, drinking him in like a glass of cool water on a hot day. It was well past five. His clothing was dirt-smeared and dusty. He tossed his saddle in his truck and removed his work gloves.

She slid out of her pickup. At the sound of the door closing, he turned in her direction.

His brow quirked and a smile played on his lips. But it vanished by the time she reached him. He smelled of horse and sweat. Why did she find even that appealing?

Clay propped himself against the closed gate of his battered truck. He was tall and handsome, his dark eyes glittering as he looked her up and down. Did he notice that she'd changed out of her work shirt and into a gauzy peasant blouse? That her jeans were clean and her lips glossed? Izzie swallowed back her nervousness. This was about business, she reminded herself. Yet she had taken time to brush out her long hair. Now she was embarrassed that she had dressed as if going on a date. She tucked her hands in her back pockets as her heart fluttered and kept walking until she was close enough to see his long lower lashes brushing his cheeks.

"You wanted to speak to me?"

He nodded. "You look pretty."

So he noticed. She blushed.

"Want to go somewhere more private?" she asked and then thought her words sounded like an invitation she had not meant to extend.

His brow quirked again.

"I mean, so we won't be interrupted." She pressed her hand to her forehead as she made matters worse. What was wrong with her? She didn't generally trip over her own tongue. Must be the lip gloss.

Clay chuckled. "I know what you mean, Isabella. My truck or yours?"

"Mine."

"Good choice." He extended his hand, and she led the way. He scooped up his saddle and followed, dropping the gear into her truck bed. She glanced at it and then to him.

"Some things have been going missing around here."

"Ah." She reached for her door, and he beat her there, opening it for her. She could get used to this, Izzie thought, as she slipped behind the wheel. He rounded the hood, giving her time to admire his easy gait and powerful frame. The good girl after the town's bad boy. The cliché made her wince. But she'd never gotten over him or her body's reaction every time she got near him.

She pressed a hand to her flushed face as he swept up into the cab.

"The quarry?" he asked, instantly choosing the place where they had spent happier days.

"Sure."

The drive took only fifteen minutes, but it felt like forty as the silence stretched. She actually blew out a breath of relief when she put her truck in Park. They walked side by side to the water and sat on the log everyone used as a bench to watch their friends leap from the top of the quarry into the deep water below.

"Do I make you that nervous, Izzie?" he asked.

"Clay, I'm all tangled up around you."

"Because of Martin?"

And there it was, the three-hundred-pound gorilla in the room, the topic they had never spoken about.

"There is a lot about Martin and me that you don't know," she said.

"That so?"

"I thought you wanted to talk about my cattle."

"Sure. My brother tells me that the three we found up on the hill all died of asphyxiation."

"What? How do you asphyxiate a cow?"

"By removing all the oxygen from the air."

She sat back and stared out at the cliffs, the still water and then back at him. "How do you do that? Like carbon monoxide poisoning?"

"Not CO_2. Blood tests aren't back yet. But if someone was cooking crystal meth up there on your land, the gases released could kill anything that got upwind."

"How do you know that?" Izzie asked as she gave him a long assessing look.

Clay sighed and looked away, his earnest expression replaced with disappointment. "I looked it up on the internet."

"Do you think that was wise?"

He held her gaze. "I've never been wise around you, Bella."

Her lips parted, and her heart seemed to pound in her throat. She slid closer turning her attention to him. He started talking.

"The poison is called phosphine and it kills things. Also causes visible damage to the lungs, liver and nervous system. Convulsions, coma, heart failure. And—" Clay drew a folded sheet of paper from his breast pocket "—a fluorescent green sputum."

Izzie took the sheet, scanning over the page. "Like my cows!"

She skimmed the symptoms, and he used an elegant index finger to point to the spot. There it was.

When she glanced up, it was to find Clay watching her closely. "So you didn't know?"

Izzie's brow knit, and then realization dawned and she stiffened. Briskly she folded and returned the printout. "What are you implying?"

He met her hard glare with one of his own. "I told you when you hired me that I won't be a part of anything illegal. Not even for you, Izzie. If you knew they were on your land, you best tell me right now."

Her hands fisted, and she folded her arms defensively over her chest.

"Izzie. I mean it. I've been down this road before. I will not do it again."

"Don't you trust me?"

"I don't trust anyone. Not anymore."

She sighed heavily and threw up her hands in aggravation. But she answered his question—again. "I did not know."

"Word is that you got money troubles."

She gasped. "Who told you that?"

He shrugged. Izzie looked away.

"Is it true?" His voice held a note of tenderness now.

"Yes. Mom has…some debts."

"Then they aren't your debts."

Izzie sighed. "Not technically. But someone has to pay

the bills. She spends everything she can get her hands on and more."

"Gambling."

Her brow lifted. "No. Not anymore. Not since I was a kid." Izzie placed her elbows on her knees and cradled her chin in her upturned palms.

"She likes nice things." And so Izzie had shut down their line of credit at the bank. Removed her mother's name from the accounts. But the damage was done. Her mother had a nice new car, leased, and Izzie had a car payment and a six-thousand-dollar loan against her precious truck.

"And you are covering for her."

"What am I supposed to do? She's my mother."

"How?"

She lifted her chin from her hands and turned to meet his stare. "I am *not* involved with manufacturing drugs, Clay."

He nodded and looked out over the lake. "I believe you."

She didn't know if she should be insulted or relieved. Izzie stared at the abandoned quarry as she thought about it. Finally she said, "That means a great deal to me."

He gave a humorless laugh. "It shouldn't. I'll believe just about anyone."

She cast him an odd look, and he shook his head and fell into silence. It hurt her to realize how much his past still haunted him. She wondered if she might make that a little bit better by sharing the truth.

"Clay, I want to tell you something…something about Martin."

Now Clay looked uncomfortable, his eyes shifting everywhere but back to her as his hands braced against the log, stiff and straight on either side of his body. He looked as if he were preparing to throw himself from the log and right into the lake.

"I want you to know why I went out with your friend."

He flinched, and then his mouth tipped down, making tight lines that flanked his mouth.

"Because you preferred him to me?"

"No. Because my parents would not allow me to go out with you after my cousin told them you were selling weed."

"I never…" He stopped, as if the arguing was useless.

She believed him. But after his father died, Clay had changed, taking his anger out in rebellion. Skipping school, getting into fights. When the drunk driver killed his mother, he'd changed from rebellion to recklessness.

"You scared me back then, Clay. You were so wild. And after my aunt caught my cousin with the pot, he said you sold it to him. My parents had just gotten back together, and I didn't want any more fighting. So I said all right."

He bowed his head as the muscles at his jaw turned to granite.

"Did your cousin tell you who really supplied him with the weed?"

She shook her head.

"Martin. He supplied everyone back then."

Izzie gasped. "I didn't know that."

"He was very careful. While I…well, I was a train wreck."

"You were not."

But he had been. Back then, Clay had so much anger in him. He wouldn't tell her why, but it had begun with the trouble between his folks. Around that time, the Twin Towers fell and Clyne had joined the marines right after. Was that really fourteen years ago? Gabe, just shy of turning sixteen, had been too young to join. But Clay said he had wanted to. She knew that things had been rocky between their parents but it had taken their mom two more years before she left Clay's dad for good. Gabe, then eighteen, had found his escape riding the rodeo circuit.

That had left Clay and Kino in the middle of the mess. Clay had skipped school to go hunting, escaping into the woods. He'd failed everything and been left back, but he'd just kept cutting class. She'd reminded him that without his diploma the marines wouldn't take him. That was when he'd confessed that it killed him to come to school and have her ignore him.

Then his father had been murdered.

"I couldn't stand it," he said. "I thought you wouldn't talk to me because of my dad. He ruined a lot of things. Then he died, and I thought, finally, it will get better."

Izzie had gone to the funeral. Clay had not. But he was back in school and his grades came up. Sometimes they would study together in the school library. He'd hit the books and studied hard. He just made it through his sophomore year and she her junior year. She'd really thought he'd make it into the US Marines. Then, over the summer, his mother had gone to that competition in South Dakota. Seven months short of his seventeenth birthday…

"Then your mother and sister died. Or we thought your sister died."

He clasped his hands together and rested his forearms on his thighs. "Did I tell you that Kino is taking Lea up to South Dakota after they see some sights? He's going to find her. I just know it."

She rested a hand on his forearm. "I hope so."

He smiled and placed his hand over hers. "Iz, I was so angry at the world and myself back then, I couldn't see straight. The only good thing in all that time was you."

She resisted the pull to move closer. That had always been the way with him. She was too old now for her mother to keep her from seeing whoever she pleased. But Clay was now working for the livestock manager, who had her cows. Would they really fire him for seeing her? And hadn't she caused him enough trouble?

"I shouldn't have gone out with him. But I was so desperate to see you."

Clay gave her a look of confusion.

"Seeing Martin was the only way I could think of to be with you."

He gave his head a quick shake as if he did not believe his ears, and he gaped. She held her breath, waiting for him to call her all the things she called herself, a coward, a traitor, a child. She had been all of that and more. But he just stared, and she exhaled, realizing the next breath had to choke past the lump in her throat.

"Is that true?" he asked, his voice now a low whisper.

"Yes." Tears stung her eyes. She lifted her chin and fought a battle against them and lost. "It was stupid. They forbade me to see you. But when I was with Martin, you were there. At least in the beginning."

"Before he started bragging."

Izzie gasped. "About us?" Shock dissipated, to be replaced with outrage. "I never once. We never! It's a lie."

He let his hand slide from hers. She returned them to her lap.

He met her gaze. Held it. Then he nodded his acceptance of her declaration. My Lord, no wonder he stayed away. And Martin had pressed her so hard.

"Did he tell you why I broke up with him?"

Clay lifted a brow. "He said he dumped you."

Izzie made a sound of frustration and swiped at the tears. Then she stared out at the blue waters where once they had all dared each other to jump from the cliffs. Clay had jumped first. Back before her parents had heard the rumors about Clay. Before they had made it impossible for her to see him. Before Clay took a gun and robbed a store.

She watched the golden sunlight of late afternoon glint on the water in wide bands. She thought that their relationship had become like that lake, just the surface visible and so many secrets hidden beneath the calm water.

Her anger burned away, leaving her hollow and more tired than she could ever remember.

"Clay, will you tell me what happened that day?"

He hesitated, then answered with his own question. "Haven't you heard the story?"

She had. Several versions. Rubin had no connections and so had gone to federal prison. Clay, the son of a drug trafficker and meth addict, had a war-hero uncle in the FBI, a brother on the tribal council and another on the police force. He'd gotten off easy. That's what folks said. But she was no longer interested in that story. She wanted *his* story.

"The paper said the records were sealed because you were a minor."

He pursed his lips and blew out a breath. "What do you want to know?"

Chapter Nine

Clay waited with a hollow resignation for the questions. In the seconds before she spoke he decided to tell her everything. Couldn't be worse than the rumors. Could it?

"Why did Rubin go to prison, when you went to a detention center?" Izzie asked. "Was it because of your uncle, like everyone says, or something else? And why did you say that you will not be set up *again*?"

He tried to think to consider his reply, but Izzie's questions buzzed about inside his head like a hive of angry hornets, stinging him. The poison of his past seeped into his bloodstream, making him as cold as the chilled lake waters.

He'd been so angry back then. Sick with anger, drowning in it. Angry at his father for getting killed and angry at Clyne for picking the marines over his miserable broken family and at Gabe for leaving to ride the rodeo circuit and then sending most of his money home. Angry at the need for that money and the way his mother watched for the mail. Angry that his older brothers found a way out that left Clay and Kino behind, at Kino for idolizing his druggie father after his death, at his mother for driving to South Dakota to win a contest only to die, and angry at the drunk driver who crossed the center line to use his pickup truck as a battering ram against his mother's Honda Civic.

All the same stuff that happened to him had happened to

Gabe and Clyne, but somehow they'd never missed a step as Clyne took over providing for the family and Gabe took over managing the household. It was as if they didn't even miss them. Only Kino had faltered, fixating on his need to avenge their father, as if he deserved it, which he didn't.

"I always meant to tell you, Izzie." He cast her a glance and was immediately sorry. She glared at him. She was not the open-minded girl she had once been. Perhaps he was lucky that she even cared to ask. Or perhaps she didn't care about him so much as worrying about what kind of a man she had chosen to read sign.

"But you never did," she said.

"Hard to. I called. Left messages."

Her jaw dropped. "I didn't know that."

He sat back on the log as realization struck. Her parents never told her. Of course they hadn't. But he had also tried in person.

"You wouldn't speak to me. I tried, that day outside Elkhorn Drugs. And again after church."

"I remember I was with my parents, who had forbidden me to speak to you. My dad threatened to turn me out if I was seen with you."

Clay dropped his head, and his blunt cut hair fell in a curtain about his face. It didn't hide his shame. Who could blame them? If Izzie had been his daughter, he wouldn't have allowed her within a mile of him.

"Clay, my father is dead, and my mom, well, she and I are having troubles. And I want to hear. Will you tell me, please? I'll listen. I promise."

It was all he could hope for.

"First, tell me what you think you know."

"All right." She looked skyward and drew in a long breath.

"I know that there was a robbery. Martin shot the clerk.

The clerk was Native and a few years older than me. I didn't know him, but I know his family. Rubin was with Martin in the mini-mart. You waited in the car. Their driver. I know you took them to and from the convenience store in that car of yours."

She didn't say it was a worse piece of junk than the truck he now drove. His first car, more Bondo than metal unless you counted the coat hanger holding up the muffler. He'd been saving up then and now, for what he didn't know. A truck, a bus ticket, a fresh start, a chance to make something of himself.

Izzie gathered a strand of hair, absently sliding her fingers along the length. "I know it was a 2001 hatchback. Terrible choice for a getaway car." She arched a brow and then continued. "I know Gabe was the patrolman who came after you. I know that Martin fired at him with a pistol, and Gabe killed him with a single shot. I know it was a closed coffin. I know that you and Rubin were arrested. You went to Colorado, and Rubin went to a federal prison for four years, the maximum they could give him because the crime happened on the Rez, and Rubin is Native."

That was all so.

"You were charged with aiding and abetting and with fleeing the scene and...what else?"

"Conspiracy to commit a crime. That means they say that I knew about the planned robbery beforehand and didn't tell anyone. Anything else?"

"I know I wrote you in Colorado, and you never wrote back."

That piece of news hit him hard in the gut.

"I wrote you back," he said. "Three times. But I never got another letter."

Her gaze flicked to him. "You wrote?"

He nodded. Izzie's generous lips pressed thin. She was

puzzling it out, deciding if he was lying or if her parents had taken them.

"Why should I believe you?" she asked.

"I don't know. Nobody does. Not even the courts."

Clay leaned back, gathering his knee and lacing his fingers around his shin as a counterbalance.

Izzie turned toward him, sitting sideways on the log.

"Why don't you tell me what happened?"

He felt so tired, but he faced her and gave her a look, making sure she wanted to hear. She nodded.

"Tell me." It wasn't a resounding affirmation of faith, but that needed to be earned. From what he'd seen since returning more than six years ago, not many folks were even willing to hear his side.

Izzie waited.

It was a start. But the telling was hard. He didn't like it because it made him look stupid. He had been a fool. A fool for Izzie. A fool to trust Martin. A fool to go with them that day.

"I got my GED," he said.

Her nostrils flared, and she angled her head, staring, still waiting.

"Okay, listen, okay…where to start?" His throat was dry. He shifted nervously and then thought that this just made him look guilty, as if he was thinking up a lie. He stretched his neck and rolled his shoulders as he once did before nodding at the handlers to open the shoot at the rodeo. Eight seconds on a whirlwind, that was what Clyne called riding a bucking bronc. This was worse. "That day, Rubin cut school. Martin and me, we'd already dropped out. Martin unofficially—me, well, my paperwork was submitted and filed."

Izzie shook her head in disapproval. "You were so close to graduating."

"I was miles away from graduating. I needed to get out of here. Thought if the marines wouldn't take me I could make a living riding broncs."

"Like Clyne and Gabe," she said.

But he hadn't rode broncs until after juvie.

"Anyway, Rubin's father is a trucker. He hauls different stuff." Clay didn't want to say anything that might make Izzie a target, so he kept it general. This kind of information was dangerous.

"He works for the cartels," said Izzie.

Clay raised his brows in surprise.

"That's what my father said. But he hauls regular stuff, too. Potato chips, cigarettes."

"Women," said Clay.

This time Izzie's eyes went wide.

"That day, well, Rubin said his dad had a big job, very hush-hush. Rubin thought it was weed. It was usually weed, but when we got to his place, there was the back of the trailer in his big barn and a blue port-a-john beside it. I saw a hose leading under the closed gate of the truck, through that little opening in the back. Rubin's dad was home, but drunk, so Rubin stole his keys and opened the back. Rubin wanted to take some pot, sell it."

"But not you."

"Izzie, Clyne was home then. Recovering from the injury. Taking charge. He was on me pretty hard. He had me working for the tribal headquarters, and Gabe had just joined the force. He thought it would be a good idea to use the new dog to check my room and car for drugs."

"Good for them."

"Yeah. I was glad to have them home. Anyway, when we opened the gate it was full of women. Girls, really. Mexicans. They were so young, and they started screaming. Rubin's father came and cuffed Rubin across the mouth. Chipped a tooth in the front. He said the girls were on their way to Phoenix that night. The cartels promised them jobs as hostesses and waitresses, but they were going to end up in strip clubs and bars and massage parlors from here to Atlanta."

Izzie looked as sick as Clay felt. "What did you do?"

"I decided to tell my brother. Gabe could come out and stop this. They were people, you know, not drugs. Kids. Younger than me, mostly. But I didn't tell that to Rubin or Martin. Martin actually asked if he could have one of them for the day."

"One of who?" Izzie's voice rang with outrage.

Clay mopped his forehead with his hand.

"A girl. He wanted one. Rubin's dad laughed and said sure, if he had two hundred dollars."

And there it was. The reason for everything that followed.

He didn't understand it because at that time Martin was still dating Izzie. Anyone who had a girlfriend as pretty and sweet and smart as Isabella Nosie didn't need to take some child. The idea of paying two hundred dollars to rape a girl made Clay sick. They hadn't looked older than thirteen.

"Then we left, and I thought it was over. But it wasn't. Martin said he wanted a pop. So I stopped at that store. I just wanted to get away from them, you know, forever. I was done. But they went in, and I didn't drive away..." God, he'd been stupid. So stupid.

"And?"

"And..." His shoulders rounded. "I had a flip phone. I used it. Called Gabe. He was new on the force then. Riding along with John Wilcox. I told him about the girls, and then I heard the shot. Gabe heard it, too. I told him it was gunfire and where I was. Later the attorney said I knew what they were doing and just got cold feet. Rubin and Martin ran back to the car. I dropped the phone between my legs. Gabe heard most of it."

"You didn't know what they were planning before-hand?"

"That's what the judge asked and the police. Everyone. No. I didn't know."

Clay met her disbelieving stare and shook his head.

"Did you tell them all this?"

"Yes. Repeatedly."

"What did they say?"

"That I must have known or at least suspected. That was why I called Gabe. That I would have seen Martin's gun. That he would have shown off with it."

"Well?"

"He didn't. But I saw the gun when he got back in the car. I saw the money, too. A fist full of it. Martin dropped it on my car mat, and they both howled like wolves. Told me to drive and I did. Martin said he had his two hundred dollars and then some." Clay wiped his brow again, remembering.

"Are you crazy?" Clay had said. "I can't be part of this. My brother's a cop." And he'd just called him and given them their location. And his phone was still connected.

"But you are a part, bro. Might even let you join the Wolf Posse. I'll talk to Randall."

The Wolf Posse was a gang, and his grandmother lived in fear that Clay would join.

"I don't want to join. I told you."

"Well, the marines don't want you."

His ears buzzed with adrenaline. What was happen-ing? The panic welled in his chest, constricting. His mind flashed an image of the last time he felt this fear, when he had opened the door to his dad's kitchen, seeing him lying in a pool of his own blood, and his little brother Kino huddled under that kitchen table crying.

"We gotta bring the money back," said Clay.

"Bring it back? I just shot a guy. I'm never going back."

"You shot him? Who?" asked Clay.

"He got one right here." Martin used the barrel of his gun to point at his own cheek. "Ow. Still hot."

That's when the siren blared. Clay saw the familiar car speeding up behind them. He knew it. One just like it was parked in his grandmother's yard every night. It was either Gabe or one of the other guys on the force. There were only twelve of them. Clay slowed down.

"Are you crazy?" yelled Martin waving the gun. "Go. Go."

He did, running like a child from a consequence, knowing he'd never outrun this. His junker hit top speed. The wheels shimmied, and the steering went mushy. Behind him the police car gained.

"Why?" said Clay.

Martin had half turned in his seat to stare out the window at the approaching car.

"Why what?"

"Why would you do this?"

"For the money, stupid."

"The money. You shot a man for money. You lied to me for money."

"I didn't lie to you."

"Yeah? So where's the pop?" Even as he said it, Clay knew how ridiculous that sounded.

Izzie's voice jarred him from his memories.

"Is that why Rubin was charged with armed robbery and you weren't? You didn't go in?"

"Yeah. Surveillance tapes showed that Rubin drew a knife. Martin shot the clerk after he opened the register.

and before the guy could hit the silent alarm. Shot him in the face. He died alone on the floor behind the counter, and Martin had his money." Clay fought against the self-loathing and the urge to go back and count all the places he could have made different choices. "Martin told me to head back to Rubin's place. I told them I had to go pick up Kino from school, which made Martin laugh."

"So you drove away?"

"He had the gun."

"The phone. Was it still on?"

"And connected. Gabe came after us. Usually the patrolmen ride alone, but Gabe was new on the force. A rookie. I kept watching for them in the rearview, and finally, there they were. Eight months on the job and here he was arresting his brother for armed robbery."

Izzie pressed her index finger to her lips and shook her head, as her eyes went wide.

"Rubin panicked and started screaming. I told Gabe I was going to hit the brakes, but Rubin thought I was talking to him and he braced against the dash.

Clay remembered that moment of perfect clarity, the moment when he realized two things simultaneously. First, he had only tolerated Martin because he couldn't stand the thought of not seeing Izzie anymore. And second, he would never again put blind trust in another person.

"I stopped. The cruiser stopped. Martin and Rubin were screaming at me. I thought I was dead. The police opened the patrol car doors, weapons drawn, and took cover. They're bulletproof, those doors."

In the rearview he had seen the driver—Gabe.

"What happened then?"

"Rubin started crying. Martin called him a baby. Martin aimed the gun out the passenger window. I hit him in the ribs, but he grabbed the door handle and fell out into the road."

Clay couldn't say the rest. The guilt was too hot, choking him. He'd kept Martin from firing at his brother. But he hadn't kept Gabe from firing at Martin.

"One shot discharged by Officer Cosen," said Izzie. "That's what the newspaper said."

"One shot." *One life lost.* He should hate Martin for setting him up, using him. Instead, he felt sad and sorry and full of regrets. Martin had been so smart. He just, he just…

Izzie's hand inched closer. He didn't look at her as her hand came to rest on his shoulder and then moved to sweep his hair back from his face, tucking a strand behind his ear.

"I'm sorry," she said and rested her head on his shoulder. She nestled there, hugging his closest arm with both of hers. Not saying a word, but just sitting beside him, her presence giving comfort.

When he had won the battle over the lump in his throat and the burning in his eyes, he drew a ragged breath. Her scent, warm and appealing, rose about him with the familiar aroma of the pines. Izzie's clothing smelled like the horses she loved, but her hair smelled like sage. He lowered his head until his cheek rested on the top of hers.

"Should I have known? Should I have said I won't drive you out to Rubin's dad's? Maybe kept driving so Martin wouldn't have died there in the road."

"I don't think you could stop Martin from doing exactly as he wanted. No one could." She pressed a hand over his chest. "That's why I broke up with him. It was his way or no way."

"But you went to his funeral."

"Out of respect." She rested a hand over his heart. "Why didn't the judge believe you?"

"Maybe he thought no one could be that dumb. But I could. Was."

"Then why didn't you go to federal prison, too?"

"I wasn't on the surveillance footage. I didn't go in the store. I didn't have a weapon. I didn't resist arrest."

"Rubin ran."

Clay nodded. "Yup. Like a rabbit. But he didn't get far. Gabe is a good runner."

"Played on the track team, right?"

"Mile and quarter mile."

"Rubin was stupid."

"Rubin was scared. We all were. But Rubin was more scared of his father than of prison. He knew his father would beat the hell out of him. His dad didn't even bail him. Just left him there."

"And you had Luke Forrest, FBI agent and decorated US Marine. The papers said he spoke at your hearing."

"He did. Asked for leniency, and he offered the program that accepted me. He was the only one who saw me during those twelve months. No contact, that's one of the rules, but FBI agents don't count, I guess. He got me the job with the tribal livestock manager. Donner is a classmate of his."

Izzie pushed off his arm and straightened. Clay had to fight to not drag her back against him. It had been so long, and he missed her so much.

"Didn't Gabe tell them about how you fought Martin?"

"He didn't see that. It happened fast. Seat blocked most of it. Just my word, which isn't worth much."

"What happened to the girls?"

"Oh, they were out there and they got them, INS and federal agencies. The women were detained, deported."

"You saved them."

"They likely came right back in the next truck."

Izzie rubbed her face with her palm and scooted away from him. "Thank you for telling me," she said.

"Thank you for listening."

They'd gone all formal again. He didn't like it.

Her eyes held a wariness that her smile did not mask. The water was now black and the sky clouding over. A cold wind blew, causing a light chop on the water.

"Best get back. Looks like rain."

Izzie stood and waited for him to rise. They walked back to the truck and slipped into their seats. She turned the key, and the truck rumbled to life. Izzie drove them back to town.

"I was going to sell a few cows to pay the fine, but they tell me I can't get them out while they are in quarantine," said Izzie.

"That's so."

"Do you think they will charge me the detention fee for the days they are in quarantine?"

"Not sure," he said.

"How long do I have to wait for the veterinary report?"

"I've never done this before, so I don't know how long it takes."

"Who takes care of my herd until then?"

"I guess I do," said Clay.

She glanced at him. "You'll see they get what they need?"

"Will do."

He wished she needed more from him than reading sign and watering cattle. He wished he could be the man in whom Izzie confided. Wished she would hold on to his arm and snuggle up against him again. But there was a mountain of troubles separating them. Talking wouldn't gain back what was lost. She'd left him and he'd left her. But Izzie had asked for his help to get her cows back. He planned to do so, and he knew exactly where to start. Rubin Fox, his old friend and convicted felon, now a full member of the Wolf Posse. If someone was cooking meth up there, Rubin would know about it.

Chapter Ten

It was end of business on Thursday before Clay could find time to go and see Rubin Fox. As he was leaving the office of the livestock manager, Clay noticed Izzie's neighbor in the parking lot. He was about to go over and say hello, but as he moved closer, he saw that Floyd was talking to Franklin Soto, the tribe's livestock inspector.

Soto was in his fifties, short and broad with an athletic physique slowly going soft. He had a ready smile, undeterred by the brown front teeth caused, Clay had heard, by a collision with the thick skull of a cow. Every year, Soto headed up the committee for the annual rodeo, which together with the tribe's casino supplied the operating budget and prize money for the rodeo events. Soto's full-time job was the health and vaccination records of the tribes' cattle, Soto was the go-between with the state officials to be certain the tribe was in compliance with all regulations.

Something about the way that Patch and Soto leaned in and spoke in hushed tones put Clay on alert, and he slowed his approach. Floyd noticed him first and called a greeting. The two men broke apart. Patch headed in Clay's direction while Soto walked past Clay without acknowledging his presence. Happened a lot.

"So, wedding tomorrow?" asked Floyd.

Clay watched Soto pass. What were they up to?

"What?" Clay asked.

"Kino. He's getting married tomorrow."

"Oh, on Saturday. He is."

"She a nice girl?"

Clay watched Soto disappear through the door and considered retracing his steps, but he had to go to a family barbecue tonight, his grandmother's party for Kino before the entire clam headed down to Salt River for the wedding rehearsal and rehearsal dinner on Friday. That meant he had limited time to find Rubin.

"Very nice."

"You got a date?"

Clay shook his head.

"Oh, I thought maybe you and Izzie were back together again, with you helping her and all."

Clay gave another shake of his head. Patch was a terrible fisherman.

"Just as well. That girl is in over her head. Best keep clear of her."

Now Patch had Clay's complete attention. He fixed his gaze on Patch, taking in his slippery smile.

"What does that mean, exactly?"

"Oh, well, just that she's got her mother's debts and those boys to look after. Hard to see how she'll make ends meet, unless she finds a man."

"She's doing okay."

"If you say so. I know exactly how much it costs to raise cattle. And I don't see her selling as many as she'd need to in order to pay her debts. What with her lack of sales and that nonsense up in her pasture, kind of makes me wonder where she found the extra money."

Clay resisted the urge to push Patch on to his scrawny backside. Instead he touched the brim of his hat and forced a smile.

"Gotta go. Family party tonight. Kino's send off."

"Oh, sure. Have fun at the wedding. Reckon half the tribe will be there."

Clay climbed into his truck, letting the anger loose on the innocent vehicle door that closed with such force it shook the interior. Could Izzie possibly be wrapped up in this? Was that why he was so mad? But she wouldn't have asked him to nose around if she were involved…unless she was playing him. Clay felt his shoulders slump. That would just kill him.

Clay turned the key in the ignition. His truck protested and then turned over. Why was he even going to see Rubin? He had no dog in this fight. He should be heading to his place to change for the party. Instead, he turned toward the worst section of the Rez. He hadn't been there since he was a teenager, but the Fox family remained in the trailer that had tilted badly even back then. Well, his mother and two sisters continued to live there and Rubin slept there sometimes. Rubin's father was still in federal prison for trafficking, second conviction, because of the illegal girls that Clay had reported. The case was one of the rare instances where the district attorney had been solicited by the tribal council, and she had agreed to try the case. Rubin's dad was four years into an eight-year sentence, and he and his son had served time in the same prison for a while.

Clay did not expect a warm welcome from the Fox family.

After Rubin had returned to Black Mountain from prison, Clay had seen him around. He'd looked different because he was different. Short hair, gaunt cheeks and a chiseled body that left no hint of the boy who had been sent away. Rubin was dressing like just what he had become—a gang member, with overlarge jeans and shirt that were ideal for concealing a weapon and a flat-brimmed ball cap that shielded his eyes. Clay had told Rubin he was sorry about his dad, and Rubin had sworn at him. Since then they had largely ignored each other. Everyone knew Rubin was a dealer, and he had his own place. But on weeknights, Rubin often ate at home, then went to work with the Wolf Posse. Clay knew that from conversation around his grandmother Glendora's table. Kino wanted to arrest Rubin. Gabe said they didn't have enough evidence.

Clay knocked at the front door. A moment later a beautiful girl stood in the door frame.

"Anna?" he asked, guessing the older of Rubin's sisters.

"Beth," she said and giggled.

Clay shook his head in disbelief. "Is Rubin here?"

"He's at the table. You're Clay Cosen, right?"

"Who?" That was Rubin's mother's voice, full of fury.

His mother started shouting, and Rubin came to the door pushing his sister back and ordering her to the kitchen. She gave Clay a seductive look of regret that made Clay's ears go back.

"Really?" said Rubin. "You come to my house?"

"I need to speak to you." Clay couldn't quite muster the courage to say he needed a favor.

"You got nerve, Cosen. Coming here." Rubin shouted over his shoulder in Apache, telling his mother to hush up. Then he followed Clay out into the night. "Why not come to my crib, coz?"

They both knew why. That's where the Wolf Posse met and conducted business. Clay was less welcome there, if that was possible.

Clay glanced at Rubin, noting that he had added more tattoos to his forearms. Wolves, of course, the symbol of the gang that Clay had come very close to joining before he'd seen that the ones who really had his back had been his family all along. His brothers. His uncle Luke. Where would he be now without them? He looked at Rubin, and a chill slithered up his spine. Rubin, a dark mirror, reflecting what might have been.

"You and I got no biz-nus, bro. How 'bout you blow?" Rubin placed a hand on the door handle, barring the entrance to his mother's home.

"I need to ask a question."

Rubin lifted a brow, curious now.

"Do you know what's going on up in Izzie's pasture?"

Rubin snorted and then gave a cruel smile. "'Course I know."

"Can you tell me?"

"What? You might be wearing a wire. You think I'm loco?"

"I'm trying to help her."

"Oh yeah? Like you helped me after the robbery? You had a lawyer, a fed and a cop in your corner. You helped me all right. Pinned the whole thing right here." He poked his chest with his thumb.

Clay was about to remind his friend that he had been innocent of every crime except being a damned fool and believing his friends. Instead Clay remained silent.

Rubin pursed his lips and then rolled his eyes. When his gaze came back to meet Clay's the bravado was gone, and his expression was deadly serious.

"You asking me and I can't tell you. But I can tell you this, stay away from Isabella Nosie. You hang around her, and you'll get yourself into trouble worse than the last time."

"What does that mean? Is Izzie involved?"

"Get off my porch, bro. And stay away from Izzie." Rubin stepped back into the house and slammed the door in his face.

Clay stood in the cool night air, feeling a different kind of cold seep into his blood. *Stay away from her.* Was Izzie involved or in trouble? Clay returned to his truck, wishing he could follow Rubin's advice and knowing that he could not.

He didn't really remember the drive to his grandmother's because his mind was elsewhere. All Rubin had done was warn him off. But it was more than Rubin had done the last time.

Clay completely forgot that he was expected for the party at his grandmother's until he drove past her house and saw the gathering of people in the yard. Tomorrow afternoon the family would head down to Salt River Reservation to meet the bride's family. Tonight, their grandmother wanted all her boys together for one last meal. Clay hung a U-turn and pulled into the overcrowded drive. Clyne's large SUV sat before him, Gabe's unmarked unit and Kino's patrol cruiser. Off on the lawn was his grandmother's late-model blue Ford sedan with the crumpled back fender where she'd backed into a concrete pole.

There were two fires in the side yard, one for cooking and one for gathering. In the firelight, Clay could make out several of Kino's friends and a few of Clyne's and Gabe's. None of his, of course, because he had forgotten to invite any of the guys from work.

From the looks of things, the party was already started. He glanced at the clock on his dashboard and winced. He was an hour late.

Glendora spotted him first and left the cooking pit. She met Clay as he exited his truck.

"Where have you been?" she asked.

"I had to see a friend."

She looked at his empty cab. "But you didn't bring him. You have the drinks?"

Clay's heart sank. He'd forgotten his one job, to pick up the pop from the beverage center. His grandmother read the truth on his face. Man, would he ever stop being the family screw-up?

"Clay?" she asked.

"I'm sorry. I'll go get it."

She clasped his wrist in a hold stronger than he would have expected from a woman her age. But then she had raised four boys after his parents had died. Clay didn't know anyone as mentally strong as Glendora, and that was including his four brothers.

"No. They'll drink water and beer. You're not leaving now."

They walked toward the makeshift banquet table, which was a large piece of plywood on sawhorses that had been covered with a blue flowered bedsheet. There was so much food he feared the table might collapse, but on further inspection, he saw that his brothers had braced the plywood with two-by-fours because they had been here early to set up.

Clay heaved a sigh as his grandmother tugged him toward the gathering.

It was fitting that they come together here, of course, in the yard where every important event of their lives had been celebrated.

His grandmother clung to Clay's arm as they moved toward the yard. There were Clyne and Gabe, tending the ribs, basting and turning. The ribs would likely be dry as they had been cooking much longer than expected. Beside them, in a circle of friends, stood Kino, laughing.

"Doesn't Kino look happy?" said his grandmother.

"Very."

"Who would have guessed that my youngest boy would marry first?" She slapped Clay. "What's wrong with the rest of you? Clyne is thirty-two and so busy with tribal business he hasn't dated in a year, and Gabe, always running from one emergency to the next. When does he have time to see a woman? You all have good jobs. Why don't you find a girl?" She sighed and looped her arm through his, leaning on his shoulder. "Kino and Lea are a good match. Do you know her Apache name?"

His grandmother referred to the name given to Lea by the shaman on the last day of her Sunrise Ceremony. Kino had told him Lea's formal name, but he could not recall. But he knew Izzie's. She was called Medicine Root Woman. It was a powerful name, grounded to the earth with a touch of magic in the strong medicine. Izzie was strong, he knew, for only someone so tough could carry the responsibility she bore.

"It is Bright Star Woman, and Lea is bright and giving. She is the balance Kino needs to keep him from seeing the world as full of nothing but bad people. Forgiveness and justice, a good match."

Was his grandmother referring to his brother's relentless hunt for their father's murderer? Clay had gone along to protect Kino, but not for any need for vengeance. His father had given them life, but he was a bad person in many ways. Much of Clay's anger had come from knowing exactly what his father was and did.

"You need balance, too."

"I'm balanced."

His grandmother patted his hand in a pacifying way. "Maybe you can take a few days off and go up to South Dakota with them."

"Grandmother, I'm not joining Kino on his honeymoon."

"But if you go, then they can have a real honeymoon instead of following your sister's trail, visiting with Bureau of Indian Affairs and the foster family we know had her as a baby. You should go instead of Kino and Lea."

"I'm not a police officer."

"You are his brother. You're smart and the best tracker on the reservation. You might even be as good as your grandfather Hex Clawson and better than my father."

That made Clay's eyebrows lift in surprise. This was high praise indeed.

"Jovanna has left no tracks."

"Everything that moves leaves tracks," she said, repeating the words Clay had heard many times and used often himself. "My husband taught me that."

"Yes, Grandmother. But I have work here."

Glendora slipped her hand from the crook of his arm. "What work is more important than finding your sister?"

Keeping Izzie safe, Clay thought.

His grandmother waited, but when Clay did not reply she exhaled and then motioned toward the gathering. "Come on, before those ribs are as leathery as jerked beef."

They moved just outside the fire's light.

"Look who's here," called his grandmother.

He was received with hugs and hoots and slaps on the back. Finally someone handed him a beer. Nice to be treated like the guest of honor instead of the lost sheep.

Kino stepped forward and hugged him.

His younger brother released him and asked, "Everything all right?"

"Sure, sure. Congratulations."

Kino gave a half smile and still managed to look happier than Clay had ever seen him.

"Good thing you didn't shoot her that day you met," said Clay.

Kino gave him a playful slug to the arm.

"Hey, quiet about that."

They exchanged a smile. Kino was getting married. The thought struck him, and Clay's heart gave a funny little flutter.

Kino's friends circled closer, returning to their conversations interrupted by his arrival. There was Bill and Javier, his brother's two closest friends. Kino's bride-to-be, Lea Altaha, was with her family at Salt River, making this a low-key bachelor's party. The woman Kino would marry was also the one he had rescued from the cartels down on the border three months earlier. Lea had worked with an aid organization, providing drinking water to those illegals crossing the desert. As Shadow Wolves, he and Kino had been charged with tracking and apprehending those same illegals. Yet somehow the two had set aside their differences and made a good, strong match.

Clay went to joint Clyne and Gabe. Clyne offered a smile, but Gabe, less tolerant of Clay's general lack of regard for the time, cast him a look of disappointment.

"Here he is. At last," said Clyne. "I'm famished." He was the one who played well with others and who was a master at both negotiation and consensus building. A leader by any measure.

Gabe, ever the investigator, was more to the point. "Where have you been?"

"I had to stop by to see a friend."

Gabe's brow swept down over his dark eyes. "What friend?"

Clay changed the subject. "Any word on the dead cattle?"

Gabe looked to the heavens as if for patience, then flicked his gaze back to Clay. "You were with Izzie Nosie?"

"No. But—"

"Good. Because you can't work for her and keep your job. You know that, right? Conflict of interest."

"She asked me to do her a favor."

"And you've done it. So stay away from her."

Clay felt the need to challenge, but a glance toward the banquet table showed his grandmother watching them from a distance with worried eyes.

"Anything from the necropsy?" he asked, hoping the dead cattle might prove his suspicions.

Gabe's face went expressionless. "Clay, you do not want to get in the middle of my investigation. And that is what this is, an active investigation. Keep out of it."

He didn't remind Gabe that it was only an investigation because Clay had tracked the cattle, found the dead cows and called him.

"You hear me?" asked Gabe.

"I do." Clay could turn his back on just about anyone and anything. But not family and not Izzie. He felt like a deer being tugged in opposite directions by two hungry wolves. Someone was about to be disappointed. But either way, the deer lost.

Chapter Eleven

Izzie had a call in at nine on Monday morning to the state veterinary offices. As an interested party, listed on their report, she was entitled to a copy of their findings, and even though Clay had raised the possibility, she was still speechless when she heard the results.

All three necropsy reports indicated that her cows died of complete cardiopulmonary collapse. There was fluid in their lungs and irritation of all respiratory membranes. The cattle also showed extreme kidney and liver damage. Blood work revealed low blood potassium and high levels of magnesium.

"Consistent with poisoning," finished the vet on the phone. "Want a fax copy or US mail?"

"What caused this?" asked Izzie.

A pause, then, "Ah, we are turning this over to the FBI. You might want to contact an attorney."

Izzie gripped the phone, blinking like an owl as that bit of information settled in. She'd never been in trouble a day in her life. She'd always done exactly what was expected even when she wanted to do otherwise.

"But I didn't do anything," she said.

"Is there anything else?"

"No. I... Thank you."

"Yeah. I'll drop a copy in the mail. We have your

address." The vet hung up, leaving Izzie gripping a phone connected to no one.

Dizziness rocked her, and she had to sit down hard in one of the vinyl-cushioned chairs at her mother's kitchen table. Next she set the phone on the plastic tablecloth festooned with yellow daisies and used the same hand to wipe the sweat away from her forehead.

Clay had been right. Those cows had inhaled something that had come out of those trailers, something that had stopped their hearts.

Izzie folded her arms on the table and rested her head on her arms. She closed her eyes. Poison, drugs, Clay had said. Something popped into her mind, and she lifted up from the table so fast she swayed.

"Clay was right! They *were* poisoned. And I have proof."

They had to give her the cattle back.

Izzie drew on her denim jacket and headed for her truck. Thirty-three minutes later she was standing in front of Dale Donner's desk demanding that he release her cows.

Donner eyed her from behind a battered, overladen desk, tipping back in his swivel chair. She recalled that her father had been happy at Donner's appointment, saying he was a fair man. His shirt stretched a little too tight over his belly, and his hands gripped the arms as if deciding if he should take the trouble to get up or not. "My cows?" she said again. "State vet says they are not contagious."

"Well, I don't have that report yet," said Donner, sounding peeved.

"Call and get it faxed. I'll wait."

He lifted his brows. "That could take a while."

She wondered if she might have had better results if she had tried a different approach. More honey and less vinegar. But she had already set herself down this road, and it was too late to backtrack.

"I want my cows back."

"I'm sure you do. But you can't have them until I have the report, and then you still owe a fine on the ones we rounded up off the road."

"But someone cut my fences and chased those cattle out of my pastures."

"I don't have the police report corroborating that, and even if I did, you have to file an appeal." Donner pushed his desk chair back and rolled on castors to the filing cabinet, where he retrieved the appropriate form. He used his legs like a child on a scooter to return to her and handed over the pages. "My advice is that you pay the fine, get your cattle back and then file the appeal. If it goes through, we'll reimburse you."

She didn't want to do that because it involved selling her cattle, which took time and cost her money. "How long do appeals take?"

"Well, you have a right to a hearing in tribal court, but you have to make a petition for a hearing within three business days of notice of impoundment, and that would be today. You just made it."

She opened her mouth to protest, but he just kept talking.

"Once the tribal court officer gets that form—" he pointed to the pages now gripped in her hand "—then the tribal court has seven business days to hear your request. Let's see, that's by next Tuesday at the latest, but they don't meet on Tuesday. So Wednesday it is. Now you have to have evidence. Can't just be your word. Witnesses and physical evidence is best. Police report, surely. Vet report and anything else you can think of."

"But you can't sell my cattle in the meantime?"

"Twenty days after notice of impoundment. We hold auctions every Thursday. Let's see." Donner consulted the business half of the wall calendar on the overcrowded bulletin board behind him. "That's October eighth."

Izzie wanted to ask where Clay might be, but resisted. She filled out the paperwork while she waited. When the fax machine chirped to life, Donner collected the pages and made a copy for himself.

"I can release the quarantine lot. Not the impounded ones, though."

"You'll bring them to my place."

Donner rubbed his neck. "You have to arrange transport."

Izzie's face went hot. "But you took them."

"As a precaution."

She flapped her arms, and the appeal fluttered against her leg. "Fine. I'll be back."

She stomped from the office and took both the appeal application and fax pages across the street to tribal headquarters.

After that, Izzie took Donner's advice and spoke to Victor Bustros about selling a few of her cattle at Thursday's auction to pay the impoundment fine and hoped she get it back on appeal. Victor Bustros handled the brand inspection and auctions on the Rez. Izzie calculated carefully how many of the cattle she needed to sell to and pointed out the cattle picked to Bustros's assistant, who marked them with paint. She hoped they got a fair price, because her checking account was dangerously low. She wondered, not for the first time, what her mother spent the grocery money on, because for a cattle family, they certainly ate a lot of beans.

Since Izzie did not have the extra money to have her recovered cattle trucked back home, she was left with only one alternative. She called her part-time hands, Max Reyes and Eli Beach. They arrived with the horse trailer and three of her horses, including Biscuit.

The rest of the day was spent moving the released portion of her herd slowly from the quarantine yard to her permitted grazing land.

By day's end she was hot, hungry and angry at no one and everyone. She thanked Eli and Max, who agreed to go retrieve the horse trailer while she saw the horses settled. It wasn't until she returned to the house, bone tired and dragging her feet with fatigue, that her mother stepped from the front door and greeted her with a worried expression. She extended her arm, offering a white legal-sized envelope.

"This came for you. I had to sign for it."

Izzie studied the tribal stamp and seal. Her mother had not opened it.

"What is it?" she asked.

"Might be the necropsy results or the official release from quarantine. Could be their acknowledgment. I've requested a hearing about the cut fences. I don't think I should have to pay a fine when someone is messing with me." Izzie slit the envelope with her finger, leaving a ragged flap of torn paper. Then she drew out the enclosed letter. She scanned the page. Her ears started ringing.

"No, no, no," she whispered. She reread the words to be sure she understood, and then her arm dropped to her side, still clutching the letter.

"What is it?"

"Notice from the general livestock coordinator."

"Pizarro?"

Izzie nodded. "They have scheduled our pastures for immediate renourishment."

"What does that mean?"

Izzie stared at her mother. "It means the cows can't graze here."

Her mother shrugged. "Good. Sell the damned things. I hate cows."

With that her mother left her only daughter standing alone in the yard. Izzie managed to wait until her mother was out of sight before she began bawling like a newly branded cow.

How was she going to keep the cattle for her brothers if she had no place to graze the herd?

Izzie retreated to the barn and her favorite horse, Biscuit. She held Biscuit's coarse mane and wept for a good long while as Biscuit listened to Izzie pour out her problems. Her horse knew more about Izzie than any person living, though all secrets were safe with her mare. It was only after she had cried herself out that she realized that something stunk, figuratively.

First her cattle were rustled to the road, then three cows were poisoned by something that stopped their hearts, and then, on the very day she got half of her cattle back, she lost her grazing rights.

"Who pulled those permits, Biscuit?" Izzie asked.

Chapter Twelve

The Monday after Kino's wedding, Clay found himself back in the saddle assigned to the tribe's communal herd and the task of separating mothers and yearlings for calf branding. The job was taxing but he thought his weariness stemmed more from the festivities than from the work. The wedding was beautiful and he'd enjoyed himself. But today, unexpectedly, the memories of the celebration filled him with an unforeseen melancholy. He wished Izzie had been there with him. If he had asked, would she have come?

The day was cold with a gusty wind that lifted stinging bits of sand and dirt. Clay drew up his red kerchief over his mouth and nose and refocused on the mother who had cut away, bringing her back with the others. She and her twins trotted through the shoot into the correct pen. Roger Tolino worked the shoot, closing them in and Clay swung round for another target, but his mind still lingered on the wedding.

Clyne had no date, either. His eldest brother had said that it was one thing to take a woman out on Saturday night but quite another to invite her to your brother's wedding. Clyne did not want to give any of the women he dated the idea that he was interested in more than a night's diversion. Clyne was a strange guy, very vested in tradition and community, yet unable to find an Apache woman who stirred him in more than the obvious places. He'd even been up to Oklahoma a time or two on business that Clay suspected involved opportunities for more than just tribal networking.

Clay wondered what Izzie would say about that. He imagined all the things that he wanted to tell her about Lea and Kino. How they met as adversaries and now were newlyweds. It gave him hope.

Clay worked his way through the morning surrounded by the bawling of calves and shouts of the men. The pounding of their hooves reminded Clay of the women's pounding feet as they danced in a circle at his little brother's reception.

The wedding had been a wonderful celebration, with a mix of a church service and Apache dancing and song. Clay had been so proud to stand with his brothers at the altar and witness the match, but was surprised by all the unexpected emotions that his little brother's wedding stirred.

His brother Gabe was the only one of them to bring a date. He had gone with his usual go-to for such occasions, Melissa Turno, a classmate and assistant to the director of the Tribal Museum. His older brother had not had a serious relationship since his fiancée, Selena Dosela, had broken their engagement immediately after Gabe had arrested her father.

Unlike Gabe, who played it safe, or Clyne, who didn't play at all, Clay *wanted* to give Izzie the wrong idea. But he didn't think she felt the same.

Still, he couldn't stop thinking about how much he would have liked to see her dance with the women of the Salt River Reservation while he beat the drum and sang with his brothers. How he would have been proud to bring her as his date. To show everyone that she was his girl. Only she wasn't. Might never be.

Clay sighted the low gray clouds sweeping in, predicting a change in the weather. He was glad he had his fleece coat and lined gloves.

After lunch they started the task of checking the mother's brands and collecting the right irons. Each member of the tribe with cattle had a registered brand and those families with only a cow or two often preferred to keep them in the communal herd.

Donner's men worked well as a team. Matching the brands, roping, tying. Since Roger Tolino was the slightest and least competent with a rope, he had the job of sorting and branding. That left Clay and Dodge to catch and rope the calves and Tolino to let them go. Clay liked roping and riding, and usually such days passed quickly. But today even the coffee could not erase his general buzz of fatigue.

Clay took off after another calf, but, maybe because of the wedding, he couldn't stop fantasizing about what it would be like to go away with Izzie and then return to make a home. Not that Izzie wanted to play house with him, and the truth was, if he didn't quit messing with her, he might lose his job.

He roped the next calf, and his horse backed up, making the rope tight and his job of flipping the yearling to his side much easier. He placed a knee on the furry side and expertly tied the front and one back leg together. Then he stood and dusted off his jeans before retrieving his lariat.

He glanced at the sun and realized they'd be quitting soon. Donner did not pay overtime. Clay turned to the north and wondered how far the newlyweds had gotten. They planned to stop in Denver for two nights and then visit Yellowstone on their way east to South Dakota.

His grandmother had tried once more to get Clay to

head up there first and track their sister. He closed his eyes and imagined what that little girl of three would look like now as a child of twelve. Would she have their mother's high arching brow or the broad nose of their father? Did she wear her hair to her waist or in a short, modern style? An image of a teen with a blue stripe of dyed hair caused him to growl, as he mounted his horse.

His boss showed up to watch. Clay heard him calling something like, "So you decided to work for me today, did you?" Clay just waved and kept riding. Keeping his head down and his seat in the saddle.

When he finished work, he might go tell Izzie that even her neighbor, Patch, was gossiping about her mom's debts. He hoped her troubles had not caused her to do something stupid. If there was anyone who knew more about doing something stupid than him, Clay had yet to meet them. He knew Izzie was smarter than he was, but desperation could cause even a good girl to go bad. Honestly, he would have used any excuse to see her again. Pathetic, he thought.

Donner called a halt, and Clay turned his horse toward the communal pasture. His mount would get some extra grain, and he'd curry him down before turning him loose with the others.

Then he'd head back to his empty house to shower and change. This morning, with Kino gone, the place had been unnaturally quiet. And he'd had the misfortune of having to drink his own coffee. He wondered if Izzie made good coffee. Then he wondered how he might get Izzie over to his empty house and keep her there until morning. He needed to separate his fantasy world from his real life, where Izzie needed only his help. That didn't mean she needed *him*. Not the way he needed her, anyway.

Clay tied up his horse and removed the saddle, carrying it to his truck and then returning to curry the horse's sweaty barrel, his strokes rhythmic and practiced.

Izzie had been in trouble, and she had called him. Him. That meant something, right? She had not let her mother's dictates control her. And he had helped her, hadn't he? Maybe there could be more between them. Maybe she was the one person outside his family who was willing to give him a second chance.

He'd left the marriage ceremony hopeful. But now the doubts had caught up with him. First, Izzie was too good for him. Second, she might be playing him.

He said goodbye to the others, turning down an offer to join them for supper. He walked stiffly back to his truck, grit covered, dirty and satisfied that he had earned his pay.

Diego Azar pulled in beside his truck. Diego was a few years younger with a persistent five o'clock shadow and a bushy mustache. His father was Mexican, giving him more beard and less height than the rest of them. Nice guy and one of the first to befriend Clay. Today he'd been manning the office so Donner could get out in the field.

The younger man's excited expression said he had news. Clay paused, waiting.

"We got the report on the cattle."

He perked up. Clay knew what cattle, but he asked just to be sure. "Izzie's cattle?"

"Yeah. They were released this morning from quarantine."

"Why didn't they call me? I could have driven them back."

Azar nibbled the ends of one side of his mustache as if considering his reply. "Donner said you'd ask that. So he told me to tell you that if he catches you moonlighting for her again, he'll fire you."

Clay stilled. He needed this job, but more than that he

needed the clean reputation that came with working for a man like Mr. Donner. In addition, it would be poor thanks to his uncle if he lost this position.

"She hasn't asked me to do anything else." Which was the truth, much to his chagrin. "When does she get her herd?"

"Already did. Some, anyway. They're keeping the strays we impounded from the road. Let loose the rest. She drove them out this morning."

"Drove? You mean we didn't offer to return them?"

"Guess not. Owner's responsibility. Right?"

Clay took a step toward Azar, who raised his hands in surrender. "Hey, not my call, man. Donner was there."

Clay knew they often used the tribe's vehicles to transport private stock. But not Izzie's cattle.

Clay looked toward Donner, who was talking to Tolino and Dodge. Clay resisted the urge to march over there. Donner met his eye, held it and then returned to his conversation.

"Oh," said Azar. "Almost forgot. He told me to give you this." Azar withdrew several neatly folded pages from his breast pocket. "He said I should wait while you read it."

Clay accepted the offering, unfolding the pages. It was the necropsy report from the state. Another glance showed Donner watching him like a raven from the top of a tall pine. Clay turned his attention to the report.

"It's bad stuff, Cosen. Really, really bad."

Clay scanned the results. The long and short of it was that the cattle had been poisoned, and the poison had been phosphine, a by-product of cooking crystal meth. He glanced from the report to meet Donner's expressionless stare.

Donner ambled over.

Clay folded the pages and offered them back to Donner as Azar looked from one man to another.

"Thank you," said Clay.

"Figured you'd get a hold of it one way or another."

Did he mean from Izzie or Gabe, or was he insinuating that Clay would resort to theft? He didn't know, and let the comment slide. But he didn't like the implication.

Donner accepted the report and thrust it in his back pocket. "I've already called Chief Cosen to notify him of the cause of death. He's bringing in the FBI. You need to stay way the heck away from this."

"This or her?"

Donner rubbed his neck. "You work for me, so I have to say it because you don't have a reputation for being the best judge of character."

And there it was. "No one tells me who I can and can't speak to. Not even my boss." But his skin was now tingling, and the hairs on his neck stood up just the same way they had that day when he'd looked in his rearview mirror and seen his brother's police cruiser with lights flashing.

He turned to go and Donner spoke again.

"Clay, they think she's involved."

There was a whooshing sound in his ears now. Had Izzie become so desperate that she would allow such things to happen on her land? He didn't want to believe it. But his stomach cramped with his doubts. He never would have thought Martin would have picked up a gun and shot an innocent man just so he could get laid. How could Clay really know what was in the heart of a man?

Or a woman?

Donner headed in the opposite direction, leaving Azar hovering with wide worried eyes.

"I gotta go," said Clay.

Clay climbed into his truck and pulled the door closed. Azar stepped forward and gripped the ledge of the open window.

"Why don't you come have a drink with us?" asked Azar.

"Rain check, okay?"

Azar released his hold and stepped back. "Be careful, Clay."

Chapter Thirteen

Supper time approached, and Izzie was still in the barn with Biscuit. She'd curried her horse down, cleaned the tack and wiped her eyes before her brothers piled off the bus. They'd headed to the house to change and grab a snack, but then they'd return dressed in work clothes and buzzing with excitement over the return of half the herd. That gave her a chance to pull her work shirt over the documents in her back pocket that revoked the family's permits and to practice her expressionless mask of stoicism. It was easier than forcing a smile and easier on the boys than crying in front of them.

"You got them back," shouted Will, by way of a greeting as he charged into the barn.

At eleven, he was one of the tallest in the sixth grade, but also one of the thinnest. All arms and legs, he did not yet resemble their father for whom he was named. He wore his hair very short, as was the style now for boys. Behind him came Jerry, a fourth grader, who was losing teeth but not yet gaining inches. As a result he was more coordinated and compact.

Izzie kept brushing, hoping that her brothers would be so preoccupied with the cattle, now filling the pasture behind their home, that they would not notice their sister's red and puffy eyes.

"Yes, most of them," she said, thinking her voice sounded nearly normal.

Will stood in the barn door, looking up at the hillside and the herd that grazed as if they had not ever left. Jerry reached her side, his eyes dancing with excitement.

"How did you do it?"

"The report came back from the state. They're not sick."

"So what killed the three we lost?"

Izzie had thought about this, wondering how much to tell them. She wanted to protect them but did not want to leave them ill-equipped to deal with what their classmates might hear from their parents. They were still children. How much did they really need to know?

"Well, nothing catching. That's the important thing." She glanced down from Biscuit's withers and met Jerry's gaze. "How about you two see to the sheep. I'll feed the horses today."

"Hurray!" shouted Jerry, pumping his fist as if he'd just scored the game-winning basket. Then he wheeled away.

"Don't forget the chickens!" she shouted to their backs.

Izzie prepared four buckets of oats and some vitamins. She placed Biscuit's feed before her and headed out to the pasture. At sight of the buckets the other three horses came trotting back to the barn for supper. That was where she was when she saw a familiar rusty pickup pull into her drive.

Clay, she realized, and her heart did a little flutter. He swung out of the cab and strode in her direction. She breathed deep for the first time since the papers were delivered. The dread, which she carried since receiving that envelope, began to slip away.

"Heard about your cattle," he said by way of a greeting.

"Yeah." She tried for a smile but fell short, managing only a grimace.

"And the report. The cows weren't sick." He reached her now, and only the thin wire fence separated them.

Izzie glanced toward the house, wondering if her mother stood at the window, watching. Izzie's stomach knotted tighter, and her need to touch him warred with the worry that her mother would embarrass her. She shouldn't care, but her mother thought him responsible for Martin's death. Martin, Izzie's mother believed, was a good boy who had paid with his life for his involvement with Clay. If she only knew the truth. But there was no point in arguing. She would not believe a word Izzie said.

"Would you rather they be sick?" he asked. He was studying her face, and his expression was as somber as a funeral mourner. He lifted a hand and placed one gloved finger under her chin, tilting her face upward. "Izzie, have you been crying?"

He noticed. Of course he did. Clay had always noticed everything about her. A new shirt, a change in mood. Her eyes started to burn again.

She drew back a step and nodded. Then she pulled the papers from her back pocket and offered them to Clay. "I got these today."

He took them and read them as the horses finished their meal and ambled back into the pasture. Izzie retrieved the buckets and placed them by the fence, then slipped out between the wires, expertly missing the barbs both top and bottom. She noticed Will and Jerry leaving the chicken coop and pausing to stare at their unexpected visitor. Will started toward them.

Clay lowered the pages. "Immediate renourishment?"

The knot filled her throat again, so she nodded.

"What's this about? You've had this grazing permit forever."

Actually since her grandfather had applied for them,

back when no one wanted this far-off corner of the Rez. Her grandfather and father had cleared many of the trees by hand, making the wooded area suitable for grazing.

"Maybe it's just time," she offered.

"No way, Izzie. This has to do with the state report. You know that, don't you?"

Before she could answer, Will and Jerry drew up, hands in back pockets, trying to look like the men of the place.

"Ya'atch," said Clay, using the Apache greeting.

They both answered in unison.

"Boys, this is Clay Cosen."

Jerry's eyes went wide, and he and Will exchanged looks. Clearly it was a name they knew.

"Clay and I went to school together."

The two stood staring like two baby owls.

"Well? Shake his hand," she ordered.

Jerry, the outgoing one, offered his hand first. Her brother stared at his hand while Clay shook, as if expecting something to happen. Then Will offered his, and Clay accepted it.

"You two done with your chores?" she asked.

"Not yet," said Will.

"Best get to them. Daylight's burning."

They hesitated and then walked toward the sheep pen, casting several backward glances.

"Afraid to leave you alone with me, I'll bet," said Clay.

"They're only boys," she said, dismissing his concerns.

"They're your brothers. No matter how old they are, they want to protect you."

"I think this is a bigger threat," she said, retrieving the papers.

"I'd say so. What do you plan to do?"

"I'm not sure. Apply for a new permit?"

Clay shook his head. "You can fight it, you know?"

She didn't know that and told him so with her blank stare.

"You appeal to the council. Call the office and ask to be placed on the agenda. They're meeting Wednesday night."

"I can't speak before the council."

"Why not?"

"I just… I've never done anything like that before."

"Izzie, you're under attack here. Half your herd is still impounded. Three were poisoned, and now your permits have been pulled. Am I the only one who smells a rat?"

He'd confirmed her fears. The tears started again, running down her cheeks as her lip trembled like a seismometer predicting an earthquake.

Clay pulled her in his arms. His hand rubbed her back, and he made soothing sounds. That only made her cry harder because it felt so good to be back in his embrace again.

"I got you, Izzie. I'll get you through this."

She sagged against him, letting him take her weight and her fear and her sorrow. He took it all, standing solid as Black Mountain as he cradled her. She finally reined herself in and straightened to find both her brothers staring at them from across the yard. She stepped back from Clay, and he cast a glance over his shoulder. Then he returned his attention to her.

"You're going to be all right?"

She didn't think so. Everything around her seemed to be breaking loose, and she couldn't hold the pieces together any longer. She should go and reassure the boys. Tell them that everything was all right. But it wasn't all right. It was so *not* all right.

"I'll talk to Clyne and make sure you get on the agenda,"

said Clay and inclined his head toward the house. "You want me to stay?"

She did. So much it frightened her.

"No. Call me, please."

"Have you seen the state report yet—the necropsy?"

"No. I heard a summary over the phone."

"Call my boss. Ask for a copy. You're entitled to one. And I'll see if I can get it."

She didn't even remember walking him to his truck. He took hold of her hand. The act was as natural as breathing. She laced her fingers with his, cherishing the warmth of his palm pressed to hers. Suddenly she didn't feel all alone. It was just like before this all happened. Back when the world was full of nothing but anticipation for their bright future. She looked up at him, taller now, changed in ways she couldn't even imagine. His smile was endearing and made her heart beat faster. How had she ever managed all this time without him? Izzie didn't know. But she did know that she didn't want to do that again.

He released her hand and climbed behind the wheel. "I'll call tonight."

"Thank you." She waved him away and then walked past her brothers, who gawked at her. She made it into the house to find her mother, red-faced with fury.

It was a confrontation that was long overdue. But this time, Izzie would not turn tail like a whipped dog.

Chapter Fourteen

Clay arrived late for dinner at his grandmother's home. He stepped into the living room and was greeted with the aroma of onions and garlic and beef. The heavenly blend reminded him how long it had been since he'd eaten. His grandmother appeared from the kitchen doorway, face bright with her smile. In her hands she held a wet dish towel showing she had already cleaned up. Clay hugged her, and she patted his shoulder, still clutching the rag.

"You're late," she said. She stood on her tiptoes and inhaled. "You smell good." Now she stepped back, still holding him by each upper arm and beaming up at him. "Showered, dressed. I hope that isn't all for me."

He recalled a time when her face had creased with disappointment in him. He never wanted to see that expression again. Glendora Clawson had already seen more than her share of tragedy, and it showed on her lined face and the silver strands in her dark hair.

"I stopped by to see Izzie."

Gabe appeared from the dining room, pausing in the doorway, an empty coffee mug held absently in one hand and a tight expression on his face.

Clay returned his attention to his grandmother.

"Have you eaten?" she asked.

Clay shook his head, and Glendora went to work, darting into the kitchen. Clay followed, watching her bustle to the cupboards and then to the stove, ladling out a portion of stew from a steaming pot.

"Just let me warm up the fry bread." She set aside the stew and recovered three large disks of the fried dough that all her boys loved. The golden flat bread was wrapped in paper towels and popped in the microwave. She handed over the stew in a bowl with a large spoon.

"Coffee, water or milk?"

"Water, please," said Clay.

She motioned him toward the dining room. Gabe followed a moment later with a steaming cup of coffee. That and the uniform he still wore meant his brother was working tonight.

Clay took the seat adjoining Gabe's. Behind Clay sat a small television on a wobbly table. A weather girl from Phoenix reported clear skies and cold nights.

"Can I get a copy of the state vet report on Izzie's cows?" asked Clay.

Gabe glanced from the television back to him. "Public record."

"Do you have it?"

Gabe fiddled with his phone and then glanced up. "Emailed as an attachment."

"Thanks."

No moss ever grew on Gabe.

From the kitchen came the long plaintiff beep of the microwave and the sound of the door opening. His grandmother appeared with three thick pieces of fry bread. She gave Clay two and Gabe one.

"I had supper," said Gabe.

"Not enough. You're too skinny. All of you." Glendora returned the salt and pepper to the table before Clay and pushed the butter closer. Then she retreated to the kitchen, leaving Gabe and Clay alone.

"Is Luke coming?" asked Clay and then dug into the stew.

"Yeah." Gabe sipped his coffee. "Oh, and he's bringing his new partner, Cassidy something. They were reassigned as a team and have agreed to review my investigation."

Most tribal police were loath to bring in the federal authorities. Not Gabe. He knew when they were needed, and he didn't hesitate.

"Is Izzie under investigation?"

Gabe gave him a blank stare and lifted his mug, taking a long swallow.

No answer is still an answer, their mother used to say.

"Luke wants to speak to you, too."

Clay nodded, shoveling the stew now, barely tasting the warm, delicious mixture as his famine took control. When he straightened, his grandmother appeared and retrieved the bowl. Clay tore into the fry bread.

"Might be best to keep away from Izzie until they clear her."

Clay sighed, knowing that once again, he wouldn't do what was best or wise or expected. His grandmother returned with another full bowl of stew, and Clay dug in, savoring this helping now that the hunger had eased. Finally he pushed the bowl away and regarded his brother.

"She's not cooking meth," said Clay.

"What if she just gets paid to look the other way?" His brother was a good investigator, and his suspicion worried Clay deeply. He was paid to get to the bottom of things. Sometimes that made him a real pain in the neck. Clay knew for a fact that it was Gabe's unwillingness to ignore things that had broken up his engagement to Selena Dosela. He just had to poke around, and Selena must have felt that he had used her, which he had and would always do to solve a crime. Clay knew Gabe would do his job even if that meant arresting his brother, again.

"If she's involved, then why ask me to track those cows?"

"A mistake, maybe," said Gabe. "Or unrelated."

"Why go up in the woods where they were cooking, and why would they shoot at her?"

"Didn't recognize her?"

"Or she's innocent."

Gabe dropped his police chief persona and gave Clay a worried look. "Don't put me through this again."

"I haven't done anything."

"I still believe you didn't do anything the last time. But being in the wrong place at the wrong time was enough. Remember?"

Clay nodded and went into the kitchen. Clyne appeared from the hall leading to his bedroom and stopped when he noticed Clay.

"Moving back?"

"Not today."

Clyne nodded and rummaged in the refrigerator for a bottle of beer. Clearly Clyne was off duty for the night. Unlike Gabe, Clyne's schedule was regular, except for the occasional emergency, but often they called the tribal council chair first.

His grandmother stowed away the leftovers as Clyne leaned against the counter regarding Clay. *Oh, boy*, Clay thought. *Here comes the other barrel of the Clyne-Gabe shotgun. Two-on-one, that's how it was and always has been.*

"I need you to put Izzie on the council agenda. She is contesting the impoundment and fine."

"Okay."

"She is also contesting her permits being pulled."

Clyne set aside his beer, and Glendora stopped shuffling. Gabe propped himself in the doorway, all ears. Clay told him about the renourishment, and Gabe chimed in about getting the orders from Tessay and delivering them in person, as required.

"I forgot about that," said Clyne absently. "Voted last week on all renourishment recommendations."

"Last week?" asked Gabe, eyes sharp.

Clay caught Clyne and Gabe exchanging a look.

"I'll make a motion for a delay," said Clyne, "if you promise to keep away from that upper pasture."

"Deal," said Clay. The trail would be cold, anyway. "You know that road on her upper pasture? The one in the woods?"

"Yeah."

"Can you find out who built it and why?"

"I'll give it a shot."

"Thanks."

Clyne retrieved his beer, and Clay headed to the living room to call Izzie. She sounded stressed but refused his offer to meet somewhere. He got her email address and agreed to send over the necropsy report. As he returned the receiver to the cradle he worried over the tension that had rung clear in her voice.

Clay wished he could see her, but he abided by her wishes and headed home alone. The house was dark and unnaturally quiet. He wasn't used to being alone, except in the woods, of course, where he preferred it.

ON TUESDAY THEY finished the branding. That night Clay ate with his brothers at his grandmother's home. Kino called during their dinner hour to check in. They expected to be in South Dakota by Friday. Their grandmother Glendora recalled for him the name of the retired trooper who Clyne and Gabe had discovered had witnessed Jovanna removed from the scene of the accident. It was a reminder that none of them needed. Clay spoke to Kino briefly and thought he'd never sounded so happy. Clay pushed down the tiny stirring of jealousy at his brother's good fortune as his thoughts went to Izzie Nosie again.

On Wednesday, Clay picked up several strays off one of the tribal highways. There was a council meeting to-night, and Izzie was on the agenda. He mentally reviewed all the information Clyne had given him on procedure for the meeting. He went home, showered, ate some leftovers and rattled around the empty place until he could stand it no longer. Then he headed to the meeting early.

Izzie was already there. She came to greet him, her eyes darting nervously about as she licked her lips. He took her hand and kissed her on the cheek in hello, then felt he had overstepped when her face flushed, and she glanced around to see if anyone had noticed them. Was she still ashamed to be seen with him? Had she accepted his help merely out of desperation?

That thought made his insides ache. If it were true, it just might kill him. All he could think of since Monday was Izzie. He was determined to do his best to help her. But was that all she wanted from him—his help?

Clay and Izzie waited in the hall until the doors to the chamber opened at six thirty and then walked side by side down the center aisle. The council table was empty, but the room was not. Filling the front row on the left side sat the tribes' general livestock board, including their clerk. On the aisle was Franklin Soto. Donner filled the next two seats, lounging back in his chair with legs crossed at the ankle and his fingers laced over his generous stom-ach. Pizarro sat next to Donner and leaned over to speak to him. Clay would have loved to know what he was up to since he had the authority to choose which of the tribe's pastures were subject to renourishment. On the end, closest to the wall, huddled Victor Bustros, Pizarro's clerk, who dealt with the mountains of paperwork necessary to hold and sell cattle including the lists of all the individual brands. Though not actually on the board, he attended all meetings with the livestock board. Bustos had his head inclined to listen toward Pizarro and Donner but was not engaged in the conversation.

Clay chose the front row as well, taking a seat closest to the general livestock board. The choice was intentional and reminded Clay of the two sides of a legal battle, prosecution and defense. Donner noticed him and sat forward to greet him, but as Izzie moved past Clay and sat to his right, Donner's smile morphed to a grim line joined with a hard stare. His boss glanced from Clay to Izzie and then back to Clay, giving him a withering look at Clay's decision to ignore his warning.

Over the next ten minutes, members of all three tribal communities filtered in. Finally, about fifteen minutes after the meeting was scheduled to begin, the tribe's council appeared. They always met in private sessions prior to the public meeting. Clyne said that was where the real business was done.

Clay knew them all—three women and three men. With Council Chairman Ralph Siqueria still absent, there was the possibility of a tied vote on any issue. Clay watched his brother take his seat behind a nameplate and smiled; the pride still rose every time he saw Clyne there among the tribe's leadership. Their mom would have been so happy. Arnold Tessay, the longest-serving member of the council, sat beside Clay. Their clerk, Martha Juniper, a broad woman notable for her fry bread and her owlish glasses, asked them to rise and honor both the American flag and the tribal flag. That done, the tribe's acting chairman, Dennis Faden, called the meeting to order.

Clay waited for their turn. When the matter of the permits was raised, Izzie asked for the explanation, just as Clyne had advised. No one seemed to know why that land was scheduled for renourishment. Pizarro, who was in charge of such matters, stated that it was a rotation, and this land was overdue.

Izzie replied that the land had not been overgrazed and then asked for an extension to allow for the council to inspect the property in question.

Tessay said they didn't have time to check every cow pasture, and that was why they had a general livestock coordinator. Clyne proposed that he and Pizarro have a look at the pasture in question and report back to the council. The council voted to delay the question, and the motion passed with Tessay and Faden against, Cosen, and the three remaining council members for. Izzie had her stay. Her cattle could remain until the council met again in one week's time.

Clay's delight was diminished when he and Izzie stood to leave and walked past Gabe, who still wore his uniform and looked less than pleased to see him here.

They made it out into the parking lot. The weather girl had been right. The sky was clear and glistening with silver stars. He tugged his denim coat closed against the chill as he halted beside Izzie's truck. For some reason, his brain chose that moment to remind him of the empty house waiting for his return and the privacy he would have if he managed to convince Izzie to join him.

"Well, you have a few more days," said Clay.

"Thank you for all your help. I never would have known what to do, procedure and all. And Clyne calling for a motion, I know that was you, too." She lifted up on her toes and kissed him on the cheek.

He froze for only a moment before sweeping her up in his arms for a real kiss, the kind he'd been wanting to give her since the tenth grade.

Chapter Fifteen

Izzie's blood surged as Clay deepened the kiss. She pushed toward him and relished the hard pressure of his mouth on hers. His hand came up, gripping the back of her neck, and she let him take some of her weight. She lifted on her toes to get even closer, sliding her tongue against his. But he pulled away, setting her at arms' distance.

She was about to object, but then she heard the voices, other members of the community moving through the lot to their vehicles. How had she not even heard them? And why was it that he had?

Izzie had been completely lost in their kiss, and it irked her that Clay still had the wherewithal to notice what was going on around them. But she was grateful, too. She did not wish to be the subject of more gossip, mostly because the idea of facing something like what Clay had endured scared her to the core.

"Isn't that your neighbor?" Clay asked and drew her farther into the shadows.

It was, and he was deep in conversation with Clay's boss. Izzie strained to hear anything of the exchange between them.

"Did you know Floyd offered to buy my cattle?" she said.

"You said he asked you out."

"Yes. But yesterday he offered to *buy* me out. Right after my permits notice arrived. It was like he knew."

"Could be. News travels fast." Clay looked back at the man in question, gesturing with his hands as he spoke to Donner. "He got that kind of money?"

"No, which is why he gave me a low-ball offer. Take them off my hands, he said. You'd have to be a fool to take that kind of deal."

"Or desperate," said Clay. "Maybe with the troubles you've been having, he figured you might be wanting to get out of the cattle business."

"Victor Bustros called me, too. This morning. Said he'd heard about my troubles and offered to auction my herd."

Bustros worked under Pizarro. But as brand inspector one of his duties was to oversee the tribe's auctions.

"I didn't know."

"They're like sharks smelling blood."

All round them came the sound of cars and trucks starting. Headlights flashed on, and vehicles pulled out from the gravel lot on to the highway. Izzie lingered, hands shoved in her pockets. She wanted another kiss, and another and another. She tried to remember why that was such a bad idea, but all she could recall was how right it felt to be in Clay's arms.

"You want to go get something to eat?" he asked.

She didn't want food. The want she had was much deeper, more primal. Izzie wanted the pressing of flesh to flesh. His heart beating beside hers. She wanted the heat and the wetness and the friction. But she didn't want to be the subject of gossip. She knew the viciousness of the wagging tongues around here. It was a small community in a small reservation. Clay was living proof that people didn't forgive or forget a misstep. She had to guard her reputation. She was a businesswoman with a mother and two brothers to provide for. She should walk away.

Instead, she asked, "Isn't Kino away on his honeymoon?"

Clay's brow quirked and he went very still. Had she really just said that? She didn't know who was more surprised, she or Clay.

"Yes," he said, not making the offer that she wanted.

"So you're alone out there." She couldn't be less subtle than that.

"I am. You like to come over for…"

She gave him a wicked smile and nodded.

"Okay. Two trucks or one?"

She didn't want to leave her truck out here where anyone could see it and make assumptions. Besides, someone would surely see Clay driving her back here in the morning.

"I'll follow you."

"Great." But his expression didn't say great. The tightness at his mouth and the lack of enthusiasm in his tone told her he'd pegged this for what it was, a quick hook-up that no one else needed to know about.

He opened the door to her truck and gently caressed her arm as she swept inside.

Izzie had ten long minutes to reconsider. But she didn't. She just sat in the parking lot for a full minute, giving Clay a head start before she drove after him. When she came to the turn that would take her home, she didn't take it. Instead she pressed her foot down, accelerating into the curve as the anticipation built. How many years had she dreamed of spending the night in Clay Cosen's bed?

"Just one night," she whispered, giving herself permission.

She saw his taillights and forced herself to slow, giving

him a few minutes to prepare for her arrival. She lingered in the driveway and stared up at the stars sparkling above. Dividing the sky from the earth stood the dark silhouette of the Black Mountain. Her people had lived in the place so long it was a part of them and they a part of it. She felt it then, the beating pulse of the earth beneath her joining in sacred ceremony with the beat of her heart.

The door to his house opened, and Clay filled the frame, dark before the light within.

"Izzie?" he called.

And she went to him, entering his home as he swept aside to make room for her passing, before he closed the door behind her.

He took her coat and ushered her in to the living room. She glanced at a very tempting couch that looked long enough for them to stretch out. They sat on the soft sofa, she by the armrest, he on the center cushion. She wondered if her mother would notice her absence. She often came in from livestock meetings to find the lights out and her mother's bedroom door shut. It was her mother's way of reminding Izzie that she did not like the cattle business or the cattle her husband had left to his daughter.

Izzie turned toward Clay, admiring his familiar, handsome face and knowing they were also strangers, separated now by years and experience.

"Can I get you a drink?" he asked.

She shook her head and pivoted toward him. She lifted a hand to caress the hard blade of a jawbone. Izzie met the intense gaze that gave Clay the air of danger. Clay sat still, as Izzie explored his face with her fingertips, becoming familiar with the man he now was. She slid closer and looped her arms around him, lacing her fingers behind his neck. She sighed in satisfaction, recalling all the prayers that Clay would be hers.

And now he would be, and she wondered why, in all that time, she'd never once asked to keep him and still keep the peace in her home. Her father had warned that this man would cost her everything. Had he been right?

She had made a promise to her father to run the business, but did that mean she had to live like a nun? For a moment she let herself imagine what it would be like to have Clay, not just for tonight, but every night. She wanted that. But if life had taught her one lesson, it was that you did not usually get what you wanted. You had to choose carefully.

His phone rang and they both jumped. He glanced down and saw it was Clyne. He turned the screen so she could see, and she nodded. His brother might have more news.

"Hey," said Clay.

"Hey. I'm not sure what's up with those grazing permits, but Tessay was adamant that we not interfere with Pizarro's decisions. Undermining him, he said. He said we've never questioned him before, and it set a bad precedent."

"All true," said Clay.

Izzie wondered if he should tell Clyne she could hear him.

"But there was something about it. Didn't feel right. You coming over to Grandma's tonight? We can talk some more."

He grimaced. "No. I'm beat."

A hesitation. Had his brother made a guess as to what was really occupying him?

"Tomorrow, then," said Clyne at last.

"Sure. Tomorrow."

Clyne disconnected, and Clay set the phone on the coffee table, turning his attention back to her. She gave him a smile that she hoped was full of sensual promise. Tonight, she would pretend that nothing would separate them.

Izzie stood and held out a hand to him.

He reached, clasping tight. He remained seated, looking up at her with what she thought might be hope. His hand gripped hers more tightly as if he was afraid she might let go. The taut lines at his mouth showed that he was unsure what she was doing. Did he think she might leave him now? She wouldn't. She wouldn't leave him unless dragged from his arms. All those wasted years haunted her, and so did her need to always do absolutely everything that was expected. Acting, not doing what was right for her, but what was right for everyone else. Well, not tonight. Tonight was about what was right for her and for Clay.

"Izzie?" he asked.

"Show me your bedroom, Clay."

He was on his feet so fast, she startled back a step. A moment later he swept her up in his solid arms, leaving the living room behind. He was bigger and stronger now. His face had changed, too, becoming more angular and his eyes showing a wariness that she had only glimpsed when he was a teenager. It came from his father back then. Now it came from being betrayed. Izzie vowed to never betray his trust.

She laughed as he hoisted her with no effort and fairly flew down the hall that led to a room cast in shadow. She could see all that was important: the large bed and headboard. He laid her down upon the soft comforter, and she was enveloped by his masculine scent. It was heady as any alcohol, and in moments she was drunk with passion.

She lifted a leg, and he tugged off her boot and socks. Then he repeated the procedure on the other leg. He abandoned her for the time it took to remove his own boots and socks.

He rested a knee upon the bed, and she realized with a thrill of dread and excitement how big his body was compared to hers. She reached, and he knelt beside her.

She reclined on the pillows, and he braced himself as if he meant to do a series of push-ups. Instead he lowered himself inch by delicious inch until he pressed her down to the bedding. Their mouths met, and her flesh tingled. She threaded her hands in his thick hair and tugged him closer. He held his weight off her, his chest just skimming against her breasts as he swayed side to side in the most deliciously sensual move. The gentle friction drove her crazy, and she surged up to meet him, pressing her breasts to the arousing hard surface of his chest. He rolled to his back and carried her with him. Her legs now straddled his denim-sheathed thighs, and her belly came in contact with the evidence of his need for her. The thrill of anticipation beat inside her with her thrumming heart. He deepened the kiss, their tongues now sliding one against the other. But she needed to feel his skin against hers, so she pulled back. Her eyes were adjusting to the light filtering in from the hallway now, and she could see the tension in his jaw as he waited for her. This was Clay. The boy she had loved and the man she desired.

His breathing was heavy. She sat up, shifting so she straddled his middle and came down on his hips. He sucked in a breath and released it in a hiss. If she didn't know better, she'd think she had hurt him. But the pain he felt was just like hers, need and longing mixed with desire.

"Oh, Bella," he said. "I've dreamed of this so many times."

She smiled and grasped at the fabric at her waist, clasping the hem of the turquoise button-up blouse she wore and dragging it over her head. Beneath she wore her best bra, which was low-cut but not extremely revealing. This was just a plain white lace B-cup that she filled. But it didn't seem to matter because Clay now stared up at her in wonder, as if she were the most erotic thing he had ever seen.

"You're beautiful," he whispered as his hands slipped up to encircle her waist. His grip slackened, and his fingers danced down her back, sending a delicious tingle over her skin. Finally, he cradled her backside, still unfortunately clad in her best black jeans. He tugged the two of them into closer contact and she thrilled as he rose up to kiss the bare skin at her shoulder. She sat straddling his waist, letting her head loll back as he showered hot, wet kisses on her neck, his tongue and teeth arousing her flesh.

She stopped him only to drag off his plaid flannel shirt and the white T-shirt he wore beneath. It was like Christmas morning, she thought, exploring his square shoulders, broad chest and muscular back. Her fingers roamed over taut rippling muscle and velvety skin. The pads of her fingers grazed over warm flesh that dimpled under her touch. She smile in triumph, relishing the reaction of her touch, but her lips fell open with a groan of pleasure as his mouth found her breasts, soaking the lace over one hard nipple and then the next.

They were so good together and it frightened her.

But it didn't stop her, not as she eased out of her jeans. Not as she unfastened his. She wasn't turning back. Tomorrow would be soon enough to deal with the fallout of this decision. Tonight was her chance to make the biggest, most wonderful mistake of her life.

Chapter Sixteen

Clay couldn't believe this was happening.

As he kicked off his jeans, he could hear the voice of doubt reminding him that she had not been honest with Martin. She had told him that she had gone out with Martin in order to be with Clay. Martin had told a different story. One that had just about killed him.

But that was in the past. Yet another past he'd never really been able to put behind him, even now when Izzie was here in his bedroom stripping out of her jeans and panties and bra. He followed suit, dragging off his remaining clothing and tossing them away. He wanted her desperately, but not so desperately that he did not stop in stunned silence at her beauty. She knelt before him on the bed, naked and mysterious as the night. Her breasts were larger than the last time he'd touched them, the nipples the same soft rosy brown and tight now with excitement. Her flat stomach and muscular thighs showed the results of many hours of physical labor. But now she had the narrow waist and flaring hips of a woman. He stared at the glossy black thatch of hair, and his mouth went dry. Gone forever was the thin, playful girl he had known. Izzie was now entirely woman in body and spirit.

Medicine Root Woman, the shaman had named her at

her Sunrise Ceremony. Grounded, powerful and somehow momentarily his.

When he lifted his gaze it was to find her surveying his body. What changes did she see?

Their gazes met, and they shared a smile as they reached in unison for each other. She pressed against him, and his body twitched and jumped with need.

He dragged the fastening from her hair, releasing the coiled rope from its neat, functional bun at the back of her head. Her glossy, deep brown hair unwound until it lay across one shoulder in a twist. He finger-combed the silky strands over her shoulder and down her back, restoring the black curtain that he had always loved. Then he captured her, bringing her head to his chest, allowing him to inhale the scent of her hair. Still sage, he realized. She inched closer until her sex met his.

He stilled, closing his eyes for a moment to thank God for his good fortune. He'd lost her for so long. Now he prayed for a new beginning. That she was no longer ashamed of him. In this moment, he realized why it was so important to keep his job and earn back the respect he had lost on that day long ago. It was for Izzic. He wanted to be the man she deserved. To make her proud.

Clay kissed her mouth, and Izzie let him take her weight, trusting him with her body. He lay her back on the pillows, tasting her as he explored the recesses of her mouth. Then he moved down her throat to kiss her perfect breasts. His reward was the soft moans of pleasure that escaped her parted lips as he continued to kiss and stroke.

He didn't know why Izzie was giving him this second chance, but he planned to do everything he could to please her. He dipped lower. Izzie's cries became more frantic, and she reached out with desperate greedy hands, whispering for him to take her. He drew back. He wanted her more than almost anything. But not so much that he would take advantage of the best thing in his life.

"Bella, are you sure?"

She opened her eyes. Her lips were swollen with his kisses, and her need called to him louder than any siren.

"Yes. Now, Clay. I need you." She didn't lie there waiting but took hold of what she wanted.

Now *his* breath came in a ragged pant. "Let me get a condom."

"I'm using birth control."

"No condom?"

She shook her head. "I want to feel you."

Wasn't that the ultimate show of faith? She trusted him, deep down and wholeheartedly. Clay felt so happy he thought he might cry. But he didn't. Instead he shifted between her legs and eased down inside her. It was that first slow, silken glide that met with resistance. He glanced up at her as a question formed in his brain, but she lifted up, and he slid deeper. Isabella stilled and then began to move. He wanted to go slow, to savor this first time, but the pleasure and the need to move won over his good intentions, and he drove hard to match the pace she set. He relished the change in her breathing and the arching of her back as she reached her pleasure. He followed a moment later. He dropped down upon Isabella and let her finish him. As the mind-blowing sensations rocketed through him, he dragged her against him, wishing he never had to let go.

As his body relaxed, his mind re-engaged, and he thought to wonder as she lay nestling in his arms, why, after all these years, had she picked this night to take what he had offered her so many times before? His grandmother, who was a very wise woman, had once told him that a woman's heart is not so easy to read as a man's. A man loves or hates. But a woman can do both at the same time. She might use her body to hurt a man or use a man or love a man. The trick, of course, was to know one from the other. That memory disturbed him and kept him from sleep. There was something else that bothered him, but he could not quite remember what. Finally, he realized what it was that had tried to break through his thoughts, back when he had no thoughts but finishing what Izzie had started.

Martin had lied to him, not once, but twice. Clay knew that because, despite all the tales Martin had told him, until tonight, Izzie had been a virgin.

Clay stroked her glossy hair and listened to her soft breathing. Finally he dozed and woke when Izzie slipped from his arms. He rose on an elbow and followed her with his eyes as she disappeared into his bathroom. Then he flicked on the bedside lamp. The evidence of his suspicion was there on his skin. Isabella's innocence and Martin's lie. He wondered why he'd believed Martin when he said he'd taken her again and again. And why he had believed Martin when he'd said he wanted to grab a pop from that store.

Now, at least, Clay understood why Martin had risked his neck to steal the money to take a frightened little Mexican girl. He felt stupid all over again.

He listened to the water run and then stop. The door opened, and Izzie paused, naked and beautiful in the soft glow of his reading lamp.

"Why didn't you tell me?" he asked.

She blushed and lowered her chin before looking at him through a forest of thick dark lashes. "Because I was afraid you'd say no."

As if he could ever refuse Bella anything.

"Are you all right?"

She nodded, but she didn't stand tall as she usually did, and there was a tentativeness about her that he didn't recognize.

"Are you sorry?" he asked and then gritted his teeth against her answer.

Her chin came up. "No. I'm not. I've always wanted it to be you. I just never expected it to take so long."

He lifted the covers. "Come here."

She did, sliding in beside him and nestling face-to-face on his pillows. He draped a leg over her and dragged her closer, then he rolled on to his back. It was hard, because he wanted her again. But he'd wait. There would be time, he thought. She rolled toward him, and one of her legs glided across his thighs. He sighed at the sweetness of having her in his arms. Clay drew slow circles over her back and closed his eyes, forcing down the desire. Had he really thought that taking Izzie would get her out of his system? She was like the drug he could not shake. The habit he would do anything to fill. Izzie's fingers kneaded his chest like a cat, and she closed her eyes.

Clay reached and switched off the bedside lamp. There in the darkness, with her heart beating slow and her breathing gentle, he held her as she drifted to sleep. It took him some time, because of the images of Izzie beneath him and the images of what else he'd like to do with her. But finally he slipped into slumber that was broken by the faraway bleating of his phone. He glanced at the clock and saw it was already 6:56 in the morning. He had to get to work, and Izzie needed to get home. He opened his eyes and stretched. His phone was on Do Not Disturb from midnight to seven, so only those on his favorites list would get through. All others had to call twice to get his phone to ring.

Izzie blinked up at him. Her hair was tousled and her

skin glowing with health. She slept on her stomach and had kicked off the covers, he realized, giving him a good long look at the slope of her back and the lovely round curve of her buttocks. When his gaze returned to her face, it was to find her grinning that wicked smile she'd cast him last night.

"Good morning," he said and kissed her brow.

She pushed the hair off her face and lifted up on her elbows. His gaze dropped and his breath caught. Lord, he was going to be late for work.

In the living room, his phone rang again. It was the tone he'd picked for Gabe.

"You going to get that?" she asked.

He gave her a slow shake of his head and returned her knowing smile.

"Good." She slipped on top of him, her breasts pressing to his bare chest. The heat of her touch made his entire body awaken.

Someone knocked on his front door. Clay's smile vanished as he sensed something was wrong. He took Izzie's shoulders and set her aside as he sat up.

"Stay here."

He slipped out of bed and into his jeans, then cast a look over his shoulder, surprised to see the worry in her face. She knelt on his bed, sheet clutched to her breasts and her other fist over her mouth. He was about to ask her what was wrong when the knock turned into a pounding.

"Clay?"

That was Gabe's voice.

"Open up."

He reached the door a moment later and pulled the door open to see Gabe wearing his uniform and a sour look.

"She here?" he asked, thumbing over his shoulder at Izzie's truck.

"Yeah."

"Get her."

Clay cocked his head. "Why?"

"I have to arrest her."

Chapter Seventeen

Rebranding. That was the charge against Izzie.

Clay stood aside as Gabe read Izzie her rights and then asked her if she had any questions. She was crying now and asked Clay to call her mother. Gabe put her in the back of his cruiser and closed the door. Clay grabbed his arm before his brother swung into the unit. Clay motioned with his head, and Gabe followed him a few feet from the vehicle.

"How did this happen?" asked Clay.

"Pizarro got a complaint of missing cattle. So he sent someone over to Izzie's place to do a count. There's a discrepancy in the number of the cattle she has and the number they released from quarantine."

"That doesn't make any sense. Who made the count?"

"Victor Bustros. Pizarro asked him to go over to Izzie's place."

Victor was the branding inspector for Black Mountain, Clay knew, responsible for keeping track of every brand for every Black Mountain rancher and all the brands for the tribe members who kept a cow or two in the tribe's communal herd. But he worked with Boone Pizarro.

"This stinks."

"Maybe. Anyway, Victor went at sunup. Carol gave permission for him to have a look. He found she had too many cattle, and so he checked the brands. Some of her cattle had been recently branded."

"That's not illegal."

"They'd been branded over a previous brand."

"Whose?"

"Those belonging to Floyd Patch."

Clay struggled to find an explanation. "*Patch* was the one missing cattle?"

"Yeah."

"And they assumed Izzie took them?"

"There's been a lot of activity up there. Logical to check the neighbors. She'd been driving cattle, possible that some of his got out and mixed with hers. They didn't think she stole them. Floyd's fences aren't well maintained. We pick up his cattle all the time. In fact I would have bet my paycheck they were his cows out on the highway that day."

"But they were Izzie's cattle."

Clay rocked back as if Gabe had punched him in the gut. He glanced back at the cruiser to see Izzie staring at him. Clay's gut churned as the disbelief gave way to a far worse feeling, the feeling of being used yet again.

"It would explain why she has been registering record numbers of calves year after year. She could have just been collecting Patch's strays."

"But wouldn't he notice the loss of cattle?"

"Apparently he did. This time, anyway." Gabe glanced back at the cruiser, checking on his prisoner.

"This is a mistake."

"You sure about that?" asked Gabe.

"She's not a thief."

"You said the same thing about Martin."

His brother's words struck him like a second punch to

the gut. Was it possible? Had Izzie been so desperate to make ends meet that she'd do something like this?

"Why? Why would she?"

"To cover her mother's debts. She's been paying them off. I checked. It's a lot, Clay."

He thought he might throw up.

"Would explain the cut fences. It would be a good place to bring in the stolen calves."

"You don't have any evidence to support that." Why was he defending her?

Gabe shrugged. "Just starting to gather evidence now."

"You drive her through the middle of town in the back of your unit, and it will ruin her reputation. You know that." Clay knew what it was like to take that ride. The shame and the humiliation. He'd done so himself, in Gabe's cruiser, up to police headquarters. Fingerprinted, photographed. He shuddered.

"It's my job. I have enough to charge her. She'll face tribal court within the month."

Clay grabbed his arm. "She can't be in jail for a month. She's got a ranch to run."

"I'm sure her mother will bail her out."

"With what?"

"She's still got cattle. Donner released half her herd." Gabe looked at his arm, where Clay still held him. Clay let him go. "I warned you, little brother. I told you to keep clear of her."

What if they were all right about her? What if Izzie was involved with the meth lab up in her pasture, and she was rustling cattle? What if she had been playing him, using him, even sleeping with him to get his help? Had she hired him to find the culprit or just to hide her own tracks? Clay swayed, feeling as unsteady as a dead tree in a heavy snow.

"I best get going," said Gabe. He paused and turned back. "Oh, Kino called Grandma. He found the BIA officer who took Jovanna from the scene and got the name of her case manager."

The news did not bring the joy it should have. Clay stared at Izzie, who stared back at him, her head lifted in stoic pride belied by the tear stains that streaked her cheeks. Was she the woman he thought he knew or a stranger?

It was happening all over again. He was mixed up in something, and once more his tribe would either assume he was a coconspirator or the stupidest man alive.

Gabe got into his car, stretching his safety belt across his body before turning on the ignition. From the seat behind him, Izzie lifted her hand in farewell. Clay kept his hands at his sides as they pulled away.

He stood in the yard long after the dust had settled and the birdsong had returned. Long enough for his toes to get cold and for him to realize that he was barefooted and shirtless.

Izzie had been arrested. And she'd been here, with the brother of the police chief, when they had found the re-branded cattle. Was she really that calculating?

Martin had been.

The thought of making another mistake, of trusting the wrong person and ruining what was left of his reputation, filled him with an icy cold. His ears buzzed as if he stood underneath a nest of hornets, and his stomach ached. Izzie wouldn't do that to him, would she? He rubbed his knuckles over his chest at the ache that was deeper than skin and muscle and bone. He thought about Gabe coming back for him. Charging him with some damn thing, like conspiracy or failure to report a crime, which was about the same charge as before and showed he didn't have an ounce of sense when it came to judging peoples' intentions.

How was it he could read sign but couldn't read the truth in a person's words?

"Not again," he said.

Time to cut his losses and protect what little reputation he had left. Clay returned to the house to retrieve his phone. He would call Izzie's mother, as he had promised, and then put Isabella Nosie and her troubles behind him.

He might just talk to Mr. Donner and then drive on up to South Dakota for a long weekend. See if he could help Kino and Lea find that case manager and locate their sister. That's where his allegiance should be, with his family. Hadn't he once told Kino the same, when his little brother had been hell-bent on finding their father's killer, instead of helping Gabe and Clyne in their search for Jovanna? Now he was guilty of the same thing.

Clay located his phone and saw three messages. The first two were from Gabe alerting him that he was coming to his house to arrest Izzie. Clay now thought to wonder how Gabe knew that Izzie was with him and realized that he'd likely gone to Izzie's place first and then made a logical guess. That meant that Izzie's mom already knew her daughter was in trouble and where she had spent the night. The third message was from Kino, telling him the good news. His brother sounded jubilant, and the happiness in his voice only made Clay feel worse.

Clay pushed the hair from his face and sank into a seat at the kitchen table, contacting something soft. He pivoted to find Izzie's coat still draped across the back of the chair. He dragged it from its place and hugged the sheepskin sheath to his chest, breathing in the scent of leather, the horses she loved and sacred sage.

His words came in Apache squeezing through his tightening vocal cords. "Ah, Medicine Root Woman. Did you use me, too?"

CLAY DIDN'T ACTUALLY remember showering or getting dressed. But he did remember making coffee, because he burned his hand on the old percolator pot he used on the stove.

His phone rang, and he checked the caller ID. It was police headquarters. He stared, knowing that his brother would call from his mobile if he needed to speak to Clay. So that meant this was Izzie calling him from jail.

He stood looking at his phone until it stopped ringing. Then he waited. She didn't leave a message. Clay stared at the missed-call notice. He just couldn't deal with her problems anymore.

He turned away. Took two steps into the kitchen, gathered his truck keys and stopped. Clay remembered making that call. He remembered when all his friends vanished and the only ones who stuck by him were his family. Who did Izzie have? A judgmental, demanding mother? Two kid brothers? She needed him to believe her, and he'd done just what everyone once did to him, assumed she was lying. Clay redialed the number and was told that Izzie was in processing, and she had already used her phone call. She'd called her mother. But he knew that she had called him first, and he hadn't been there for her.

Truth from lies. That's what it all boiled down to. Did Clay believe Izzie or did he believe the evidence of the rebranded cattle found among Izzie's quarantined herd?

Clay slipped his phone in his pocket and gripped his truck keys in his fist. Izzie was being set up. He felt it. And he should have believed her when Gabe escorted her out. She wasn't using him like his old dearly departed friend, Martin. She was asking for help from a friend.

During his eighteen months away, he'd learned to climb and navigate. He'd learned to meditate and to engage in trust activities. And he'd trusted the other guys there with his life. But he'd never trusted anyone with his heart. Until now.

If Izzie was playing him, then he'd find out the hard way, just like he did everything else. He was not leaving Izzie on her own in jail. He couldn't. Because he still loved her.

Clay called his boss but got Veronica. He wasn't coming in today. He had to help a friend.

Then he headed over to the police station in Black Mountain.

There he was told to go to work as he couldn't see her until after processing. Clay knew what that meant, remembered every detail, right down to the gray-green chipping paint on the bars of the holding cell. Clay hung his head in shame as he recalled how he had just stood there as his brother drove Izzie to jail. What had he been thinking?

He couldn't get to her, so he went to work, not to the livestock offices.

His brother had enough evidence to make an arrest. His brother was a very good judge of character, but when he erred it was on the side of being too cautious. He didn't leap before he looked. That was why he was who he was and why Clay was about to take the biggest leap of his life.

Because he was going to prove her innocent and get her out of jail.

The place to begin was where this had started, Izzie's land. Clay headed back over to Izzie's pastures to see if there was anything he had missed at the original sight. He hadn't, but he did find something newer by several days, a portion of the fence that had been cut and expertly mended.

He also found tire tracks and boot tracks, two sets. He called Gabe who came over.

"I'll photograph them," said Gabe. "What do you reckon?"

"Only reason to break a fence is to let something out or in." Clay pointed at the ground. "See?"

Gabe squatted and looked, but Clay thought his brother didn't really see.

"Cattle tracks?" said Gabe.

"No," said Clay. "Those are too small for cattle. Have to be calves. Old enough to be weaned, from the size. And they are coming in, not out."

Gabe stood and dusted the sand off his knee.

"I'm going to talk to Patch," said Clay.

"No, you are not. You're not interfering with my investigation, or I'll arrest you, too."

Gabe must have seen Clay's face redden, or maybe it was the intake of breath. Anyway, Gabe removed his hat and ran his thumb over the brim, silent for a moment. Then he faced his younger brother.

"I'm sorry, Clay. But you need to let me do my job."

Clay wanted to tell him to do it then. Or yell at Gabe that he was trying to help him. But he just managed to hold his tongue. Clay stared at Gabe, who rested his hands on his hips and scowled.

"What do you want me to do?" asked Gabe.

"Come with me to see Patch. I'm sure these are the kind of boots he wears."

"Lots of folks have construction boots."

"I'll match them."

"What do you think he did, exactly?"

Clay studied the ground. "Someone chased Izzie's cows out through the cut a few days ago. She'll prove it when she gets her hearing. Here someone has added cattle to her herd. Gabe, someone is messing with her."

Gabe nodded, agreeing with that. "This cut is newer. See how the tracks are dried all round? Yesterday."

Gabe's mouth went grim. "You think someone re-branded those cows with Izzie's brand and then set them loose in her pasture."

"Yes."

Gabe's eyes shifted down the hillside. "How did they get her brand?"

Clay shook his head, unsure.

"Let's go have a talk with Floyd," said Gabe.

Clay grinned, feeling the first ray of hope finally break-ing through the clouds that had surrounded him all day.

Gabe nodded, and the two drove down the hill to Floyd's place. They got out of their respective vehicles together and headed to Floyd's home, where they were met by his sister, Celia Batista. She lived there with her husband, Ron, who worked the place with Floyd. Celia had a round face, dark eyes squeezed by her pudgy cheeks and a body that seemed a series of ever-increasing rings of fat. She wore a shapeless flowered shirt, knit slacks and flip-flops pressed flat from overuse. Celia directed them to the barn.

"There's soft sand out here in the drive. Get him out here so I can see his tracks," said Clay.

"Wait here." Gabe left him and returned a few minutes later chatting with Floyd. "Just need you to sign a com-plaint," said his brother, motioning to the truck.

Floyd's smile dropped when he saw Clay. "What's he doing here?"

"Asked him to come on out to read some sign."

Floyd's stride lost its confident swing. He seemed less willing to follow Gabe out on to the dirt drive. Gabe looked back, waiting.

"Something wrong?" he asked.

Floyd was sweating now, but he shook his head and followed Gabe to his cruiser. Clay made a careful study of their passing and then nodded to Gabe.

Gabe asked Floyd to wait and retraced his steps, being careful not to walk over the tracks they had made.

"You sure?" he asked Clay.

"Positive."

"Well, now." Gabe returned to Floyd who sputtered and demanded to know what was going on, so Gabe told him.

Celia hurried out in the yard, but her bluster vanished when she saw her brother's face turn ashen.

"So," said Gabe to Floyd, "you going to tell me how you got a hold of Isabella's brand here or at the station?"

Floyd said nothing. Ron and his wife exchanged a long look. His wife shook her head, her hands now clasped stiffly over the most prominent roll of her belly.

"Floyd, I've got you for cutting fences and tampering with Izzie's herd. I've got your tracks leading right into her fence line. And I suspect you're the one who rebranded your own cattle and you're the one who let some of her herd out on the highway last week. So someone would notice the rebranding."

Floyd was rubbing his neck as if he were a chiropractor.

"I hope that's the worst of it," said Gabe, sounding conspiratorial now, as if showing serious concern over Floyd's welfare. "But there's things going on here, Floyd. Serious federal crimes."

"Don't say anything, Floyd," said his sister.

"Hush up." He turned to Gabe. "I got the branding iron from Eli Beach. He helps her out, and sometimes he works over here with Ron and me. I said I wished I could get her to sell out, and he suggested rebranding."

"Eli suggested it?"

"Yeah." Floyd's hand dropped back to his side.

"Where is he?"

"Not here."

"Well, that was real helpful of him," said Gabe. "You pay him?"

"No."

"Strike you as strange that a man would do something like that for free?"

Floyd hiked up his jeans. "Well, it does when I hear you say it."

Clay couldn't keep the smile from forming on his face. Izzie was innocent.

"Why'd you want her cattle?" asked Gabe.

"Not her cattle, really. I wanted those permits. Her land is better."

Because Izzie's dad had busted his hump clearing trees instead of complaining about it like Floyd, thought Clay.

"If she sold, she wouldn't need them," Patch went on, his voice now whiny as a mosquito. "Isn't right that she gets those permits year after year. She can't hardly keep that place running, even with help."

Especially with help from a man who was stealing her branding iron, thought Clay.

"Your brother-in-law in on this?"

"Floyd," screeched his sister. Then, seeing Floyd hesitate, she hopped right in. "He didn't know."

"Except he drove the four-wheeler through her pasture," added Floyd.

Gabe had a heck of a time keeping Celia from beating her brother, and Clay found he was enjoying himself for the first time in days. Gabe got Celia off Floyd but had to threaten to arrest her before she calmed down. Gabe lost his hat in the scuffle, which Clay retrieved and returned. Gabe replaced it on his head and turned back to Patch.

"You know anything about those meth cooks up there?"

Floyd lifted both hands in a gesture of rejection. "I surely do not."

Gabe leaned in toward Floyd who cowered back.

"If I find out you are helping the traffickers or the cooks," said Gabe, "I swear I will fight for federal prosecution, Floyd, unless you come clean right now."

The color drained from Floyd's face, and he pressed both hands over his heart as if fearful it would stop. It was one thing to be caught rebranding. But it was quite another to face a federal charge for narcotics, a drug-related offense that the tribe would most likely turn over to the district attorney to be tried by the State of Arizona.

"I don't know nothing about the crystal meth cooking. I swear."

Clay's smile vanished. If Floyd was telling the truth, then Izzie's troubles were far from over.

Chapter Eighteen

Izzie waited in the cell all morning, expecting her mother to come bail her out. But her mother didn't come. Her mom wouldn't like idle talk about her daughter being mixed up in something like rebranding. Was her mother's reputation more important to her than her daughter?

When Izzie had paced herself out, she settled on the narrow stainless steel bench that was bolted to the wall and wondered if this would be her bed tonight.

As soon as she stopped moving, her mind dragged her right back to the look on Clay's face when Gabe put her in the squad car. It hadn't been indignation or worry or even disbelief. She would have loved to see disbelief on his face, because that would have meant that he thought she was innocent, that some mistake had been made.

No, what she had seen on his face was shock as he reached the conclusion that she had betrayed him, just as Martin had done. A moment later his jaw had turned hard as setting concrete.

But she had not used him. She had called him from the station to tell him so. He had ignored her phone call. Cut her loose. Decided already that she was guilty.

It didn't matter that she hadn't done it. What mattered was that he could believe she would. He didn't trust her. Oh, he'd slept with her. He might even have loved her once.

But he just wasn't willing to take the kind of risk involved with trusting her with his whole heart.

She could just smack Martin Ethelbah right in the teeth, if he wasn't already dead. Gone but not forgotten, she realized. Never forgotten because his ghost still haunted Clay Cosen. Maybe he always would.

She didn't recall Martin's exact last words to her before she broke it off, but it was something to the effect that if she wouldn't have sex with him, he would find a girl who would.

She cradled her head in her hands and wondered why, with all her problems, the thing that cut her straight across her heart was Clay's face when she drove away.

He'd let her call go to voice mail. Izzie sagged and then straightened as she remembered his call to her after *his* arrest. How he left a message telling her he was innocent and begging her to believe him. She'd never picked up and never called back. Now he had done the same thing. The shame hit her deep. What a horrible thing, to be denied the chance to explain. Yet she had done that to him for *six years*. Perhaps she deserved to be sitting in this cell, if for no other reason than it made her realize what she had done to him. No. To them.

As the morning turned toward midday, Izzie began to wonder who was setting her up.

"Izzie?"

She startled at the sound of her name, rolling off the tongue and ringing with a familiarity that made her tingle and the hairs on her arms lift straight up. Clay stood before her, his hands on the bars as if he were the one in the cage.

He glanced up and around.

"Still looks the same," he said and then gave her a gentle smile.

A ray of hope entered her heart.

"Clay?" She rose. "I didn't do it, Clay."

She went to him, expecting him to pull back. But he didn't. Instead he extended his arms through the bars and took hold of both her hands, dragging her to him until they were separated only by the vertical steel.

"I know," he said.

"How?"

"Because I know you, Isabella Nosie. I know you promised your dad to look after that place for his sons. I know you'd do just about anything to keep the ranch going, but just about is a far cry from anything."

She beamed at him. He believed her.

"Your brother thinks I'm guilty."

"Naw. He just had enough evidence to make an arrest. But I've been doing some investigating myself." Clay held up a ring of keys.

She gasped and stepped back. "Clay, you cannot break me out of here."

"See," he said. "Still the good girl. Won't even leave the jail when the door swings open."

He tried a few keys before finding the right one and then grinned.

"Gabe asked me to bring you out. He's dropping the charges."

She peered through of the open door and down the hall to the police offices in the tribal headquarters.

"Why?" she asked.

"Because you're not guilty and because we found who is."

He took her arm and guided her out past the series of desks and into the office of the chief of police. Clay positioned them between the chairs before Gabe's desk and the bank of glass windows looking out to small desk-filled room that was the tribal police station.

"Thought you'd like to see this." Clay pointed, and Izzie watched from behind the clear glass as Floyd Patch and their shared ranch hand, Eli Beach, were marched past them toward the booking area.

"Eli?"

"He took your brand and gave it to Patch. Might have been his idea. Patch rebranded some of his own weaned calves and then he and Ron broke into your pasture again to add them into your herd."

"And they were spotted in impoundment."

"Yes, as you left. Bustros, the brand inspector, noticed it. I believe Gabe is looking into that. Trying to sort that out. Matching stories up. Looking for inconsistencies. He's really good at that—details, I mean. Scary good."

The tears Izzie had swallowed down all morning erupted like a thundercloud, and she wept. Clay gathered her in.

"Shh, now. Everything will be all right."

When she finished choking and sputtering, she asked Clay why they had done this to her.

"Permits," he said. "Floyd wants them, and he can't have them unless you give them up."

"What about the pasture renourishment? I still have the permits, but I won't be able to graze my cattle there for over a year."

"Something stinks about that, too. Gabe is looking into that, as well."

She stepped back and tilted her head to study his face. His smile was a little too fixed and did not reach his eyes, which she knew sparkled with his smile and danced when he laughed. His smile faltered.

"It's not over, is it?"

"No."

"What should we do now?"

"I'm not sure."

Gabe arrived, looking rushed and overworked as usual.

"He's got a strong alibi for the seventh." Gabe glanced to Izzie. "Hello, Izzie. I see he figured out which key." He extended his hand to Clay, who gave him a large ring of keys. "Patch says the veterinarian was over at his place in the morning of the shooting. He recalls seeing the police vehicles go by. If it checks out, then he might not be tied up in the drugs."

"Can we go?" asked Clay.

"Sure. I might have more information tonight if you want to come to Grandmother's for supper. And Friday, Luke will be there."

Luke Forrest, the war hero, FBI agent who folks around here either idolized or despised. He'd gotten off the Rez. He'd made good. But he was a Fed and that was something that Apache just didn't do.

How had Clay's uncle done it? Clay's father, Luke's older half brother, had been a drug trafficker who had been murdered in his kitchen, and Forrest had ended up enforcing the law against such things. Strange world, she thought.

"Can I bring Izzie?" Clay asked.

She could tell from the long pause that Gabe didn't like that idea.

"Tonight?" Gabe asked, clarifying.

The brothers exchanged a long look that Izzie could not read. Finally Gabe nodded and then went back to the interrogation room. She watched him go.

"Ah, Clay? I don't think I'm coming over for supper. I've got things to do." The auction was tonight. She had cattle to sell and a fine to pay.

Clay's shoulders sagged, and his mouth went tight. The muscles at his jaw twitched.

"Sure."

She'd hurt him. She knew it. She just didn't know how.

"Come on. I'll drive you back to my place."

"Your place?"

"To get your truck."

She felt her face flush, as she realized what was happening. Clay thought she didn't want to be seen with him. And why wouldn't he? There had been a time when that was true. But that was before he helped her prepare to face the tribal council. Before he figured out what was happening on her land. Before he came and got her out of jail. Before she spent the best night of her life in his bed.

"Clay, I think you have the wrong idea about this. I'm not ashamed to be seen with you."

His brow arched and he cast her a hard look.

"Sure. I understand."

But he didn't. And she didn't think telling him otherwise would do a thing but waste her breath. Since Clay's return to the Rez, so many people had turned their backs on him. And she had been no different. The shame of that now ate into her bones like cancer.

Clay was exactly the kind of man she had always wanted, and now she needed to be the kind of woman he deserved.

Chapter Nineteen

Clay took Izzie to his place, and she kissed his cheek good-bye. He didn't try to hold her or to kiss her back. He had freed her from jail. And she said she wasn't ashamed of him. But there were six years that said otherwise. As Clay saw it, the only way to know whether Izzie was really willing to accept him was to solve her troubles and then see if she still wanted to become a part of his life.

Until then, he would keep his head down and his eyes open. Clay headed inside alone and found the place too quiet, but it was only Thursday, and Kino wouldn't be back until next Sunday at the earliest. He spent the evening haplessly moping and packing some of his belongings. He opted to sleep on the couch to avoid the memories of Izzie in his bed, but they just followed him out to the living room. He slept badly and was up and to work so early on Friday morning that he found the office was still locked. The morning chill chased him back to his truck, where he was when Donner rolled in twenty minutes later. He gave Clay an odd look as he parked beside him.

The two men exited their respective vehicles simultaneously and headed toward the office together. Donner's face was inscrutable, and Clay slowed to a stop at the door as dread hit the lining of his stomach. Hadn't Veronica told Donner that Clay was taking a personal day yesterday?

Clay thought of the time he'd been away with Kino and the days he'd missed all or part of the day while helping Izzie.

"I can make up the hours," offered Clay.

Donner made no answer.

"I'm fired. Aren't I?" asked Clay.

That made his boss's brows lift in surprise. "No, you're not. Gabe was here yesterday. He wanted to ask me some questions. He wouldn't tell me exactly what was happening, but I gather that you figured out how Isabella's cattle got loose and how they got rebranded. That's good work."

"You're not firing me?"

"Clay, you are one of my best men. I wanted to offer you my help. I'm not the tracker you are, but I'm a good shot and good with cattle. Plus, Isabella's father was a friend of mine. So if you need a man, call me."

Clay blinked in surprise.

"I also wanted to tell you that if you think Izzie's pastures don't need renourishment, then you should look to Pizarro. He's the one who makes that call, and until this happened, I'd have said he was an honest man. But when I questioned him, he told me that I should mind my own business. That's no answer."

"Really?"

"He did. So I thought you might want to send Gabe to see him."

Clay looked at his boss with new eyes. "Why are you doing this?"

"Same reason as you. Someone is messing with Izzie Nosie, and I don't like it."

The two shook hands, and it felt different somehow, as if he and Donner were equals. Clay left the office a few minutes later with orders to move the branded yearlings and cows to a new pasture. First he called Gabe and told him about Donner's suspicions. Then he went to work. It wasn't enough work to keep his mind from Izzie. It was hard not to call her. He checked his phone often to find no message, texts or missed calls. Finally, he gave up and called Gabe again, asking for an update, but Gabe told him if he wanted information, he should come to supper at their grandmother's that night.

At quitting time Roger asked if Clay wanted to go grab something to eat, but Clay turned him down in favor of dinner at his grandmother's table.

Clyne had sent him a text that their uncle Luke had arrived. Clay wanted to find out if his visit was official business or social, so he headed over to his grandmother's, stopping only long enough at his place to shower off the dust and grime earned from a hard day's work.

At his grandmother's, Clay was greeted to the mouth-watering aroma of a roast in the oven. The beef, potatoes and onions all combined to make Clay's salivary glands fire and his stomach rumble. He closed the front door, and Clyne called a greeting from the dining room. He found both his eldest brother and his father's half brother sitting at his grandmother's table before the remains of a pumpkin pie. Luke rose to hug Clay and slap him on the back.

When they drew apart, Luke took a long look at him.

"More good news about your sister," he said.

Clay's gaze flicked to Clyne.

"I don't think he knows yet."

"Oh," said Luke. "Well, let me be the first to tell you. Kino spoke to the case manager and found out that Jovanna was in a foster home on the Sweetgrass Reservation until 2008. When it shut down, she was moved off the Rez with a foster family."

Clay's gaze flicked to Clyne. He knew how strongly Clyne felt about Native American children being removed from Indian homes and raised by white families. Clyne's expression was stormy, as expected.

"Is she still in that foster home?" asked Clay, as the hope began to rise in him, becoming real. Kino was getting close. His little brother might not be able to read sign as well as he could, but he sure could do investigative work. The only one better was Gabe.

"We don't know yet. He's on his way to Rapid City to find out."

"Well, that's great." He looked about the kitchen. "Where's Grandma?"

Clyne chuckled. "She's off to talk to her sisters. Planning an invitation list for the Sunrise Ceremony. I think she's going to invite the entire tribe. We'll need every bit of the cow Nosie is going to give you."

Luke knew about that? What else did he know?

"So," said Clyne, "what's up?"

"Gabe said that he got tipped about the rebranding from Victor Bustros," said Clay.

"The livestock brand inspector?" asked Luke.

"Yeah," said Clyne.

"Bustros works for Pizarro," added Clay.

Clyne picked up the story. "And at the council meeting, last week's, not this week's, Pizarro—he's the general livestock coordinator—listed Izzie's land for renourishment with several others. I've looked at her pastures since. They're healthy. Tessay seemed in a hurry to call the question, and he had the votes, four to two. It's a routine matter. Motion passed. I never knew until afterward that none of the four who voted to renourish had seen the pasture beforehand, which is unusual."

"Why unusual?" asked Luke.

"Most times one or two of the council members go to look at the overgrazed pastures."

"Isn't that Pizarro's job?" asked Luke.

Clyne shrugged. "Never popular, closing a pasture. Sometimes he wants the backup."

"But not this time," said Luke.

"No."

"So you've got Patch, guilty of rebranding, releasing another rancher's cattle and actually slipping his cattle in with hers. And the second problem of the permits," said Luke. "And that little trouble with the gunfire, dead cattle and the evidence of someone cooking crystal meth on Izzie's soon-to-be-renourished land."

"Also the improved road," said Clay.

"Right," said his brother. "I checked into that. And we have no order for road improvement from the tribe. Yet there it is on Nosie's upper pasture, big as life."

"The kind of road you would need to bring in big trailers?" asked Luke.

"Yes," said Clay. "But why is it there?"

"I can handle that one," said Luke. "We have intel that the cartels are moving the ingredients for cooking crystal meth over the border. Because of what Gabe has told us, we believe they are setting up on the reservations to avoid federal jurisdiction. According to our contacts in Mexico, we have got a lot of agricultural precursor unaccounted for, and they would need that to make the drugs. And that area, where Izzie lives, is just inside the reservation boundaries but in a spot way off the beaten track. The road in and out is easy to defend, because you can see traffic coming from both directions."

"Gabe should hear this," said Clay.

"He has," Luke said. "What you can't see is someone riding up on them from the lower pasture."

"Like you and Izzie did," said Clyne.

"Also, since that spot is secluded and close to the main

highway, it would be easy to move product. Good place to store product, too, except for the problem of the rancher and her cattle. So they need to get Izzie off that land."

"Who?" asked Clay.

"That's what we aim to find out," said Luke.

"Are you going to the council?" Clay asked.

"Nope."

"I thought you needed permission to bring in the FBI or any outside agency on to the Rez," said Clay.

"That's so," said Clyne.

"But I can come back home visiting anytime I want," said Luke, "because I'm still a member of this tribe."

"This is an unofficial visit. That way there is no paperwork."

Clay turned to his brother. "But word will get out that Luke is here, and everybody knows he's with the FBI."

"We don't need much of a head start," said Clyne.

Clay put it together. "You think someone on the council is involved."

Clyne shrugged. "Gabe says the bad guys always know when the Feds are around."

"And where they will be," added Luke. "So while I'm here, I might ride along with Gabe or come chat with Clyne. Unofficially. I was hoping you might bring me over to Izzie's for a visit."

"I could do that."

"Great."

"What about your partner?"

"She's close. In case I need her."

"She ever been on the reservation?"

"Not this one. She worked up in South Dakota. Covered the same territory where Kino is now."

"She Indian?" asked Clay.

Luke laughed, and he and Clyne exchanged a look of confusion.

"She's white. Very, very white. And serious." He whistled. "She has a daughter, so that proves she's human, but other than that...well, all business. She's a widow and a mom, so..." He shrugged.

"That's tough," said Clyne.

"What happened to him?" asked Clay.

"She never said. Doesn't talk about it. Anyway, she worked in South Dakota and then in California and now down here with me."

Clyne jumped in. "Gabe met her. Said she's so white she's really pink. Got blond hair the color of corn pollen and blue eyes. He said she looks like she's from Sweden or something."

Clay knew that Clyne, with his traditional values and aesthetics, had never even dated a white woman. Though he had many white friends. Political friends, activist friends. Clyne never seemed to be off duty.

"Norway. Her ancestors, I guess. Anyway, they didn't hire her for her looks," said Luke. "She's tough as rawhide. Officially, she's trout fishing. I also suggested she visit Pinyon Fort and the museum for a little culture."

"You should bring her and her daughter over for supper," said Clyne. "Grandma will want to meet them."

"Her girl is staying with her mom, I think. And I don't want Cassidy connected to me. Not yet. Far as anyone knows, she's a tourist."

Before Clyne could respond, his phone rang and he excused himself. Luke and Clay settled at his grandmother's table and Luke helped himself to another generous slice of pie.

"She know you ate that pie?" asked Clay.

"Not yet, but I plan to be gone before she finds out." Luke grinned.

Clay debated waiting for the roast, but opted for the last slice of pie, destroying the evidence.

"So, how are you doing with Donner?" asked Luke.

"It's a good job, and I'm grateful to you for getting it for me."

Luke waved away the thanks. "I just got him to give you a shot. You're the one who's kept it. I admire you, Clay."

Clay lowered his fork. "Me?" He couldn't keep the surprise from his voice. His uncle was a shining example of what a man could make of himself. And he'd done it all on his own.

"Yes. You. *You* stayed. *You* faced your past, and you are making a name for yourself. Folks speak highly of your honesty and work ethic."

That was just nonsense. When folks spoke of him, it wasn't to mention his work ethic.

Clay pushed away the remains of the pie and studied his uncle. He looked like his father in many ways. Same shape to his face. Same easy smile. Same peaked hairline. Only Luke's hair was bristling short, and his father had always worn double braids.

"My work ethic?" He snorted. "I wouldn't have had a chance at that position if not for you. That job means everything to me, and I know how lucky I am to have it."

Luke's smile dropped, and he sat back in his chair. "Everyone needs help sometimes. Like the help you've been giving your girl."

"She's not *my* girl." Though he was thinking that was what he really wanted her to be.

"My mistake," said Luke.

Clay held back his frustration but made a poor job of it, judging from his uncle's curious expression.

"What?"

"You've never made a mistake," said Clay.

"*Everyone* makes mistakes."

Clay cast him an impatient look and then dropped his gaze. Luke was his elder. Even if he were not, he was also family and due respect.

Luke patted his arm, and Clay met his gaze. Something had changed, but he didn't know exactly what.

"Okay," said Luke, "I think it's time I came clean about a few things. You're family, and so I think you have a right to know just what kind of help I had."

Clay placed his fork on the empty plate and directed his attention to his uncle. What had he done? Stolen loose change off their father's dresser?

"You know I wanted to join the US Marines. You might even know how *much* I wanted it. But when I was seventeen, I got drunk at the quarry, and your dad didn't want me to drive. He was drunk, too. Not as bad as me, but pretty drunk. I wouldn't give him the keys to the truck. *My* truck. So I drove." Luke's hand settled on his own neck. "I drove right into an embankment. Six months from graduation and enlistment papers all signed and I crashed my truck. Your dad was nineteen. He'd already been expelled from school. You know what he did that night?"

Clay leaned in, waiting, hoping this wasn't another story of his father's failings. It was a long list. But this was before Clay was born. Before Clyne was even born. Before his mom and dad were married, before the drug charges.

"He switched places with me. Told me he was driving. Told me not to say otherwise. And you know what? I did. That sound like a hero move to you?"

Clay sat back as understanding came and, with it, all the implications.

"Your dad was a dropout and a troublemaker, but he

was still my big brother. It wasn't the first time he hauled me out of a jam. Like Clyne does in your family. I wasn't perfect, despite appearances. My brother, your father, told me to shut up when the police came. I did that, too. Your dad was arrested for DWI, and I joined the US Marines and shipped out. You know the rest. Except, if he didn't have that prior, then two years later, when he was on his honeymoon with your mom, his DWI would have been a first offense. He wouldn't have gone to prison. He wouldn't have met the gang members and begun driving for the cartel. You see? All that might not have happened. And yet, he never said a word about it after. Never told a soul. When I tried to thank him, he told me I could thank him by taking care of his sons. So I've tried. I didn't just plead your case because it was the right thing. I did it because I know that a nineteen-year-old makes stupid mistakes and that teenagers shouldn't be treated like adults. You deserved a second chance, Clay. And you've earned it many times over. I only wish…" He let go of his own neck and clutched his coffee mug. "I wish your dad had been given a second chance, too."

Luke sipped his coffee. Clay sat in silence as he realized that the uncle he'd always idolized was human. Flawed. Did that mean they all were? Mistakes. Punishment. Redemption.

When was it enough? He glanced at Clyne, standing in the hall, speaking on the phone. What mistakes had he made in Iraq or on the road with the rodeo circuit? Was the difference between him and his perfect older brother only the difference of getting caught?

"Thank you, Uncle," Clay said formally. "For telling me this."

Luke gave his nephew's cheek a pat, as if Clay were still just a boy.

"So who do you think is setting Nosie up?" said Luke.

Clay brought his attention back to Izzie's problems. "Arnold Tessay, one of the tribal council members, pushed for the vote that revoked Izzie's grazing permits. Victor Bustros is Tessay's man, and he is the one who first noticed the rebranding. Eli Beach is a part-time ranch hand who stole Izzie's brand. My boss oversees impounding cattle and sits on the general livestock council with Boone Pizarro. Pizarro also ordered the renourishment. I think her neighbor only wanted her permits, but who knows?"

Clay wondered if he was not also under suspicion.

"That all?"

"All I know."

"Long list," said his uncle. "You in touch with your old friend Rubin Fox?"

"I went to see him when I suspected meth cooks."

"What did he say?"

"To stay the hell away from him and also to stay away from Izzie."

"What do you think he meant by that?"

"At the time, I thought he was implying that she was involved, but now I think he might have meant that she was in the middle of some big trouble."

"So he cares enough about you or about Izzie to give you a warning. Surprising."

"Yeah. He's involved with the drug trade. Just like his dad. He's hooked into…"

"Distribution. Yeah. We know him. His dad was a minor player with a small box truck. Ran drugs from the border with Frasco Dosela. Worked with your dad, too, actually."

Clay had not known that. But he knew Frasco because he was the father of the woman Gabe planned to marry. Now Frasco was in federal prison and Gabe was still single.

"Someone else is moving product now. Not sure who. Rubin is protected by his Native status and by the fact that he never leaves the Rez. I'm sure Rubin has got prospects and probably information. Will he talk to you?"

"I doubt it."

"Well, try, anyway. See if he'll meet you somewhere, somewhere public. I'll speak with my friend Donner. I already put Cassidy on Tessay."

"Cassidy?"

"My partner."

"Your partner's name is Cassidy, like Butch Cassidy?"

"That's her first name. Last name is Walker."

"Cassidy Walker? Sounds like the name of a Texas Ranger."

Luke gave a chuckle. "Yeah, well, I told you that she's here trout fishing? Guess who I got for her guide?"

Clay shrugged, giving up without a try.

Luke smiled. "Tessay's son, Matt. And she's very persuasive, charming when she's not being a bad-ass."

Gabe arrived, in uniform and in a rush, as usual. He motioned to Luke, and the two stepped out into the backyard and closed the door behind them.

His grandmother came in, and Clay helped her set the table, then kept her company as she removed the roast from the oven to cool down. Clyne returned from his phone call and glanced out the back window at Luke and Gabe but gave them their privacy. When the food was ready, his grandmother broke up the meeting, calling Gabe and Luke to the table. It was nice to share a meal with his family. His uncle took Kino's usual place, and the table was filled again. After supper, Clay bid the group farewell and kissed his grandmother good-night. Then he returned to the dark, empty house.

He thought of Izzie, wished he could call her and take

her out. But though she had shared his bed, she was not willing to share a cup of coffee with him, at least not in public.

Clay understood. Funny that he'd never appreciated how important a man's reputation was until it was lost.

On Saturday morning, Clay called Rubin and got his voice mail. He left a message and then continued packing for his move back into his grandmother's home. When he stripped the bed, he lifted his sheets to his nose. Izzie's scent hung faintly to the linens. By the time he had the laundry packed, his phone rang. He fumbled in his pocket for it, hoping it was Izzie. He stared at the caller's name.

Rubin Fox.

He answered.

"Rubin?"

"You call?"

"I need to talk to you."

There was a momentary pause. "Come on, then."

"Where?"

"You know where."

Clay's heart sank. He had let Rubin set the location, and his uncle had told him to meet his former friend only in a public place.

"Well? You coming?"

"Yes," said Clay.

"See you in twenty, coz."

The phone went dead. Only now did he think to wonder why Rubin had agreed to meet.

The Wolf Den. The hangout of the Wolf Posse and the last place in the Rez Clay should go. He grabbed his keys.

Chapter Twenty

Clay headed to Rubin's place of business, a house on the eastern side of the Rez community called Fort Pinyon, after the stronghold of the same name. Past the museum and the fort lay an area closed to all but Apache tribal members. Inside that area was an unofficial community that folks called Wolf Canyon, but the only wolves there were members of the Apache gang, the Wolf Posse. They operated here, far from the tribal headquarters and close to the most sacred ground outside of Black Mountain itself.

Most of the tribe avoided Wolf Canyon except when looking for trouble or a score. There was always plenty of traffic. The homes were boxy, colorless and old like everywhere on the Rez. He glanced at the peeling paint on stucco walls, dry rotting wood, sagging gutters and windows repaired with packing tape. Everything looked like a postcard sent to those philanthropists back East asking for money for the Indian College fund.

He pulled up before the wolf den, a washed-out beige stucco ranch, notable because of its position at the end of the road and because the windows were secured with metal bars. For a moment Clay thought of the irony of Rubin leaving prison and then creating one here. He noticed Rubin's black pickup. His vehicle was dusty but too new for a man who supposedly existed on government subsidies.

Beside it was a beige four-door sedan with a tribal license plate. That made Clay frown. Who was the tribal official visiting the wolf den?

Clay left his truck, looking past the two vehicles to posse headquarters. The door, designed to keep unwanted visitors out, stood wide-open. The small hairs lifted on Clay's neck, and he reached for his phone to call Gabe. Then he remembered what his brother would say, what he always said. *You're not an investigator. Wait for the police.*

But Rubin wouldn't leave that door open. Never. That meant Rubin was in trouble. Clay shouldn't care but found he still did. Once Rubin had been a friend. Clay had thought that their friendship had died long ago of neglect. Did he owe Rubin anything? He didn't know, but he did know he wasn't waiting for the police.

Clay stepped out of his truck and onto the tufted mounds of yellow grass that no one bothered to mow. The silence was chilling. Where was his posse, the gang of men whom Rubin always said had his back?

Clay wished he carried a gun and then remembered Gabe saying the best way to get shot was to carry a gun. He thought walking into the wolf den unannounced and unescorted was also an excellent way to get shot.

Clay brought up Gabe's number on his phone and let his thumb hover near the green call button. Then he entered the house. The light was muted because of the brown packing paper someone had secured with gray duct tape over every window. What happened in this house was private, from the sale of drugs to the plans to move shipments around the reservation. As far as Clay knew, Rubin had never moved up to trafficking off the reservation, and his uncle said the same. Had Rubin learned his lesson from his father's mistakes? Staying on the reservation reduced his chances of facing federal prosecution. After all, he was

Apache and so not subject to the laws of the US government, as long as he stayed here, with his people, and as long as his people didn't turn him over to the Feds—again.

Clay called a hello and was met with silence. There was a rifle propped against the wall between the entrance and living room.

Clay hugged the wall, the dread making his stomach drop. He glanced at the firearm but left it where it was.

"Rubin?" Clay said and was met with no reply. "It's Clay."

He peered through the entrance toward the living room. His gaze swept the room before snapping to the body that lay between the living room and the adjoining room beyond. Two legs poking out and arms spread wide as if the man was falling backward into cool water. The legs were clad in jeans and the two feet sheathed in the expensive unlaced sneakers Rubin favored.

Clay stepped through the door, already smelling the blood. Rubin laid face up, eyes open, mouth open and hat still on his head. But his head seemed to have settled too far onto the floor. And behind him on the carpet was a large crimson stain that Clay knew must be blood. Lots of blood. Clay stared as his skin rose into gooseflesh. He didn't remember backing out of the room but found himself standing in the room's entrance, one foot in the hallway as if the sensible part of him was preparing to run.

Apaches did not associate with the dead. It was the worst kind of bad luck. Rubin's ghost might follow him. But Clay was also a Christian, and a Christian did not leave a friend's body unattended. Still, Clay wished he could be like his ancestors and burn the entire place to the ground before striking camp and moving away forever.

He caught movement from the dining room, and then the sound of a pistol shot pinged. Clay ducked back into the hallway, crouching behind the wall, knowing from the bullet hole that now pierced the Sheetrock above him that the wall offered no protection.

He pushed the call button on his phone. Dropped the phone in his breast pocket and then reached for the rifle.

"Don't shoot. It's Clay Cosen."

"Clay?"

He knew the voice but could not place it.

"Who's that?" he asked.

"Arnold Tessay. Don't shoot."

Arnold Tessay? What was the councilman doing here? Was that his vehicle? Clay tried to recall if Tessay was related to Rubin. Apache family trees were complicated. It wasn't hard to trace everyone back to a mutual relation. Then Clay's brain reengaged. Tessay had fought hard against Izzie's permits. He'd insisted on the quarantine of her herd. And he was cousin to Rubin's father.

"Did you shoot Rubin?" asked Clay.

"I'm putting down my gun. Come out."

Clay thought he wouldn't do that just yet. He hoped Gabe had picked up but couldn't check without releasing one hand from the rifle.

"I called Gabe. He's on his way." He said that loud enough for his brother to hear, if he'd picked up. "Why are you here, Mr. Tessay?"

"If you're staying, I'm going."

There was a thump, like something heavy hitting the bare floor. A moment later Clay heard the back door open and close. He took a look into the room, where Rubin's body remained. But now there was a pistol just beyond his outstretched right hand as if he'd died with it in his grip. Clay turned and saw the bullet hole in the wall and a new kind of terror welled.

Through the open front door, Clay saw movement in

the yard. He rushed to the entrance. Arnold stood beside the sedan.

Clay stared in confusion. "You can't leave the scene of a crime."

"Hell, boy. I can do anything I want. I'm a tribal councilman. And you're a convicted criminal who just killed a man."

"I didn't kill Rubin."

"Well, that rifle in your hand says different. It's the murder weapon, and it's got your prints all over it. The pistol shot came from Rubin's gun. Unfortunately, he missed. Won't matter. You didn't." Tessay removed the work gloves he wore. "Have fun in prison."

Clay stared in horror at the rifle as Tessay laughed.

The councillor slid behind the wheel. "Two drug dealers. They'll believe the worst and think they're better off with you both gone. Be hard on your grandma, of course. But she's got three good boys. That's something."

Clay couldn't even speak. His numb fingers extended, and the rifle clattered to the ground.

Tessay pointed at the rifle at Clay's feet. "See now, I thought you would have shot me. That's why I took out the bullets."

"You made Rubin call me. Lie to me. Get me over here."

"Well, he works for me. Worked. And it's no lie. Izzie is in trouble. Big trouble. Cartel is on the way to her place now. We tried to get her off that land. Lord knows, I tried. If it hadn't been for that stupid, greedy Floyd Patch, she never would have been up there in that pasture counting her herd, nosing around. I got to go." He started the engine.

"Why? Why take Izzie's land?"

"It's the perfect spot for a mobile meth lab. I'll have it under renourishment for three years or so. That gives the cartel boys time to cook product without worrying about the Feds. As tribal council member, I'm alerted to any joint initiative with the federal authorities. Gives me time to warn them and them time to move. Scourge of our community—drugs. But very lucrative."

Clay now understood why Gabe could never find the meth labs they knew were operating on the Rez.

"You betrayed your people."

Arnold snorted. "Like hell. The cartel don't sell here. They sell to the whites. I'm just doing my part to help them destroy themselves. Think of it as a modern version of the Ghost Dance, a way to make them all disappear." He closed the door and placed an elbow on the lip of the open window.

Clay took a step in his direction and met with the snub-nosed barrel of a pistol.

"I'll tell them what happened here."

Arnold laughed. "Great. You do that."

"They won't believe you," said Clay, his stomach twisting tighter then the cinch around a bronco's belly. They *would* believe him. Every word.

Tessay grinned like a man holding a winning hand. "Wait for your brother and find out who he believes. You or the evidence. Or you can run after your girlfriend. You might get there in time to get shot, too. If I were you, I'd be heading to Mexico. Give me a call from there. I'll hook you up as a driver, like I did for your dad."

That information staggered Clay a step. He regained his balance as Tessay backed out and drove away. Before the dust had settled, Clay heard Gabe's voice, far away and tiny. He drew out his phone.

"Did you hear that?" Clay asked.

"Some. Just you, really. Stay there."

Clay was already running to his truck. "You've got to get to Izzie. She's in trouble."

"Stay there. I'm sending units to her now."

"I'll meet them." He was closer to Izzie's place than police headquarters. Closer than home where Gabe had been. He'd get there first. He had to.

CLAY MADE IT to Izzie's place in record time. He found the house empty, and so he headed to the barn to find Max Reyes sitting on a roll of hay, his head in his hands as if he were crying. Max was a hand for hire, but since Eli had been providing her branding irons to Patch, she was shorthanded.

"Where is she?" asked Clay.

Max Reyes startled and shot to his feet, reaching for the closest weapon, which turned out to be a flat shovel used to clean stalls. His hands trembled, and his eyes were wide.

"I couldn't stop them. They would have killed me, too."

The idea that Izzie was already gone washed over him like cold rain. Clay stepped forward, and Max swung the shovel. Clay caught it and wrenched it from his hands. An instant later he had Max off his feet and pressed to the wall of Biscuit's stall. Clay's gaze flashed from Max to the place where her horse should have been.

"Where is she?"

"They called me. Told me to tell her that her cattle was wandering on the road again up by the drug cook site. An accident, they said. It would look like an accident."

"How long ago?"

"I don't know."

Clay banged him up against the stall, and his hat fell off.

"Fifteen minutes, maybe."

"Why didn't she take you?"

"I told her I'd follow in the truck."

Clay dropped Max, who sprawled on the dirty ground. Clay glanced around. He needed a horse. A fast horse.

He made his choice and was lifting the saddle when Max came at him. He should have stayed down. Clay dodged the punch and countered with one of his own, hitting him square in the forehead. Max's eyes rolled up, and he fell so hard that Clay felt the impact of his head hitting the dirt-packed floor through the soles of his boots.

He took one more moment to look at Max, who was breathing but unconscious.

"I ought to kill you," muttered Clay. Instead, he tied Max like a roped calf, with all four appendages locked behind him. He had to get to Izzie.

Clay lifted his phone to warn her and saw he had no service. Izzie had no service, either. Not until she got up to that improved road and he hoped like crazy that she wasn't there yet. The urgency pressed him on.

Clay gathered from her barn what he could in a hurry. Rope, saddle, blanket, machete that Izzie used for cutting bailing twine. He always carried a lighter, knife and phone. And from his truck he grabbed his saddlebags that held his fishing kit, hooks, line, sinkers and some hunting gear. As he mounted up he wondered if having a gun would just get him killed quicker or keep Izzie alive. For the first time since returning from the elite Native American tracking unit of Immigration and Customs, known as the Shadow Wolves, he wished he carried a rifle in his car like every other Apache he knew. But everyone he knew wasn't a convicted criminal. Everyone he knew didn't understand the difference between a conviction with a deadly weapon and a conviction with none. The difference between him and Rubin Fox.

He had no idea how many they'd sent to kill Izzie or how they intended to make it look like an accident. But the images of her in different deadly encounters swam before him as he pressed his heels to the powerful mustang she called Red Rocket and hoped the gelding lived up to his name.

He rode to the upper pasture, hugging the fence line. Praying he wasn't too late.

Chapter Twenty-One

Izzie kept glancing over her shoulder. Max should have been up here by now, and the longer he took the more unsettled she became. She used to be at home here, on this land, in the pasture. And if not happy, at least content with her purpose. She used to look forward to fulfilling her promise to her father, turning over the ranch to her brothers and finally beginning a life of her own. But gradually, year by year, her dreams and goals had begun to disappear. She was nearly twenty-five now. Was it already too late?

Back when she had received her Apache name, Medicine Root Woman, at the Sunrise Ceremony, she had known what she wanted to become. Then her father died. And she learned that she was good with cattle. Managed to increase her herd. But she didn't like cattle. They were stupid and needy and fearful. She liked horses. Thought she might raise them one day. In her heart, in the places she didn't admit aloud, she wanted to be a large animal vet. Schooling took time and it took money. Neither of which she had. Her time was not her own. The money belonged to her brothers, or it would, someday.

What would happen then, when the boys could do a man's work and she gave them what was theirs? What would she do then?

Her eye tracked movement, always looking for gopher

holes that could break a horse's leg and harm the cattle that got themselves in every manner of predicament despite her best efforts to give them safe pastures. She spotted the large black SUV the moment it appeared from the road that led up the mountain. The size, clean exterior and shiny newness made the vehicle stand out. As it approached she noticed the tinted windows, and the hairs on her neck lifted. It looked like what she imagined might be used in the president's motorcade. But here, on Apache land, such trucks meant only one thing: drug business.

She glanced about for the nearest cover and found the rocky slope and wooded area that led to the improved road. As she turned she saw Clay, charging up the hill on her chestnut mustang, Red Rocket. He was waving her toward the woods. His speed and the wild gestures only liquefied her unease into a cold breaking wave of panic.

She didn't look back toward the fence or the approaching vehicle but tore across the open ground at a full gallop, scattering the cattle that separated her from cover. The first sound she heard over the cattle's mooing and snorts was a single pop. Her heart, already pounding in her chest, seemed to stop.

She'd been around enough firearms to recognize the sound of a rifle shot. She flattened to her horse's back as more shots sounded. It wasn't clear if they were shooting at her or at Clay or both. She glanced to him, seeing Clay motion her down and then dropping out of sight himself. Now all that was visible of Clay Cosen was his leg swung over the saddle as he gripped the cantle between his thigh and calf muscles. His mount, Rocket, continued on, familiar with this unusual mode of riding.

They used to ride like this as children, imagining themselves in a time when her people wore red headbands marking them as army scouts and warriors.

Izzie swung herself from the saddle, looping her elbow over the saddle horn and her knee over the cantle. The cattle surrounded her as Biscuit continued at a lope through the herd that swallowed them up.

Beyond the fence the pop, pop, pop of gunfire continued. She hoped they didn't hit her cattle. Glancing forward, she saw the trees and the exposed gray rock. She and Clay broke from the herd together, separated by only fifty feet.

"Who are they?" she shouted.

"Cartel. Here to kill you."

Her fingers still gripped the reins, but they were numb now and bloodless.

Why, she wondered. Why did they want her dead? The land. The permits. It had to be.

Their horses climbed the steep outcropping of rock, Izzie first, Clay just behind on the narrow animal trail. Another series of shots sounded, and Biscuit stumbled, dropping to her forelegs.

Izzie cried out as her weight shifted, and she fell beside her horse. She was on her feet and tugging the reins, her gaze fixing on the stream of blood now flowing from her mount's shoulder.

"Oh, Biscuit!" she cried.

"Leave her!" shouted Clay. He landed beside her, still gripping Rocket's reins, and tugged Izzie to her feet.

"No," she howled, but he propelled her along, using Rocket's large body as a shield between her and danger. They reached the cover of the series of large boulders and pines. Bullets sparked off the rock, sending sharp shards of stone flying. Only when all three of them had reached cover did Clay release her arm. Rocket's barrel heaved, and foam fell from his mouth as the gelding recovered from the hard ride up the steep hill.

Izzie dropped to her knees, also panting as she struggled to fight the urge to vomit.

Clay was pressed to one of the boulders, peering back at the shooter's position.

"Three I can see," he said. "Can't tell how many still in the car. Two, maybe."

Izzie swallowed and then crawled next to him, gathering Rocket's reins. Behind them, Biscuit gained her feet and was limping painfully up the incline after them.

"I have to get her."

Clay reached out and grabbed Izzie's shoulder.

"They aren't shooting at Biscuit. You go out there, and she'll get hit again."

Izzie dropped to her seat as tears burned from her eyes and flowed down her cheeks in splashes of hot pain. Biscuit didn't deserve this.

She glanced at her mare's wound and the blood, then up to Biscuit's head. There was no blood coming from her horse's nose. It looked like the bullet had hit muscle and bone. Not her lung. Izzie rubbed her own chest in sympathy. Then her eyes went to the rifle sheathed and tied to the front of her saddle, mostly for killing snakes and gophers.

"The gun."

Clay glanced back to Biscuit. Then without a word he leaped up and exploded over the ground, running. He grabbed the rifle from the sheath tied to her saddle, and Izzie heard the sound of more gunfire. Clay threw himself down, and Izzie sat with both hands clutching her throat. Had they shot him or was he taking cover?

Clay began moving, using the downed logs and low rocks as he crept back up the incline. Izzie wished she could return fire as the gunshots continued, pinging off the rock. It was the longest thirty feet she had ever seen.

But as Clay made his heroic approach, Izzie realized something. She was a fool.

All these years she had let her need to be the perfect daughter ruin her chance at the one good thing in her life, her love for Clay Cosen. She loved him, irrationally and with all her heart, and if that made certain members of this tribe turn up their noses, then so be it. She didn't need them. She didn't need her spotless reputation or her mother's approval, either. She needed Clay.

And she needed them both to get out of this alive.

Clay fell in beside her, breathing heavily. She threw herself into his arms, and he hugged her with his one free arm.

"Thank you for coming for me."

"Thank me when we get out of here," he said. He moved to rise, and she let him go. She'd always turned to him in times of trouble, and he had always been there for her. Izzie felt the creeping unease as the truth crawled over her skin like spiders. She had used him. Was using him right now. This wasn't his fight. It was hers. Clay deserved better than a fair-weather friend. And that was exactly what she had been. When he'd turned to her, she had turned her back.

"I'm so sorry," she said as the tears came harder.

Clay squeezed her hand. "Izzie, I need you to pull it together."

"I was so mean to you."

"What?"

"I didn't even come see you when you came home."

He looked at her as if she'd gone mad. "Izzie, there are guys shooting at us. Can we talk about this later?"

She sniffed. Nodded and wiped her nose on her sleeve.

Clay peered over the rise.

"What are they doing? Are they coming?"

"No. One got in the car."

Leaving? They were leaving.

"Thank God," she whispered.

Clay continued to watch. "Where are the other two?"

Izzie peered over the rock and watched the SUV as it climbed the road and then turned.

"Where are they going?"

"Going to pull in above us. At least that is what I'd do."

Izzie's heart hammered. They were now trapped between an open pasture and the road.

"Gabe is coming," said Clay. But his gaze was flicking about as he took in their position and the enemy who was now capturing the higher ground.

Izzie looked toward the road. "They're waiting for us to leave this cover."

Clay looked back across the open pasture. "Can't go that way. They'd pick us off. But we gotta move. Now."

Chapter Twenty-Two

"Stay low," Clay said as he grabbed Rocket's reins and hoisted Izzie up on the horse. They left the animal trail and made for deeper cover. Behind them, the men on the road disappeared into the woods.

"Should I shoot at them?" she asked.

"No. Save the bullets. Come on."

They continued on. When the branches encroached, she slipped from the saddle, following beside Rocket. A moment later the shooting resumed from the direction of the road as their attackers below caught glimpses of them through the pinyons. One bullet splintered the bark of a tree trunk just inches above where Izzie had placed her hand. But she kept going, following Clay deeper into the thicket. Clay knew the woods. He knew how to track and trap. But he had always been the hunter. Now they were the hunted.

From here she could see the gravel road just above them. Was he trying to get past it, to the woods beyond? It would make sense not to be trapped between the men behind and the road ahead. But it was too late.

"I can see them," she whispered, pointing. "Coming up the road."

"Can you still climb, Izzie?"

She nodded. Clay boosted her up the tree trunk and then

instructed her to throw his lariat over a branch above her. She did as instructed, and before she had even thrown the rope, Clay had shinnied up a nearby sapling and used his weight to bring the top of the trunk to the ground. It was a game they used to play, bending saplings for the ride down. But she knew the other purpose of such a setup because her father had taught her. A snare, a big one, used to capture a large animal. Clay secured the bowed tree and then moved rapidly on the ground, fashioning a large noose that he hid in the branches of the shrubs on either side of the path. One side of the loop lay on the ground, but the other was a few inches off the forest floor. The noose was so artfully camouflaged that she thought she might walk right into it even knowing where it encircled the path. He secured the other end of the rope to the bowed branches he had staked and covered the line with debris. As she watched, the snare vanished. She hoped the cartel members were city boys.

"Come down," he whispered, and she scurried back to him. They moved on. Clay stopped three more times, using his fishing line to run invisible threads across the path and again to make a lasso of wire line, which he placed partially in the stream. This one he set with several hooks. Above them, the men neared.

"Can't we just hide? Wait for Gabe?"

Clay shook his head. "I don't want my brother shot."

Had she actually just suggested they crawl away and hide while his brother face the danger directed at her? Izzie's cheeks flushed hot as she decided it was past time for her to stop running from trouble and expecting everyone else to face down her problems.

"You're right. What can I do?"

He gave her instructions. It was dangerous. They'd have

to separate. She needed to lure them but keep them from getting a good shot at her.

"Don't use the gun unless you have to." He handed it to her. "That will give away your position and lead the ones on the road to you."

"Okay." She turned to go, but Clay stopped her by capturing her by the arm.

"Izzie, I have to tell you something else. Tessay's working with them."

"Why are you telling me this now?" And then she knew. If it came to it, Clay would give his life up for hers, and he wanted her to know what he knew.

"Oh, no, you don't. Don't you die on me, Clay Cosen."

He grinned and saluted. "Yes, ma'am."

A moment later the killers' arrival was punctuated by the sound of gravel crunching under tires followed by car doors slamming.

"You remember what I said?" Clay asked. "Use the horse to startle them and take cover."

"What if they shoot Rocket?" she asked, the anticipation and worry broiling inside her.

"What if they kill you instead? Who will look after your brothers then? Rocket?"

Izzie straightened her spine and prepared to do what must be done. She gripped Rocket's reins in one hand and the rifle in the other. She nodded her readiness. Clay clasped her chin between his thumb and curved index finger. She leaned in and gave him a kiss. Their mouths met greedily. Then he left her, running fast in the opposite direction.

Izzie led Rocket to the place where he could be seen from the trail, a living decoy should the men get past Clay's traps. Then she dropped the gelding's reins. Rocket was a good horse and knew that a dropped rein meant to stay put.

She tied a lead line on the side of his bridle and walked as far from the animal path as the line allowed, taking cover behind a cluster of rocks. As she settled in against the cold stone and damp moss, she wondered if, like Geronimo, this would be her final stand. She understood now what it meant to fight against terrible odds for your family. Like those warriors of old, she fought because she was left with only two choices. Fight or die.

Izzie took the red bandanna from around her neck and folded it carefully. Then she tied it in the fashion of her people, like a male warrior would with a wide band tight across his forehead. She lifted her rifle and waited. From somewhere uphill she heard a war whoop and knew Clay had engaged the enemy.

CLAY ALLOWED THEM to see him for just the briefest instant, not long enough, he hoped, to get a bead on him before he rushed away down the trail. He veered off before the first snare and was gratified to hear orders shouted in Spanish and then the heavy footfalls of pursuit. He watched as the first man caught his boot on the trip wire that sent the section of log he had suspended above them crashing down. It glanced off the first man's shoulder but struck the second of four squarely in the face. Clay winced at the crunch of wood splintering bone. The second man dropped to the trail. The third man fell to a knee and lifted his semi-automatic machine gun, scanning the area for a target and finding none. Clay had already dropped from view. He knew enough Spanish to understand that the downed man was alive and heard the order to leave him. Too bad. He had hoped they would order one of the three to carry him back to the SUV.

Clay waited until they had continued down the trail before retrieving the abandoned man, dragging him into the shrubs and tying him wrist to ankle in a series of knots Clay had learned from his brothers. He also knew from firsthand experience that the more the victim struggled, the tighter the knots became.

The men were moving cautiously now. So slowly that they might see the snare only a few feet before them. He had hidden the noose well, but the trip line had only some greenery disguising it. He knew that it would not fool any of his siblings, but the lead man, now inching carefully along, still placed his silver-tipped cowboy boot squarely in the noose, and a moment later he was rocketing into the air, his semiautomatic firing in a wild arc that sent his two remaining comrades diving for cover. One man landed close enough for Clay to disable him.

Clay did not like to cause pain, but all he needed to do was think of Izzie, just fifty yards down this very path, and it was easy to draw his knife and slice cleanly through the man's hamstring. The suspended man's howling was so loud, he wondered if the final man even heard Clay's victim's scream. Clay punched the blade of the knife into his other thigh and then relieved him of his guns. He left him howling and rolling from side to side under a bush beyond the edge of the trail.

The last remaining man was now trying to cut down his friend, which was a terrible idea. Likely the man would land on his head and break his neck. Clay sent the man running down the trail with a blast of gun fire. Less than a minute later he heard his screams and knew he had blundered into the spider web of monofilament and fishing hooks that Clay had rigged to come loose on contact.

He followed and reached the final man at the same time as Izzie. She trained her rifle on their foe as Clay ignored the hooks that tore the man's forehead, neck and body and quickly tied him.

By now the two men who had been left behind would be hearing the screams and cries of their comrades. They had no vehicle. These were not the men in charge. No, the leader was the coward who had abandoned his team at the first sign of trouble and run into the net. But still, Clay thought they would be coming. And he was out of traps.

IZZIE DID NOT want to leave Clay, but she thought his plan was a good one. With only two men left, it would be best if she could draw them from cover. Unlike Clay, she did not wish to bring them in alive. They were on her land. They were trying to kill her, and she was more than willing to protect her family and the man she loved.

An even match now, Clay said, with two of them and two cartel killers from Mexico. Two Apache versus two Comancheros. It was an old match, and each side had their share of victories and losses.

Clay wanted to get behind them. Izzie wanted to shoot them on open ground. But it was already too late for that, because when they retraced their path it was to discover that their attackers had already crossed the pasture and had reached cover. She saw their position, below them, hiding in the rocks. Clay had left two men disabled, howling in pain and shouting orders and threats at the remaining men. They were living decoys, but Clay needed time to get behind the approaching men. He took the semiautomatics. But he carried them across his back. What he carried in his hand was his knife and his rope. She had seen what he could do with that rope; she had watched him practicing his throw for hours. She had seen him ride at a full gallop, rope a calf, leap from his horse, flip the animal and rope its hind and forelegs all in less than five seconds.

But none of the calves he'd ever roped had carried guns.

One man was making his way between rocks. Clay told

her to let them get closer, let them separate. Then keep them distracted and apart, so he could take them out. Had she given him enough time? They were only thirty feet below her now. One man moving and then the next. She needed to stop their advance. So she watched through her rifle scope as the first man made his next move, leaving the rocks for the more flimsy cover of a downed Ponderosa pine. Then she pulled the trigger, shooting high, and he predictably flattened to the ground. She sighted him, hoping for another shot. Her fury battled with her desire to follow Clay's orders. He wanted them alive.

The man stayed down for a long time. Then he shouted for his comrade and was answered by silence. He called again, a note of hysteria now entering his voice. But his partner did not reply. Izzie smiled. Clay had reached the other man.

The final man's voice was frantic now. He swore and called out in Spanish to the Virgin Mary. Izzie scowled.

"She won't help you," she called, and then closed one eye, watching for her chance. Behind him came the snap of a branch. Clay would never be so careless. The man lifted up and looked back, responding like a gopher to a whistle. Izzie pulled the trigger and heard the scream.

Then Clay leaped on the man. The man's gun flew into the air, and she saw Clay lace both hands together and bring them down hard. The woods went silent. Behind her came the cries of their leader, calling for his men, swearing vengeance and death as the hooks gaffed him like a trout. Beyond that came the sound of steady sobs. The one Clay had dispatched without killing him, she supposed. At the moment he did not seem grateful.

Clay stood and waved.

"All clear."

"Dead?" she asked.

"You got him in the shoulder. Good shot."

"I was aiming for his head." She scrambled down toward him.

"Oh," he said, regarding the man in question. "Bad shot."

She kept her rifle ready until she saw their attacker lying motionless, facedown, with his hands neatly secured behind his back. Blood welled through a hole in his jacket like a running stream.

Izzie let the rifle slip to her side as all the fight drained out of her. She began to shake and reached with her free arm. Clay pulled her close. Izzie let the sobs come.

"You're safe, Izzie. I've got you."

He had always gotten her, always been there.

"What if they send more?"

"With the FBI wise to the location of their cook site? With my brother patrolling this area?" He stroked his hand over her head. "With Tessay under arrest? No, Izzie. They won't be back."

Not here, anyway. But they would be back on the reservation. The protection of Indian land was just too tempting to the cartel, and the money was too enticing to some members of their tribe.

Izzie burrowed her face into the soft flannel of Clay's worn shirt and breathed in the warm reassurance of his scent. How had she ever made it so many years without him?

From somewhere below their line of sight came the sound of sirens. Clay's brother Gabe and likely his uncle, Agent Forrest, were on their way.

Clay set her back and took a long look at her, scrutinizing her face.

"You going to be all right?"

Her stomach dropped. Something about the way he said that made her think he was saying farewell. One look at his face and she knew the truth. What he was really asking was would she be all right without him?

"Yes," she whispered. "Or I will be."

He gave her a sad smile.

"Go on," she said, giving him permission to go.

Clay moved toward the open pasture. Waving his arms toward the approaching police cruisers. She knew what he would do now that she was safe. He would leave her alone again, give her her privacy, let her keep her stellar reputation among the ranching community, because that was what she had always wanted. But she didn't want that now. Now she wanted Clay Cosen just as he was, because there wasn't a better man anywhere. The only trouble was, she didn't know if he wanted her.

Was it already too late? Had she hurt him too deeply and too often to ever make amends?

She watched Clay walk out to meet his brother and felt what Clay must have experienced when she walked away from him, a sense of hopeless loss. Izzie's breath shuddered as the tears came again.

Chapter Twenty-Three

Clay watched Gabe directing his men to wait and then ducked through the fencing. A moment later, he and their uncle came striding forward together in a perfect matched gait. They made an ominous sight, Gabe in his police uniform, gold tribal shield flashing in the sunlight, and Luke, dressed in a dark gray suit and tie that made him look every inch the G-man.

There was no easy way to tell his brother that he had fled the scene of a crime. Luckily, Gabe opened the conversation without waiting for him.

"She okay?"

Clay nodded.

"You okay?"

Another nod.

"I told you to stay put."

"Did you expect me to?"

Gabe's mouth quirked for just an instant as he struggled to keep hold of his stern expression.

"Did you pick up Tessay?" asked Clay.

"Not yet. Brought all the horses," he said, motioning toward the six cruisers that covered the 1,800 square miles of Apache reservation. He glanced back toward the woods, where Izzie emerged from the rocks leading her horses.

"I need you to call a vet. They shot Biscuit."

Gabe got on his radio. Then he rested a hand on his pistol as if it was the armrest of a familiar chair.

From the woods came howls of anger mingled with the high-pitched screams of pain. Luke and Gabe exchanged a look.

"Who's that?"

Clay went through it in sequence, the call from Rubin, finding his body. His conversation with Tribal Councilman Arnold Tessay and then coming to help Izzie face five cartel killers.

"How many dead?" asked Luke.

"None."

That made both men exchange a look. Gabe shook his head in clear disappointment, and his uncle cocked his head to stare at Clay.

"What?" asked Clay.

"You should shoot to kill," said Gabe, repeating what he knew from law enforcement. If you use your weapon, aim for mass.

Clay knew that philosophy. But he had a record. That made him see things differently.

"Very dangerous," said Luke.

"More witnesses for you," said Clay.

"Let's go mop up." Gabe lifted his radio. One of the cruisers headed up the mountain, to the improved road and the abandoned SUV.

Luke called his partner. She exited the car by the road, and Clay was struck with two things. She was small, and she was so blonde that her hair seemed to be a reflection of the sunlight.

"*That's* your partner?" asked Clay.

Luke glanced back. "Yeah. I know. But she's tougher than she looks."

"I sure hope so."

"Young. On her third assignment. Before that she was in US Army."

"Oh, boy," said Clay, knowing army and US Marines didn't always get along.

"It's okay. Let's go find some illegal aliens."

Clay walked them across the pasture where Izzie waited with Rocket and Biscuit, comforting the horses. Biscuit now stood with her front leg raised and her chest oozing blood.

After Clay had pointed out all the wriggling bodies of their attackers, Gabe took him into custody. Izzie left Biscuit the minute she saw Gabe put Clay in the back of his cruiser. It was the ride Clay had never wanted to take again, and this time Izzie was there to witness his humiliation. Somehow, despite all his efforts, he was in custody again. The look on Izzie's face made Clay feel sick. He read her expression as a kind of acceptance that he was what they all said, the black sheep, the black eye, the raw wound, the lost child or worse…just like his father.

Clay went through another round of questioning at the station. Gabe told him all the men he'd captured would live and that Luke and his partner, Agent Walker, had taken custody of them. He also told him that Clyne had called a special meeting of the tribal council and that Tessay had been suspended pending investigation. It seemed that Arnold's prediction was wrong. The federal and local law did not take his word at face value and were investigating Rubin's death with Tessay as the prime suspect.

Clyne appeared after the meeting at police headquarters with an attorney for Clay, whom Gabe said he didn't need. It was a rare instance when his two older brothers disagreed. Clyne won the argument, as usual, and Clay's new attorney began the process of securing Clay's release on bail, which Clyne generously posted.

Clay was released to Clyne's custody, and he picked up his personal items at the main desk to discover Izzie had called twice. He didn't call back. He was too tired and his heart was too sore to hear her goodbye.

He had a late meal with Clyne and his grandmother; Gabe and Luke were too busy to make an appearance. He'd never gotten a chance to move his things here, so he returned to his place, and it was not until he hit the shower that the exhaustion really took hold. He barely got dried off before he stretched out on the couch and was out as if someone hit him on the head.

On Sunday morning, he woke to the far off buzzing of the alarm in his old bedroom because he had forgotten to turn it off. He groaned and buried his face under the sofa pillow until he recalled that Izzie regularly attended church. That got him up and moving. He threw his packed possessions into his truck. It was discouraging that everything but his saddle fit in only two large duffels and a single box. He made it to his grandmother's in time to join her and his brothers for services. But he was disappointed to find Izzie was not in attendance. Her brothers and mother were there, and her mother seemed to spend the entire service staring at Clay in stony silence and then formally thanked him for saving her daughter's life. It was the most awkward moment of his life, followed by the next as Clay accepted the offered kiss on the check and then excused himself, leaving his grandmother and Izzie's mother deep in conversation.

On Monday, Clay was back at work and was surprised when his boss told Clay that he was proud of him. On Tuesday, Gabe arrested Boone Pizarro. According to Donner, the shamed councillor implicated Pizarro while looking for a plea deal. Pizarro was accused both of rebranding

Izzie's cattle and ordering Victor Bustros to check Izzie's cattle's brands. No charges were made against Bustros yet.

Wednesday morning Clay's new attorney stopped by his work to tell him the forensics came back on Rubin's murder. Clay's prints were all over the murder weapon, which was bad, of course. But a partial print of Arnold Tessay's was found on one of the empty bullet casings at the scene. It was enough to hold Tessay, who had secured a defense attorney, a "damned good one" who had already requested a bail hearing.

Clay wondered if Tessay would get it because he'd heard his uncle Luke predict Tessay was a flight risk and, if allowed bail, might flee, but perhaps that was because Luke was hoping he would run. Leaving the reservation meant Tessay would lose his protected status. Clay knew that Luke and his partner were building a federal case against him, which he would present for the tribal council's approval and, if successful, press the district attorney to accept the case.

Clyne showed up on Wednesday evening to take him to the closed session of tribal council and told him that their youngest brother, Kino, and his new wife, Lea, were due home tomorrow.

"Ready?" asked Clyne.

"Yeah." They climbed into his older brother's SUV, but Clyne didn't start up the vehicle.

Clay lifted his brows in an unspoken question.

Clyne drummed his fingers on the wheel. "She's speaking to the tribal council tonight, same as you."

He didn't need to ask who *she* was. Izzie. He'd see her. It would be hard, as hard as every chance meeting he had suffered through since his return from the detention center in Colorado.

But when he entered the council chambers, it was worse

than he imagined. He saw her. No, he *felt* her. Just being in the same room caused a physical pain in his chest. He rubbed his knuckles over his sternum, but it only got worse.

Izzie stood when he entered and walked down the center aisle to meet him. His shoulders went tight as if every muscle there had suddenly seized up. He clenched his jaw, and sweat rose on his brow.

Before him most of the tribal council were already seated. The council members, minus Arnold Tessay, sat on one side of the table. Their chairman, Ralph Siqueria, had returned from DC and presided over the closed session with only invited speakers. Gabe, Luke, his blonde partner and Izzie all sat on the opposite side of the table but pivoted as Clyne and Clay entered.

Izzie waited as Clay approached. He didn't know what kept him moving.

"Hello, Clay," she said.

He nodded, hoping to move past her to his seat, but she blocked his path.

Clay glanced to the witnesses and grimaced. They all sat motionless as if afraid to miss a moment of this personal drama.

"You've been avoiding me," said Izzie.

"That's so."

"Why?"

"Izzie, let's just get through this?"

She shook her head. "Not until I tell you something."

He gazed down at her soft brown eyes, taking in the image of her pointed chin and the angle of her brow and her smooth skin and, well, everything that made her so beautiful. In that moment he had time to consider all the mistakes that kept him from being what she needed. Clyne took his seat across from Gabe. Clay looked at his older brothers. Their presence seemed to mock him. Neither of his brothers had let their mother's tragic death or their father's train wreck of a life derail theirs.

"Are you listening to me?" she asked.

Had she been speaking? His face went hot. He wished she would not do this now, so publicly. But perhaps she wanted all to know she was grateful and their business was finished. He could bear it. Couldn't he?

"Clay, I said that I made mistakes. That I let my obligations and the opinions of others keep me from doing what *I* wanted. But I won't let that happen anymore. It is *my* life and *my* decision what man I choose to share it with."

Clay wrinkled his brow in confusion. This was not the speech he had expected to hear.

"I don't understand."

"When I was young, I listened to my mother. I pretended to avoid you, but I went out with Martin just to be near you. When he died, I didn't grieve for him. I grieved for you and for us, and that shames me. Then when you came back, I was so certain that I had to fulfill my promise to my father and to keep the herd for my brothers before I even considered a family of my own."

Clay's heart was beating so fast that his ribs ached.

"I understand, Mizz Nosie."

Izzie stamped her foot. "Don't you dare call me that. Not after the night we spent together."

His gaze snapped to hers. Behind him, he heard the intake of breath from someone on the council. Was that Clyne, shocked at Izzie's admission?

Why would she tell them all? She had always guarded her reputation. An Apache woman's virtue was important. Her honor like a living thing, to be nurtured...but she had told them all—publicly.

He scrutinized her face, but she had adopted the blank expression of a woman who did not wish to reveal her emotions. He felt the first stirring of hope. She had stood here before her tribal leadership and told them, every one of them, what they had done.

She must have lost her mind. He tried to control the damage.

"It was the fear, the need, that's all."

"No." She grabbed the front of his shirt, bunching it in her fists, and gave him a little shake. But she didn't need to, because she had his full attention. "It was not the fear or the need. I am not ashamed of you. I am ashamed of myself. I am proud of you. You are brave, honest, smart. You put the needs of everyone first. You helped Kino down on the border, and you are giving up your place so he can make a home there with his wife. You helped Gabe and your uncle solve this case. And you kept me alive."

His breathing was so fast that he was dizzy with it. He had to widen his stance just to regain his equilibrium.

"Bella?"

"I love you, Clay Cosen. I have loved you since I was a little girl, and I will love you all my life."

He looked at her, trying to understand what was happening, afraid to believe his ears. She nodded, confirming what she had said.

"I love you," she whispered.

She said that here, aloud before the entire tribal council. Clay's jaw dropped as he looked from one smiling face to the next.

She loved him.

"Clay, can you ever forgive me?"

The buzzing in his ears silenced all sound. He could not hear the men and women behind him at the council table, because his senses were too full of Isabella Nosie.

And possibilities.

"Is it true?" he asked.

"I love you so much."

He turned to his brothers, his voice hushed with astonishment. Clyne was wiping at his eyes, and Gabe had puffed up like a Tom turkey.

"She loves me," he said to them.

Clyne called for a recess.

Several of the council members glanced at Clay and Izzie as they rose and made their way out of the chamber.

IZZIE STARED AT Clay, but he just stood there with a stunned look on his face. She had bared her soul to him, and he was silent as the room in which they stood.

Was this how he had felt after the shame of his arrest, standing in the judicial chamber? What if he didn't love her? What if she had waited too long? What if he could not forget, could not forgive?

Her cheeks burned with shame. Why should he forgive her? She had done nothing to earn his love.

"You said that in front of everybody. The entire council."

"I know. I'm sorry. I just—just…" She was a fool. "I wanted everyone to know." She dropped her gaze. "I didn't mean to embarrass you."

She stared up at him, willing her lower lip to cease its trembling. He remained silent, and she could not read his thoughts. All she knew was that she was too late.

It was hard to speak now. The pain lodged in her throat like a wedge, choking her. There was no saving face, no way to keep her pride. She had taken the risk and lost.

"I'd understand if you can't forgive me. I was so caught up in what my father wanted and what my mother wanted that I lost sight of us."

She sank into the closest seat, set up for the public meetings. Clay dropped to a knee before her.

He took her hand and gave a little squeeze. "Izzie, look at me."

She did.

"There is nothing to forgive. You took care of your family. And I repaid my debt for the mistake."

"But you didn't make a mistake."

"I trusted Martin. I knew him well enough to know he wanted that two hundred dollars. I even knew him well enough to recognize the lengths he'd go in order to get it. That alone was worth eighteen months in detention. As for us, well, most folks can't look past a single mistake. But you did."

"Oh, Clay."

"And I love you for that. I love you, Isabella. I've loved you since I was ten years old. And I want you to be my wife."

"Your wife?" Now she was the one staring in shock.

He smiled and brought the back of her hand to his mouth brushing his lips against sensitive skin.

"Would you like time to think about it?" he asked.

She shook her head. "No. I've had too much time to think. Too much time away from you."

"So…?" His mouth quirked.

She threw herself into his arms, nodding her head against the warm strength of his neck and shoulder.

"Yes, Clay. I will be your wife."

Chapter Twenty-Four

The following Sunday afternoon preparations were well underway for the barbecue lunch following church to welcome home the newlyweds. When his grandmother had mentioned her plans for the gathering to Clay, he had immediately asked if he could invite Izzie.

"She's your girl, isn't she?" Glendora had replied and then insisted that he invite Isabella's entire family.

His girl. He liked the sound of that.

Because of Gabe's investigation and Clyne's political responsibilities, this was the first time the brothers had all been together since Kino's wedding.

Clay joined his older brothers at the fire pit in the backyard. They had the smoker going, coals ready. The ribs, rubbed with a mix of seasoning, waited in the cooler.

Their uncle was, unfortunately, unable to attend. Gabe said they had leads to follow, thanks to the suspects they had in custody. Of course, the men were not talking, but Luke knew which cartel they belonged with. The FBI was anxious to cut this supply line while the trail was hot.

Gabe said they had some new leads to follow because both Tessay and Pizarro were now anxious to cooperate to avoid federal prosecution.

All three brothers turned at the sound of tires crunching in the gravel drive beside the house. There was Kino's truck pulling to a stop. Glendora hurried out of the house and rushed past them, hugging Lea, who looked rosy-cheeked and happier than Clay had ever seen her. After Glendora had hugged Kino, she captured his bride and left her youngest grandson to his brothers. The men hugged and slapped each other on the back.

"Any more news?" asked Gabe, ever the investigator. He was referring to the hunt for their missing sister.

"Yes, actually. Grandma is going to flip. You know I spoke to Jovanna's case manager."

Clay didn't know. Somehow he'd missed that piece of news in all the excitement of the past two weeks.

"Well, after the foster home closed, she handled Jovanna's placement in a temporary foster home and then her permanent adoption." Kino turned to Clyne. "I did what you said. I hired an attorney up there, and he has filed papers to get the adoption unsealed. He says that's the first step, and then we can seek to have the adoption overturned." Kino drew out three business cards from his front pocket. "Here is his name."

Gabe accepted a card and passed the other cards to Clay and Clyne.

"He said there will be a hearing. One of us should go."

"I'll go," said Clay. They all looked at him. Clyne and Gabe had been up there already, and Gabe was in the middle of investigating the biggest case of his career. Clyne had council business, including electing a new member to replace the vacancy left by Tessay's resignation. Kino had spent much of his honeymoon tracking Jovanna through the foster-care system. It was Clay's turn to help find their baby sister.

The brothers turned to Clyne, who nodded his approval.

"How long will it take to get her back?" asked Gabe.

"I don't know," said Kino.

"Better be before this July. Grandma has her dress half done. She's beading the yoke every day."

"And she's already spoken to the shaman," added Clyne.

"We're going to need another cow," said Clay.

"Who will be her sponsor?" asked Clyne. It was a position of honor, but one only an Apache woman and member of Jovanna's tribe could fill. It was customary for this to be a close friend of the family. This woman would act as both teacher and guide. The brothers looked blankly at each other for a moment.

"We have to find her first," reminded Clay.

"We'll get it done somehow," said Clyne. "Grandma's not the only one who wants her back. We all do. She's our sister, and she belongs here with her people."

"One more thing," said Kino. "The case manager slipped up. She said that Jovanna's parents weren't Indian."

"What!" roared Clyne.

"They're white?" asked Gabe.

"I don't know. Maybe. Not Indian, that's all he said."

"What does that mean?" asked Gabe.

"It means they're not Indian," said Clyne. "We have to get her home. Now!"

Clay had seen that look before. Clyne would not rest until he retrieved Jovanna.

Their eldest brother was a staunch advocate for Indian children being raised in their communities. Especially since so many Indian children had been removed from their families and lost to their culture.

"We need a court order," reminded Gabe.

Kino placed a hand on Clay's shoulder. "I heard you and Izzie are back together."

"Yeah." Clay grinned. He was so happy. The only dark spot in his world right now was his baby sister's absence.

"About time. You going to marry her?" asked Kino.

His brother was always blunt, and only he could get away with it.

Clyne and Gabe exchanged a glance. They always seemed to know what the other was thinking.

Clay shrugged. "I already asked her."

"And," said Gabe.

"She said yes."

Kino gave a whoop of excitement. The brothers clapped Clay on the back.

"Have you got a ring?" asked Clyne, ever the practical one.

"Not yet."

"I have Mom's," said Clyne.

The brothers went silent as Clyne opened his shirt, revealing the traditional medicine bundle carried by warriors of old. Inside were items of power, and the contents of each man's bundle was private. They had each made such a packet as part of their education in the tribe. Both Clyne and Gabe wore theirs about their necks. Gabe now pressed a hand over his, making Clay curious as to what the leather pouch contained. Meanwhile, Clyne drew his over his head and opened it. A moment later he held their mother's diamond solitaire ring between his thumb and forefinger.

Clay felt the lump in his throat. His brother had carried this next to his heart for all these years. The ring his father had given his mother with his promise. A promise he did not keep. Clay knew that he would not ask Izzie to wear that ring.

"That should go to *your* wife," said Clay.

Gabe nodded his agreement.

"I don't think I will marry. There is no one." He shrugged.

"That's because you want to marry the next Miss Apache Nation," said Gabe, but his kidding tone gained only a scowl from Clyne.

"How are we going to survive as a people, if we don't marry other Indians? We've got a culture to preserve and a responsibility."

It was another thing Clyne felt very strongly about, the survival of the Apache people.

"Then you better get married and have lots of Apache kids," said Kino.

Clyne made a noncommittal sound and tucked the ring back into his pouch.

Gabe clapped a hand on Clay's shoulder. "Does Grandmother know yet?"

"We told her."

"What kind of wedding?" asked Gabe.

"Small, soon."

"And you'll return to work with Donner?" asked Clyne.

"Not sure. Izzie will need help with her cattle for a while. Until the boys are old enough to handle them."

"Will you live there?"

Clay shook his head. "We want our own place."

"There is a position open on the tribal council," said Clyne.

Clay turned to Gabe to see his response, and then he realized Clyne was speaking to him. Clay laughed, thinking they were teasing him. Neither of his older brothers smiled.

"Me?" he said, pressing a finger into his chest. "They don't want me."

"Actually several of the council have approached me and asked me to speak to you about this. People of the tribe are all talking about you and your courage. Your heroism has gotten you noticed."

Clay blinked in astonishment. "Me," he said with wonder. He realized that he had lost many things the day of the robbery—his pride, his friends—but never his integrity and never his family. Izzie had believed in him, though he didn't know it at the time. Now others did, as well. Most importantly he believed in himself.

He grinned. "Let me talk it over with Izzie."

The brothers laughed and slapped him on the back.

"I want to hear all about what happened," said Kino. "Everything! I already heard Gabe's version, but he makes everything sound like a police report."

"I gave you the facts," said Gabe.

Izzie pulled into the drive with her mother. A moment later her two brothers spilled out of the backseat. They seemed to grow by the minute.

"Later," said Clay, and went to meet them.

He approached with his hands in his pockets, not sure how to greet her. He wanted to sweep her up in his arms for a kiss, but with Carol and her brothers here, he was uncertain.

Izzie came bounding forward, keys jangling in her hand as she leaped into his arms and kissed him on the mouth in front of his brothers, her brothers and her mother. Clay froze for just a moment, and then he did what he had dreamed of doing all day. He kissed her back, hard and possessive. Her mouth was soft and yielding and full of promises he intended to see she kept.

Someone cleared his throat. Clay stepped back, and Izzie moved away, grinning up at him with such pride and love it made his chest swell. His brothers stood behind him, as they always had. Her brothers stood behind her.

Glendora moved between the two groups and took Izzie in her arms for an enveloping hug.

"It is so good to have you back at my table, Isabella." Then Glendora turned to Izzie's mother, relieving her of the large casserole she gripped. Glendora passed the glass container to Clay and then looped her arm with Izzie's mom, steering her toward the house as if the gathering was completely natural. Clay and Izzie shared a smile.

His brothers parted to let the two older women pass.

"I hear that my grandson has asked for your daughter's hand."

"He asked me for her hand," said Carol, which was true. Somehow he and Carol Nosie had both survived that awkward conversation and he had gained her mother's guarded consent.

Clay could not hear some of the reply, but then his grandmother's words were clear.

"Too long coming, I say."

"A good match," said Carol.

Clay felt he could breathe again, and Izzie beamed up at him.

"I told you," she whispered.

Clay wrapped an arm around Izzie. It was the gift he had most wanted, her mother's approval. The men headed for the fire pit to put the ribs on the coals. Izzie's brothers hesitated between Izzie and the men.

Clay motioned the two after his brothers. "Go on."

The two bounded off like deer joining the herd.

Izzie squeezed his hand. "Did you tell your brothers?"

"Yes."

"And?" she asked.

"They're happy. Said it was about time."

She laughed. "And they're right about that."

"Izzie? I have something to ask you."

She turned, her dark brows lifted in the middle like the wings of a perching bird. "Yes."

"Clyne says, that is, he's been asked by the council if I would be interested in seeking a place on the tribal council."

"Tessay's place?" she asked.

"You don't sound surprised," he said.

"Surprised? That they would pick a hero? A man of great integrity? Clay, you deserve this. Don't you know that?"

"I'm beginning to. What do you think?"

"It will be hard work, but I don't know anyone who could represent our tribe better than you."

He warmed under the glow of her faith in him.

"You approve?" he asked.

"Yes, and I am so proud of you."

He kissed her again, there on the land that had belonged to their people for longer than memory. Here in the shadow of the sacred Black Mountains where they would make a home and build a life—together.

* * * * *

"Did you know I was here?" he demanded. "Or did you just get lucky?"

"I wouldn't call this lucky."

Keira pulled emphatically on the rope around her arms, and in spite of himself, Graham winced.

"If you're not going to answer my questions," he said, "then I'm going to go back to our previous arrangement."

"What previous arrangement was that?" she replied, just shy of sarcastic.

"The one where I don't speak at all."

He started to turn away, but she snorted, and he stopped, midturn, to face her again.

"More of the silent treatment? What are you?" she asked. "A ten-year-old boy?"

For some reason, the question annoyed him far more than her lack of candor. Graham strode toward her, and once again, she didn't cower. She raised her eyes and opened her mouth, but whatever snarky comment had been about to roll off her tongue was cut off as Graham mashed his lips into hers messily. Uncontrollably. And when it ended, Keira was left gasping for air—gasping for *more*.

TRUSTING
A STRANGER

BY
MELINDA DI LORENZO

MILLS & BOON

First Published in Great Britain 2016
By Mills & Boon, an imprint of HarperCollins*Publishers*
1 London Bridge Street, London, SE1 9GF

© 2016 Melinda A. Di Lorenzo

ISBN: 978-0-263-91893-9

46-0116

Our policy is to use papers that are natural, renewable and recyclable products and made from wood grown in sustainable forests. The logging and manufacturing processes conform to the legal environmental regulations of the country of origin.

Printed and bound in Spain
by CPI, Barcelona

Melinda Di Lorenzo is a Canadian author living on the West Coast of British Columbia. She is an avid reader and an avid writer. Her to-be-read and to-be-written lists are of equal overwhelming length and she plans on living to be 150 years old so she can complete them both. Melinda is happily married to the man of her dreams and is a full-time mum to three beautiful girls. When she is not detangling hair, fighting for her turn on iTunes or catching up on sleep, she can be found at the football pitch or on the running trail.

As always, I owe the deepest gratitude to my family. Without them, I would never have been able to add the title of "writer" to my list.

Prologue

Mike Ferguson crossed and uncrossed his legs, then crossed them again.

Even though the swanky hotel room was loaded with testosterone-fueled tension, the movement was the only indication that any of it affected him.

So far anyway.

Unflappable. It was a characteristic he valued above most others. A characteristic each of the two men in front of him lacked utterly.

The one with his meaty fingers around the other's neck…he was on edge. On *the* edge, maybe. He should've been calm. Self-assured. Those were the things that would make a man good at a job like his. Instead, he used ego and coercion tactics to get his way.

The one on his knees was just as bad. A blubbering mess. Or he would've been blubbering, if he'd been able to do more than gurgle. Had he shown a little more fortitude, the first man would've released him long ago and traded violence for a reasonable conversation.

Ferguson sighed.

Either way, both men were weak, as far as he was concerned. An embarrassment to work with.

Ferguson cared so little about them that he couldn't even be bothered with their names. Unfortunately, they were a necessity for this particular issue. Because they were also the only two men on the planet who knew as much as Mike did about his activities. The only two men who could implicate him for the one time in twenty years that he'd lost his cool while trying to protect everything he'd worked so hard to achieve.

"You think you found Mike Ferguson," the first man growled at the second. "What were you going to do about it? Turn me in?"

Gurgle, gurgle.

"Or were you going to tell our mutual friend and let *him* turn Mike in? Or maybe just skip the preamble and kill me?"

Gurgle, gurgle, gurgle.

"Fat chance you'd get to that badly disguised weapon of yours before my palm crushed your trachea."

Gurgle.

Ferguson was tired of the theatrics.

"Drop him." The command came out as if he was talking to a dog about a bone and, truthfully, it was kind of the way he saw them.

Beta dog. And even *more* beta dog.

The presently dominant one flexed his hand once more, then released the submissive one to the ground.

"You know I'd never turn him in," the second man croaked.

"We *all* know that," the first replied. "Takes a hell of a lot more guts than you've got to do the job that I do. You've been looking for Mike Ferguson for how long? And nothing. You couldn't find him until *I* let you."

"You think that's what happened?" The other man finally sounded a little gutsier. "I've suspected all along that he was under my nose. What I was looking for was *proof.* Because that's how *I* do things."

Ferguson rolled his eyes, came to his feet and stepped between them. "Your pissing contest is starting to get to me, boys."

"Waiting is starting to get to *me*," the first man snapped. "I want the other half of my money."

"Relax," said Ferguson. "Both of us want to be paid. And I agree. Enough time has passed, and we've all exercised enough patience for one lifetime. Your *friend* has stewed long enough. He needs to be smoked out."

"He'll never leave," said the second man. "And he's stupidly stubborn. Bad enough that if we go to him, he'll probably die before he tells you where he's hidden what you're looking for."

"So motivate him."

"Motivate him? It's been four years," pointed out the first man. "I'm tired of hanging around, waiting for him to show his face, hoping he'll turn up and lead me to the painting. I think *I* could motivate him just fine."

Ferguson gritted his teeth. "This doesn't need muscle. It needs finesse."

He reached into his pocket and pulled out his preferred weapon of choice. Photographic evidence. He held it out, knowing it was far more menacing than any gun.

"You recognize the kid?"

"Yes!"

"His life is in your hands."

The man on the ground was immediately blubbering all over again. "Please don't!"

"Motivation," Ferguson stated coldly. "Just enough to get the man to his own house. Then we can decide whether we move on to muscle. Two days, no more. Understood?"

"Yes."

The reply was barely more than a whisper. It didn't have to be. Ferguson knew the beta dog had been motivated enough.

Chapter One

Keira Niles stepped on the gas, checked her rearview mirror and smiled.

Admittedly, it was kind of a forced smile.

But it was a smile nonetheless.

Because today was going to be the day.

The one where she said yes.

The one where she gave in to Drew Bryant, the handsome, friendly neighborhood businessman whom she'd been flirting with for four years.

Today, she would tell herself—and believe it—that his business-minded attitude was a complement to her socially conscious one instead of a sharp contrast to it.

Yes, she was finally ready to dismiss the doubts in her mind that had never seemed all that reasonable to start out with.

Drew was as close to a perfect man as she'd ever met. Calm and predictable, financially stable and kind. Tall enough that when they kissed for the first time, she'd probably have to tip her head up at least a little, and good-looking enough that he'd probably stay that way until both of them were too old to care anyway.

It was a good list. A good cross section of pleasant characteristics that were totally at odds with the nervous butterflies in her stomach.

Go away, Keira grumbled at them.

But no. She was nervous, and the butterflies were prevailing. So she did the only thing she could—she beat them down as forcibly as she knew how.

No more excuses, no more waiting for this, that or the other thing.

She straightened her dress over her thighs and glanced at her bare ring finger on the steering wheel one more time. Maybe soon it wouldn't look so naked and exposed. So free.

Don't be silly, Keira, she chastised herself.

But it wasn't that silly, if she thought about it.

Her parents would be happy if she settled down. They weren't getting younger, and neither was she. Or Drew. He was nearly forty, and he'd hinted enough times that he was just waiting for the right girl. He'd also hinted enough times that maybe *Keira* was that girl. Jokingly called her his girlfriend on repeat since he moved in beside her parents just a few years earlier.

He was a good, stable man. Handsome. Friendly. A catch.

Just this morning, when she'd come by to water her mom's rhododendrons, he'd paused to say goodbye before he left for his business trip. He'd given her a peck on the cheek—and while it hadn't lit her up with fireworks, it hadn't felt bad, either. It wasn't until he drove away that Keira saw that he'd left his briefcase behind.

And a man on a business trip needs his briefcase.

It was a sign. A subtle push that she ought to take a spontaneous, romantic leap.

After only the briefest hesitation, she'd decided to do it. No call, no warning. Just a seizing of the moment. So she grabbed the overnight bag she kept at her parents' house and set out on the four-hour trip to the Rocky Mountains and the aptly named Rocky Mountain Chalet.

It was a chilly oasis right in the middle of the mountains—a hot spot for honeymooners who preferred ski hills to sandy beaches and hot toddies to margaritas. The surrounding resort town had year-round residences, too, but the chalet was really the hub of activity.

It would've surprised Keira if her parents' soft-spoken

neighbor had chosen a place like this for a weekend of business, but she doubted he'd picked it himself. His clients, who often stopped by his house, and whom she'd had only a few occasions to meet over the past few years, seemed like the kind of men who liked nice things. Bespoke suits and menus that didn't have any prices.

Not that Drew was any less classy. He was just a little more understated than overpriced. A little more golf shirt and chinos, and little less glossy necktie and cufflinks. A square-cut diamond versus a marquise.

You're stalling.

Keira realized that she *had* stopped, her hands on the wheel at exactly ten and two, her eyes so glazed over that they almost didn't see the forbidding sign that pointed out cheerily how solidly she was about to seal her fate.

No Turnaround, Twenty-Two Miles, it read.

The drive time had passed far more quickly than she thought. The hours had felt like minutes, and the resort was close now.

Was what she was doing crazy and impetuous? Maybe. But it was also the perfect story to tell their friends. Their kids, if they had them. Plus, she got the feeling that settling into a life with Drew wouldn't allow a whole lot of wildness.

Which is a good thing, she reminded herself.

She was mild mannered and easygoing, too. So they were kind of perfect for each other.

And she was almost there. That final turn up the mountain was all it would take.

"Well," she said to the air. "This is it."

Somehow, the second she clicked on her turn signal, the air got colder.

And when she depressed the gas pedal and actually followed through on the turn itself, Keira swore she had to turn the heat up.

GRAHAM WOKE FROM the nightmare far too slowly.

It was the kind of dream that he deserved to be ripped away from quickly, not dragged from reluctantly.

In it, he'd been chasing Holly through their home. She'd started out laughing, but her laughter had quickly turned to screams, and when Graham caught up with her at the bottom of the curved staircase, he saw why. Sam's small body was at the bottom. Graham had opened his mouth to ask what Holly had done, but she beat him to it.

"What did you *do?"*

The words were full of knowing accusation, and try as he might, he couldn't deny responsibility for the boy's death.

The image—and the question—hung in Graham's mind as he eased into consciousness.

In reality, he'd never seen Sam's body—just the aftermath and the blood.

In the dream, though, it was always the same. Holly alive and Sam dead, and Graham left broken and unable to shake the false memories. He wished desperately that they would disappear completely, or at least fade as he opened his eyes. Instead, they tightened and sharpened like a noose around his psyche.

Survivor's guilt.

Graham was sure that was a large part of what he felt. The problem was he was increasingly sure he *wasn't* surviving.

The leads had dried up long ago, his investigation into who had pulled the trigger growing frustratingly colder with each year.

Even the name—Michael Ferguson—the one thing he'd had to go on, had never panned out.

Graham had always believed the truth would come out and, with it, justice. It had never been a part of his plan to live out his days—to *survive* them—in the middle of the woods in a cabin no one knew existed. He sure as hell never thought he'd wake some mornings wondering if he was as guilty as everyone thought he was.

What kind of man admitted publicly that he didn't love his wife just days after being accused of her murder?

Did an innocent man escape police custody and promptly disappear?

In the early days, those questions seemed easy to answer.

An innocent man ran only so he could give the authorities enough time to *prove* his innocence.

Four years had gone by, though, and instead of gaining traction and credibility, Graham's story had at first exploded in hatred and bitterness. Then faded to obscure infamy.

Dreams like the one he'd just had made him question every choice he'd made since the second he picked up his cell phone on that morning.

What if he hadn't answered it at all?

What if he'd called 9-1-1 himself instead of giving that nosy neighbor the time to do it?

What if—

The squawk of Graham's one and only electronic device cut off his dark thoughts. The bleep of the two-way radio was so unexpected that he almost didn't recognize it.

The mountain range that held the cabin hostage also insulated the location from uninvited transmissions. The two-way mounted to the underside of Graham's bed could only be reached one of two ways. Either the message sender had to be less than a hundred feet away, or he had to be right beside the tower at the top of the mountain, tuned to exactly the correct frequency.

The first would mean initiating lockdown mode. Which Graham wasn't in the mood for.

The second meant someone was trying to reach him on purpose.

And only one person knew where he was.

"G.C., do you read me?"

Dave Stark. A friend. A confidant. The only person who'd stuck by him over the years. He was the man who'd placed the call to Graham on *that* morning. Whose voice threw Graham back every time he heard it.

"You there?" Dave asked.

Graham swung his legs from the bed and reached down to flip the switch.

"I should be asking if *you're* there. And why you're calling me sixteen days ahead of schedule. We're regimented for a reason."

"G.C., stop being your bullheaded self for one second… I have good news."

Graham went still. *Good* news? He wasn't sure what to do with the statement.

"Come again?"

"I found the man we've been looking for."

The world spun under Graham's feet. His mouth worked silently. Four years of waiting to hear those words, and now that he had, he couldn't think of a single damned thing to say.

"You still there, G.C.?"

Graham cleared his throat. "Where is he?"

"A place you know well."

"Stop being cagey, Dave. It doesn't suit you. Or the situation."

"Home."

Home. Forty-nine miles of nearly inaccessible terrain and two hundred more of straight highway driving is all that stands between you and the man who very likely killed your wife and son, and robbed you of your life. Michael damned Ferguson.

Hmm. Graham was far from stupid. What were the odds? And why had he surfaced now?

"He's there on business. Must've thought enough time had gone by that no one would be looking," Dave added as if in answer to Graham's silent question. "Booked in a hotel under another name, but I swear to God, G.C., I'd recognize the man in my sleep."

"You've got the snowmobile ready to go?" Graham asked.

There was the slightest pause. "Yeah. But there's a weather advisory out. They're expecting a blizzard and the whole town is shut down already. No one can get in or out. Blockades up and everything."

"You can't get around them?"

Another pause. "Of course I can. But I won't. Had to flash my ID just to get away long enough to come up to the tower."

"So flash it again."

"It's taken me this long to find him, I don't want to get caught because of a stupid decision. The blockades will be up all night, and probably into tomorrow. If it's clear enough by morning, I'll find a way out. One that won't arouse the suspicion of every rent-a-cop in the area."

"If he gets away—"

"He won't. His hotel reservation in Derby Reach is good until Wednesday morning, G.C., and I paid the clerk a hundred bucks to watch him. Two full days is plenty of time."

Graham stifled his frustration. "Fine."

"Over and out."

By the time the radio screeched, then went silent, Graham was already pulling clothes from his freestanding closet. No way was he waiting another twenty-four hours to get to Dave.

And Ferguson.

Chapter Two

Keira stepped on the gas and squinted into the snowy on-slaught, then glanced in the rearview mirror, trying desperately to see…anything. It was a hopeless endeavor. Someone could be right on her bumper, and she wouldn't know the difference.

Just minutes after she pulled her car onto the road that led up to the resort, the big, friendly flakes had turned into tiny, angry ones that threatened her vision.

Then she'd heard the announcement. They were closing the roads down. Emergency access only. She couldn't turn around, even if she wanted to. She just prayed that she'd get there in one piece.

In fact, if her calculations were right, she was kind of sure she should *already* have gotten there

She gripped the wheel tightly.

The terrain underneath her car seemed to be growing steadily more uneven and the front-wheel drive hybrid was starting to protest.

But she pushed on.

"So much for signs," she muttered, and shot Drew's briefcase a dirty look.

Keira looked at the rearview again.

If someone was behind her, would they be able to see her, even with the lights on?

Unconsciously, she pushed down on the gas again, and her car heaved underneath her.

"C'mon, you stupid thing," she muttered. "Any second we'll reach the turnoff for the resort and you can go back to being your eco-obsessed self again."

After another few minutes of driving, the trees on the

other side of the road still hadn't thinned out, and there was no break in the blizzard.

It really did seem to be a blizzard now. Even though it was technically daylight, the whiteness of the snow somehow darkened everything in Keira's line of vision.

So that's what a whiteout *means.*

She flicked on her high beams. They made no difference.

At last, Keira turned to the logical voice in her head for guidance.

Its reply was an unexpected shout.

Moose!

The huge, hairy beast stood out against the blank whiteness. It stared down the car. And it wasn't moving.

It's not moving!

"I know, dammit!" Keira yelled back at the voice.

She swung the steering wheel as hard as she could. In reply, the tires on the hybrid screeched their general disapproval of the maneuver. As the speedometer dropped down to ten miles an hour, the car skidded past the moose and, for just a moment, relief flooded through Keira's body. But when she tore her eyes away from the animal, she saw that she'd simply traded in one disaster for another. A yawning chasm beckoned to her hybrid.

And all she could do as she sailed over the edge was close her eyes and pray.

As GRAHAM STOMPED through the ever-thickening storm, his feet grew heavier. Even his snowshoes seemed to protest the slow trek. The route was steep and a lot of it bordered on treacherous. The bonus was that vertical climb turned a forty-mile hike into a ten-mile one instead.

Sweat built up on Graham's skin, dripping down his face and freezing in his beard. He flicked away the ice and paused to take a breath. The air was cold enough to burn. But neither the snow nor the wind were enough to block out the raging of his thoughts.

You knew the storm was coming but you picked this path anyway and you don't have a damned thing to complain about. You're sure as hell not giving up.

He slammed down his snowshoes with even more force and moved on. His internal monologue was right in so many more ways than he'd meant it to be. He hadn't just picked this particular path at this particular moment. He'd picked all the paths that led up to the metaphorical storm—perfectly matched to the actual one—which was his life.

The king of bad decisions.

With a crown of regret.

He almost laughed. Today of all days was not the day to turn into a poet.

Been alone far too long, he thought.

Then he *did* laugh. Solitude was so much more than a choice. It was an absolute necessity.

So, no. He didn't need poetry or cynicism or even hope. Cold, hard facts. That was where this was leading. A long-awaited resolution.

He laughed again, and the rumble of his baritone chuckle punctuated the cold air for just a second before the wind cut through and carried it away. As the laugh faded, another rumble followed it, this one far deeper, and so loud it echoed over the sound of the storm.

Graham froze.

An avalanche?

This thought was quickly overridden as he realized the noise was actually a human one.

A car engine and tires on the icy pavement.

It had been years since he'd been close enough to any kind of traffic to hear the sound. Graham's eyes lifted in search of the road above. With the snow as heavy as it was, he couldn't see anything more than a few feet ahead.

The rumble continued, growing even louder.

What kind of maniac is out in these conditions? Graham wondered, then shook his head.

Clearly someone who had even less regard for their own safety than he did.

Graham took another few steps, expecting the noise to fade away. It didn't. In fact, it seemed to be building. And then it stopped abruptly.

Something wasn't right.

Graham's ears strained against the muted broil of the storm and caught a high-pitched shriek, almost indiscernible from the wind. Then his eyes widened. The horizon was blank no more.

A purple streak shot off the cliff above, crashed through the trees, dropping first a dozen angled feet, then another ten. Then—incredibly, unbelievably—it slammed to the forest floor somewhere ahead.

Move!

He didn't stop to think about the consequences, but tore across the snow, beating branches out of his way as he ran. He was too determined to reach the site of the crash to let his awkward, snowshoed gait slow him, and in only a few minutes, he reached the car.

A girl.

He went very still for a very long second.

The driver was a young woman. With a flaming crown of auburn hair and her head pressed into the steering wheel, arms limp at her side.

The smell of gasoline was all around him, and the threat of explosion was very real.

And Graham felt something shift inside him.

Every part of him that had gone numb with shock now went wild with a need to save her.

Chapter Three

Keira couldn't open her eyes. She had no idea if minutes had passed or if had been hours. She only knew that she was cold. Frozen right through her secondhand, designer sweater and her teeny-tiny dress to the bare skin beneath. A little pseudodrunkenly, she wondered why she hadn't dressed for the weather.

She should probably move. Try to get warm. But the chill was the bone-freezing kind that makes it impossible to move anything but chattering teeth.

Sleep threatened to take her, and though she knew instinctively that she should fight it, she was really struggling to find a good reason to stay awake.

The click of a seat belt drew her attention.

A car.

Her car. She was driving. Then falling.

Now she was being lifted.

Good.

But her relief was short-lived.

Next came the ripping, and the tearing off, of her clothes.

I'm being attacked.

The assumption slammed home fear and brought with it a burst of furious energy. Keira's arms came up defensively while her feet lashed out with as much aggression as she could muster. She wasn't going down without a fight.

Her knee connected with something solid, and for a moment she was triumphant.

Her eyes flew open, and this time when she froze, it was from something other than cold.

A pair of dark-lashed eyes, so gray they were almost

see-through, stared back at her. They were set in a fully
bearded face, partially obscured by a knitted hat, and they
were pained. And angry. Furious, even.

Keira tried to shy back from their icy rage, but she was
positioned in a deep dip in the frozen ground, and the
hard-packed snow all around her was as unyielding as
the man above her.

Roll over! Roll away!

Except she couldn't. Because the man had one hand
over her collarbone. His palm was just shy of the base of
her throat.

"Please," she gasped around the pressure he was exert-
ing just below her trachea. "Please don't hurt me."

His eyes widened in surprise. Then very, very slowly,
he shook his head. Then he let go of her neck. Cold air
whipped across the exposed skin, making her shiver uncontrollably.

The man pulled away and disappeared from view. And
the *r-r-r-rip* of fabric started up again immediately.

Oh, God.

In spite of the way Keira's body was shaking, she attempted to sit up. But in less than the time it took to draw
in one ice-tinged breath, the man's hand shot out once
more, closing over the same spot he'd released just moments earlier. He pursed his lips, and in spite of the cover
of the beard, Keira could see the frustrated set of his jaw.
He shook his head again.

What did he mean? Did he want her to just lie there
while he stripped her down?

Keira didn't realize she'd spoken aloud until he nodded.

She tried to tell him she wouldn't do it—that she *couldn't*
do it—but when she opened her mouth, the wind swept in
and cut the words away.

She thought he must've taken her silence as acquies-
cence, because he disappeared again, and suddenly Keira

was stripped almost completely bare. Her dress had been so skimpy that she hadn't even bothered with a bra. And without the dress, all she had left were her lacy boy-cut undies, and if she remembered correctly, they didn't leave much to the imagination.

Very abruptly, Keira didn't feel cold anymore. She had a bizarre urge to look down and check if her panties were as revealing as she believed them to be.

Not a good sign.

She tried to lift her arms, and when she found them to be too leaden to move, frustration shot through her.

"I need to see my panties!"

The words came out in an almost shout, and they struck Keira as hilarious. A giggle burst from her lips.

The bearded man was at her side in an instant, concern evident on his face. Keira thought *that* was funny, too. One second he had her by the throat, the next he was worried about her.

"What are you staring at, hmm, Mountain Man?" she asked.

Her laughter carried on, and even though it sounded a little hysterical, she still couldn't stop it.

The man stood up abruptly. From her position on the ground, Keira could see he was huge. Strikingly tall. Wide like a tree trunk.

And he was dressed in clothes that her mind couldn't make sense of. His enormous shoulders were draped in white fur, but underneath that was a Gore-Tex jacket. The hat—which she'd noted before—was incredibly lopsided and almost laughable. His pants were leather, but not the kind you'd find on a biker or on badly dressed club rat. Tucked into boots crafted of the same suede and held together with wide, sinewy stitches, they looked like something out of a seventh-grade social studies textbook.

Keira's giggles finally subsided, but only because her jaw had dropped to her chest.

In a move that made Keira concerned for his safety, the man began to undress.

What the heck?

He tossed the weird ensemble off without finesse.

For several long, inappropriate seconds, Keira had an opportunity to admire his naked form. Her gaze traveled the breadth of his muscled torso, taking in the cut of perfectly formed muscle. He had well-defined pecs and biceps, and a puckered scar just above his left collarbone.

Unclothed, he looked less like a mountain man and more like…well, more like a mountain itself.

Keira's eyes moved south, even though she knew she should stop them. Just as her gaze reached his belly button, though, he tossed the long underwear–style T-shirt he'd had under his jacket in her direction. It ballooned up, then settled about four inches above her head, suspended there by the walls of the dip where she was lying.

Before Keira could ask what he was doing, the man dove in beside her.

Very quickly, he slipped his boots onto her feet, then used the rest of his clothes to build a cocoon around them. His pants hung over their chests. The white fur that had been on his shoulders covered their legs and feet.

When he was done, he rolled Keira over forcefully. He wrapped the jacket around them and pulled her back into his chest. The world seemed to be vibrating, and it took her a long moment to realize it was because she was still shivering.

Without her permission, Keira's body wriggled into the stranger's, trying to absorb all the heat he was emitting. She attempted to fight it. She told her hips they shouldn't fit against his legs so perfectly. She mentally commanded her head not to tuck into the crook of his arm.

But it was a losing battle.

He inhaled deeply. And with his exhale, he flung his free arm over her waist and dragged her even closer. His bare leg slipped between Keira's newly booted feet and she couldn't even pretend to fight the need to be right there, exactly like that.

At long last, her shaking subsided.

Don't fall asleep.

But that, too, was an inevitability.

Great. Crash your car, then get stripped down and forcibly cuddled by an equally crazy man. Only you, Keira.

His heat lulled her. His solidity comforted her. His presence made her feel unreasonably safe.

And as she drifted off, she finally clued in to the Mountain Man's intentions. He wasn't trying to hurt her at all. He was just trying to keep her warm.

And he was very likely saving her life.

NAKED FLESH PRESSED to naked flesh. The oldest trick in the Boy Scout handbook for staving off hypothermia. It was effective, too, judging from the amount of heat in the snowy alcove.

The girl beside Graham adjusted a little, and one of her hands grazed his thigh.

Okay maybe Boy Scout *is the wrong choice of words*, Graham amended.

Every bit of movement reminded Graham that he was the furthest thing from a do-gooder kid in a uniform. Especially now that the panic that she was going to die on his hands had worn off.

The girl shifted beside him once again, wriggling ever closer and heightening his awareness of her petite form all the more. Her mess of auburn hair tickled his chest, and its light scent wafted to his nose. Her silky skin caressed him.

I'm in hell, Graham decided. *The worst kind of hell.*

She murmured something soft and breathy in her sleep, and Graham groaned.

Saving her might have been a mistake. An impetuous decision fueled by the man he used to be.

That...and her pretty face.

Her still, lifeless body behind the wheel had been almost too much for him to bear.

Bend. Lift. Drag.

She was easy to carry. So small. Almost fragile looking. Fair in that way that redheads often are, but with no smattering of freckles. In fact, the paleness of her skin rivaled the snow, and Graham wasn't sure whether it was a natural pallor, or something brought on by the accident and the cold. It didn't matter; she was entrancing.

Then he'd pulled her into the clearing, shaking and shivering and seemingly so needful.

Graham grimaced. She *was* beautiful, no doubt, but she definitely wasn't frail. An accident like that should have killed her. Coming out alive was a feat. But the fight in her when she'd woken up...that was a whole other story. It had impressed him as much as it had ticked him off.

Under the fine bones of her face, she was a firecracker, no doubt about it.

Graham slipped his hand to hers, touching the soft pad of her open palm, just because he could.

And because you want *to*, scolded an internal voice that sounded a little too much like his late grandmother.

It was true, though. He did want to. It had been a long time since his fingers last found residence in someone else's hand.

The girl's hand closed reflexively, and Graham jerked away.

Nice work, he thought. *Save a girl, then get creepy. You could at least wait until she tells you her name.*

Her name.

He felt an impatient compulsion to know what it was and, after just a second of considering it, he decided to see if he could find out. Maybe check for her ID in the car. She was warm enough now that she wasn't at risk of dying, and he could safely give her—both of them—some space.

He pushed aside his clothes-turned-blanket and tucked them around the girl's body. Then he slipped from the dip in the ground, stood silently and surveyed the area. The cold air buffeted against his skin, but he was accustomed to the weather, and as he came to his feet, the strong breeze in his eyes bothered him more than the temperature did. The storm had slowed quite a bit. The snow was light, mostly blowing around from the residual wind.

He glanced down at the girl and adjusted the overhanging shirt so she wasn't bared to the elements. She'd be fine alone for a few minutes while Graham had a closer look at her car and attempted to figure out who she was. Then he'd have to decide whether it was better to keep her close, or try to get her back into town.

Into town.

In the heated excitement of saving her, meeting up with Dave had gone out of his head. In fact, *everything* had gone out of his head, and he wasn't sure how that was possible.

Graham turned back to the girl.

In the past four years, his pursuit of justice had been relentless. Single-minded to the point of mania. He'd thought of nothing but finding the man who took Holly and Sam from his life. Now, very suddenly, he was distracted from his purpose.

By this girl.

He took another step closer to the car. The front end dipped down from the pressure exerted by Graham's body as he'd clambered across it on his insane rescue mission. The purple paint had been slashed to hell by the branches surrounding it, and the rear wheels were completely flat. Remarkably, the rest of the car was intact.

Graham stood underneath the vehicle, frowning. Damned lucky. The vehicle could have smashed to pieces, taking the girl with it. Or she could've gone off the road just a few miles up, and Graham would never have found her. She had to have some incredible karma stored up.

What if someone's waiting for her?

Graham's gut roiled. He had to assume that time wasn't a luxury he had. The second they—whether it was an emergency crew or someone else—found that car in its weirdly whole state, with its empty driver's seat, the relatively far distance to his place in the woods grew that much smaller.

Get control, man, he commanded himself.

He needed a plan.

His gaze sought the car and the spot where the girl lay hidden. A small, greasy puddle—presumably the source of the gasoline smell—had formed under the driver's side door and it gave him an idea.

They can't find the car in one piece.

He would make it harder for anyone to locate her. Harder to locate him.

Graham squinted up at the sky. Clouds obscured the waning sun.

Graham didn't own a watch. It had been years since the batteries in his old one wore out, and it had never seemed like much of necessity. Right that moment, though, he wished he had one so he could pinpoint the hour, predict the sunset and time it just right.

But you don't *have one*, he said to himself. *And you don't have time to wait, either.*

All he needed was a spark. One that could easily be generated with some of the electrical wires in the car engine.

Once he got started, it took less than an hour for Graham to render Keira's car satisfactorily unidentifiable. The dark, sour-smelling smoke was already dissipating, though he was sure he still reeked of fuel himself.

He took a step back to survey his handiwork once more. He thought it looked as natural as any burning car could. A branch puncturing the fuel line, the angle of the car conveniently leaking accelerant from the line to the engine, and the rest had gone up in smoke.

So to speak.

Graham was actually a little surprised at how efficiently the fire took hold. Not to mention how well the whole thing cooperated. Several minutes of blistering, blue-green flames, an enormous puff of black smoke, then a fade-to-gray cloud that blended in nicely with the fog that had rolled in from above.

Not that Graham was complaining—it sure as hell made his task a lot easier. The husk of the car continued to smolder, but with the fuel burned up and the decidedly frozen state of the surrounding area, he wasn't even worried about it spreading any farther.

Not bad for my first arson attempt.

The thought only made him smile for a second. The last thing he needed was to add another felony to the list that already followed his name around.

"Is that my car?"

At the soft, tired-sounding question, Graham whipped around. For a second, he just stared down at her, mesmerized by the way her long, dark eyelashes brushed against her porcelain skin, and entranced by the enticing plumpness of her lips.

He'd never seen a more beautiful girl, or felt an attraction so strong.

"Is it?" she said again.

Reality hit Graham.

Saving her had been a hell of a lot more than just a

bad idea. If Graham's instincts were right—and they usually were—then this walk in the storm turned impromptu rescue mission…would be his undoing.

Chapter Four

Keira met the stranger's wary gaze with one of her own. For a moment she saw something heated and intriguing in his eyes that cut through the cold air and sizzled between them. Then it was gone, replaced by the guarded look he wore now, and Keira was left wondering if she'd imagined it.

Maybe it was a hallucination brought on by a head injury, she thought.

Her brain did feel fuzzy, and when she blinked, the snowy world swam in front of her. Even the big man—who was as solid a thing as she'd ever seen—seemed to wobble. Then a wicked, head-to-toe shiver racked Keira's body, and the Mountain Man's face softened with worry. Very quickly, he undid his own big red jacket and stepped closer to offer it to her.

Keira only hesitated for a second before she took it gratefully. She vowed silently to give it back as soon as she was thawed. But right then, it was warm *and* it offered her a decent amount of cover, and with it wrapped around her body, she felt a little more in control. Still woozy. But better.

"My car..." Her voice sounded hoarse, and her throat burned a little as she spoke.

When the Mountain Man didn't answer her third inquiry, she tipped her head toward the smoking mess of metal, then looked back at him again. He just stared back at her, a little crease marking his forehead.

Keira let out a rasping sigh. "Do you speak English?"

He nodded curtly.

"So…what? You're just testing me out? Deciding if I'm *worthy* of speaking to?"

Her question earned a crooked smile. An expression that said, *Yeah, that's about right.*

Keira sighed again. A few silent hours with this stranger, and she could understand him perfectly. She doubted she could read Drew that easily, and she'd known him for years.

Drew.

Damn. A kicked-in-the-gut feeling made her shiver once more, and the Mountain Man reached out a hand, but she waved him off.

"I'm fine," she lied.

He raised an eyebrow. *Liar.*

"I don't care if you believe me or not," Keira stated. Her eyes narrowed with an irritation to cover her embarrassment, and then she muttered, "I'm just not used to sitting nearly naked in the snow."

He chuckled—a low, attractive sound that warmed her inexplicably—sat back on his heels and waited. Those piercing gray eyes of his demanded answers, and Keira found herself wanting to tell him the truth.

Her job as a child and youth counselor had given her the ability to form good, quick judgments. And something in this man's handsome face made her think she could trust him.

Handsome?

The descriptor surprised Keira, and if her blood had been pumping through her body properly, she might've blushed.

Because yes, he *was* handsome.

He had full lips, an even brow and in spite of his facial hair, he had strong features. Keira was close enough to him that as she realized just how attractive he was, her heart fluttered nervously in her chest.

She was alone with him. In the middle of nowhere. She was injured. Maybe badly. And now she was remembering that glimpse she'd caught of his muscular torso when he'd stripped off his clothes so he could warm her up. Keira had been too out of it to think about it before. She was wishing she could see it again so she could memorize it.

What's the matter with you? she chastised herself.

She couldn't remember the last time she'd looked at a man like this. At least not long enough to notice how prettily translucent his eyes were, or how their wintry appeal so sharply contrasted with his burly frame. She certainly hadn't come close enough to one to know how well his body fit beside her, or how comfortable it was to be in his arms.

No way could Drew come close to this kind of magnetism.

Mountain magnetism.

And he was watching her again, that same not-so-muted heat in his eyes.

Maybe he's remembering the way you *felt cuddled up beside* him.

That thought was finally enough to draw the color to her cheeks, and Keira could feel the heat spread from her face down her throat and across her chest. She was sure she must be the same shade of red as the borrowed coat.

In an attempt to ease the increasingly palpable tension between them, Keira shifted her gaze back to her smoldering car.

Midway between the vehicle and spot where she was sitting a black flash caught her eyes.

My phone.

She knew that's what it was, and that she had to get it. And for some reason, she also knew that her benefactor—if his intentions were even good enough to call him that—wouldn't let her just go grab it. Not willingly.

Butterflies beat against Keira's stomach as she offered him a weak smile.

"Can you excuse me for a second?" Her voice was weak, even to her own ears. "I think I need to…uh…use the ladies' room."

GRAHAM NARROWED HIS EYES and considered calling her bluff. He was sure whatever reason she had for suddenly getting up, it had little to do with the most basic of physical needs.

Graham had to admit that he was surprised she could stand at all. What surprised him more, though, was that she took off into the dark. The borrowed boots flew off, and she moved at a hobbling, barefoot run.

What the hell?

Graham was so startled that he almost forgot he should chase her down. He stared after her, a puzzled frown on his face. Her creamy legs poke out from under the big coat, as sexy as they were ridiculous.

She really should tuck those away before she ruined them with frostbite, he thought absently.

She glanced over her shoulder at him and stumbled forward a little farther.

Where the hell did she think she was going? Her ridiculous flight was going to run her straight into the thickest part of the forest. It was going to tear up those pretty little feet of hers. And was going to create unnecessary work for Graham.

First World, fugitive-about-to-turn-kidnapper problems.

Still, Graham might've been tempted to let her go a little longer if he hadn't spied the wound on her thigh.

Dammit, he growled mentally.

How had he not noticed the slash before?

Her movement across the snow opened up the cut, and

even from a few dozen feet away, Graham could see the blood ooze out of it.

Belatedly, he jumped to his feet and strode after her, his long legs closing the gap between them.

In seconds, he was on her, and without preamble he reached down, wrapped his arms around her knees and threw her unceremoniously over his shoulder. She beat weakly at his back, but he ignored it.

"Let me *go!*" Her order was almost a squeal, and Graham ignored that, too.

He carried her across the ground like a sack of potatoes, and when he had her right back at the spot she'd run from moments earlier, he dumped her to the ground—not quite hard enough to hurt, but just hard enough for her to squeak.

He shot her a look that commanded her to keep still and, although her eyes flashed, she didn't try to get up again. From the shallowness of her breathing and the deep flush in her cheeks, Graham doubted she *could* get up.

But as soon as he leaned back, she was off at a crawl.

If we were at the hospital, Graham thought, *I'd insist that an orderly strap her down.*

For a moment, he considered calling after her.

No. Speaking to her will only create more issues. Make you slip up and give something away. Too much risk.

He watched her shimmy helplessly over the snow for another second—she barely got more than a few inches—then stretched out, closed a hand over one of her ankles and dragged her back.

He righted her, set her between his thighs and held her there.

Using his teeth, Graham tore his T-shirt into strips—one to bind her hands together, another to bind her feet together, and a third to stop the flow of blood from her thigh. She fought him on the first two things—and he couldn't blame her for that—but when she finally spotted the wound, she stopped struggling.

Graham could feel her eyes following the quick, sure movements of his hands as he fashioned the stretchy cotton into a tourniquet. He was disappointed that the blood soaked through almost immediately. He tore off another strip from his T-shirt, bundling the wrapping as thick as he could and as tight as he dared.

The flow of blood ebbed, but she was going to need stitches, and Graham had nothing on hand that would do the job.

"Mountain Man?" Her voice was soft. "I'm really hurt, aren't I?"

Graham nodded curtly.

She was silent for a minute, leaning her back into his chest. Then she shifted a little, tipping her head just enough that he could see her tempting, pink lips.

"I should warn you," she murmured. "I'm not going to make this easy."

Graham rolled his eyes. As if *that* surprised him.

In spite of her words, though, she turned sideways and settled her face against him. Then her eyelids fluttered shut, and her knees curled up as if she *belonged* in his lap.

With a frustrated groan, Graham tried to ease away, but the sleeping girl wriggled closer and then she murmured something else, and instead of trying to disentangle himself from her, Graham found himself straining to hear what it was. He tucked the coat over her legs and leaned down, pressing his face close to hers.

She shifted in his lap, and her lips brushed his ear.

Graham's body reacted immediately. Desire shot through him, and his grip on her tightened.

Slowly, he untied her wrists. He breathed out, waiting for her to wake up, realize she was free and level a punch at his face. Instead, she flexed one free hand, then slipped it up to his shoulder, her thumb grazing his collarbone.

Graham groaned and crushed down the ridiculous longing coursing through him.

A lock of auburn hair slipped to her cheek. Graham reached to brush it away reflexively. When his hand slid against her cheek, he realized the heat he felt could be blamed on more than just desire. Her skin was hot to the touch, and though her face was still pale, two spots of pink had bloomed in her cheeks.

Graham frowned and placed the back of his hand on her forehead, then trailed a finger down her face. Yeah, she was definitely far warmer than she ought to be.

He needed to get her somewhere safer, cleaner and functional enough for treatment. The clinic in the resort town was out of the question. Anywhere public was.

Home.

It was the best option.

Graham glanced up at the sky. The sun had completely set, and the sky was pitch-black. Travel now would be dangerous.

More dangerous, he corrected silently.

The climb down was steep, and he would have to carry her. Graham had no idea how long he'd be able to do that.

He looked back to the girl.

He didn't have any other choice.

Whatever circumstance had brought her to him, she was still in need of medical care, and however long ago it had been, Graham still held fast to his oath.

First do no harm.

Chapter Five

The ground beneath Keira was moving. It thumped along rhythmically like a conveyor belt made of nearly smooth terrain. It was soothing. Almost.

A sudden bump jarred her and sent her head reeling. Her eyes flew open, and the world was upside down. She realized it wasn't the ground that was moving. It was *her*. Them.

The big man had her cradled in his arms, and he was traveling across the snowy ground at an alarming speed. She could see the bottom of his bearded chin. His neck was exposed and a sheen of sweat covered it. His breathing was a little heavy, but he seemed oblivious to her added weight.

"Excuse me?" Keira's voice was far weaker than she wanted it to be, and if he heard her, he didn't acknowledge it.

She struggled to right herself, the quick pace making it difficult for her to do more than lift her head. All she could see was sky.

She blinked, and the sky stayed. The expanse of it was so big above her that it was almost dizzying. No moon. No stars. Just a solid spread of grayness. Keira closed her eyes to block it out as she tried to orient herself.

The big, red jacket was still wrapped around her, cinched at the waist and tied at the throat. A scarf was wound tightly around her head, insulating her face as well as her skull. The Mountain Man had used the white fur to cover both her feet and her legs. She wasn't in danger of freezing anymore, though the terrible cold she'd felt right before slipping into oblivion wasn't completely gone.

She felt weak. Really weak. She sought something tangible to grasp at in her sea of straw-like thoughts.

Wrists tied together. Not that. *Blood.* No. *The smoky, woodsy scent of the Mountain Man's skin.* Definitely not.

And at last she found something.

My phone. Yes.

She'd managed to grab it in her stumble across the snow. She'd shoved it into the coat pocket just seconds before the Mountain Man caught her and hoisted her over his shoulder, caveman-style.

Was it still there?

She desperately wanted to reach into the coat to find out.

But right that second, her hands—which were no longer bound together, she noted—were actually *under* his shirt, pressed into his nearly rock-hard chest. And there was no hope of drawing away with any chance of subtly. Her fingers fluttered nervously, and even though he didn't react, Keira was sure the stranger's pulse jumped with the movement.

Curiosity fueled her to see if she was correct.

She uncurled her fingers slowly and moved her palm up, just an inch. The big man's heart was already working hard with exertion, but there was no mistaking the double beat as her hand came to rest on his sternum.

Oh.

Keira moved again, and this time she couldn't tell what was more noticeable—*his* heartbeat, or *hers*. Because she was definitely reacting to the way his skin felt under her hand, and the tightening of his arms didn't help, either. A lick of heat swept through her, and her light-headedness increased, too.

Focus on something else, she told herself. *Think of Mom and Dad. Think of work and the kids who need you. Think of Drew.*

But right that second, she couldn't even quite recall what Drew looked like. When she tried, his features blurred away, and the rugged looks of the unnamed Mountain Man overtook her mind instead.

Ugh.

Keira was *not* the kind of girl who rebounded from the idea of a marriage-potential relationship into the arms of a grunting, hulking man straight out of a hunting magazine.

Well. Not figuratively anyway.

Because she *was* quite literally wrapped in his firm grip, her head pressed into the crook of his arm.

Just how long had the Mountain Man been carrying her? And to where?

"Hey," she called, happy that her voice was a little louder.

But she still got no response. She tried again.

"Mountain Man?"

He didn't slow.

"Hey!" This time, she said it as loudly as she could manage, and from the way his grip tightened on her, Keira was sure he'd heard her.

But he still didn't acknowledge her directly.

Stubborn.

With a great deal of effort, she wiggled an arm free from inside the jacket, snaked it out and yanked on his beard.

He drew in a sharp breath, snarled and released her. Keira tumbled to the ground. Hard. Her back hit the snow, nearly knocking the wind out of her.

He looked down at her, regret in his gray eyes made visible by the moonlight behind him. Except then she opened her big fat mouth.

"You jerk! You dropped me!"

His expression tightened and he rolled his eyes.

Yeah, you think this is my *fault, don't you?* Keira

thought. *Well, I didn't ask for the car accident. Or for the damned moose.*

"And I especially didn't ask for you and the stupid beard," she muttered.

He reached for her, concern evident on his face, and she shuffled backward along the snow.

"What?" Keira said with a head shake that made the world wobble. "You're worried about me because I don't want to be manhandled? I've got news for you. Non-forest-dwelling women have high expectations nowadays. No way are you getting those Sasquatch hands on me again. Not unless I ask you to."

She colored as she realized how that sounded. And she strongly suspected that underneath that beard, he was trying to cover a sudden smile.

"Jerk," she muttered again.

He crossed his arms over his wide chest and gave her an expectant, eyes-narrowed glare. Silently daring her to stand up on her own.

"Yeah, I will," Keira snapped.

She pushed both hands to the ground and came to her feet. Rocks dug into her skin. Ice bit at her toes. And worse than that, her head was spinning again.

There was no way she was going to be able to walk more than a few feet. But there was also no way she was going to admit it to the smug Mountain Man.

And sure enough, his expression definitely said, *You need me.*

No way was she giving in to *that*. No matter how true it might be.

Keira straightened her body, grimacing as pain shot through her pretty much everywhere. In particular, her thigh burned, and she had to resist an urge to lift the jacket and have a closer look. Instead, she made herself meet the Mountain Man's stare.

"Where to?" she asked through gritted teeth.

He shrugged, then pointed to the black horizon.

"Great!" Keira said cheerily.

She had no idea what she was looking at. Or for. Vaguely, she thought again that she should probably ask him what he intended to do with her. But she was feeling rather stubborn, and the longer she was on her feet, the foggier her head was getting.

The Mountain Man stood still, watching her as she took two agonizing steps. He probably would've watched her take even more, except he didn't get a chance to. Because the world swayed, and Keira was unexpectedly on her rear end, staring up at the sky, transfixed by the few stars that managed to shine through the snowy sky.

Apparently, her little nap in the Mountain Man's arm hadn't done much of anything to renew her energy.

And now he was standing in front of her with that frown growing deeper with each heartbeat.

As he stared, Keira *did* begin to feel warm. But it had nothing to do with the weather or the accident, or anything at all that she could pinpoint.

Except maybe just…*him*.

Keira swallowed a sudden thickness in her throat and forced herself to look away.

Immediately she wished she hadn't, because the first thing that her eyes found was the fabric that had been wrapped around her thigh. When she'd struggled futilely to escape, it had slipped off and fallen into the snow. Keira frowned at it. It *had* been a light color, grayish or tan, it was hard to say which. But now it was dark.

Blood.

Instinctively, she knew that's what it was. And not just any blood. *Her* blood. Lots of it.

She brought her slightly floppy arm up so she could feel her leg.

Yep. It was damp and sticky. No wonder she was so woozy. And no wonder the Mountain Man had been in such a hurry.

She sat there for a long second, then sighed in defeat.

"Hey, um, Mountain Man?"

He raised an eyebrow and looked down at her.

"So, yeah," she said. "I've decided we're not going to get very much farther if you stop carrying me."

His brow furrowed for one moment, then a wry chuckle escaped from his lips, and he plucked her from the ground as if she weighed nothing. But he only carried her for another minute. She looked at the run-down cabin that appeared before them. It screamed "horror movie."

They'd reached their destination.

Chapter Six

Graham could read Keira's expression perfectly as she looked from him to the wooden house.

Seriously? it said. *You're taking me in* there*, and you expect me to go without a fuss?*

If he'd felt inclined to speak, he would've replied, "Actually, I don't expect you to do anything without a fuss."

Instead he just shrugged, which made her emerald eyes narrow suspiciously. She went back to assessing the single-story structure with its rough shingle roof and its wide porch hung with ancient wind chimes. And likely found it lacking.

For the first time since he'd moved in semipermanently, he wished it was a more impressive abode.

The outside was purposefully left in disrepair, meant to deter anyone who saw it from wanting to enter.

He moved up the stairs, but as he reached the threshold, Keira's hand shot out, and Graham was too startled to realize what she was reaching for before it was too late. Her fingers closed on the well-worn sign. It was handcrafted by Graham's great-grandfather almost a century earlier when he'd built the cabin as a hunting outpost. Graham had meant to remove the handmade plate a long time ago.

"Calloway?" she said as she ran her fingers over the barely discernible lettering, then wriggled a bit so she could look at him. "That's you?"

She eyed him with patient curiosity, and a battle waged inside Graham's head. The last name wasn't an entirely common one, but it clearly hadn't sparked any recognition in her.

Given time, would she make the connection between

him and the crime attached to the surname? If she did, would she simply chalk it up to coincidence, or would she investigate further?

In the end, Graham took a leap of faith and nodded tightly.

"Calloway," she repeated thoughtfully and added, "Is that a first name or last name?"

Graham tensed, but after a second, she smiled—the first genuine one Graham had seen since he found her—and he relaxed again. Her teeth were even, but not perfect, and the grin transformed her face. She went from porcelain perfection to devilish beauty.

"Or are you one of those people who just has the one name?" she teased. "Like the Cher of the survivalist world?"

Graham rolled his eyes, loosened one of his arms, tore the sign from its chain and tossed it with perfect aim into a wood bin on the porch. Then he carried her up to the door, turned the knob and let them into the cabin.

The heavy curtains ensured that it was almost dark inside, but Graham kept his modified woodstove on low, even when he wasn't in the cabin. As a result, the air was an ambient temperature. The only light—not much more than a dim glow—came from the same stove. At that moment, it highlighted the Spartan decor.

The furniture was limited to a set of rough-hewn chairs and a matching table, and Graham's own lumpy bed. He carted the girl across the room and deposited her on the latter. She tried to stand, but Graham pushed her back down and shot her a warning glare before he slipped to the other side of the room.

He wasn't doing anything else until he'd given her a more thorough look-over and tended to the mess of a wound on her leg.

Whether she likes it or not.

He dampened a clean cloth, then set some water to boil. He refused to think about anything but the immediate tasks at hand, and once he had the pot on the stove, he moved back to the bed.

As he seated himself beside her, she crossed her arms over her chest, and her mouth set in a frown. Graham ignored her expression, raising the cloth to her face. She snatched it from his hand.

"I can do it," she told him, but there was no bite in her words—just exhaustion.

Graham watched as she wiped away the grime left behind from sleeping in a hole and several hours of being carried through the woods. He was unreasonably pleased when she handed the cloth back and he saw that she only had the tiniest of abrasions on her otherwise perfect face.

Perfect face? Calm your raging manhood, Graham, he growled at himself. *It's clearly been far too long since you've seen a woman. And her prettiness is not your focus anyway. Her health is what's important. She needs to heal so you can get on with meeting up with Dave.*

He stood up stiffly, filled a tin mug with spices and pressed juice, topped it with the now-boiling water, then added a generous helping of his homemade booze. It wasn't as good as a painkiller or a sedative, but even if either had been available, he doubted she'd take one from him.

In moments, Graham was back at her side, offering her the steaming liquid. She eyed it suspiciously and didn't reach for it.

"I don't think so," she said.

Graham rolled his eyes, then grabbed the mug and took a pointed swig. Even the small mouthful warmed his throat as he swallowed.

He offered it to her again.

She still sniffed the drink, and Graham had to cover a smile.

"Fine," she muttered. "I guess you're not trying to poison me."

At last, she relented and took first one cautious sip, then another.

Satisfied that she was going to drink it, Graham slipped away again. He banged through the cupboards until he found each item he thought he might need and placed them on a tray. None of it was ideal—he didn't even seem to own a Band-Aid—but it would have to do.

Once he had everything ready, he opted to get changed. His clothes were dirty, and in some places soaked with the girl's blood. All of it risked contamination, and the last thing he wanted was to give her an infection.

Graham shot a quick glance in her direction. She was still engrossed in sipping the spiked drink, so Graham dropped his pants and stepped into a fresh pair of jeans instead. Then he stripped off his damp shirt and doused his hands and forearms with soap and some of the boiled water, then rinsed the suds off into a metal pot.

When he turned back to the girl again, the tin mug was at her side, and her eyes were fixed on him. They were wide, their striking shade of green dancing against the fairness of her skin. The orange firelight glinted off her hair, adding otherwise invisible hints of gold to the red.

Another bolt of electric attraction shot through Graham's blood.

Damn.

She really was beautiful.

Without meaning to, he let his gaze travel the length of her body. The white fur that had been covering her legs had slipped to the floor, leaving her calves bare. She still wore Graham's big, red jacket, but it didn't cover anything past midthigh. She tried to tug it down, but when one side lowered, the other rose, and after a second she gave up. It didn't help at all that he knew she had nothing but panties on underneath the coat.

Even from where Graham stood, he could see two spots of pink bloom in her cheeks. The added color in her fair skin did nothing to dampen his desire.

Double damn.

He forced himself to turn away and take a breath, re-arranging the items on his tray until he was sure he could trust himself to get closer to her. He had to count to twenty to normalize his breathing, and even when he was done, he wasn't sure he was completely in control.

As he turned back, she looked as if she was bracing herself for an attack, and Graham couldn't say he blamed her. He felt unusually animalistic as he took careful, measured steps toward her. When he sat down, he made sure to leave a few inches between their knees.

Graham balanced the tray of makeshift first aid supplies between them and took her horrified expression in stride.

He met her eyes and raised a questioning eyebrow.

"What? You're going to start requesting my permission *now*?" she asked.

Graham didn't cover his eye roll at all. He let her have it full force. Then he tipped the tray in her direction and waited as she inventoried the items there.

A white square of fabric he was going to use as a bandage. A mini airplane-serving size of vodka that would double as a disinfectant. A homemade, gelatinous salve Graham had created for treating the occasional burn. A punch-out package of antibiotics labelled Penicillin in bold letters and, finally, a hooked needle, threaded with fishing line.

Graham had to admit that the last thing glinted ominously in the dim light, but the rest was pretty innocuous.

Though clearly the girl didn't think so.

"Hell. No," she said.

She pushed the tray away and took a long pull of cider. Then she moved to set the mug down, but Graham closed his hand around hers, and he forced her fingers to stay wrapped around the handle. He tipped the mug to her lips. She swallowed the last of the cider, and he gave her an approving nod.

For one second, she looked offended.

But her eyes were already growing glassy and unfocused. Graham took the cup from her hands and placed it on the tray, opened the vodka, dabbed it onto the square of fabric and reached for the wound on her leg.

Keira batted at his hand, and when Graham frowned irritably, she just giggled and threaded her fingers through his. Startled, Graham didn't pull away immediately. Instead, he stared down, admiring the way her hand looked in his. Small and delicate. Soft and comfortable. In fact, it fit there. Just the way she'd fit in his lap.

"Hey…Mountain Man?"

Graham dragged his gaze up to hers. Her eyes were far too serious.

"You're not exactly my type," she said. "But if—*if*—I went for the angry, brooding hero kinda thing. I'd pick you." She paused, frowned a little, then added, "I don't think I meant to say that out loud. Am I *drunk*?"

She wobbled a little, almost slipping from the bed. Graham caught her. He eased her back onto the bed, smoothed back the mop of hair from her face and waited for her eyes to close.

Chapter Seven

Keira woke slowly, feeling slightly unwell.

Which should have alerted her to the fact that something was wrong even before she remembered where she was and how she got there.

She'd always been a morning person, awake and ready to go before the coffeepot finished brewing. When she'd lived at home with her parents, she and her dad got up at the crack of dawn. The two of them often watched the sun rise together. Then he would read the paper while she made breakfast for her mom, who would get up a solid hour after they did.

Keira valued those early hours, and when she'd finished her degree three years earlier and taken a job in social work, moving into her own place, she continued with the rise-before-dawn ritual.

So if she felt sluggish, as she did right at that moment, she was either hungover or seriously sick.

Which is it now? Keira wondered, somehow unable to recall quite what she'd been up to.

Then she pried her eyes open, and the sight of the cabin sent a surge of recollection and panic through her. A half a dozen thoughts accompanied the memory.

Calloway and his cider. Calloway, holding her hand, easing her back onto the bed.

And worse…Keira telling Calloway he wasn't her type.

Keira blushed furiously as she recalled the last few moments before she passed out. She'd been distracted by the way his palm felt over top of her hand. It was warm. Warmer even than the mug. And rough in a way she'd never experienced before. If she took the time to think about—which she now realized she hadn't—she supposed that Drew's hands were probably soft from the hours he spent sitting in an office and the occasional indulgence of a MANicure.

But not Calloway's. He had calluses on top of calluses, and Keira had had a sudden vision of him *actually* wielding an ax. Chopping wood for this very toasty fire. Topless. Because even in the snowy woods, that kind of manual labor worked up a serious sweat.

And there was no denying the potentially romantic ambience.

Secluded location. Check.

Tall, dark and handsome stranger. Check.

The gentle crackle of a fire. Check.

So maybe it wasn't that she *couldn't* recall what she'd been up to. Maybe it was that she hadn't *wanted* to remember it.

Clearly, what she needed was a minute to collect her thoughts and assess her surroundings. So she held very still and took stock of everything she could.

She was on her side, lying with her back pushed to the wall and her hands tucked under a pillow. She had a blanket wrapped around her, but there was an empty space beside her. The last bit made Keira swallow nervously. There was no denying that the spot was just the right size to hold a big, burly man.

Had he slept beside her?

Keira's face warmed again—both with embarrassment and irritation—at the thought.

Somehow, lying in the bed beside him seemed much more taboo than curling up beside him in a desperate attempt to keep warm postaccident in a snowstorm.

Still without moving, she scanned the limited area that she could see, hoping to find proof that she hadn't actually spent the whole night cuddled up next to Calloway. But it was a one-room deal—not huge, not small—with a table and chairs in one corner, and the still-burning woodstove in another. She supposed the bed where she lay was in a third corner. So, unless the fourth and final corner was home to a recliner or a second lumpy mattress, her fears were true.

She'd officially slept with the Mountain Man.

An inappropriate giggle almost escaped her lips as she pictured telling her best friend that she had no problem getting past the failed, so-called sign that was supposed to lead her to Drew. At all. She'd simply climbed into bed with the next man she met instead.

Keira knew her cheeks were still red, and she was glad Calloway wasn't there to see her reaction. If just the *idea* of sharing a bed with him made her feel so squirmy, actually confronting him about it would be a nightmare.

Where was he anyway?

"Calloway?" she called.

Keira wasn't expecting a spoken reply from the thus far mute man, but she did half anticipate his looming presence to step from some hidden alcove so he could stare down at her with that smirk on his face. But right that second, the cabin was completely silent. Which wasn't too terrible, considering the dull ache in her temple. The rest of her hurt, too, and she wondered if she needed medical attention beyond that of a serving of liquored-up cider, a questionable dose of penicillin and the makeshift care of a bona fide mountain man.

She pushed herself to a sitting position, and was pleased that her head didn't spin and that the ache eased off a little. But when she stood, her legs shook, and she realized she was still far weaker than she was used to. With a dejected sigh, she glanced around the room in search of something that would approximate a crutch. She spied a fire iron beside the stove, decided it would do and hobbled toward it.

Maybe there was something in the cabin itself that

would answer her questions. She took another slow look around the single-room cabin.

Most of what she saw appeared to be pretty basic. The kitchen contained a wraparound cupboard, an ancient icebox and a rubber bin full of cast-iron pots.

She walked over and opened the icebox. It held the required slab of ice, several flat, wrapped packages that looked like steaks and—

"Beer?" Keira said out loud, surprised.

Calloway seemed more like the moonshine type than Bud Light. But there it was anyway. She closed the icebox and moved on to the cupboards. She didn't know what she thought she'd find, but it definitely wasn't instant hot chocolate and packaged macaroni and cheese. A bag of oatmeal cookies peeked out from behind a stack of canned soup.

So he wasn't that much of a survivalist after all.

As Keira let her gaze peruse the cabin a third time, she took note of some of the more modern accoutrements.

Sure, there was no television or microwave, but there was a dartboard and a current calendar and a digital alarm clock. A stainless-steel coffee mug sat on one window-sill, and a signed and mounted baseball adorned another.

For all intents and purposes, it was a middle-of-nowhere man cave. Minus the requisite electronics, of course.

Her curiosity grew.

Keira took a few more steps and banged straight into a dusty cardboard box, knocking it and its contents to the ground.

Dammit.

She reached down to clean it up. And paused.

A notebook—no, a scrapbook—lay open on the floor. An ominous headline popped up from one of the newspaper clippings glued to its page.

Heiress and Son Gunned Down in Ruthless Slaying.

A gruesome crime scene was depicted in black-and-white below the caption, and Keira's fingers trembled as she reached for the book. She flipped backward a few pages.

Home Invasion Turns Deadly. And a photo of a tidy house on a wide lot.

She flipped forward.

Debt and Divorce. Police Close in on Suspect in Henderson Double Murder. A grainy shot of a short-haired man covering his face with the lapel of his suit jacket.

Something about the last headline struck Keira as familiar, and she frowned down at the page, trying to figure out if it was a case she'd heard about. She scanned the article. It was enticingly vague, just the kind of sensationalist journalism that baited the reader into buying the next edition. The suspect was listed as someone close to the victims and the words *unexpected twist* were used three times that she could see with just her quick perusal, making her think the "twist" was probably not "unexpected" at all, but that the reporter wanted to play it up anyway.

Then she clued in.

Derby Reach.

A chill rocked Keira's body. It wasn't just a familiar case. It was *the* case. The affluent community where she'd grown up, home to doctors, lawyers and judges—like her father—had been blown away by the double murder.

Keira remembered the day it occurred, but embarrassingly, not because of the tragedy itself. She'd met Drew that day. While the neighbors stood on their porches, gawking and gossiping, Drew had been walking through the street, totally clueless, as he searched for an open house he'd been booked in to view. She'd been the one to explain to him why no one was thinking about real estate at that moment. And his casual romantic pursuit of Keira started the moment he knocked on her parents' door by accident.

Now Keira wished she'd paid more attention to what was happening in her own backyard.

But why did Calloway have the scrapbook in his house? What connection could a man like him have with a wealthy socialite's death?

With the book still in her hands, Keira took a cautious, wobbly step back to the window.

Across the snowy yard stood Calloway. In spite of the subzero temperature, he hadn't bothered zipping up his coat. The wind kicked up for a second, tossing his thick hair and ruffling his beard. Calloway didn't seem to notice at all.

As Keira squinted through the glass, she frowned. A narrow figure in full protective gear—helmet, fur-lined hood, thick Gore-Tex pants and knee-high boots—stood facing Calloway, his hand resting on a parked snowmobile. Something about the way the two men faced each other made Keira nervous. And as she tried to puzzle out the source of her distinct but unspecific unease, the wind changed and a loud voice carried in her direction.

"I've had a change of plans."

The breath Keira had been holding came out with a wheeze, and she stumbled back in surprise.

Calloway.

It was he who'd spoken.

Even though he'd turned so that his back was to her and he was blocking her view of the other man, Keira knew it was him. The deep, gravelly nature of the voice couldn't have suited him more perfectly.

Keira pressed her face almost right against the glass, and gasped again, this time not at Calloway. The other man had a gun, hooked menacingly to his side.

Keira took a step back. Her head spun. She needed to get away. From Calloway *and* his armed friend.

"My phone," she murmured, then looked toward the window again as she remembered.

It was in the pocket of the coat Calloway wore right that second.

Chapter Eight

The silence of the woods, combined with his habitual alertness, usually gave Graham plenty of notice whenever someone got even close to near to the cabin. More often than not, he could hear them for miles out.

This afternoon had been an exception.

A stupid exception, considering you knew *he was coming.*

But Graham had spent the whole night lying awake beside the girl, worrying about every pause in her inhales and exhales, overthinking every shift of her body, and second-guessing both his stitching job and his decision to ply her with the booze.

Was the fishing line too coarse to be effective? Were the stitches evenly spaced? Would the alcohol worsen the side effects of her concussion?

Graham had been so distracted by his concern that he didn't hear the approaching snowmobile until it was so close he could actually look outside and see it. He'd barely had time to close the door behind him before the man in front of him—who was currently struggling to unfasten his helmet—parked his vehicle at the edge of the house.

Graham worked at fixing something like a smile on his face.

As much as he trusted and relied on Dave Stark, he had a feeling that the girl's presence might jar the man's loyalty. It was one thing for the two of them to keep Graham's hideout a secret—adding an innocent unknown would be a whole different story.

So Graham stood with his hands in his jeans' pockets and waited with as much patience as he could muster for the familiar man to unclip and remove his helmet, and was careful to keep his gaze forward. He didn't let his eyes flick worriedly toward the cabin. Toward *her*.

The other man finally got his helmet free, and when he whipped it off, Graham frowned. A deep purple bruise darkened one of Stark's eyes, and a long abrasion led from his left eyebrow to the corner of his lip. He seemed indifferent to the damage.

Graham gave the other man's appearance a second, more scrutinizing once-over. Even aside from his injuries, he did look unusually worse for wear. His jacket was dirty and torn in a few places. When he turned slightly, the cold sun glinted off a metallic object at his waist.

A pistol.

Graham's eyes skimmed over it, then went back to Dave's face. Never before had his friend seen a need to bring a gun to the cabin. He wasn't brandishing the weapon, but he wasn't trying to disguise its presence, either. There was something about the way he wore it that Graham didn't like.

"What the hell's going on?"

"I was about to ask you the same thing," Stark countered.

"Me? I'm not the one who looks like he just rolled out of a bar fight."

Dave shrugged. "Occupational hazard. You wanna tell me what you meant by 'change of plans'?"

"I meant that I'll make my own way into town."

Dave couldn't hide his surprise. Or the hint of fear in his eyes.

"Why would you do that?" he wanted to know.

"Few loose ends to tie up."

"Four years, we've been waiting for this. You've sunk every available penny into finding the man. What loose ends could possibly—" The other man cut himself off and narrowed his eyes shrewdly. "What's this about?"

Graham held his gaze steady. "I can't just walk away from this setup, Dave. If things go south with Mike Ferguson, I need to know that my space isn't in danger of being compromised."

Dave sighed. "It's *already* compromised."

"What do you mean?"

"Been an accident up on the road that comes in from the resort town," Dave replied. "Happened to catch it on the radio right before I left town. Car went over a cliff yesterday. Burned to a crisp. Couldn't even get a discernable VIN."

A dark chill crept up Graham's spine. "Not sure what a car accident's got to do with me. Or you, for that matter."

Dave's eyes strayed to the cabin. "You wanna rethink that?"

Graham refused to follow the other man's gaze. "Why? I've been up here four years and nothing has ever turned the radar my way."

"Is this how you want to play? Because if you can't trust *me*…"

It was Graham's turn to let out a breath. He trusted Dave about as much as he trusted anyone.

Which isn't much at all.

But there was no way he was admitting that. The man had been his best friend for two decades, and the only person he could count on for the past few of those.

"Explain it to me, then," Graham said instead. "Tell me how the accident affects me."

"I know cops, my friend. That radio chatter—it's suspicious. They think the burn was a little too perfect."

"So?"

"So, the only thing I know better than cops is *you*. And I know exactly what was going through your head yesterday when we talked on the radio. You were champing at the bit to get to Ferguson. I spent the whole day assuming you'd show up at the resort and that I'd have to hold you back. So I think maybe you *did* leave the cabin yesterday. And I think maybe something stopped you. Something that started out as a vehicle and ended up as a burned-up piece of trash."

"The road is forty miles from here. You think I could've trekked through that and made it back here already?"

Dave shook his head. "I don't think you took the traditional route. The back way is only ten miles. Really rough terrain. But again…this is you we're talking about, isn't it? You've never done things the easy way."

Graham refused to take the bait. "The road is the last place I want to be. So I'm still not seeing what the accident has to do with me."

"It wasn't just a little crash. They're going to be looking for answers. And this isn't all that far to look. Come with me now. Unless you have some other reason for staying…"

As Dave trailed off, all the hair on the back of Graham's neck stood up.

"Get on your snowmobile, Dave," he replied, just short of a growl. "I'll come to you when I'm ready."

"C'mon, Graham—"

"*Now*, Dave."

"All right. This is your deal."

The other man slipped on his helmet, swung one leg over his snowmobile, then flipped up his protective visor and met Graham's cool stare.

"One other thing," he said. "She's a neighbor."

A neighbor? What the hell did that mean?

"She?"

"The driver."

"How could you even know the driver was a she?" Graham scoffed. "You said the car was burned to a crisp."

"It was. But I found *this* right alongside those snow-shoe tracks."

Dave reached to the side of the snowmobile, unsnapped a storage compartment and pulled out a black purse, then tossed it through the air. Graham caught it easily. He didn't have to open it to know it was hers.

"Best guess, it'll take them two days to expand their search out this way," Dave added. "Tops. But that won't matter, right? Because you'll be on your way back home."

"Right," Graham agreed, hoping the word didn't sound as forced as it felt.

As Dave's vehicle disappeared into the snow, Graham's hand squeezed into a tight, angry fist, crushing the purse for a moment before he regained control.

Very slowly, he peeled his fingers from the purse. Even more slowly, he unsnapped it and opened the zipper. He reached straight for the wallet and slid out the driver's license. And there it was in black and white.

Keira London Niles. Resident of Derby Reach. The city where Graham had found Holly's broken body. What were the odds?

Slim to none.

Graham took three determined steps toward the cabin, then paused.

The front door creaked open, just a crack.

What the hell?

Graham took another cautious step. No way had he forgotten to close the door properly. He spun around just in time to see the girl—dressed in a pair of his boots and too-long sweatshirt—lift a metallic object behind her shoulder as if she was wielding a baseball bat. Her legs were more than a little shaky, but her face was set in a determined glare as she swung the fire iron straight at his chest.

Chapter Nine

The big man was too slick. As Keira swung with all her might, he leaned back like an action-movie hero, easily dodging the blow.

You might have overestimated your own abilities, too, she thought as she lost her footing and stumbled forward.

Keira shoved down the nagging voice. She preferred to blame it on him. Especially since he had his arms outstretched as if he was going to *catch* her of all things.

Ignoring him, she drew back the weapon again. And Calloway took a half a step back.

Good.

"Give me the coat," Keira commanded.

He frowned wordlessly, and Keira rolled her eyes.

"You can drop the silent, brooding stare," she said, just the slightest hint of a tremor in her voice. "I heard you talking to that other man. Who is he?"

Calloway gave her a long considering look before replying gruffly. "Drop the weapon and I'll drop the stare. Tell me what you heard."

For a moment, Keira went still as her brain caught up to her ears.

Calloway's voice had that same gravelly tinge she'd noted when it had carried on the wind into the cabin, only this close, it was amplified all the more. It was a good voice.

"I heard just enough to know you're a liar," she snapped. "Give me the coat and tell me who that man was."

He stared at her again, then shrugged and slipped the Gore-Tex from his shoulders.

"I don't know why you care," he told her. "And it's funny that you think *I'm* the deceptive one."

"What does *that* mean?" The defensive question slipped out before Keira could stop it, making her blush.

He held the jacket out. "It means I don't believe in coincidence."

"That makes two of us. Throw it."

Calloway tossed the jacket, and Keira caught it in the air, careful to keep one hand on the fire iron as she did it.

"I played all-star baseball in high school," she warned as she started to dig through the pockets in search of her phone. "And I once hit a home run with a broken arm. So don't assume that my injuries will make me any less willing to swing with everything I've got."

"I wouldn't dare."

Keira narrowed her eyes. She strongly suspected he was trying not to smile.

If he laughs, I'll hit him anyway, she decided.

But he stayed silent.

Keira stuck her hand into another pocket. One she was sure she'd already explored. Where the hell was her phone?

"Are you looking for something in particular?" Calloway asked, his voice just a little too innocent.

She glared at him. "Listen. You might have saved my life—"

"Might have?" Graham interrupted. "You were unconscious. In a blizzard. I'm not sure *might* is the right word."

Keira's cheeks heated up. "I didn't mean it like that."

"So how did you mean it? The way *I* mean it when I say I might be standing outside, freezing, while a woman who I carried for ten miles, who I took into my house, who I gave my own *bed* to, aims a weapon at my head?"

The pink in Keira's face deepened to a cherry red, and he noticed her hand wavered. "I—"

Graham shook his head and cut her off again. "Or did you mean it like how I mean it when I say I might just be considering tossing you over my shoulder—again—carrying you *back* to the crash site and leaving you there?"

"You wouldn't!"

"I *might*."

His voice was dark, and Keira's eyes widened in surprise. She took a step back, her gaze no longer fixed on his face, but on his hand.

"That's my purse." She heard the tinge of fear in her statement.

"Keira London Niles of Derby Reach. There has to be a story in that name. Active member of Triple A. Twenty-four years old, just last month," he reeled off. "Happy birthday, by the way. Did you know your license was expired?"

"Give it back!"

He held it out, but there was no way for her to take it without losing her already tenuous hold on the fire iron in her hands.

"You don't want it anymore?" he asked.

"I'm not stupid," she grumbled.

"Far from it," Calloway agreed.

He set the purse down on the railing, reached into his pocket and pulled out a familiar black object. Keira felt the color drain from her cheeks, and the jacket slipped to the ground.

Well. That explains why I couldn't find it, she thought.

"Who were you going to call?" Calloway wondered out loud.

It was a good question. One Keira wasn't even sure of how to answer. Calling Drew seemed out of the question. Her parents were away on their annual European cruise. And her best friend would probably just laugh her butt off.

"The police," she whispered, not certain why she sounded so unsure.

Calloway tipped his head to one side, as if curious,

and tapped the phone on his chin. "Not someone from *Derby Reach*?"

Why had he said it like that, with the tiny bit of emphasis on the name of her hometown? She recalled the scrapbook full of newspaper clippings about the murder in her hometown, and a little chill crept up her spine.

GRAHAM EXAMINED THE little crease between her brows, then the probing look in her emerald gaze. His gaze traveled down her face to her pursed lips. He almost believed the puzzled look to be genuine. And as a result, he also almost missed the subtle adjustment in her stance as she pulled an elbow back and prepared to strike.

I'm a sucker, he realized. *One pair of big green eyes, one bossy mouth, and I'm a mess.*

She swung and Graham ducked backward. He charged at her, and she lost her balance, stumbling toward the stairs. Automatically, Graham switched from an attack mode to defense mode. He reached out to stabilize her, and realized a moment too late her clumsiness had been an act, her near fall a feint.

Rookie mistake, he growled at himself.

She was already off at a run.

"What the hell!" Graham yelled after her.

She had to know she didn't stand a chance of getting away from him. Even if she hadn't been weakened by her injuries, Graham was at an advantage. His legs were longer, he was far more accustomed to the terrain than she was and he wasn't wearing boots five sizes too big.

Apparently, she wasn't going to let that stop her from trying.

Graham caught up with her just inside the tree line on the edge of the clearing. His arms closed around her shoulders and the fire iron dropped to the ground. With a mutual grunt, the two of them fell straight into the snow.

She wriggled away, kicking viciously. Keira's foot met his chest, and when she drew it back for another round, Graham flung himself backward.

"Dammit!" he cursed as he landed hard on his rear end.

"Damn *you*!" Keira countered angrily.

She crawled along the snow, found a tree trunk and pulled herself up. But Graham was there in a flash.

"You can't win," he cajoled.

With desperation clear in her eyes, she charged at him. The surprise of the attack—more than the force of her body weight hitting him—knocked him to the ground once more. Graham let out another annoyed growl and sprung to his feet. By the time he was upright, Keira had the tire iron in her hands again, this time raised over her head.

"Stay back!" she yelled, and waved it around a little wildly.

Graham eyed the weapon dismissively, then focused on Keira instead. "Put it down."

"Fat chance."

"Put it down, or I'm going to *make* you put it down."

"I don't think so."

"Fine. Let's do things the hard way."

He stalked toward her, and with a cry, she tossed the fire iron at him, then turned and attempted to flee once more. She didn't make it more than four steps. Graham counted them. Then he slipped his arms around her slim waist and he lifted her easily from the ground.

Keira screamed, probably as loud and as long as she could, but her voice just echoed through the forest, bouncing back at her uselessly. She flung an elbow in the direction of Graham's stomach, but the attack didn't elicit more than a grunt. In a slick move, he flipped her around and pinned her to a large evergreen, then fixed his eyes on hers.

Keira continued to struggle, but Graham wasn't even pretending to let her get away. She finally seemed to give in, and she stopped fighting. She slid to the ground, but he continued to hold her arms as he glared down at her. Her breath was coming in short gasps and her limbs were shaking.

On the ground, she looked small and fragile once more.

For a second, Graham felt guilty. He'd made himself responsible for her well-being. Taken her in to care for her. Yeah, she'd lashed out at him for some reason he couldn't understand. But she was probably scared as hell and still shaken up. And maybe her hometown *was* just a coincidence after all.

Graham loosened his hold, just slightly. Then she attempted to twist away, and guilt evaporated. He squeezed her wrists together over her head, pressed a foot—as gently as he could while still being firm—into *her* feet and immobilized her.

"I'm done playing games," he told her in a low voice.

She lifted her chin defiantly. "What are you going to do? Kill me?"

Her question hit him hard, square in the chest. She *did* know him. Or thought she did.

No coincidences.

"I'm not a murderer," Graham replied coldly, and dropped her wrists. "And what I'm going to *do* is take you back inside. Where we're going to eat breakfast like two normal adults. And where you're going to tell me exactly what the hell you were doing up this mountain in the first place. Understood?"

She nodded meekly, and Graham had to shove down the reflexive regret at dampening the fire in her eyes.

You need answers, he reminded himself.

He pulled back, and as he did, Keira tipped up her head. The new angle gave him a perfect view of her eyes, and Graham saw with relieved satisfaction that the fire—quite clearly—wasn't extinguished. Just banked.

Chapter Ten

As Calloway's seemingly enormous body eased away from Keira's own petite one, she realized how ridiculous it was to think she could have overpowered him in the first place. The self-defense training she received at work was no match for his brute strength. No makeshift weapon would outdo him.

"Let's go," he said.

Even if his voice hadn't demanded obedience, he didn't release her, and that gave her little choice but to go where he propelled her. They moved toward the cabin, Graham's hands pressed firmly into Keira's shoulders, her feet dragging a little in the oversize boots.

Stupid, stupid, she cursed herself as they moved along. *I would've been better off taking my chances by running into the woods instead of thinking he owed me some kind of explanation.*

Because he really *didn't* owe her one. And if Keira thought about it, she was probably the one who owed *him* something. Had she even thanked him for saving her? She couldn't remember. She opened her mouth to do it now, then paused as she second-guessed the impulse. Should she still thank him now that she suspected he had something to do with the four-year-old homicide in her hometown?

I'm not a murderer, he'd said.

Did that make it true? Keira desperately wanted to believe him. And not just because she was trapped on the mountainside with him, and her only way out—so far—was a man with a snowmobile and a gun. Something about Calloway felt intoxicatingly *right*. Especially when he was standing as close to her as he was now, his hand on her body, guiding her where he wanted to go.

When they moved up the stairs, and he reached around her to push open door, his clean, woodsy scent assaulted her senses, rendering her brain temporarily nonfunctional. Her booted toe caught on the transition board at the bottom on the door frame, and before she could stop herself, she was falling forward. She braced herself to hit the ground. But the impact didn't come.

She still fell, but not the way she'd been thinking she would. One of Calloway's arms slipped under her legs, and the other closed around her shoulders. As she went down, he took the full force of the ground to his own elbows and knees. He had one hand on the back of her neck, the other on her thigh, and his gray eyes held her where she was.

They were both breathing heavily, and Keira refused to acknowledge the treacherous parts of her body that demanded to know why it felt so good to be looking into one another's eyes, chests rising and falling in near unison.

A drop of water fell from his face to hers, and he eased his hand out from behind her hair to wipe it away gently. His fingers burned pleasantly against her skin, and it didn't help at all when he looked her straight in the eyes and gave her the clearest understanding of the term *white-hot* that she'd ever had. It was the perfect way to describe the way ice gray met fierce need in Calloway's eyes. They were burning so bright, she almost had to look away. But couldn't.

Lying above her, looking at her like that, Calloway wasn't just handsome. He was gorgeous. The perfectly rustic look had basically turned him into the supermodel version of his Mountain Man self.

And, oh, he smelled good, too. Even better than he had when he was carrying her up the mountainside. Raw and woodsy and tinged with smoke.

He was unpredictable and dangerous, and it was totally unreasonable to be this attracted to him. The smart part of her brain knew it. But the smart part didn't seem to be attached to the rest of her. In fact, there were a few distinct bits that seemed *remarkably* detached from her brain altogether.

Keira's whole body was alight.

Kiss me, she begged silently.

And as her heavy gaze continued to hold Calloway's, she knew he was going to.

Thank God.

Then, so slowly she was sure he was very carefully gauging her reaction, he slid his hand from her cheek to her chin and tipped it toward him. He inched forward. Keira fought an urge to speed it up, to drive her lips into his, to close the miniscule gap between them and take what she was dying to have. What she suddenly realized she'd been dying to have since the second he put his arms around her in the snowstorm.

Don't rush this, whispered a small voice in her head.

And Kiera suspected that the voice was right. This kiss—this first kiss with such an intense, unusual and mysterious man—was something to be savored.

His mouth touched hers, his eyes still wide-open.

It was the softest kiss. The gentlest one. But it ignited more passion in Keira than she'd felt in her entire quarter-of-a-century-long life. She gasped because she couldn't help it. She closed her eyes because she had to. And when Calloway's palm skidded to the back of her neck again, her arms came up, all on their own, to encircle his waist. She pulled him close, and he let her. The aches in her body eased away as she let the rest of the kiss take her, as his lips became hungry, and everything but Calloway faded to the background.

But it was painfully short.

He pulled away, ending the embrace with an abruptness that contrasted sharply with its slow beginnings.

It left Keira full of longing.

"Calloway," she whispered.

He leaned in once more, grazing her mouth, and then—without warning—he abandoned his pursuit of her lips to swoop in and lift her up instead. He carried her straight to the bed, and for a dizzying moment Keira thought he was going to skip the preamble and go straight for the main attraction.

Quicker than she could decide whether or not she should protest, he reached beneath the frame, grabbed a rope, wrapped it around her wrists tightly and secured her to the bed.

DAMMIT.

Complications were low on Graham's list of priorities. Liking Keira Niles was *very* complicated.

And he did like her. Even before they'd shared the most intense kiss he'd ever experienced.

He liked that she was wearing his clothes. He liked the way the lithe muscles in her thighs disappeared under his shirt, hinting at what lay farther up. He even liked the way she was glaring at him right that second, mad instead of scared, a hint of residual passion evident in the way her lips stayed slightly parted and the way her gaze kept flicking between his eyes and his own mouth.

Beautiful, resilient, strong and smart.

His *like* was making it hard to see her as a threat, and he really needed to overcome that. Somehow.

"What do you think you're doing?" she snapped.

"Did you know I was here?" he replied softly, ignoring her angry question. "Or did you just get lucky?"

"I wouldn't call this lucky."

Keira pulled emphatically on the rope around her arms,

and Graham winced. Coercion didn't suit him, and in spite of what people thought, he wasn't a violent man. Not habitually anyway. He just did what he had to do, when he had to do it.

"If you're not going to answer my questions," Graham said, "then I'm going to go back to our previous arrangement."

"What previous arrangement was that?" she replied, just shy of sarcastic.

"The one where I don't speak at all."

He started to turn away, but she snorted, and he stopped, midturn, to face her again.

"More of the silent treatment? What are you?" she asked. "A ten-year-old boy?"

For some reason, the question annoyed him far more than her lack of candor. Graham strode toward her, and once again she didn't cower. She raised her eyes and opened her mouth, but whatever snarky comment had been about to roll off her tongue was cut off as Graham mashed lips into hers. Uncontrollably. He kept going until he'd possessed her mouth completely, and when it ended, Keira was left gasping for air—gasping for *more*. For good measure, he dug his hands into the hair at the back of her neck and trailed his lips from her chin to her collarbone before he stopped.

"When you're ready to talk—with some honesty— I'll be just over there, waiting," Graham growled against Keira's throat.

Then he stood and moved across the room to dig out the things he needed to prepare breakfast.

Just a morning like any other, he told himself.

Except that he needed two plates and two forks instead of the usual one of each. And twice the amount of pancake batter and extra coffee. Oh, and there was also the faint feminine perfume that somehow managed to override the scent of fire that usually dominated the air in the cabin. Those things, coupled with the way her heated gaze followed each of his movements while he stoically ignored her presence, left no doubt that the morning wasn't *any*thing like any other.

Why couldn't he have rescued a hideous beast of woman with no spark in her whatsoever? Why did it have to be a girl who so thoroughly piqued his interest and so easily distracted him from finding Mike Ferguson? He should be trying to think of a way to get her out of his house as quickly as possible so he could get back to his mission. Not standing there daydreaming about her. He could barely blink without seeing her enticing form on the back of his eyelids.

"If I answer your questions, will you answer mine?"

Keira's voice startled Graham, and he spun toward her. The pan went slack in his grip, and the golden breakfast item flew right past both it and him, and landed on the floor at his feet. They both stared at it for a moment before Graham bent to snatch it up.

"Well?" Keira prodded.

Graham shrugged. "Depends."

She blinked, looking surprised. Had she just expected him to agree with no further terms? Not a chance in hell was he giving her the freedom to ask anything she felt like.

"It depends on what?" she asked.

Graham took a breath, popped the floor pancake into his mouth, then chewed it slowly and deliberately before swallowing it and answering her puzzled question. "On whether or not I think you're telling the truth. And whether or not I think giving *you* an honest answer will put you in danger."

"Shouldn't I be the one who decides if I'm in danger?" she countered.

Damn, he liked her stubbornness. He ran his fingers over his beard to cover his smile.

"Not today," he told her.

"Listen to me, Mountain Man. You might have saved my life—" Keira paused when Graham raised an eyebrow, and quickly amended, "You *did* save my life. But you also lulled me into a drunken stupor with your liquored-up cider, then crawled into bed with me, and now you've tied me up, and—"

He cut her off. "I also stripped you down, searched your body for signs of any other deep cuts or contusions, or internal bleeding. Then I stitched you up as best I could."

With each word, Keira's face grew redder, and by the end of Graham's speech, she was nearly purple.

"You *stripped* me?" she asked, her voice a squeak. "Why would you *strip* me? And then *tell* me about it?"

Graham shrugged. "I thought it best that I get that out of the way now. And it would've been hard to be thorough if you'd been clothed. That's two questions you owe me now, by the way."

"I don't owe you anything," she almost yelled. "You cannot touch me or kiss me, just because you feel like it. You cannot carry me around, just because it's easier than asking me nicely."

"You think I did all that for *me*?" Graham argued.

"I'm sure it was horribly inconvenient for you to get me naked."

Graham bit back an admission that it *had* actually been damned inconvenient. He'd covered her body carefully while searching for anything more serious than the slice in her thigh. For the first time in his life, he'd been barely able to keep his professional detachment in place, and the guilt of it had made him want to perform the careful examination of her body with his eyes closed. Except the thought of a hands-only exploration brought with it a whole host of other, far from clinical, ideas to mind. He had never been so happy to finish an exam.

Now he was sorry he'd brought it up.

"You were asleep," he growled.

"And sleep made me what? Unwomanly? Unattractive?"

Hell. No.

"High on yourself, aren't you?" Graham asked, his voice just a little too dark to be called teasing.

"What does that mean?"

"You clearly think your nudity is enough to turn a man into nothing more than a slobbering sex-crazed maniac," he stated.

"That's not what I said!"

"That's what I heard."

Keira's face was still pink. "It's just that that stuff makes it a little hard to trust that you've got my best interests at heart."

He *had* done all of those things she'd mentioned. He'd also covered her each time she kicked off her blankets in the night, panicked each time her breathing changed and had his own night thoroughly ruined.

Ruined? he thought. *Or made more worthwhile.*

He growled at the voice in his head and pushed it away.

"You're welcome," Graham said.

"You're—I'm—what?"

Ignoring her incomprehensible, sputtering reply, Graham walked over to Keira and unfastened the rope. Then, in a quick move that made her squeak, he scooped her from the bed, carried her over to the little table and secured her to one of the chairs.

"I'll let those first two questions go, and even let you ask another. In the name of chivalry," he said, and raised an eyebrow expectantly.

Chapter Eleven

If her hands hadn't been tied together, Keira would've crossed her arms over her chest in indignant frustration.

"You think you're chivalrous?" she demanded.

The big man grinned smugly. "Yes."

"You may want to buy a dictionary."

"Either way…it's my turn. You've asked three questions, and I've asked none."

"I haven't even asked my *first* question yet!" Keira protested. "And you said you were going to let the first two go."

"Changed my mind. My house, my rules," he replied.

"You are an infuriating man."

He nodded. "I'm also loyal, thorough, a tad controlling and a damned fine cook. Are you hungry?"

"Is that *your* question?"

"As a matter of fact…it is."

Keira rolled her eyes. "No, I'm not hungry."

"First question and already you're telling me a lie," Calloway said and he pushed a plate of pancakes toward her.

She shoved it back. "It's not a lie."

Calloway gripped his fingers on the edge of the plate and pushed it across the table. When it reached Keira, she tried to send it back again, but he didn't let it go.

"I'm not going to eat just because you tell me to," she informed him.

In reply, he dragged the pancake away.

Ha, Keira thought triumphantly. *Take that.*

But he wasn't letting her win. He was just upping his game. He smiled and began to cut the pancake into bite-size pieces. Then he scraped his chair over the floor so that he was right beside her. He jabbed a fork into one of the pieces and held it up to Keira's mouth.

It smelled damned good.

She turned her head away anyway.

Calloway exhaled, clearly frustrated.

Keira tipped her face back in his direction, prepared to snap something mean and clever at him. But the second she opened her mouth, his fingers were there. A piece of pancake slipped into her mouth, and it was syrupy and sweet and so soft it practically melted away when it hit her tongue.

Oh, my God.

It was the best pancake Keira had ever tasted. Maybe the best *food* she'd ever tasted. All thoughts of ropes versus chivalry went out of her head. When Calloway lifted another piece from the plate, there was no hope in hell she was turning it down. She opened her mouth eagerly, and he popped it in. Keira couldn't even act embarrassed as her mouth closed quickly and she nipped his fingers. It really was that good.

A little noise—just barely shy of a *yum*—escaped from her lips as she swallowed.

Calloway raised an eyebrow.

"Fine," Keira relented. "I take back the breakfast thing. But on the other one, I stand firm. No touching."

He smiled as if he didn't believe her, lifted another piece of pancake from the plate, raised an eyebrow and held it out. After the briefest hesitation, Keira opened her mouth, and Calloway popped it in. He let out a deep laugh, and the fourth piece he offered to her a little more slowly. When Keira parted her lips eagerly, he drew the pancake away.

"Hey!" she protested.

Graham leaned his elbows on the table. "You ready to answer another question? Truthfully, this time?"

"I wasn't *lying*," Keira argued. "I just didn't know I was hungry."

"Uh-huh."

"Besides which. I'm pretty sure it's *my* turn to ask a question."

"We both know that's not true," Calloway said, and grinned again.

He held the pancake positioned between his thumb and forefinger, just out of biting distance. Keira bent forward to grab it. This time, when he tried to tease her, she jerked her bound hands up, and just barely managed to get enough slack that she could close them on his forearm.

Calloway chuckled, but he let her take the pancake. She made an exaggerated *mmm* noise as she sucked it back, not realizing that she wasn't nibbling on just the pancake. Calloway's fingers were still sandwiched between her lips, pleasantly smooth and soft on his calloused skin. Heat shot through her, and when she relaxed her jaw to release his fingers, he didn't pull away. Instead, he swiped his thumb over the corner of her mouth, collecting a drop of syrup. Then he pushed it back to the tip of her tongue, and Keira gave his thumb a little lick, relieving it of the wayward syrup.

"Thank you," she said softly. "For helping me and fixing me up."

"Anytime."

There was a weight behind his tone that didn't match the typically dismissive expression. As if he meant it literally. *Anytime.*

Keira's pulse raced, and her heart swelled pleasantly at the thought that Calloway would drop everything just to help her. That maybe he had *already* dropped everything to help her.

In the soft, wintry sunlight filtering through the cabin,

there was no mistaking the want in his eyes. A matching one flowed through Keira.

Slowly, he loosened the rope on her wrists. And when she was free, she didn't make a run for it. Instead, she let him twine their fingers together, then lift their joined hands to her cheekbone. He ran them across her skin. She leaned closer. Her mouth was so near to his that she could already almost taste him.

At every turn, she wanted him more and cared less about what had brought her there in the first place. Two more seconds of his knee pressed between hers under the table, and she was going to be insisting that he take her back to that lumpy bed in the corner.

"You okay?" he asked.

The question threw her a little.

"Am I okay?"

His shoulders went up and down. "Give me a sliding scale? One through ten."

He really did sound serious.

"My head aches. So three out of ten for that. You untied me, so five out of ten for that. And I'm not dead. So I'll concede a ten out of ten for that."

"So…an overall of about six out of ten. Sixty percent isn't too bad."

"It's not exactly A material."

"Maybe you could bump it up to a C if I lent you some pants?"

The burn of desire, just under Keira's skin, came back, full force. Her legs *were* bare. And they were wrapped around one of Calloway's denim-clad ones. Put that together with the way his beard was close enough to tickle, the deep rumble of his voice making her chest vibrate, and Keira knew she was in a completely different kind of trouble. One that had nothing to do with Calloway's secrets or the armed man with whom he was acquainted.

That stuff—that dangerous stuff—seemed ridiculously far away at the moment.

But she needed to remember it. And to do *that*, she needed space. Reluctantly, she pulled away.

Forcing a measured tone, Keira whispered, "Pants don't outweigh the left-me-tied-to-a-bed, rifled-through-my-purse creep factor. Can I ask my question now?"

"Can you…" Calloway trailed off, looking at her as though he couldn't quite understand the request.

Then he cleared his throat and shoved back his chair, irritation making his eyes flash as he stood up and yanked away the nearly empty pancake plate.

Guilt tickled at Keira's mind, but she pushed it down.

"Can I ask my question?" she repeated.

With a coolness that didn't match the burn of his gaze, Calloway replied, "I think you're still in the red, as far as questions are concerned."

He crossed his arms and glared down at her.

Refusing to be intimidated, Keira jumped to her own feet and opened her mouth to argue, but an abrupt wave of dizziness made her head spin.

Immediately, Calloway seemed to sense the change. His eyes filled with concern. And then his hands were on her, easing her close with a gentleness that contrasted dramatically with his bulky form. He lifted her from the ground and cradled her to his wide chest.

Right away, Keira felt better. Sleepy, but better. Almost content.

He brushed her hair back from her forehead, letting his palm rest there for an extra second.

"Overdid it," he murmured.

His apologetic tone made Keira want to absolve him of responsibility. It had been her careless disregard for that weather that had led to the accident. Her attempt to come after Calloway with the fire iron that made her arms ache.

But she couldn't form the words.

After a moment, she gave up trying and pushed her face into the soothing firmness of his body instead. She could hear his heart. It was beating loudly, and she liked its steadiness. Appreciated its strength. Appreciated *his* strength.

A little sigh escaped Keira's lips as she let both him and his heartbeat surround her.

As Calloway moved across the floor, she noted that his pace matched the thumps. And in a light-headed way, she wondered if the blood rushing through her was going to match it soon, too.

But in a few steps, he reached the bed, drew back the blankets and laid her down, and Keira realized she wasn't going to get a chance to find out.

Regret made her heart ache.

Why was I arguing with him?

Keira couldn't remember.

Using the last bit of her strength, she reached for him. "Stay," she managed to whisper.

Keira knew the muddled way her head felt was what made her say it. Or what *let* her say it.

But she didn't care.

He met her eyes, and some undefinable emotion brimmed over in their silvery stare, and he peeled back the blanket and slid into the bed, and Keira didn't just not *care* that reason had slipped away...she was glad.

GRAHAM WOKE ABRUPTLY, inhaled deeply, then froze as Keira's scent filled him.

What the...

Then he remembered. She'd looked up at him with those half-closed eyes, issued the one-word plea, and he'd been unable to do anything but indulge her, crawling in beside her and cradling her close until she was sound asleep.

She wasn't the only one being indulged. You could've at least tried to resist. Would have, if you really wanted to.

That was the truth.

He could use whatever excuse came to mind—checking her breathing, making sure she was just exhausted and not injured further or feverish—but when it came down to it, Graham simply wanted her close.

Not just close...in your bed.

He couldn't even remember the last time he'd even *thought* about taking a girl to bed.

Somewhere between four years and never again.

Or longer.

Because even before your life fell apart, things on that front were less than satisfying.

Graham ran his fingers through a loose strand of Keira's hair and watched her eyelids flutter. He sure as hell didn't lack desire right that second. Or any second since she'd appeared out of thin air. In fact, his desire for this girl seemed more central to his life than any other thing.

Keira shifted a little beside him, and her slim fingers found his shirt. She tightened her grip on the fabric for a moment, and then she stilled again. As if she'd just been making sure he was still there. Graham's heart squeezed a little in his chest before he could stop it.

Stupid.

Very carefully, he put his hand over hers and loosened her hold on his clothes, then eased out of bed.

As silently as he could, he slipped on his favorite plaid jacket, then let himself out onto the porch.

Graham was startled to see that the sun had dipped down behind the mountain and that dusk was already settling in. He'd done none of his usual chores, performed none of the ritualistic tasks that had occupied him for the past four years. No perimeter scan, no check to make sure everything was ready to go should he have to leave suddenly, nothing. He'd somehow slept the day away. With Keira London Niles.

Graham took a deep breath, trying to clear the thoughts in his head and her delicate aroma out of his nostrils. The inhale of cool air helped with the second, but did nothing at all in regard to the first.

He fought to keep from heading straight back inside, then tightened his jacket and shoved aside a pile of snow so that he could slump down onto the rarely used porch rocker. The wood underneath him was icy enough to creep through his jeans, but Graham continued to sit there anyway. It seemed like a suitable punishment for the heat that stirred in him each time his mind drifted toward Keira.

Dammit.

He couldn't afford to be feeling like this about a girl he barely knew.

Hell. He couldn't allow himself to have feelings at all. His soft side was what got him into this mess in the first place.

What *was* she doing there? Was she telling the truth about not knowing Graham was on the mountain?

The second she was well enough, he was going to demand answers. Not because he wanted to, but because he had to. To protect himself, and more important, to protect her.

Graham's chest constricted again as he thought of how dangerous it was for Keira to be there with him. She couldn't have picked a worse savior. Even just knowing his name was enough to pull unnecessary, unwanted attention her way. If she repeated it, the authorities would descend on her.

Or worse.

Mike Ferguson might come looking.

Graham needed to ensure that didn't happen. More than

he needed anything else. And sitting around thinking about that didn't help any more than lying in bed beside her did.

He started to stand, but only got as far as putting one hand on the arm of the rocker.

Keira was up. Awake. Standing in the doorway. Even though she'd draped a blanket around her shoulders, Graham could see that she'd taken the time to get dressed in one of his T-shirts and a pair of his sweats—cinched tight, but still hanging off her hips. She looked sleepy and sexy and about as perfect as one person could.

Graham stared for a long second, mesmerized by the way the waning light brought out the creamy tone of her skin and deepened the auburn in her hair.

He took a breath, then wished he hadn't because her sweetness was in his nose once again. He did his best to ignore it and forced himself to speak.

"You shouldn't be up," he greeted gruffly.

"Morning to you, too, Mountain Man," she replied.

Graham's eyes flicked to the moonlit sky.

"Evening," he corrected.

"Always have to have the upper hand, don't you?"

He gave her a considering look, wondering how she could possibly believe he had the upper hand. Just looking at her made him feel…not exactly helpless. Not exactly powerless.

Spellbound, maybe.

"You should go back inside," Graham said, deflecting her question so that he wouldn't have to admit just how out of his element he felt right then.

In reply, she narrowed her eyes in the already-familiar way that told him she wasn't interested in doing what he thought she ought to do.

With the same stubborn look on her face, Keira moved toward him instead of away from him.

Graham opened his mouth to point out that she might

not like the way things turned out if she did as she wanted instead of as she should, but he didn't have to say a word. Right before she reached the porch swing, the slippery ground did it on his behalf.

Keira's feet, which were dwarfed inside a pair of his socks, skidded along the ice and with an "Oomph," she landed in his lap.

She made as if she was going to get up, but Graham wasn't going to let her go so easily; she felt far too good, right there in his lap.

"Stay."

He realized immediately that he'd echoed her earlier request—the one he hadn't been able to deny—wondered if she noticed it, too. If she did, she didn't say.

But after a minute, she leaned against him and tucked her feet up. Automatically, Graham's arms came up to pull her even closer. It was strange, how natural it felt to hold her like that.

"At least this way, I know you're not freezing your rear end off," he said into the top of her head.

There was a tiny pause before she asked, "Is that why you want me to stay?"

"No," Graham admitted.

"But you're still not going to tell me anything, are you?" she replied.

He ran his hands over her shoulders, then down her arms and rested his palms on her wrists.

"No," he said again. "Not because I don't want to."

"What's stopping you?"

"My gut."

"Your gut tells you not to trust me?"

Graham chuckled. "Actually, my gut tells me that I *should* trust you."

Graham moved his hands from her wrists to her hands and threaded his fingers through hers.

He suddenly found himself wondering if *she* trusted *him*. What *her* gut had to say.

Maybe she hadn't even considered it.

Did he want her to?

She really shouldn't trust him. His past was too troublesome, his heart too marred. He might hurt her in his attempt to keep her safe. Hell, he had nothing to even offer. Not until he'd taken care of Mike Ferguson and all that went along with finding the man.

But he wanted her faith, and not blindly. He wanted to know that he hadn't lost the quality that made a girl like Keira believe in him.

"So…" she prodded after his long moment of silence.

Graham jerked back to the present moment. "My gut tells me to trust you. But it's warning me even louder that if I tell you my story, it'll put your life at risk."

"Isn't that my risk to take?"

"It should be, yes," he agreed.

"But not now?"

"I didn't save your life just to let you get killed, Keira."

Her hands tightened on Graham's. "Are you sorry?"

"Sorry about what?"

"That you saved me."

The quiet, trying-not-to-sound-hurt voice cut into Graham's chest. He couldn't stand the thought of her believing that.

He released her hands so he could reposition her, so he could see her face and she could see his.

"No matter what happens, Keira," he stated softly, "I'll never be sorry that I saved you."

A little smile turned up the corners of her so-kissable lips, and Graham wanted to make it even wider.

"I'll tell you what," he said. "If you come inside and let me feed you dinner *and* you manage to stay awake for more than five minutes after, I'll answer one question. Your way."

"Carte blanche?"

That smile of hers reached her eyes.

In spite of his head screaming at him *not* to say yes, Graham couldn't help but give in.

"If you promise not to ask me anything too terrible during dinner, then yes."

"What do you want? Small talk?"

Graham nodded. "Small talk. In exchange for carte blanche."

And her full lips widened into a grin, and that spellbound feeling slammed into Graham's heart once more.

Chapter Twelve

True to his word, Calloway kept the conversation light. He fed the woodstove and heated up some thick soup and told her he hadn't seen so much snow in the mountains in a long time. With a head shake, he deflected her question about precisely how long.

And in spite of her resolve to stay awake, and her nearly daylong nap, the second she finished her soup Keira could feel her eyes wanting to close and sense her mind wandering. She tried to keep it focused. But when she pushed her bowl away, a yawn came out instead of a question.

If she did manage to stay awake...what would she ask?

Just a few hours ago, she swore that she had a dozen all-important, totally articulate things she *had* to know about who Calloway was and what he was doing there on the mountain. About his interaction with the man outside. About the box of newspaper clippings.

Now all the specifics were muddled.

"Keira?"

His voice, rumbling with amusement, made her jerk her head up from its unintentional resting place on her hand.

Calloway had cracked one of the beers from the fridge and looked far more relaxed than Keira expected.

He looks so...normal.

Which was somehow comforting. A beer and a fire and cozy evening. Keira wished wistfully that it could be that simple.

"You awake?" he asked.

"Yes," she lied.

Clearly, she'd drifted off enough to give him time to get the beer from the fridge. Funny that she was already so comfortable with this man—complete with all his dangerous edges—after such a short time. And not a single alarm bell was going off, either.

Calloway took a swig of his beer and gave her a considering look that matched her own. "So. Does this mean you have something to ask me?"

Keira tried again to recall what, specifically. She'd had something in mind. It eluded her now.

"Did you feed me soup to make me sleepy?" She wanted to know.

A grin broke out on Calloway's face. "I give you carte blanche and that's the question you choose?"

"You know perfectly well that wasn't it at all." Another yawn took away from the emphatic way she meant to make the statement.

"Why don't you lie down while you think about it?" he suggested.

"Nice try."

Calloway's smile widened. "I could carry you over to the bed again."

"You'd like that, wouldn't you?"

"Maybe I would."

His eyes did a slow head-to-toe inventory of Keira's body. They rested on each part of her just long enough to make the object of his attention warm, then moved on to the next.

Feet and ankles. Knees and thighs. Hips and waist. The swell of her breasts.

He paused at her lips and lingered there before he raised his gaze up again, and then he came to his feet and began to clear their table.

And even though Calloway had broken the stare and his eyes were otherwise occupied, Keira knew there was no *maybe* about it.

He would enjoy taking her to bed.

And if Keira was being honest, she craved the closeness, too. She wanted the feel of his arms around her and she wanted to taste his lips again.

Maybe the heated desire she felt was amplified by her surroundings, maybe it was made more intense by how close she'd come to death just yesterday.

Probably.

It made sense psychologically—reasonably. Her training in the social work field had taught enough about transference.

But underneath that, Keira felt a stronger pull.

He'd rescued her, at the risk of his own safety. And he was still putting her life ahead of his own.

A man like that...he deserved appreciation.

Appreciation. Yeah, that's *what you feel.*

She shoved aside the snarky thought and watched Calloway rinse their bowls, then dry them.

His body moved smoothly and confidently, undaunted by the stereotypically feminine activity. Keira liked the glimpse of domesticity. A lot.

"Keira?"

She jumped in her seat. "Yes?"

"Nothing. Just checking."

"Checking what?"

"Whether you'd fallen asleep or whether you were staring at my rear end."

"Very funny."

Calloway chuckled. "It was the only reason I could think of for you *not* offering to dry while I washed."

Keira's face warmed, and she stood up quickly. But the big man was at her side in a second, his hand on her elbow.

"Hey," he said. "I was kidding. You need to rest, not do dishes."

"I've rested an awful lot already."

"Not enough."

Warmth crept from his palm into her arm and through her chest, and she couldn't argue as he led her across the room to the bed. And she felt a little lost as he released her.

Definitely more than transference.

She looked up at his face, wondering how she'd ever questioned whether or not he was handsome. He was near perfect.

"In my other life," he told her, his voice low, "it was my job to take care of people. I want you to get better, Keira. Soon. So all I need right now is to make sure you're all right."

He pulled up the blanket from the bed, tucked it around her face, then cupped her cheek. And that second, Keira remembered what he'd said about his gut and trust, and something clicked home for her.

"I work for child protective services," she said slowly, "and I have to form snap judgments sometimes. I need to know if I'm leaving a child in a potentially unsafe environment, or decide if someone is trying to deceive me into thinking it's safer than it is. And I know this is different, but I'm used to listening to my gut, too, Calloway. And it's telling me that even if you're not sharing everything… I should trust you, too."

For a brief second, a mix of emotions waged a war in the Mountain Man's stormy eyes. Relief. Worry. Fierce want. Frustration.

Then he kissed her forehead and strode across the cabin.

Keira considered going after him, but something told her she didn't have to. Calloway wasn't holding his secrets as tightly as he had been, just hours earlier, and she could be patient.

She leaned her head down on the pillow and squished up against the wall, making room for him. Whenever he was ready.

GRAHAM BUSIED HIMSELF with tasks around the little house. None of them really needed doing, but none of them took him very far from Keira, either.

He wasn't so bogged down in denial that he didn't recognize the burgeoning feelings he had for the injured girl. Nor was he naive enough to believe that a relationship between them was possible.

Which was a good enough reason for not climbing in beside Keira.

The bigger problem was: it wasn't a good enough reason to stop him from *wanting* to do it. From wanting *her*.

He paused in his counting of his emergency candles to look over at her. She was pushed to the far end of the single-size bed, leaving just enough room for Graham's body. More than enough room if he wrapped his arms around her and held her close.

Her position on the bed wasn't an accident. It was an invitation. One that made an uncomfortable ache spread out from his chest and threaten to take over the rest of him.

You owe her an explanation.

Yes, she deserved some honesty about who he was and what he was doing there.

He just wasn't sure how he was going to go about telling her.

He leaned forward and put his head in his hands.

There just didn't seem to be an easy way of letting someone know you'd been accused of murder.

His eyes slid over Keira, then away from her.

And abruptly, he went still.

Maybe he wouldn't have to tell her after all. Maybe she knew already.

A box—one he'd shoved aside and forgotten about and hadn't touched in long enough to let it get covered in dust—sat across the room, its lid askew.

KEIRA WOKE TO FIND the bed empty and she couldn't quite deny her disappointment that Calloway's warm body wasn't beside her. And her heart dropped even further when she sat up and spied him slumped over a cup of coffee. He was still dressed in the previous evening's clothes, his hair wild.

Did he sleep at all?

"Calloway?"

He turned her way, and she saw that his face was as ragged as his appearance.

"I need to ask you something, Keira."

"Carte blanche?" she replied, managing to keep her voice on the lighter side.

He nodded, but instead of asking a question, he made a statement. "Holly Henderson."

The murdered woman from Derby Reach. Keira felt the blood drain from her cheeks. Why was he bringing her up now?

"You know the name." Calloway said that like a statement, too, but Keira seized on it.

"Yes. I know her name. But so does every person in a hundred-mile radius of Derby Reach. And you saw my driver's license, so you know that's where I'm from."

"True enough. Holly Henderson was killed four years ago," Calloway said. "Big news in Derby Reach. And you're right, everyone did hear about it. But for some reason, I think it's a little fresher in your mind. When was the last time you heard the name, Keira?"

Without meaning to, she flicked her eyes toward the corner of the room. Toward the box full of incriminating news articles. Immediately, she regretted the slip. Calloway's gaze followed hers. And when he looked back in her direction, his face was dark.

Not with guilt, Keira noted. Regret, yes. Sorrow, absolutely. And hurt. Yes, there was that, too.

And it managed to cut through her apprehension and froze her tongue to the roof of her mouth. Before she could regain the ability to speak, Calloway was on his feet, moving toward her. He reached down, grabbed the rope she'd all but forgotten about and looped it around her wrists. He cinched it just shy of too-tight and fastened her there. Lastly, he snapped up the box, gave Keira a furious, achingly heartbreaking glare and stormed out of the cabin.

Damn, damn, damn.

For several long minutes, she stared at the door. Her heart was still beating at double time, and she was sure he was going to come running back any second and offer an explanation.

What *was* his connection to Holly? For some reason, she was sure—so sure—that he wasn't responsible for her death.

But the door stayed shut, and the cabin stayed distinctly quiet, and she had to resign herself to the fact that he wasn't returning anytime soon. And she wanted to get free.

Keira followed the length of rope with her eyes.

It disappeared at the edge of the bed, so she shimmied toward the end. She still couldn't see where it was tied, but sliding to the edge of the mattress gave her enough slack to move a little more. She inched forward so that her whole head hung off the bed.

Aha!

There it was. The rope went from her wrists to the woven metal frame underneath the mattress. As Keira leaned down a little farther in search of a possible way to free herself, she lost her balance and toppled to the wood floor.

She decided to take advantage of her new position.

She worked her way under the bed, ignoring both the few slivers that found their way into her back and the fact that the frame was low enough to the ground that it dug into her chest.

She brought her fingers to the knot on the bed frame. It was as solid as the one on her hands. But a warped piece on the metal bed frame caught Keira's eye.

If she could twist it, even just a little bit, she might be able to create a gap wide enough to slip the rope through.

She began to work the metal. It hurt a bit. The fibers of the robe rubbed unpleasantly against her skin, and she jabbed herself twice on the metal, hard enough the second time to draw blood.

C'mon, c'mon.

When she finally saw some progress—a tiny space between the bits of metal—tears of relief pricked at her eyes.

With an unladylike grunt, she twisted the already bent piece of metal frame as hard as she could while shoving the rope forward at the same time. It sprung free.

"Yes!" she crowed, and propelled herself out from under the bed.

She crossed the room quickly, but paused at the spot that had housed the cardboard box.

Knowing it probably wasn't the best idea, but unable to resist an urge to do it anyway, Keira made her way to the front door. She cracked it open and a blast of chilly air slammed into her.

Too cold.

She snapped up the Gore-Tex jacket from its hook just inside, put Calloway's too-big boots back on and stepped onto the patio.

She limped down the stairs and into the yard, holding her arms tightly against her chest to fend off the cold.

How Calloway was able to stand it with no coat was beyond her.

Where had the man gone to anyway?

There were plenty of footprints at the base of the stairs

and along the edge of the cabin, but no distinct ones that led away from the cabin.

She scanned the tree line. It was so thick that, had it not been for the tracks in the snow, Keira wouldn't have been able to tell where Dave, Calloway's not-so-friendly friend, had come in on his snowmobile. There was no evidence of a footpath in, either. But there had to be a way out. Didn't there?

She had the uneasy suspicion that if she climbed up one of the very tall trees surrounding her and looked out, she would see nothing but even more trees for miles on end.

Keira shivered, a renewed niggling of doubt brought in by the yawning forest before her. Her stomach churned nervously, too, and she had to look away from the suddenly oppressive view of the woods.

Trying to distract herself, she turned back to the cabin and planted her feet in the snow at the bottom of the stairs so she could give the wooden structure a thorough once-over. It *was* old. She'd noted it in the dark the night before. The logs were all worn smooth, and the roof sagged in some places.

But it wasn't falling down at all.

In fact, it looked like someone had made an effort to keep it looking rough while in fact reinforcing it. Near the top of a particularly high snowdrift, several strips of fresh wood had been nailed over top of one area, presumably to fix a hole. Even though the porch was covered in leaves and debris, it was actually quite new, with no sign of rot. The window from which Keira had watched Calloway argue with the armed man had a new frame, too. The front door was marked with pitting and the hinges looked rusty. But Keira knew that it was solid on the inside. The whole interior was airtight.

To the casual observer, the cabin appeared run-down.

Not worth a second glance. But examining it closely, knowing what was on the inside…

"He's not just hiding something," Keira murmured. "He's hiding *himself.*"

She took one more step back. And bumped right into Calloway.

Chapter Thirteen

When Keira stumbled, Graham's hand came up automatically to steady her, then stayed on her elbow.

"For almost four years," he said, his voice full of poorly disguised emotion.

She twisted a little in his grip, but not to get away. Just to face him.

"Since just around when Holly Henderson and her son were killed," Keira stated softly.

He met her gaze. What *had* she seen inside that box? What had she read and then believed? And why the hell did what she thought matter so much more to him than the fact that she'd had a peek into his darkest secrets?

"Calloway?" she prodded.

Graham's heart burned a little inside his chest as he replied. "Yes. You're right. Since they were killed."

"She was your wife, wasn't she?" Keira asked gently.

Graham closed his eyes. "Yes."

"I'm sorry."

"Me, too."

There was a brief pause, and Graham wondered if his agreement had seemed like a confession. An apology. It wouldn't be the first time. But her next words, spoken in a devastated voice, refuted the idea.

"And the little boy…"

"Not my biological son." He opened his eyes again and saw that the pain on her face was genuine. "But I loved him like one. Every day for the last four years, I've ask myself if I could've done something differently. Something to save him."

"Four years…" Keira said. "And you've been on the run ever since."

"Not on the run," Graham corrected bitterly. "Running implies forward movement. I've been hiding, just like you said."

More than hiding.

Graham was stagnant. Stuck in the woods, surrounded by nothing but his own haunted thoughts.

When had he gone from using the cabin as a head-quarters to using it as a home? He'd never meant for it to be permanent. Just a place to stay while he hung back as the details sorted themselves out. As Dave Stark did the legwork and searched for the man responsible for Holly's and Sam's deaths.

Graham had wanted to feel useful. He'd started collecting the newspaper articles, brought in by Dave, and made the scrapbook to keep things linear. He was so sure something in those stories would spark something in *him*, and set off a chain of events that would lead to proving he had nothing to gain from his wife's death.

A motive.

That's what he'd been looking for, hidden under the piles of half-truths.

Instead, the perpetual hounding, the mudslinging, all of the ignorant hatred directed Graham's way, laid out in black and white—and sometimes color, too—left him with the feeling that he would never become a free man. Not truly. How could he, with the details of every mistake he'd ever made on display for the whole world to see?

The collection of articles had the opposite effect that it should have anyway. The finger pointers seemed right instead of wrong. Graham understood why they hounded him, why the accusations came hurling his way. His and Holly's unhappiness was well documented. Hell, sometimes it was on public display. Some of it was on paper. If

Graham had been on their end, he would be giving himself the exact same scrutiny.

Insurmountable.

That word was tossed around a lot and it stood out to Graham particularly. It's what the evidence had become. It's what his circumstances had become. The reason he felt it was better to stay here, locked behind his cabin door, rather than face a jury and tell a story that seemed unlikely, even to him.

When Graham realized just how desperate—how insurmountable—his situation had become, he'd tossed everything into that damned box and pushed it into a corner.

Before long, the media attention died off, and with the waning interest in the murder, the clippings became few and far between. There was a little resurgence on the anniversary date each year, but aside from that, Graham had nothing to add to his collection.

Ignoring the box had become easy.

Except he couldn't ignore it anymore. Keira had opened it. Now she was staring at him, worry and curiosity plain on her face.

"Just ask me," Graham commanded gruffly.

"Ask you what?"

"The same question that every person who ever heard the story, who ever saw the news, who ever read an article in that box has asked me."

Graham braced himself for her version of it.

Did you kill them? Were you angry? In a fight? Was it an accident, maybe?

Instead, she looked him square in the face and said, "I don't think it's my turn, actually."

Graham couldn't keep the surprise from his reply. "Your turn?"

Was she kidding? Deliberately misleading him?

"I wasn't really counting anymore," she told him, her voice serious. "But I think I owe you at least one."

He thought for just a minute. She wasn't the only one who could throw a curveball.

"Are you still a six out of ten?"

"Is that what you really want to know?"

"Right this second...yes."

Keira pursed her lips as if she was really considering it. "Still a six."

Graham frowned. "I don't know if it's better than a six or worse than a six, but I know you're lying again."

"You sound awfully sure of that."

"I *am* awfully sure of it," he countered and took a step closer to her so he could run a thumb over her cheekbone. "When you lie, you get a little spot of red right *here*."

"I do *not*."

"You do."

The color bloomed further, covering the rest of her cheeks. He didn't release her face, and she didn't pull away. Graham stroked the curve of crimson. His palm cupped her cheek, the tips of his long fingers reaching just above her delicate brow and his wrist at her chin.

A perfect fit.

"Ask me something *real*, Calloway," she said. "Something you really want to know."

"Did you know I was up here, when you came?" Graham replied. "Did someone tell you where to find me?"

Keira's eyes widened. "No! Why would I... No."

The blush drained from her face, and Graham knew she was telling the truth. He released her face with a sigh. The realization disappointed him—no, not disappointed. That wasn't the right description. It sent a swarm of angry wasps beating through his chest, and he couldn't pinpoint the reason.

"Let me show you something," he said.

Graham didn't give her a chance to respond. He slid his hand down her shoulder, then her arm, then threaded his fingers through hers. He guided her gently to the back of the house, following an unnamed compulsion.

The box of newspaper clippings sat just where he'd tossed it, right between his wood bin and the rear of the cabin. Graham ignored it.

"Right there," he stated.

He let go of Keira's hand and pointed at a snow-free, almost perfectly circular patch in the snow at the bottom of the cabin. It wasn't huge and only seemed out of place when looking directly at it. Anyone walking by wouldn't even notice the anomaly.

Graham watched as Keira's stare traveled upward and landed on a narrow spigot, sticking out from between two of the log beams. A nearly indiscernible puff of steam floated from the metal cylinder, then dissipated into nothing.

"You could put your hand right into that and it wouldn't even burn," Graham told her.

"What is it?"

"It's what you don't see up on the roof," Graham replied.

Her eyes widened with immediate understanding. "That little bit of steam comes from that big fire in the stove?"

"That. Or from out here."

Graham bent down and lifted up a large, flat stone, revealing a hidden, in-ground fire pit.

"Oh!" Keira exclaimed.

Still not 100 percent certain why he was doing any of it, Graham snapped up the cardboard box and moved it a little closer to the pit.

It was high time he got rid of them. They'd never done him any good anyway. Only served as a reminder of how very little had been done in solving the case.

He slipped the lid off and reached inside for a stack of newspaper. Then he tossed it into the pit.

"I modified the woodstove into a rocket stove with a heating component. So I feed the fire—from inside or from outside—and the fire exhausts into a specialized section of wall, where it then helps to heat the house. It cools significantly before it's finally filtered out, and by the time it gets *here*, it's not much more than vapor," he explained as he grabbed some more paper. "It took a year to do it, and it was worth the time."

Graham reached into the box once more, and as he did, his hand hit something cool and metal. He shoved his hand into the mess a little farther and yanked out a familiar container.

The flask was silver. Real silver, trimmed with real gold.

A little shake told Graham it was still full.

He disregarded the nagging voice in his head that pointed out that it was barely even noon, twisted off the cap and downed a healthy gulp of the amber liquid inside.

The Macallan.

It was a Scotch Graham would never choose for himself. Just like the flask, the drink inside was a gift from his wealthy father-in-law, a man who had never tired of putting Graham into his lower place on the evolutionary scale. A man who perpetuated the witch hunt that drove him underground.

Even the smooth flavor couldn't quite drive away the bitterness that came with it. Which was the very reason he'd dumped it into the box in the first place. To stash away the memories.

He took another swig, then offered it to Keira.

"If that's what you gave me the night before last," she said, "count me out. I don't want to wind up drunk and tied to another bed."

Graham managed to smile through his beard. "I'm afraid I only have the one bed. My alternatives are a wooden chair and a closet full of flannel."

He meant it as a joke, but Keira shot him a serious, searching look. "Or not tying me up at all."

"That would require a certain level of trust."

She didn't avert her gaze. "Does it look like I'm going anywhere?"

And Graham suddenly realized what he was showing her. What he was telling her. Why it made him wish she hadn't found him by accident.

Because it means I really am the one putting her in danger.

"Does it look like I'm offering to let you leave?"

Her eyes went a little wider as she caught the underlying darkness in his voice. He held out the flask again.

"This is plain old whiskey. Liquid courage." He sloshed it around.

"Do I need to be courageous?" Her question made her sound anything but.

"Always," Graham told her firmly.

Keira took the whiskey. Graham waited until she took a sip before he spoke again.

"My great-grandfather built the cabin here for its inaccessibility. He told no one but his son—who told my dad, who told me—it was here. And as close as the resort is, to get to this spot, you need an ATV in the summer or a snowmobile in the winter. Or you need to *crash* in, I guess, like you did. And who wants to make that kind of effort? So no one knows it's here. No one knows *I'm* here."

"No one except for the man with the gun," Keira pointed out.

He met her eyes. "Him. And now you. Which is a bad combination, I think."

"A bad combination?" Keira parroted.

Graham nodded. "They found what was left of your car."

Fear crossed her face, and he knew she was thinking about the consequences of being found. But she covered it quickly. "Who did?"

"The police found it. The man with the gun—Dave Stark—told me."

"The police? They'll come looking for me and—" She stopped abruptly, relief replaced by worry. "That's not good for you, is it?"

"No, it's not."

"Which is what makes it bad for me, too."

Graham nodded slowly. "I can't let them find me up here. And I can't let Dave get to you, either. As much as I rely on him, I'm not sure he'd make the right decision."

That same bit of fleeting fright passed through her features. "Who is he?"

"A friend. And a business associate, I guess. I pay him well to do the things he does for me. Food. Supplies. Information. Someone I trust." Graham paused, wondering if the last was still true. He heaved a sigh, then went on. "He suspects you're here, Keira. If he finds out he's right, I think it will upset the balance between us."

"Just tell him he's wrong."

"It's not that simple. Dave came up here because he was expecting *me* to come to him."

"Why?"

"He found the man we've been looking for—the one who actually killed Holly and Sam. He's come back to Derby Reach." Graham shook his head. "I'm going after him."

Keira stared back at him and swallowed nervously. Damn, how he hated being the source of her fear.

"What are you going to do to him?" she asked.

Graham had a list of what he'd *like* to do, and none of it was pleasant. But he wasn't that man.

"I'm going to get a confession," he said. "I'm going to find irrevocable proof. And I'm going to let Dave take him in."

"That's where you were going when you found me," Keira stated.

"Yes."

"I'm sorry."

"No. I'm sorry, Keira," he said softly.

She took a small step away. "You are? Why? This means what? That you're holding me hostage?"

"Not because I want to."

"You could just let me go," Keira suggested.

"And then what?"

"And then I walk away."

"Keira, just the accident by itself left too much of a chance that the wrong someone will poke their nose around and find my place. Which is what Dave pointed out. And I can't keep you *here*, either."

"I won't tell anyone about the cabin. You could always take me back to the crash site and I'll find my way out from there."

"And you'll do this wearing what? *My* clothes? Or that tiny dress you had on that's barely more than a rag now? And how will you explain these stitches on your leg?"

He knew his words had an edge again, and he tried to soften them by reaching for her. But she jerked away, and that cut to the quick.

"I could tell them I don't remember," she offered, the worry in her tone growing stronger.

"Selective amnesia?"

"Yes."

"Even if that wasn't as ridiculous as it sounds…could you make it believable?" Graham asked. "Could you make them think you'd forgotten me? I sure as hell couldn't forget you, Keira." He didn't give her time to respond to the admission. "Besides that…even if they bought the story, it would spike their curiosity, don't you think? A young woman miraculously survives when her car goes over a cliff. She not only lives, but receives medical attention. You think the cops will just walk away from that?"

"But if you don't let me go…they'll think I'm dead," she whispered.

"I'm aware of that possibility."

"So why *did* you even bother to save me, Calloway, if you're just going to hold me prisoner forever?"

Graham heard the desperation in her voice and when he answered, he heard it in his own, too. "Redemption."

The word hung between them, meaning so much, but saying so little.

Chapter Fourteen

In spite of what she'd said just minutes earlier, Keira found her feet moving away from Graham. She wasn't running. Not really. She just needed to clear her head. But she still ignored him as he called after her.

She knew with absolute certainty that Graham hadn't killed his wife and son. She'd felt no need to ask when prompted.

But she also had a job and a life. Kids in the system who counted on her. And she sure as heck didn't want her family to assume she was dead. Just the thought of her mom hearing about the accident made her heart squeeze.

But she also knew she wouldn't expose his secret location. She couldn't risk his life just to go back to her own. Not if she could avoid it.

Not that Calloway was about to let her go anyway.

And suddenly she *was* running again. Not away, but as a release of emotion. Back around the house and toward the woods.

It only took seconds for Calloway to catch up to her. His arms closed around her waist, and he spun her to face him. She railed against his hold, her small fists driving into his wide chest. He let her do it. His hands ran over her head and through her hair, and he whispered soothing things as she let all the emotion, all the stress of the past few days fly from her body into his.

At last her energy waned, and she stopped fighting him off. It wasn't what she wanted to be doing anyway. She realized that at the same second she realized she was crying. Soft sobs that shook her shoulders.

She inhaled deeply, trying to stop the tears, and Calloway adjusted, sliding his hands to the small of her back. As if she belonged in his arms. As if they belonged together. As she looked up at him, his expression was soft.

"Have you noticed that every time you try to hurt me, you wind up in my arms?" Calloway asked, somehow teasing and serious at the same time.

"Have *you* ever noticed that I keep trying to get away?" Keira breathed, and now she could *feel* the telltale spots of color in her cheeks that went along with the lie.

"You sure about that?"

Keira shook her head, not sure if she was answering his question, or if she was just expressing her frustration with the whole situation.

"I've been meaning to ask you…were you really going to club me to death with that fire iron yesterday?" Calloway asked.

Keira managed a smile. "I was going to aim for your legs. I just wanted to knock you down."

"A peg?" This time, there was no mistaking the teasing tone.

"That, too," Keira confirmed.

He touched her face, cupping her cheek with a familiarity that warmed her insides.

"I just want to keep you safe," he said.

His sincerity almost made her break down again.

"Two days ago," she said, sounding as choked up as she felt, "I woke up thinking I knew where my life was going. *Exactly* where it was going. But today, it's like I woke in someone *else's* life."

"Every day," Calloway murmured, his voice heavy with understanding. "That's the exact feeling I've had every day for four years. It's been a living hell for me. Waking up thinking it will be the one when the truth comes out. Wanting justice. Or, if I'm being honest, craving revenge. I can't even remember if it started that way, or if time somehow changed it. Changed *me*. It's been so long since I even thought about anything else that I'm not sure. Yesterday, I could've had it. Revenge. But I saw you in that car. Pretty and fragile and so still. I pulled you out before I could even think about whether it was the right thing to do, considering my situation. It was instinct, I guess. I wasn't even sure you were still alive until I saw the blood seeping from that wound on your leg. Saving you reminded me that there are other things out there for me. You gave me purpose, Keira."

He said her name like he owned it, and her pulse skittered nervously through her veins.

Had any man ever looked as good as Calloway did right that second, with his brooding eyes and his half-apologetic frown? Had anyone else ever put themselves in danger to save her life? Had she ever been someone's *purpose*?

Even though he wasn't holding her tightly anymore, his eyes still held her pinned in place. And she felt a tether form between them. An inexplicable, inescapable bond from her heart to his.

Keira tilted her head in his direction. His lips were less than an inch from hers. She could feel his warm breath on her cheek. She could see the longing in his eyes. His whole body was tense with need. But he didn't make a move.

Keira was sure it should be her, not him, who was offering the most resistance. After all, it had only been two days since she decided she might date Drew. Might marry him. Though it felt like a lifetime now. And Calloway had been alone for a long time. Four years since his wife died, and who knew how many of those he'd spent in isolation?

But in the end, it was Keira who reached for him.

She threaded her fingers into his thick hair, stifling a little moan at how warm and soft it was, and how the longer bits curled against the back of her hand. She made herself caress it only lightly, afraid he was going to pull away. But he didn't. He leaned into the attention for a moment, pressing the back of his head into her palm. Then he let her explore the contours of his lips in slow motion, her mouth tasting his and igniting something in her that was so hot she was surprised the snow underneath them wasn't melting.

Calloway's hands slid over her shoulders, gently kneading her sore muscles, mindful of her most damaged areas. For the first time, Keira was glad he'd stripped her down without asking. He knew where her bruises and scrapes were, and his fingers were adept at avoiding them. But his hands never stopped moving.

They traversed over Keira's face and smoothed her hair back from her face. They tripped softly over her shoulders and down to her hips, not quite tickling, then slipped between the enormous jacket and the borrowed T-shirt to rest on her hips before sliding out again to creep up to her throat.

It was an incredible feeling, to be touched like that. His palms and the strong pads of his fingers and thumbs laid claim to Keira. They worshipped her. She wanted it to go on forever, and when Calloway finally pulled away, a regretful sigh escaped her lips.

GRAHAM STARED DOWN at Keira, committing her features to his memory. He wanted to keep that worshipful expression—the one that believed in him, that trusted him—in his mind forever.

Kissable lips.

Curved cheeks.

Elegant nose with just the slightest bump, making it interesting.

And her eyes. God, they were stunning.

Green, so vibrant and dark, they looked like the Caribbean Sea after sunset, and in the cold sun, her hair was like a crown of fire.

This time, Graham was perfectly content to let himself have the poetic moment.

In mere days, her fiery temper and moments of vulnerability and misleadingly fragile appearance had gotten under his skin. He could barely wrap his head around how badly he felt the need to protect this girl he still knew so little about. He needed more of her story.

"Tell me what you were running from in that little purple car of yours," he commanded softly. "What was so bad that you were willing to risk your life by going out in that storm?"

She looked away. "Lately the only thing I've been running from is you."

Graham knew she was trying to deflect his question. "Do I need to bring out the list of checks and balances to see whose turn it is to ask a question?"

"No." Her chest rose and fell as she took a breath and went on. "His name is Drew. And I wasn't running *from* him, I was running *to* him."

Graham couldn't keep a hint of jealousy out of his voice. "Boyfriend?"

"Potential."

"Does he appreciate your very recent total and complete disregard for your own life?"

"No."

Jealousy morphed into irritation, which was ridiculous. He couldn't dampen it, though.

"Drew must be a complete idiot," he grumbled.

Keira smiled a small smile. "No. That's not it. He just didn't know I was coming."

Graham touched each upturned corner of her mouth before asking, "So you drove all the way up here, unbeknownst to Drew, based on potential?"

"Kind of."

"Kind of yes, or kind of no?" Graham teased.

"It seems silly now," Keira replied.

"Tell me anyway."

"I thought maybe I was meant to be with him," she admitted. "I thought I saw a sign."

"Fate?"

She blushed. "Something like that. It was dumb, though. I took a chance, and instead of it being a sign, I wound up here."

"You don't think it could *still* be fate?"

The blush worked its way from her cheeks down to her throat. "You think my near-death experience was fate?"

"You know that's not what I meant, Keira. And to tell you the truth...I just straight up don't believe in coincidence, Keira. Fate, though, I'm onboard with, one hundred percent."

The pink of her blush extended from her throat to the top of her chest. Graham had an urge to reach up and unzip the rest of the jacket just to see how far down the pretty color went. He closed his hands into fists to stop himself from doing it.

"So what's fate got lined up for me next, then?" she asked softly.

"Getting you somewhere safe," Graham replied. "Somewhere that the man who killed Holly and Sam wouldn't be able to get anywhere near you."

"I'm sorry, Calloway."

"*You* are?"

She nodded. "If I hadn't been so reckless, taking off in the snowstorm when I did—"

Graham cut her off. "Listen. It was stupid of me to save you, Keira. Risky as hell. But it was *my* risk to take." He paused, released her to run both hands through his hair, then spoke again. "I'm glad I did it. In four years, nothing has seemed as real as the moment you opened your eyes and I realized you were alive."

Keira reached up and put a hand on his face, that same look of awe and appreciation on her, and forget unzipping her coat—it took all of Graham's willpower to stop himself from lifting her up and carrying her straight to his too-lumpy bed.

"In fact," he added gruffly, "you're the realest damned thing I've been around for as long as I can remember. So I don't ever want you to be sorry on my behalf."

She opened her mouth, but Graham didn't get to hear whatever she'd been about to say.

A boom echoed around them, and without taking the time to think, he threw himself into her, knocking her to the ground and shielding her with his much larger body. There was a long moment of silence, and Graham wondered if he was being paranoid. There were minor avalanches in the area all the time.

But as he jumped into a defensive crouch, a second bang—possibly closer than the first—shook the air.

It was a gun, no doubt about it. Not the first time he'd heard one out here, but the first time it had seemed so close.

And it's nowhere near *hunting season.*

Was someone firing *at* them?

It seemed unlikely, but...

A third shot rang through the air, and Graham was certain this one was closer again. Keira moved, then let out a muffled shriek as Calloway slammed into her and knocked her to the ground again.

"Can you do something for me?" he asked in a low voice.

"But—"

"Please."

After a breath, her head bobbed against his chest in assent.

"Stay down until I say otherwise."

He felt her nod again and he eased off her body. He was reluctant to let her go, even a little bit, but he needed to assess where the shots were coming from and figure out if they were targeted.

He scanned what little he could see. It wasn't much. The trees provided a perfect hiding place for a shooter. But Graham could use them, too. He and Keira could move quickly between them, using them for cover. If he could figure out which direction the shots came from, they could duck from tree to tree until they reached the cabin. Then Graham would shield Keira again. He'd grab his rifle and—

The rest of his thought was lost as a fourth shot rang out.

Bloody hell.

Graham yanked Keira to her feet, shoved her to the other side of the wide evergreen, then positioned himself in front of her, shielding her from whatever was about to come next.

Chapter Fifteen

As much as Keira preferred to think of herself as strong, she was indescribably grateful to have Calloway between her and whoever was shooting at them. She was shaking so hard, her teeth were chattering, and Calloway was reassuringly solid.

Solid, yes. But not bulletproof, pointed out a small voice in her head.

Her hand slid up to his back, and she opened her mouth to remind him of that fact. But without looking, his hand closed on her wrist, stopping her midway. As if he could sense her movement before she even followed through.

The air was eerily silent now, and they stood like that for what felt like an eternity.

Is it over? Keira wondered.

Calloway spoke in a hushed voice, his eyes still scanning the forest. "You all right back there?"

Keira took a measured breath. "If it wasn't for someone potentially shooting at me in the middle of a forest... Nine out of ten on the sliding scale."

There was a pause, then, in spite of the situation, Calloway let a wry chuckle. "Are you going to tell me what gets me that all-important tenth point? Or am I going to die not knowing?"

"One small thing," Keira breathed.

"Which is?"

"Just keep us alive."

"Nothing would make me happier."

There was another long silence, then Keira asked, "Do you think someone found you?"

He spoke right beside her ear. "I don't know. If they

did… Keira. Did you mean what you said about trusting me?"

She managed a nod.

"Good. Because I need you to do something for me."

"What?"

"Run."

Keira blinked. "What?"

"If someone *is* firing at us, it's me they're after," Calloway stated. "I'm going to go in one direction, into the woods. You're going to count to ten and go in the other, toward the cabin."

"I'm not going to do that!"

"Yes, Keira. You are."

He didn't wait for her to argue anymore. He took off across the snow, leaving Keira counting to ten silently, a little more dread filling her with each number.

GRAHAM LOPED OVER the terrain, waiting for another shot to come his way and cursing his own stupidity. He'd left them exposed. He'd put Keira's life in danger even though he'd been trying to do the opposite.

He didn't bother to hide as he dodged from tree to tree. If the shooter was looking for him, he wanted his undivided attention. And to put some distance between Keira and the bad end of the gun.

"C'mon," he growled. "Follow *me*. Shoot at *me*."

The woods were silent except for the sound of his own feet hitting the ground. He finally slowed, acknowledging that maybe—a big maybe—he'd been overreacting. That possibly some off-season hunter had taken advantage of the aftermath of the snowstorm and was on his side of the mountain in search of some big game.

But what if he wasn't?

What if, somehow, the man who'd taken Holly and Sam from him found him? Found *them*?

Graham moved faster, getting angrier at himself by the second. Which is why he didn't notice the armed man in front of him until they were just a foot apart.

When he did spot him, Graham didn't stop to think. He just reacted, determined to use his strength to overpower the assailant, gun or no gun. It wasn't until he'd already pounced on the other man and smacked the weapon away that he recognized him.

Dave.

"What the *hell* is going on?" Graham demanded.

His friend was sucking wind, and when he opened his mouth, all that came out was a groan.

Graham eased off. "Explain yourself."

"Talk. To. You," Dave wheezed.

"And you were getting my attention by shooting at me?"

"Not. Me."

"Who?"

"Don't. Know."

Graham resisted an urge to shake a proper answer from him friend.

"Heard shots," Dave offered, still inhaling rapidly.

"Did you see the shooter?"

He finally seemed to have caught his breath, shaking his head. "Maybe it was a hunter. But it doesn't matter. You have to admit that it's too risky to stay here now. I can tell from your face that you know it."

Graham exhaled. Keira was safe. At least for the moment.

He opened his mouth to ask what Dave was doing back so soon—what he wanted to talk about—but before Graham could get an explanation, an engine sputtered to life in the distance, and both men turned toward the sound.

KEIRA TIGHTENED HER already strained grip on the handlebars of the snowmobile. The seat was icy under her bare legs, but she ignored the discomfort. She needed to get the vehicle moving, to get it to Calloway. She'd run blindly, obeying this command even though so many parts of her mind—of her heart—protested against it. But halfway back to the cabin, she'd spotted the big machine. It was not quite hidden behind a low bush, and it seemed like a godsend. A way to get both of them to safety. Quickly.

"How hard can it be?" she muttered aloud to herself as she looked over the components another time. "Throttle. Choke. Kill switch if I need it."

She squeezed the gas, just a little, and the machine bucked as the skis snuck to the snow.

"Easy," she cautioned, not sure if she was still speaking to herself or if she was talking to the snowmobile.

She supposed either would work.

Keira climbed off, moved to the front of the vehicle and kicked away some of the snow blocking the way, then climbed back on.

She put a little more pressure on the throttle, and the machine jerked forward hard enough to send her flying against the handlebars. She held on for dear life as it rode forward a few feet, then stalled.

Damn.

Tears threatened to form in her eyes, and Keira forced them back. She didn't have time to waste being upset. Angrily, she pulled out the choke, yanked on the pull starter as hard as she could and willed the stupid thing to cooperate.

It roared to life, and this time when she closed her fingers over the throttle, she did it softly. The snowmobile slid over the snow at a crawl. It growled a little as she held it steady.

Apparently her options were very slow or very fast. No in between.

So, fast it was.

Keira gritted her teeth and squeezed.

GRAHAM WATCHED IN awed horror—and with more than a little bit of admiration, too—as the enormous piece of machinery came tearing around the corner. Keira sat atop it, her stance awkward, her eyes almost closed and her hair flying out behind like a blazing red cape.

Her beautiful determination was clear, even through her obvious fear.

Then she spied him, and her eyes were no longer half-shut. They were so wide that their green hue was visible even from where Graham sat.

She seemed to clue in at the same second that Graham did that she was on a crash course, headed straight for him and Dave.

Sure enough, she tipped the handlebars, trying to angle away from them. Her motions became frantic, her arms flailing. Then the snowmobile bucked, and Keira was suddenly barely hanging on, her legs tossed to the side and her hands gripping the bars. The machine bounced along wildly as if it had a mind of its own.

Almost too late, Graham realized that the snarling vehicle was still aimed in his direction. At the last second, he dove toward Dave and shoved the other man out of the line of fire.

He wasn't swift enough to save himself.

The last thing Graham saw before the snowmobile clipped him, and his head exploded in pain, was the terrified look on Keira's face as she flew up and sailed through the air.

I'm sorry, he thought weakly.

But there was nothing he could do as the world blurred and he collapsed to the ground.

Chapter Sixteen

Keira landed hard against a raised snowbank, taking the brunt of the hit straight in the stomach. All of the air left her lungs in one gust, and abruptly she couldn't breathe. She couldn't inhale or exhale or force the oxygen into her body no matter how badly she wanted.

I'm going to die. Calloway's going to die. And it's going to be my fault.

How cruel was *that* for fate?

For a second, the world stayed dark.

Then it was full of spotted pinpricks of light.

And at last, Keira felt her chest rise and fall, and the white-covered ground evened out in her vision.

She pulled herself across the snow until she reached Calloway's still body.

Please let him be okay, she prayed, her heart banging against her ribs so hard it hurt.

She dropped her head to Calloway's chest. It rose and fell evenly, and when Keira put her fingers to his throat, his pulse was strong.

Thank God.

And then a hand landed on her shoulder and Keira remembered they weren't alone.

She brought her eyes up nervously and, through her tears, stared at the man above her.

He looked rough and dangerous, with a cut in the corner of one lip, and one of his eyes looked almost black. Like the kind of man who would be firing a weapon in the woods.

"Ms. Niles," he said.

He knows your name.

And for a second, he looked vaguely familiar.

No. Impossible. She knew no one who matched his description.

"Ms. Niles," he repeated, this time a little more urgently. "Stay calm."

His words had the opposite effect that they should have, and panic set in.

She had to get away.

Keira's eyes flicked around the clearing in search of safety. Of protection.

The snowmobile.

Too complicated.

The cabin.

Too far.

A glint of silver in the snow.

Yes. The gun.

Keira sprang up and hurled herself past the worse-for-wear man in front of her and dove for the weapon. She caught sight of the expression on his face—first full of surprise, then understanding—and he moved, too.

But Keira was faster.

Her hands closed on the gun and for a second she was thoroughly triumphant.

Thank God.

Then the blond man was on her, one hand wrapped around her ankle and the other clawing to get the weapon away from her.

"Don't do something you'll regret," he said through clenched teeth.

"I won't," she promised, then drew back her free foot and slammed it into his chest.

He flew back and Keira leaped up once more. With a sharp stab of remorse about leaving Calloway where he was, she took off at a limping run.

The thump of feet on snow told her that the man was following her. And gaining ground.

C'mon, c'mon, she urged herself.

She was close enough to the cabin that it was a viable option now.

Come! On!

Pushing through the throbbing pain in her thigh, Keira forced herself to keep going. And at last she reached the wooden patio. But as her hand found the doorknob, her head swiveled and she saw that her pursuer had caught up to her.

She spun, cocked the gun and pointed it at the blond man just as one of his feet met the bottom step.

"You're making a mistake," he told her, looking far less frightened than she thought he should.

"I do know how to fire this thing," Keira warned.

"You might want to rethink actually doing it, Ms. Niles."

"People love a good self-defense story," she retorted.

"Maybe. But the law rarely favors people who fire on those working with the police. Especially when they're shooting while in the home of a known criminal."

The police? A criminal?

Keira eyed the other man disbelievingly. Maybe the last part made sense.

Calloway *was* on the run from the police, after all. But nothing about the man standing in front of her screamed law enforcement. No uniform. No readily proffered ID.

No. He has to be lying.

"You expect me to believe that you're a cop?" she asked. "And Calloway is what, then…the robber?"

"This is hardly a game, Ms. Niles. My name is David Stark and—"

The rest of his statement was lost as Keira finally clued in to who this man was.

Dave Stark.

Calloway's friend. His business associate. Whom he'd known for years. And trusted.

A cop?

"I know who you are," Keira said.

"Then you know Graham and I are friends."

"Calloway told me about your business arrangement."

"But he didn't happen to mention that I work for the Derby Reach PD?"

"If you're a cop, and you knew he was here, why haven't you just arrested him?" Keira countered.

"Because I've been his friend for far longer than I've been a policeman. And because I've been helping him for as many years as he's been on the run."

"Prove it," Keira challenged.

"Fine. I have three things in my pocket," he said. "My badge, my driver's license and a pay stub to prove the ID is real. I'd like to reach in and get them. Do you mind if I do that?"

"Go for it," Keira conceded.

Slowly—as if *she* was the unpredictable one—he unzipped his jacket, pulled it open to give Keira a view of what he was doing, and stuck his hand into a side pocket. Just as slowly, he dragged out a little leather case and held it up. The front flapped open, revealing a gold badge.

He closed it up again, then traded it for a wallet, which he held out to Keira.

"*You* take the stuff out," she ordered.

He complied, first flipping out the plastic-covered license, then unfolding a piece of paper.

Without letting the gun go, Keira moved just close enough that she could read each of them. And as much as she wanted them to be fake, she was sure they were legitimate. "David Rodney Stark. Employee number 102 of the Derby Reach PD." Even Keira's desperate brain couldn't come up with a reasonable explanation for carrying around a phony pay stub.

Her body sagged.

Dammit.

Calloway had been paying a cop to…do what exactly? Bring him mushroom soup and information? Why was the other man even agreeing to it?

Then a low groan came from behind the man in question, and Keira traded in her concern about the cop for concern about Calloway, who was half standing, half slumping on the snow.

GRAHAM LET DAVE slide an arm across his back and guide him into the cabin.

His attention, though, was on Keira.

Her hair was still wild from the crazy ride on the snowmobile. Even though she held a gun in her hand, she'd sucked her bottom lip between her teeth and looked like she was trying not to cry.

Because of you.

If he'd had the energy and the time, he would've cursed himself out for somehow managing to twist the situation so that instead of him worrying about her, she was worrying about him.

But you don't *have time*, he reminded himself. *And you can't protect her, get the cabin ready in case you don't make it back and keep your own body breathing at the same time.*

Which somehow seemed important now. Guns-out revenge wasn't an option. Not if he wanted a chance at something he hadn't thought about in a long time. A future.

So he spoke, and he wasn't sure if it was because of his recent brush with unconsciousness or if it was because he was saying something he really wished he didn't *have* to say, but his words sounded hollow and far away.

"Dave, you need to take Keira off the mountain. Now."

Keira stiffened and her mouth dropped open as if she was going to argue, but Dave beat her to it.

"The crash is all over the news, Graham. Which is what I came here to talk to you about. They're looking for a body, trying to identify the driver. What do you think they're going to do when they find out she's not so dead, after all?"

"You're not going to let them find out. You're going to take her to your hotel and stay there."

His friend ran a frustrated hand through his hair. "I came here to convince *you* to come with me. To remind you again that everything we've been working for is about to slip through our fingers. Not to transport some girl you just met, keep her hidden for you and *still* not accomplish what we've been trying to accomplish for the last four years."

Graham met his friend's eyes. "I'm asking for two days, Dave."

"This has nothing to do with her. You said it yourself just two days ago."

"What other choice is there?"

"Let the cops find her."

"And if they find out who she's been with? If that info gets back to the wrong person before I catch up to him?"

"Graham, something's gotta give. I'm tired of chasing down bad leads and using resources I have no right to be using. I'm sick of making excuses to my wife and not seeing my kids and worrying all the time that I'm going to get caught helping you. Four years is a long time to live like this. I thought we were done. Now I feel like we're starting up all over again."

Graham's temper flared. "I *lost* my wife, Dave. I *lost* my kid. And you come up here and expect me to lose someone else because you think things have been too hard on *you*? I won't take the risk that Ferguson might get ahold of Keira, too, and use her as leverage. The only way to ensure her safety is to take her away from here."

"You could turn yourself in instead."

Graham's gut clenched. "Turn myself in?"

"You'd rather have me help you with a kidnapping?"

"Stop!"

The emphatic protest came from Keira, who was shaking her head and fixing Graham with an achingly sweet glare. "Calloway isn't turning himself in to save me. He sure as hell didn't kidnap me. And you guys need to quit talking about me like I'm not here and not capable of making my own decisions."

"I can't let you stay here," Graham told her.

"And you can't make me leave," she replied.

He moved closer and lifted a hand to Keira's cheek. "You *have* to do this. It's the only thing that's going to keep you out of danger. Let Dave take you somewhere safe. I promise you, I won't be far behind. I'll take care of what needs to be taken care of and I'll come for you."

"And if you get killed in the process?" Her voice shook. "Calloway, I—"

Graham leaned down and cut her off with a kiss, not caring if Dave was watching. She brought her hands up and buried them in his hair, and he didn't let her go until her could feel her heart thumping through both layers of their clothes.

He leaned away. "I have a damned good reason to stay alive, Keira."

"Two days?" she asked breathlessly.

Graham exhaled and made a promise he hoped he could keep. "Forty-eight hours, no more."

Get in, get Mike Ferguson and get back to Keira. Then he'd figure out his next move.

Minutes later, he bundled her up—thoroughly if not comfortably—and was leading her to the snowmobile.

There he kissed her again, this time tenderly, then helped her straddle the vehicle.

Dave looked unhappy, but Graham didn't care. His eyes were stuck on Keira's slim form, and they stayed there as the snowmobile roared to life and the two of them sped off into the thick woods.

Chapter Seventeen

Keira quickly gave up trying to keep a reasonable amount of physical space between herself and Officer David Stark. Her helmeted face was pressed between his shoulder blades, and her legs squeezed his hips. She rode that way not because she was any more comfortable with him than she had been since the first second she'd laid eyes on him, but because he navigated the mountain with reckless abandon.

Trees whipped by in a blur. Snow kicked up and into Keira's shirt, then melted there. It made the wind hit her that much harder and made it that much more necessary to crush herself into Dave's back.

She was holding on to him out of necessity. And she wasn't happy about it.

The only good thing about it was that it helped to keep her mind from everything else. She deliberately blocked out her thoughts and focused on the scenery instead. It was nothing more than a blur of white, and they rode for so long that Keira was sure they were going to run out of gas.

Parts of her were frozen. Parts of her ached. And *all* of her wished she could go back in time to before her accident so she could just go back to being herself. No gunshots, no makeshift stitches, no crazy ache in her chest over a man she just met.

But her concern for Calloway's well-being overrode her efforts. And try as she might, Keira couldn't shake the fact that the most pressing of her worries was that he might never be able to keep his promise and come to her.

So maybe it wasn't that the accident skewed her view. Maybe she'd known all along that Drew wasn't right for her. Maybe she hadn't really been leading a full life at all. It just took crashing into the Mountain Man's life to reveal it.

Somehow, she was sure she could pick any moment from the past few days and attach more meaning to it than she could to any other part of her life.

So, no. She *wouldn't* erase the accident. Because without it—without Drew and her stupid trip to the chalet to make her move—she wouldn't have almost died and she wouldn't have had the best kisses in the world with the most interesting man she'd ever met.

And yes. She'd take those little glimpses of heart-pounding excitement over another twenty-four years of never realizing what she was missing.

As she came to that conclusion, a final blast of snow flew from underneath the snowmobile, and she and Dave ground to a halt.

The seed of doubt in Keira's mind grew as she leaned away from him and took in her surroundings. The trees were well behind them, and there was nothing but a snow-covered hill in front of them.

Keira swung her legs off the snowmobile uncertainly, and Dave did the same, but with far more self-assurance. Then he tipped his goggles to his head and helped her pull off the borrowed helmet.

"Here's the deal, Ms. Niles," he said, his voice sounding extraloud now that the roar of the engine had cut off. "On the other side of that crest is the side road that leads into Mountain View Village. If we head into town, we might be walking straight into a sea of press. But what *I* want is to avoid them—and everyone else—if at all possible."

Keira stared at him. "You're not taking me to the hotel?"

"I want the same thing you do—to protect Graham. And to do that, I think we should steer clear of the resort town altogether. Get you somewhere safe and sound and far away from here," Dave told her.

"But Graham—"

"Hasn't thought this all the way through. Up here, I can't keep you hidden. Not effectively. Too many people are looking for you. If I take you off the mountain completely, I at least stand a chance of keeping you out of the limelight."

Keira waited for him to add something else about Calloway, something hopeful. But he just handed her the helmet again.

"We all set, then?" he asked.

So Keira nodded. She didn't see that she had much of a choice.

As much as Graham wanted to toss aside everything and throw on his snowshoes and start moving, he knew better.

Four years of waiting had taught him the value of patience, and as desperate as he was to get to Keira, his experience told him that he needed to be prepared. There was no way for him to avoid going back to the place where it all started. But if he had to do it, he could do it right.

He started with his hair, hacking it to nearly respectable length, revealing far more gray than he'd had when he went underground. Then he moved on to his face, shearing it so that the formerly bristly beard was gone completely. When he was done, the skin underneath it was almost raw with the effort.

He bathed head to toe, and though he kept himself fairly well-groomed anyway, he made an extra effort this time to scrub away every ounce of dirt. There was no sign of grime under his nails, no campfire scent lingering on his skin.

Toss on a white coat, Graham thought humorlessly as he gave himself a final once-over, *and I might be able to go straight back to the office.*

Right then, though, he laid out something far more practical. Snow-proof, waterproof pants. Lined, but not so thick that they would impede movement. On top, he'd wear a matching coat with good breathability and a removable interior. Both items were unused—Graham would have to rip the tags off before putting them on—bought long ago with the assumption that one day, he would have to abandon his home. Underneath those, he'd put on running gear, completely practical and also in new condition.

He had sharp jeans, a still-in-the-plastic T-shirt, and just in case, a dress shirt and tie, ready to go into his bag.

The cabin itself had been transformed, too. Graham boarded up the windows, careful to use well-worn pieces of wood and nails that had seen better days. He tore apart the bottom step in a way that made it appear to be natural rot, and punched a hole through the front part of the deck, too. He used a shovel to throw up several mounds of snow in front of the house, as well, and another snowstorm or two later, they'd look completely natural.

When Graham glanced up at the sky, he thought he probably wouldn't have to wait long for Mother Nature to help him out with that.

Finally, he stood back to survey the house once more, looking for any other signs that would give away its most recent use. He was satisfied that there were none, and anyone who thought it was worth getting past the snow and the broken patio would be sorely disappointed when they got inside. Everything that *could* be burned, *had* been burned. From the mattress to the curtains to—regretfully—the food, it had all been incinerated.

Only the most necessary items had been saved, and they fit neatly into Graham's backpack beside his extra clothes. *Be Prepared. Back to the Boy Scout analogy.*

FROM THE MOMENT Graham drafted his to-do list, to the second he completed it all, took less than four hours.

The sky was dark, the stars a speckled tableau above his head, and he was ready.

Traveling at night wasn't for everyone.

But to quote Dave, this is me *we're talking about.*

Graham turned away from his home, not even bothering with a second look. He'd once walked away from a thirty-year-long life. This was nothing.

THE GRUELING HIKE brought Graham all the way to the edge of the resort town. He was covered in sweat, aching and no less determined.

He kicked out a shallow hole in the snow, then stripped off his travel gear in favor of his jeans and T-shirt. He stuffed his cash and falsified ID into his jacket pockets, and filled the hole with his discarded items and marked the spot with a distinctly shaped rock as big as his head. Graham was sure he could locate it again, but there was nothing personal left in the pack, so if found, it wouldn't arouse suspicion in the finder.

It wasn't ideal, but it would do. It had to.

From his spot, the lights were too close and bright enough to make his head hurt.

No time for self-pity, he growled silently and stepped back into the trees.

Graham traipsed up the road, mentally recalling the name of the hotel Dave used each month.

I'm not going to go in, he told himself.

He just wanted to make sure they got there before he found a way down to the city.

He paused at a large overblown map at the top of Main Street. He found the place—Rocky Side Hotel—quickly. As he scanned the location, he realized that even if he skirted the perimeter streets all the way in, he'd still have to pass through a very busy area in order to reach the hotel itself. He cursed the fact that Dave had chosen somewhere so public as his monthly stopping point. Mountain View had plenty of more out-of-the-way places to stay. Romantic bungalows. Three-star hotels. The only place more attention-drawing would've been the chalet itself.

Graham forced himself to keep going.

It was well past any reasonable hour to be out on foot anywhere else, but in Mountain View the second the sun went down, the skiers became partiers and they stayed out until it rose again. As a result, even keeping to the edge of town didn't stop Graham from running into people.

After so many years in isolation, it was overwhelming.

So he was nervous. Far more on edge than he should have been.

Maybe he *would* go in. Maybe he'd just check on Keira, then see if Dave had a reasonable line on a vehicle.

And to breathe.

He knew it was ridiculous to assume that someone would know him, but that didn't make the feeling go away. When he finally had no choice but to head into the busy square in front of Dave's hotel, and a grinning club rat caught and held his eye, he expected to see some flicker of recognition. Some frightened spark that said, *Oh, that's him. That's the man accused of killing his wife.*

When he tried to cross a street a little too soon and a stranger grabbed his shoulder to stop him from falling in front of a party bus, he just about punched the Good Samaritan in the face. Even after Graham stumbled through an apology, the wary look didn't disappear from the man's eyes.

Graham didn't breathe easily until he reached the building with the large hand-painted sign that declared it as the correct hotel. His hand closed on the metal door and he pulled. It didn't budge, and when Graham took a step back he saw why.

The Rocky Side Hotel was closed for renovations.

What the hell?

Graham squinted at the sign giving the closure dates. Dave hadn't been there at all. Not in the past thirty days anyway.

So where had he taken Keira? Another hotel?

No.

A sinking feeling hit Graham straight in the gut.

He must have taken her home.

What for? To give her up, like he'd wanted to? For a misguided sense of right and wrong?

Graham reached up to yank on his hair, but came away empty-handed. It was too short for the habit to be satisfying.

His friend *knew* how much danger Keira would be in if Ferguson learned about her. To bring her that much closer, even if he thought it was because he was doing the right thing...

Graham shook his head and took another few steps away from the closed hotel and smacked into an unsuspecting passerby. The guy stammered an apology, but Graham cut him off by grabbing his arm.

"What's the easiest way to get out of town?" he demanded harshly.

The stranger's eyes widened. "Now?"

"Yes, now."

"It's two in the morning."

"I'm aware."

The man scratched his head, looking drunkenly puzzled, then grinned brightly. "Truck stop!"

"Truck stop?"

"Yeah. The delivery guys come and go all night so they don't mess with the tourist mojo during the day. Six blocks of back alley will get you there."

Graham released his arm. "Thanks."

"No problem."

The partier stumbled away, and Graham moved quickly.

Chapter Eighteen

Keira stared out the window of Dave's car, blurry-eyed. The hours it took to drive from the mountain to Derby Reach had passed quickly, mostly because she'd spent them sleeping. Or *pretending* to be asleep so she wouldn't have to make small talk with the man in the driver's seat.

Now they'd stopped.

But they weren't anywhere near her apartment. It only took Keira a single second of peering into the dim pre-dawn to clue in that they *were* somewhere familiar, though.

"This is my parents' house," she said, sounding as puzzled as she felt.

"I know," Dave replied.

"Why are we here? How did you even know where it was?"

"I looked up a few details about you. One of the perks of being a cop. And as much as I hate the idea, Ms. Niles, I need to leave you alone for a bit to take care of a few details. I figured it was safer to bring you here than it was to drop you at your own place. I hope you don't mind."

Keira's head buzzed with worry. And actually, she *did* mind. It felt like an intrusion of privacy. But she could hardly complain about the policeman doing his job. Assuming that's what he *was* doing. And when had he had time to look up the details of her life? He'd barely left her alone for longer than a bathroom break.

"My own apartment would've been fine," she said a little stiffly.

But Dave shook his head. "And take the chance that some well-meaning neighbor spots you and sees the news and reports it?"

"Right," Keira replied uncertainly.

"Besides. Your parents' house is empty, and this neighborhood is known for its privacy."

A sliver of worry crept up Keira's spine. Had she mentioned her parents' monthlong vacation? Or was that another detail he'd uncovered in his miniature investigation into her life?

And if he can find out those things in a few hours, how come he couldn't prove Calloway's innocence in four full years?

Dave put his hand on her arm, and she flinched.

"If you're worried about Graham finding you…don't. He's as resourceful as he is single-minded. And if things go wrong, having you here instead of at home will give me the extra time I need to get you out safely."

The sliver became a spike. "Wrong?"

"I'm not trying to scare you, Ms. Niles. I want you to feel safe and secure. But I'd be lying if I didn't admit that in the past, Graham has lashed out on the people he thought wronged him. There was a time when I would've called him dangerous. It's been years since he's done anything truly violent, but it's also been years since he had any reason to. He won't give up until either he's taken care of the threat, or until taking care of the threat becomes more dangerous than the threat itself. I don't want you in the middle of that."

Keira opened her mouth, then closed it again. She wasn't sure she agreed with Dave's analysis. Calloway might very well be single-minded, but it was only out of necessity. Who wouldn't want to prove their innocence in a case like this one? And as far as self-preservation was concerned…she was living proof that he was capable of caring more about others' safety than he did about his own.

She had a funny feeling that in spite of what Dave

claimed to the contrary, he *was* trying to scare her. She just wasn't sure why.

"Can I trust you, Ms. Niles?" the policeman asked abruptly.

"Trust me?" she replied.

"To lie low until I've done what needs to be done to ensure that there's no danger to you. Or to the people close to you."

His words had an ominous undertone to them, and Keira bit back an urge to point out that leaving her alone seemed counterproductive to keeping her safe. And to be honest, she was just plain eager to be rid of the man.

"I can do that," she agreed.

Dave seemed satisfied. He opened the glove box and pulled out a business card, which he handed to her.

"This is my direct number," he said. "If you have any problems at all, call me first. Do *not* contact anyone else. Do *not* reach out. And most importantly, do *not* tell anyone where you are."

He squeezed her hand. She let him hold it just long enough to not seem unappreciative.

"Thank you," she murmured.

"Another thing," Dave said. "If you doubt what I've said, keep this in mind. Your car might've crashed, but the fire that consumed it was man-made. The cops have ruled it arson. And we both know there was only one man up there."

Keira almost laughed. But then she caught sight of the serious look on Dave's face. Yes, he was still definitely trying to scare her.

Except for the first time, she was also sure he was telling the truth.

"Like I said, just keep in mind that he's the type of man who will cover up evidence at someone else's expense."

She gave him a level stare. "I'll do that."

Then she pulled away, and as she did, Dave reached for his own seat belt. Keira realized he was probably planning on accompanying her up the driveway. It was the last thing she wanted.

"It's all right," she said quickly. "I'm fine by myself."

"I'd feel better if you let me walk you to the door."

She shook her head and forced what she hoped looked like a genuine smile. "I'm lying low, remember? The last thing we want is my parents' neighbors talking because a strange man is dropping me off. If you come up, they'll have a fit."

Dave frowned, but Keira swung open the door before he could argue. Then she slammed it shut and ran up the driveway. Without looking back, she retrieved the key hidden under her mom's near-dead potted plant and let herself into the house. She counted to sixty, peeked out the curtains and finally let out a breath when she saw that Dave's car was completely out of sight.

GRAHAM JERKED HIS head up from the condensation-laden window, his hands closing tensely on the jacket between his thighs. He wasn't sure how long he'd been in the restless, close-to-sleep state, but the city lights were visible on the horizon.

"You all right?"

The question—asked in a voice that sounded full of genuine concern—came from the senior-aged trucker who'd agreed to bring Graham down the mountain.

Graham cleared his throat and did his best to answer like a normal person would.

"Fine. Just tired."

"Might wanna ease up on the death grip of the coat, then," said the trucker.

"Thanks for the tip." Graham's reply was dry, but he did let go and force his hands to his knees instead.

The driver was silent for a long moment, staring out the windshield.

Maybe you really are *incapable of normal*, Graham thought.

Seconds later, the trucker confirmed his suspicions. "I don't know what you're running from—or to—and I don't want to. But if you act that suspicious everywhere you go, you can bet the cops'll be on you before you can demand to have your rights read."

"Trust me. I'm so far past the reading-the-right part of things that it's not even funny."

The trucker laughed anyway. "Makes me glad that this is the end of the line, my friend."

He nodded out the front window. A brightly lit truck stop beckoned just a mile or so ahead. Graham knew the spot. It was just outside Derby Reach.

For the first time since his flight from the cabin, he hesitated. It was there that his original escape started. Five hundred and fifty dollars slipped to another trucker—one far less friendly than the one who sat beside him now—to take him 482 miles.

He'd worked hard to put the town behind him.

Graham had been smart about his movements. Careful. He'd created a trail. Money here and there. Verifiable appearances at gas stations and hotels and grocery stores. One overblown fight in a bowling alley and a faked slipup of credit card use in a city on the other side of the country. Until he deliberately tapered off in his endeavors to be seen. It only took four months to create the perfect wild-goose chase. Two months after that, he was well settled at the cabin. Dave knew where he was, but no one else was looking in the right place. No one was even *thinking* about the right place.

Now I know how they felt, he thought grimly. *Clueless.* Where would the other man have taken Keira?

Not to her home. Too obviously risky.

Even Dave would know that.

Graham stared down at his hands, considering all the options.

But not to his own home, either. Keira would never agree to that.

Dave would want her to feel safe. Comfortable. Familiar.

Family.

Had Keira mentioned any? Graham couldn't remember, but his gut told him Dave would've found out. Then what?

"Too many damned possibilities," Graham muttered.

"Buddy?"

Graham's gaze flicked back to the trucker. "Sorry."

"Don't apologize for being scared. We all got stuff to worry us."

Scared?

Graham opened his mouth to deny it, but when he met the trucker's eyes, and the other man gave him a knowing nod, he realized it was true. He *was* scared. For himself, a little. For Keira, a lot.

He held in a growl.

Twenty years, he'd known Dave. Twenty damned years. More than two-thirds of his life. He knew—more than most—that Dave's priorities could get a little skewed at times, but Graham would never have thought he'd do something like this.

Whatever this *is.*

It didn't really matter anyway. Graham was responsible for what had happened to Keira. What might happen to her still. Damn, how he hated this helpless feeling.

I have to save her.

But first he had to find her.

"You sure you're all right?" the trucker asked.

Graham managed a forced smile. "Six out of ten."

The big rig came to a rumbling halt then, and the diner loomed in front of them, and Graham couldn't decide if it felt like a starting point, or the end. He just knew he *needed* it to be the former. Would force it that way if he had to.

"Have they got public internet in there?" Graham asked.

The trucker shrugged, reached into his pocket and handed over a smartphone.

"Not in there. But I've got it out here," he said. "Probably less traceable anyway. You can feel free to clear the browser history after, too."

Graham punched a button on the screen, then paused. One of the last things he wanted was to make this man culpable for his mistakes. The phone became a lead weight in Graham's hand.

"If I told you that you were aiding a fugitive, would you still hand this over?" he asked.

The driver met his eyes evenly. "Been working the routes for forty-two years. Picked up a lot of hitchhikers. Means I'm pretty damned good at two things—navigating the roads and navigating people. If you're one of the bad guys, I'll hand over my license right this second."

"Thanks," Graham replied gruffly.

He fumbled with the phone for a second, but in a couple of taps, he had a home address for H. Gerald and Karen Niles.

And it gave him another chill. Their house was just a block from the home where he'd lived with Holly and Sam.

He shoved aside the increasing concern and, as suggested, he swiped away the browser history before handing the phone back. If nothing else, it gave the man plausible deniability.

The trucker gave him one more long stare. "You sure you don't want to walk away from whatever this is? As soon as I'm done my pie, I'm turning left and going straight for a hundred more miles."

An image of Keira—worried eyes, fiery eyes, soft, caring eyes—flashed through Graham's mind, and any doubt fled once again.

"Thanks," he said. "But some things are more than worth the risk."

The trucker smiled smugly, as if he was expecting the answer and knew just what Graham was talking about. "She must be one hell of a girl."

"Damn right," Graham agreed and hopped from the truck.

A hell of a girl in a hell of a situation. And only another five miles away.

Chapter Nineteen

Keira paced the length of her parents' living room, wishing she could shake the restless feeling that kept her moving.

Everything she normally found comforting about the house was putting her on edge.

The food she'd taken from the freezer, heated according to the note taped to the lid, then eaten, sat heavily in her stomach. It was shepherd's pie. One of her favorites and it had never given her such bad heartburn.

She'd bathed. But the light lavender-scented body wash she'd used reminded her of her mother and made Keira lonely for her. Why had she promised Dave Stark that she wouldn't call anyone? Just hearing her mom's voice, listening to her complain about the heat or the way the humidity made her hair puff out, would've helped. Even if she didn't tell her mom anything, even if she just sat quietly while her mom spoke…it would've gone a long way to ease her mind. But she didn't want to endanger her parents. She didn't even want to risk it.

And now that she was clean and fed, Keira didn't know what to do with herself.

The quiet—so different from the perpetual noise of her thin-walled, one-bedroom apartment—was stifling. And each time an unexpected sound cut into the silence, whether it was the rumble of the furnace or the bark of a neighbor's job, Keira jumped.

Even the twelve snow globes—one for each Christmas they'd spent in Disneyland when she was a kid—that lined the fireplace mantel offered little comfort.

And the policeman's actions and decision had done

nothing to ease her worry. He'd created even more questions for her than she'd had before.

Keira sighed, overwhelmed by frustration. For a second, she considered whether or not she should go against her word and sneak over to her apartment. Even if it was just to grab some of her own clothes.

She plucked at the pajamas borrowed from her mom's drawer, wondering if they were part of what kept her from feeling comfortable. From feeling like herself.

She picked up the first snow globe from the mantel and shook the little white flakes over Mickey's head. It was a mistake. The snowy display sent her mind immediately to Calloway.

Was he okay?

Keira set the snow globe down, and her gaze found her parents' antiquated computer in the corner of the living room.

Dave had asked her not to contact anyone. But he hadn't asked her not to research anything on her own.

A little guiltily, she slid out her dad's office chair from its dusty spot under the mahogany desk, sat her still-aching rear end in the cool leather and booted up the old machine. It took several minutes for the thing to chug to life—just enough time to chew one pink nail to a ridiculously short length and to assess whether or not she was being a little crazy.

A police officer had just all but warned her outright how dangerous Calloway was. And really, just the fact that Calloway had a hideout should've been enough to set off a hundred warning bells. Or at least make her question her attraction to him. Instead, every self-preserving instinct she had reared its head when she thought of David Stark. And every bit of intuition she had encouraged her to seek answers.

At last, the computer beeped, announcing its somewhat reluctant readiness to oblige Keira's amateur sleuthing.

Calloway, crime, she plugged in.

And right away, a series of news articles popped up. Keira scrolled through the list. Some were the same as the ones she'd found in Calloway's scrapbook. Some were different.

Home Invasion Gone Wrong? Or Cover-Up Done Right?

Police Seek Husband for Questioning in Gruesome Double Homicide.

Graham Calloway. Doctor. Husband. Stepfather. Killer?

Keira's hand pressed into the stitched-up wound on her leg. A doctor. Well, that explained that.

She sighed, clicked on the last article and began to read.

For Holly Henderson, a fairy-tale romance has ended in tragedy. The twenty-five-year-old (heiress to the Henderson fortune) and her young son were killed in their home nearly one year ago today. It was Dr. Graham Calloway, her estranged husband and the primary beneficiary of the young woman's will, who discovered the murder. Now the police have issued a countrywide manhunt in search of Calloway, who will officially be charged with his wife's and stepson's murders.

Keira read through article after article, piecing together both the murdered woman's life and her death.

From her teenage years on, Holly was a favorite of the local media. Her late mother was old money, her father on the rise politically. Holly herself lived wildly, partying hard and often, until a surprise pregnancy brought her craziness to a grinding halt. While quite a bit of scandal accompanied the announcement, by all reports, it was the best thing to happen to the young heiress. After the birth of her son, Holly's name faded to obscurity, with the only notable events in the papers being her mother's passing and her father's election to city councilman. She met and married her son's pediatrician, Graham Calloway.

Then came the murder.

Keira's heart hammered as she read the details.

The call came in to the 9-1-1 center at two in the afternoon, and in minutes the police were on the scene. When the officers got there, they found Calloway holding his wife's body tightly in one arm, a gun in the other hand.

In spite of the circumstances, Calloway was initially taken at his word. They accepted that he'd found the house and his wife and hadn't called 9-1-1 immediately, but instead tried to revive her. Property damage, missing items, forced entry — all of it pointed to a home invasion gone wrong. But as quickly as the theory was accepted, it began to be discredited. A grieving husband became an angry husband.

And that's when things grew scandalous again.

Calloway became a target, his squeaky-clean reputation dragged through the mud. Troubled, precollege years surfaced. Several articles noted an assault charge at eighteen, and a weapons charge at seventeen. Although the former was pardoned and the latter sealed, somehow each became public knowledge.

The whole marriage was called into question. Calloway reportedly accused Holly of having an affair. A restraining order was said to be in the works. Domestic disturbance calls from the neighbors were rumored. And there were hints at a custody battle over the young boy.

A neighbor came forward, stating she'd heard a noisy

argument just minutes before the gunshots. Finally, it was leaked to the press that Holly, who had long ago made Calloway the beneficiary in trust to her massive family fortune, had been about to divert the funds away from her soon-to-be ex-husband.

More and more rumors abounded.

Formal charges were pending.

And then Dr. Graham Calloway disappeared, making every reporter scream about the surety of his guilt.

Keira paused in her reading, wondering why the revelations from the online news sources didn't fill her full of doubt. All she felt was sadness for Calloway. It hurt her heart that he'd lost his family to that kind of violence.

And she was sure that it was something done *to* him, not something done *by* him.

Maybe she could chalk up her conviction to an inability to accept the truth rather than a gut feeling, but she didn't think so.

Keira looked back to the computer, flipping through the last few articles about the investigation.

The police chased down dozens of leads, followed every rumor. Nothing. They'd chased him countrywide. Assets were frozen, the property and her mother's family's fortune tied up in red tape. Even her politician father couldn't get ahold of a cent.

Eventually, the case was put aside for newer, fresher, solvable ones.

Henry Henderson, Holly's father, catapulted to political stardom.

And Calloway remained at large.

Except he's not at large at all, Keira thought as she leaned away from the computer.

A perfectly capable policeman knew exactly where he was hiding. Where he'd been hiding for years. So why hadn't Officer David Stark turned him in? Somehow, friendship didn't seem to cut it.

Puzzled, Keira punched in Dave's name to the search screen. Unlike Calloway, he had very little digital presence. The usual social media, security settings on high, a mention of community service in the local newspaper and nothing more.

But there *had* to be something more. Some really good reason for not just handing Calloway over to the higher-ups and being done with it.

Keira stared at the screen for a long time, willing herself to see something she'd missed.

Nothing.

She blinked at the computer screen, the words blurring in front of her, and she wondered if it was time to give up, at least for now.

Her finger hovered over the Close Window button.

Keira immediately felt guilty. This wasn't some internet search for cute cat videos. It was a man's innocence. Or guilt. It was his life.

And then an article at the bottom of the screen caught her eye. It didn't have Dave's name in the highlighted link, but the fact that it had popped up in her search struck her as odd.

Paternity Suit Dropped.

Keira brought the pointer down to the article and clicked.

Link not found.

She tried again.

Link not found.

Keira sighed. She rested her chin on her palm, trying to decide if the dead link was even relevant. Irritably, she typed in its title, added a plus sign, then typed Dave's name.

The moment she hit Enter, the computer chose to stall, an evil little circle spinning around on the screen as it took its sweet time thinking about what she'd asked it to look for. It held Keira's sleepy gaze for a good three minutes before her eyes drooped again. Her lids got heavier and heavier, and her shoulders slumped tiredly, and she had to force herself to keep from putting her head down on the keyboard. She could barely make her eyes focus on the information anymore.

She rested her head on the crook of her elbow.

Just for a second, she thought. *While I wait.*

But minutes later, she was sound asleep.

Chapter Twenty

The neighborhood was eerily the same as it had been four years earlier. Though Graham didn't know why he'd expected it to change at all. A lifetime might've passed for him, but it was little more than a blip in the lives of people who lived in these houses with the well-manicured lawns, and the carefully pruned trees and the six-foot-on-the-nose fences. Graham knew, because he'd been one of them not that long ago.

It had seemed ideal. The perfect, ready-made life. So much better than his overpriced bachelor pad in the heart of downtown.

It was Holly—fun, and sassy and a little bit wild—who had brought the neighborhood into Graham's life. She'd thrown a first birthday party for her son at her inherited house, and even though he didn't usually make social visits to his patients' homes, Graham had felt compelled to go.

In retrospect, it was Holly's cherubic son who drew him in.

And probably who held me there, Graham admitted.

At the party, the little boy had been toddling straight for the in-ground pool in the backyard when Graham spotted him. He'd rushed to the kid's side, grabbing him seconds before he'd plunged in, and just moments after *that*, Holly had latched on to Graham's arm in a rather permanent way.

It was the life Graham had always dreamed of, but struggled to find. His upbringing was hard, his teenage years harsh and lonely, and it had taken every ounce of will to fight his way out. A pretty wife, a perfect son and a nice place to come home to had still seemed far off.

Until that party.

The first thing Graham did when he moved in was to have the pool filled. Which was probably the perfect piece of foreshadowing.

Graham was practical, but Holly liked *nice* things. *Fun* things. *Shiny* things. Things that could hurt Sam, or hurt her, and things that always left Graham wondering just how the hell the package—that perfect-from-the-outside life—could be so different from the contents.

Nothing reminded Graham more of that fact than standing at the end of the street that led into the heart of that neighborhood. Shiny and nice.

False advertising.

Except for Sam, of course. The kid was heartbreakingly golden. Smart and sweet and full of life. The last part came from Holly, undoubtedly, while the first two were prime examples of the simple ability to overcome the odds. Which Graham related to perfectly. And ultimately, that's what broke him. Not Holly's affairs, or alcohol abuse, or the feeling that he was living on the periphery of some could-have-been life.

Graham wanted that kid. He was willing to fight for him, tooth and nail, and when Holly finally came out of her boozy haze long enough to realize what was happening, to see that her shiny doctor husband was going to take away her shiny son, she sobered up. Just long enough to kick him out. Just long enough to make him hurt. And just long enough to get killed.

Graham eyed the fork in the road warily.

One direction led to the Niles home and to Keira; the other went straight to Graham's old place and his bad memories.

Funny that he and Keira had lived so close to one another at some point, but never crossed paths.

Though maybe not so funny, if Graham was being honest. The two years he'd called this area home had been a closed-door hell. He hadn't had much time for making new friends. Between putting in sixty hours a week at the clinic, chasing down Holly at every turn and still trying his damnedest to be a good father to Sam.

Graham ran a hand through his shorn hair. As much as the past was to blame for his current predicament, he really didn't have time for dwelling on it.

He planted his feet in the direction of his former life for one moment, then swung toward Keira's parents' house.

Toward my future.

If I have one.

Three blocks brought him to the correct street, and that's where he switched from a comfortable own-the-place swagger to a don't-belong-here skulk. There weren't many people out, but that wasn't terribly surprising. It was noon on a Tuesday, and the residents were mostly at work.

Graham wove through the backyards, grateful for the owners' preference for shared good-neighbor gates and large hedges rather than sparse trees and bolted fences. They offered plenty of cover.

He didn't know what he'd find when he reached the Nileses' place. Maybe Dave would've taken up residence on the couch—a thought that made Graham's lip curl—or maybe he was just watching the place from some panel van on the corner. Either way, Graham was going to tear a strip off him. The man had jeopardized his hope of keeping Keira alive.

Alive?

That thought didn't just make his lip curl. It didn't even just make him pause. It stopped him dead in his tracks.

He'd been making his plans—a little spontaneous and uncharacteristically reckless—and the resulting moves with the idea of keeping Keira safe. What he *hadn't* been doing was focusing on what it might really mean if he wasn't successful. He hadn't truly considered the fact that

her life might be in jeopardy. If she met Michael Ferguson,
if Dave somehow put her in contact with him…

Graham closed his hands into fists, flexed them open,
then closed them again.

Damn.

Keira would be a witness. She'd become someone who
could do something even Graham himself couldn't do—a
person who could identify Holly and Sam's murderer on
sight. A liability. No way in hell would the cold-blooded
killer let her just walk away at the end of it.

Graham moved a little quicker and he didn't slow again
until he was two doors down from the Niles residence.

Once there, he stopped and did a careful visual perusal
of the perimeter.

It revealed no sign of his cop friend. There wasn't a
single car on the cul-de-sac.

So Dave had either left her alone completely, or Graham's instincts were off and he hadn't brought the girl
there at all. A niggling of self-doubt crept in.

What if he was wrong?

Moments later, though, he spied a solitary light in the
otherwise-dark Niles home. It was like a tiny beacon from
behind the closed blinds, quashing any question Graham
had about his gut feeling. He knew he was right; Keira
was in there, completely unguarded.

Waiting for him, possibly.

Hopefully.

Graham cut through the final backyard that lay between him and the girl, then paused on the other side of
the fence. After a quick glance around to make sure no one
was watching him—at least not overtly—he grabbed ahold
of a low-lying branch on a sturdy tree and pulled himself
up. He shoved down thoughts of how ridiculous he would
seem if caught—*a grown man climbing a neighborhood
tree*—and surveyed the Nileses' landscaped yard. It was

tidy, but not manicured, well-cared for, but not overdone. A yard *he* might've liked to have when he lived in the area. Holly had been partial to all things marble and all things floral, and with the removal of the pool, had commissioned an elaborate gazebo.

Yard envy is not *the point of this mission*, he reminded himself and moved his gaze around the lot, looking for ways to get to the house without being detected.

A big tree, much like the one where he sat now, offered ample coverage between the edge of the yard and the fence. Just a few feet from that was a line of shrub, a storage shed, then another tree, which was right beside a wide porch.

The layout of the home was familiar to Graham—his had been larger, but otherwise very similar.

The porch hung from the rear of the house. It was topped by a country-style door that undoubtedly led directly into the gourmet kitchen. Glossy wooden steps led up to the second floor. At the top of those was another deck, this one long and narrow. It would be home to sliding glass doors that would lead into the master suite.

And that's your best bet, Graham decided.

He didn't hesitate. He didn't look around as he moved from one spot to the next. If anyone was watching closely enough to catch his stealthy entrance, he didn't want to see them coming. He'd fight, if he had to, but if he was going to be taken out by a sniper, he'd rather not be looking down the barrel of the gun when it happened.

Graham made the transition from one yard to the other easily, and no one stopped him as he sidled up the back stairs. No alarm sounded when he found the sliding glass doors unlocked and slid them open. In fact, the only noise he heard other than his own shallow breaths was a tiny squeak as he slipped from the master suite into the hall.

Careful to tread lightly, Graham eased past the requisite

family photos that lined the stairwell. When he hit the middle of the steps, he froze.

There she was, straight across the expansive family room. Her head was down, her face pointed in the other direction, and for a very long, very slow heartbeat, Graham feared the worst. His stomach dropped to his knees, violent waves crashed inside his head and, try as he might, he couldn't breathe.

I'm too late, he thought, an indescribable thrum of desperation weakening his whole body.

His eyes closed and he grabbed at the railing to steady himself, unexpected moisture burning behind his lids.

He sank down to the stairs, racked with despair.

Chapter Twenty-One

Keira had woken with a start, her heart thumping in her chest and her head pressed into her dad's sports-car-themed mouse pad. It only took her a second to remember where she was and why she was there. The only real question was, what had woken her so abruptly?

Her eyes sought the clock above the mantel.

It was 1:03 p.m.

Three hours in a face-plant. And she didn't feel at all refreshed. She rubbed her cheek, trying to smooth out the little marks left by the mouse pad.

Then the ceiling above her squeaked, and she went still.

That's what woke me, she realized.

Keira knew the sound well. The culprits were three loose floorboards, one right outside the master bedroom, one on the very top stair and a final one, three up from the bottom step. When she was a teenager, her dad refused to fix them because there was no way to navigate through the hall without triggering one, making it next to impossible for her to sneak out—or in. Now, her dad said the squeaks added character to the house. But right that second, all they added was fear.

She cursed her own stupidity.

She hadn't bothered to bolt any of the doors or check any of the windows. And someone with good intentions wouldn't sneak in through the upstairs.

Keira glanced to the other side of the room, through the formal dining room to the French doors just off the kitchen. It was the quickest way out. But the back door had a notoriously rusty handle, which often stuck.

Her eyes flicked to the hall at the edge of the living

room. It led to the front door. And straight past the stairs—
the only way for the intruder to get to her.

She decided to take her chances with the kitchen.

But she waited a second too long. Before she could
move, the final squeaky floorboard sounded, and Keira
was stuck.

In a panic, she snapped up the nearest thing she could
use as a weapon—an egg-shaped marble paperweight—
palmed it, then closed her eyes and waited.

She heard the trespasser hit the last step of the stairs
softly, then the pause at the bottom. Keira tensed. Whoever was attached to the footfalls didn't come any closer.

Why is he holding back?

She was afraid to breathe. Afraid to move. And her
hand, clasped so tightly around the paperweight, was
growing sweaty.

Her fingers wanted to move.

They were going to move.

They *did* move.

And even the slight adjustment drew a sharp inhale
from her potential attacker.

Dammit.

Keira leaped to her feet, the paperweight slippery in
her palm. She zeroed in on the invader.

He was standing on the bottom step. The relative dark
created by the tightly drawn blinds obscured his face and
bathed it in shadows.

He took a tiny step toward her.

"Stay there!" Keira commanded, only a slight tremor
in her voice.

He paused, but only for a second. And Keira wasn't
taking any chances. She drew her arm back and prepared
to launch the marble egg with all her strength. It might
not hit him, he might duck… It didn't matter. What Keira
wanted was time.

She tossed the paperweight and turned to run.

He called something after her, but she ignored it.

Go, go, go!

She wasn't anywhere near fast enough. Strong arms closed around her, pinning them to her sides and lifting her from the ground.

"Stop!" His harsh tone not only demanded attention, it required obedience.

She wasn't going to give him the latter, and she was only giving him the former because she had no choice. And she sure as hell wasn't going to make it the *good* kind of attention, either. She kicked her legs, hoping to hit something—anything—important. He just squeezed her tighter.

"Keira!"

She ignored the fact that he knew her name. "Let me *go!*"

He ignored her, too, and backed up until they hit the stairs. He pulled her to a sitting position, his thick, muscular thighs wide around her, hugging her hips snuggly.

Keira wanted to yell, to holler for help, but her throat was dry, and she was scared that a scream might prompt him to do something worse than whatever he was already planning.

A little moan escaped from her lips. "Please."

"Keira."

Her name, the second time, was spoken much more softly. And finally she recognized the voice.

"Calloway," she whispered, her whole body sagging with relief.

"It's me," he murmured into her hair.

For a second, Keira just let herself lean against him, appreciative of his solidity. But it didn't take long for the heat in her body to rise. It bloomed from each part of Calloway's body that touched her. His inner thighs to her outer thighs. The bottom of his forearms on the top of hers and his chest pressed into her back. Her rear end pushed straight into his—

With an embarrassed gasp, Keira pulled herself away.

Clearly, all it took was the feel of his body against hers to turn her blood into lava and her mind into mush.

Which isn't so bad...is it?

"What are you doing here? You said two days. You're okay?" she made herself ask, trying to calm the blood rushing through her system and failing completely as she took in his changed appearance.

Dr. Graham Calloway.

The title seemed at odds with the man she'd met in the woods, but at that moment, she had no problems imagining him in the role. He'd shaved his beard, revealing a strong jaw and showcasing those amazing lips of his. The clean-cut look suited him and took years off his face. A white T-shirt hugged his thick, well-muscled body, and a pair of slightly too-big jeans hung a little low on his hips. He sat on the step above her, the extra height making him look even bigger than usual. From where Keira was, she had to tip her head up to meet his gaze.

God, he looks good.

He brought his hand up to push back his hair and gave her a clear view of his gray eyes. The want in them burned brightly. Keira's pulse thrummed even harder.

"Will a sliding scale do?" Calloway wondered out loud, and Keira had to struggle to remember what question she'd asked him in the first place.

"Sure," she managed to get out.

He tipped his head to one side thoughtfully. "All right. Three out of ten for having a hard object thrown at my head. Eight out of ten for having found you alive. Two out of ten because I'm a little disappointed that you're finally wearing pants."

Keira blushed, jumped to her feet and smoothed the borrowed pajama bottoms. "Are you just going to sit there?"

"Did you have something else in mind?" he teased.

Keira shook off the innuendo—and what it did to her—and headed straight for the kitchen without turning to see if he followed.

GRAHAM WATCHED KEIRA walk away, just because it was a nice view. He waited until she'd fully disappeared down the hall before he rose to follow her.

He felt markedly different now that he knew she was okay. Almost relaxed. He knew it was a bit—*okay, a lot*—premature to be letting down his guard, but for some reason, he couldn't quite help it. Seeing Keira in her own element probably had something to do with it. Even though it wasn't *her* home, it was a home she was clearly comfortable in.

Silently, she filled a kettle. She skirted the island with familiarity, rummaged through the cupboards, found what she was looking for, then set up two mismatched cups with chamomile tea bags. She didn't speak as she worked, but Graham had no problem imagining her humming as she went along, pulling out some kind of loaf from the freezer, thawing it in the microwave, then setting that on the counter beside the tea.

It was nice. Normal. Graham liked it.

So he stayed quiet, too, waiting as she laid everything out. When she was done, he took a small sip of the tea and let the floral flavor lie on his tongue for a moment before swallowing.

Keira climbed onto an island stool beside him, her knee almost touching his. Her delicate hands wrapped her mug, and she shot him an expectant look.

Graham wished immediately that the meeting wasn't about to take a serious turn. He wanted to make her blush again and laugh. He wanted to kiss those lips and drag that hair from its tight ponytail and forget that they were in any kind of danger.

But you can't.

There were other far more pressing matters to deal with. He needed to ask her why Dave had brought her here instead of staying in the resort town. And why he'd left her alone. When he opened his mouth, though, something else entirely came out.

"I'd like to turn that sliding scale into a ten out of ten."

"What—"

Graham didn't let her finish. He put one hand on the back of her head and the other on her chin. She trembled a little in her seat, but she remained glued to the spot as Graham lifted her face gently and kissed her lips. And as light as his touch was, desire surged through him.

Slow it down, Graham cautioned himself.

He trailed a finger down her cheek, then leaned back and smiled.

"Eight," he joked. "Maybe nine."

There was that blush.

Damn.

He drew her close again. He dragged his mouth down her cheek, tracing the curve of it, and the pink spread from her face to her throat. Then lower. He pulled away so he could look at her, so he could admire the arch of her brow and the swell of her breast and see that she wanted him as badly as he wanted her. He wasn't disappointed. Keira's lids were half-closed, and what little he could see of her eyes was glossy with heat. Her chest rose and fell against his enticingly.

To hell with slow.

Graham's grip on her neck tightened, and she gasped. He pulled her forcefully into his lap, making her teeter a bit on his knee, her legs dangling down. Her choice was between holding him tightly and falling to the ground. Thankfully, she chose the former. Her arms slid up to Graham's neck while his arms slipped to her waist.

He kissed her again. Forcefully. Possessively. She opened her mouth, welcoming his exploration. Her hands were in his hair and then they were sliding down his back, then holding him as if he was her lifeline.

"Graham," she said against his mouth, and he liked the way his name sounded on her lips.

"Yes, love?" he breathed back.

"I'm scared."

Fierce protectiveness filled his heart.

"I won't let anyone hurt you," he promised, and he meant it. *Not as long as I'm alive.*

Keira shook her head slowly. "No. I'm not scared for me."

"What're you scared for?"

"You. And us. If there *is* one, I mean. Or could be. I don't want this to be it."

Graham heard the need in her voice, and he had a matching one—an almost painful one—in his own when he answered. "I like you, Keira. More than like you. I have since the second I saw you in that car. That's the real, selfish reason I pulled you out. I wanted to know you. As crazy as it is, I felt like I *had* to. Or maybe I felt a little like I already did. The line is kind of blurred. I don't know if I can promise you a future—hell, maybe that's not even what you're asking—but I can give you now. I can give you honesty. I can give you *us*."

Her eyes were wide and hopeful. "All right."

Trust, unexpected and almost unbelievable, expanded in Graham's chest.

"I'm not a perfect man," he warned her.

"I know," she replied.

Graham grinned. "Oh, you do, do you?"

She went pink. "I meant I don't *expect* you to be perfect."

When in doubt, go for shock.

"I lit your car on fire," Graham stated.

Keira face went a little redder. "I know that, too."

Graham raised an eyebrow.

"Dave told me," Keira admitted.

"Did he tell you *why*?"

"To cover up the evidence. But he meant it in a bad way. I know better."

Graham swallowed. His throat was raw with appreciation of her understanding, but his heart was dark with guilt at needing it.

"How do *you* think I meant it?" he asked.

"You were buying time. Protecting yourself."

"I don't know if you know this, Keira, but most men don't commit a felony in the name of self-preservation." He was half joking, but she didn't smile.

"I'm glad you're not most men," she said.

He leaned in to give her a soft kiss. "Did Dave tell you anything else about me?"

"Not really."

"But?" Graham pushed.

"I searched you on Google."

"I'll bet *that* didn't have anything nice to say about me."

"I don't believe everything I read."

"But some of it?"

"Not most of it."

Graham closed his eyes for a long moment, but he could still feel Keira's gaze on him. It wasn't judgmental or even assessing. Just patient. She put a hand on his cheek.

"You can tell me," she said.

Graham opened his eyes and nodded. "Holly was wild. Impetuous. A little crazy, sometimes. Her mom died when she was young—just nineteen—and left her a lot of money.

Her dad was never able to control her and, believe me, he tried. Screened her boyfriends, put a tracking device on her car, recorded her phone calls, you name it. But she was an adult. At least in the strictest sense of the word. She refused to be reined in. She wasn't even trying. It's just who she was. The baby—Sam—slowed her down for a while. But as soon as she was settled, as soon as *I* was settled... she started up again. Drinking and other men..."

"It's not your fault," Keira said, sounding very sure.

Graham was sure, too. Holly *couldn't* be controlled, and it had nothing to do with Graham. That didn't stop him from feeling guilty about her death.

The truth.

"I didn't love her." The admission came out hoarse, and Graham cleared his throat and tried again. "I didn't love her, but I was a good husband. A faithful husband. And that kid... I loved him more than I've loved anyone before or since." His voice was rough once more, and this time he let it stay that way. "I couldn't let anyone think I had anything to do with his murder. I'd rather die myself. That's why I ran. Why I paid Dave to search for the man who killed them. Why I've never been able to walk away and start fresh, even though I've got the means." He looked at her face and saw the tears threatening to overflow, and his heart broke a little more. "I'm sorry, Keira—"

Her lips cut him off. Her fingers dug in to his hair, then ran smoothly, soothingly, over the back of his neck. She was pouring herself into the kiss, and Graham accepted it. Reluctantly at first, but with increased acceptance. Then with enthusiasm. He met her attention forcefully, his tongue finding purchase between her lips, his hands getting lost in her auburn tresses. She sank into his arms. She belonged there. When she pulled away, Graham felt the loss all over.

Then she spoke, and the loss was forgotten.

"My bedroom is upstairs," she said, her words loaded with promise. "Third door on the left."

Wordlessly, Graham scooped her up and moved at double time to the staircase.

Chapter Twenty-Two

They were a tangled mess of arms and legs and bedsheets and sweat. Calloway's muscular, oversize body took up three quarters of the available space. Never before had Keira's double bed in her childhood room seemed so small.

But it's the perfect size, too, she thought as she opened her sleepy eyes and looked over at him.

His face was still peaceful, and Keira was a little envious. A silly grin was plastered on her own. And her mind refused to sit still because it was too full of sweet nothings.

Beautiful.

Incredible.

Amazing.

And the way he said her name. The way he whispered it. The way he called it out, as if there was no one else in the world.

And what he'd said earlier was right. It *was* crazy to feel like this. It would be crazy to feel like this even after a few months. But after only a few days... That pushed it right over the edge. But damned if Keira cared.

She examined his face carefully, memorizing the lines of it in the soft morning light. She liked the thick crest of his eyebrows and the dusting of silver in his hair. Already, the shadow of a beard peppered his cheeks. She liked that, too.

Her heart wanted to burst through her chest with its fullness.

But there was a heaviness there, too. One the allover glow couldn't quite mask.

Because Calloway wasn't safe, and their time together was finite. His hideaway was no longer an option, her parents' house wasn't any better and her own apartment was the first place the man who'd killed Calloway's family would look.

Their only option was to run somewhere else.

"No."

Calloway's statement was soft but decisive. And he hadn't even opened his eyes.

"No, what?" Keira replied.

"I can feel you thinking."

"Someone else's thinking can't be felt," she argued.

He cracked one lid. "Yours can."

Keira made a weak effort to detangle herself from his arms, but he held her firmly in place. She didn't struggle too hard. Truthfully, she was happier to rest her head against him than she was to resist him.

"I didn't even know you were awake," she said as she trailed her palm across his chest.

"Little hard to stay asleep while you're plotting something that's going to kill you."

"That isn't what I was doing."

Calloway eased his hold and rolled both of them to their sides, so they were facing each other.

"No?" he said. "What *were* you thinking about, then?"

"Leaving."

"Leaving?" he repeated, sounding surprised.

"Leaving together," she clarified. "You don't have to find Ferguson. Or risk *your* life. Not if we run."

"Keira…"

"They already think I'm dead," she reminded him. "Dave told me the media was all over the story."

Calloway's expression clouded. "And you're just going to walk away and let it stay that way?"

A lump formed in Keira's throat. "They'll mourn and move on."

"How long will you last? What if one of *them* dies? Will

you stay away when they have the funeral? Or one of your parents gets sick or has an accident?" He shook his head, then added in a harsh voice, "You have no idea what you're saying. What you're committing to."

"I don't see what other choice I have."

"You can stay here, and let your family and friends know you're alive."

"And what happens to you?"

He smoothed her hair back from her face. "Are you asking what happens to *me*, or what happens to that *us* we talked about?"

Keira didn't answer him. She *was* worried about Calloway directly. She didn't want the police to catch him or for him to be arrested for a crime he hadn't committed. But she also had to admit—at least to herself—that she was scared of losing him. She was just too embarrassed to make the declaration out loud.

Two short days, and you need this man as badly as you need air.

Even thinking it was enough to make her face heat up.

When she stayed silent, Calloway sighed. "I've spent a long time isolated from the people I knew. It nearly killed me to hear the rumors. It nearly broke me a hundred times. Hiding is the hardest damned thing I've ever done. I would never forgive myself for dragging you into that life."

"I don't care," Keira said, her voice full of residual post-lovemaking conviction.

"You *think* you don't care."

"Don't tell me what I think."

"I wouldn't dare."

Calloway leaned forward and gave her bottom lip a little tug with his teeth. Then he released it and ran a hand over the same spot, sending renewed sparks of desire through her. Keira stifled a pleasure-filled sigh. Calloway's face was determined, his jaw set and his eyes not in the slightest bit tired. And Keira had the distinct feeling that he was trying to distract her. He formed a lazy path from her mouth to her shoulder to her hip, then traced a circle over her sheet-covered abdomen.

Two more seconds of that *and it's going to work.*

Keira grabbed his hand, determined herself. She needed to make him understand that she wasn't going to just let him slip away. He tried to pull his hand out of hers. She held firm. *Take that.* But his thumb was still loose, and it began to move up and down, just below her belly button, and it was far more distracting than his whole palm had been.

She willed herself not to give in to the temptation he presented.

"You've been gone for a long time," she said. "So maybe you've forgotten how to compromise. Relationships are a two-way street, Calloway."

He didn't even blink at her use of the *R* word. "What do you want me to do, Keira? Let Dave take me in? Say the word, and that's what will happen. But there is absolutely zero chance of me allowing you to abandon your life on my behalf."

Keira's stomach dropped. "You can't go to jail."

"I will, if it means keeping you safe."

"I'm not letting you sacrifice yourself for me any more than you're letting me sacrifice myself for you!"

In an unexpected move, Calloway flipped her from her side to her back, then propped himself above her, his biceps flexing with the effort.

"You're a stubborn girl, aren't you?"

"No."

"That blush tells me you *know* you're a stubborn girl," he teased. "I *have* to prove my innocence, Keira. Or we don't stand a chance. Do you know where Dave went?"

"He said he had to take care of a few things." She paused. "Calloway…"

"Yes?"

Keira pulled the sheet over her chest, then propped herself on her elbow, facing him. "Why would he suddenly start thinking you're guilty?"

Calloway's expression clouded with surprise. "Is that what he said?"

"Not exactly. It's what he implied. Or maybe what I inferred. But it was like he was trying to scare me."

"But he *knows* I'm innocent," Calloway muttered.

"He knows it?"

Calloway gave her tight nod. "Dave's the one who found Holly. Hours before I got home."

Keira frowned. "But the papers said it was *you* who found her."

He ran his fingers over the ridges in her forehead. "I thought you didn't believe everything you read."

"I don't. But that's a pretty big discrepancy."

"Lie down with me again."

Keira opened her mouth to tell him no, they had more important things to worry about. But when she caught the pleading look in his eyes, she was powerless to resist. She curled up beside him, her body tucked beside his, her head resting on his chest.

GRAHAM WAITED UNTIL Keira was settled, the soft scent of her hair flooding his senses, calming the thud of his heart.

"If you want to listen, I'll tell you the story," he said, his voice low.

"Okay," she agreed.

And for the first time, he told the full truth, and shared the hard thoughts that kept him awake for four years.

"Dave and I met in high school. We started out hating each other. We fought, actually, in one of those parking-lot

fights, with the crowd of guys egging us on and screaming for blood. God knows what it was about. We both got
suspended. Not a first for me, but Dave's dad was a cop,
and he was royally pissed off that I was ruining his kid's
life. He turned up at my house, demanding to know what
I had done. When he saw my living situation, well, I guess
he took pity on me. Absentee mom. Drunk dad. So instead
of giving me hell, he took me home and commanded Dave
to take care of me." Graham paused and laughed as he remembered it.

Dave's father was everything Dave wasn't. Hard and
decisive on the outside, kind and insightful on the inside.
He didn't take anyone's garbage. Graham admired him.
Loved him.

"He changed my life," Graham told Keira, curling a
strand of her hair around one of his fingers. "He gave me
value. Helped me get that scholarship for med school and
made me believe I could do it. He died when we were
twenty, and I promised him I'd see it through. He even
left me a bit of money to help out. But Dave took his death
badly, and pretty soon it was me carrying his weight instead of the other way around. Sorting out his fights and
saving his rear end every weekend. If it hadn't been for his
father's name, I doubt he would ever have made it past the
first day as a policeman. He developed a hell of a gambling
problem and I was always bailing him out of one debt or
another. We went on like that for years, Dave messing up
and me picking up the pieces."

"Just like you did with Holly," Keira added.

"Just like that," Graham agreed, then took a thick
breath. "Which brings me to the next bit. Things moved
fast for Holly and me. Met and married in less than a year.
I adopted Sam…and Holly adopted Dave."

"They had an affair?" Keira asked.

"There were things…a pattern, I guess, that took me

a while to notice. Money moved from her account on the same day he paid off a car he could never afford in the first place. Every time Holly made a cash withdrawal, Dave would show up with something newer and shinier. A suit. A computer. A vacation in the Bahamas. And he stopped asking *me* for money. Holly got more and more distant. And once, I overheard a very heated conversation between the two of them. Holly was yelling about jealousy and entitlement, and Dave was yelling back about sharing what should never have been mine."

"But you never asked either of them if your suspicion was true?"

Graham shook his head. "I rationalized *not* asking. What if I was wrong? I didn't want to ruin nearly a decade and a half of friendship. Or worse, jeopardize what I had with Sam. So I just started the divorce process on the sly. I hired the best lawyer I could afford, who promptly figured out that we were near to broke. My income and our assets were the only thing keeping us afloat. All of Holly's savings were gone, her investments mostly sold off, her cards maxed out. Which meant I had no choice but to confront her. But I never even got as far as asking about Dave before she flipped out. She threw everything I owned out on the street. Then threw me out, too. Three days later, the cops were at my hotel room door. Holly had drunk herself into a stupor, fallen down the stairs and called 9-1-1, blaming *me*. For the first time in a long time, Dave had to come to my aid. He bailed me out, dropped me off, then went to reason with Holly. Instead... Well, you know what he found."

"That's terrible." Keira's voice was full of the same ache that plagued Graham's heart, but then she spoke again, and her tone was also puzzled. "Why didn't he just report it himself?"

"I told him not to," Graham admitted. "I thought I was protecting him. And what was left of Holly's reputation."

"And that's why he helped you all these years?"

"Yes."

Keira pushed herself up and met Graham's eyes. "But, if he just admitted that he was there first, wouldn't that exonerate you?"

Graham shrugged. "Exonerate? No. Create reasonable doubt? Maybe. Or it might just implicate Dave, and as much as I question his motives at the moment…he's not a killer."

"You know that for sure?"

"I believe it one hundred percent."

"So we're back to wondering why he suddenly changed his mind about you being the good guy."

Graham stared at her pinched-up features and couldn't suppress a smile.

"Is that where we are?" he teased. "I thought we were in bed, getting ready to—"

She cut him off. "I'm going to ask him."

Graham's grin fell off his face immediately. "No."

"Are you telling me what to do again, Mountain Man?"

"This time, yes, I am. Do *not* ask Dave Stark why he changed his mind about protecting me."

"Asking him is the only thing that makes sense," Keira argued. "And you're supposed to be chasing after Ferguson."

"You take priority, Keira. I'll deal with Dave first," Graham said grimly. "He owes me an explanation for what he said to you, and for leaving you here alone."

She opened her mouth as if she was going to protest again, then closed it and laid her head back on his chest.

"Calloway?" she said after a minute.

"Yes?"

He braced himself for another spiel about how and why

she should endanger herself. Instead, her fingernail traced his collarbone, then his pectoral muscles, then found the edge of the sheet, just below his waistline.

"What were you saying before?"

"About?" The word came out throaty and full of heat. Now her hand slipped *under* the sheet.

"About what we were getting ready to do in this bed," she filled in.

With a growl that made her laugh, Graham grabbed her by the hips and lifted her over top of him.

Chapter Twenty-Three

Keira eyed Calloway guiltily. He was definitely sleeping this time, his handsome face slack, his breathing even.

Seduction had never been Keira's strong point, but she'd worked her hardest to wear him out.

Not that it wasn't rewarding for her, as well. Graham was a fierce and attentive lover. And that made her feel even worse.

But there's no way he'll willingly let you out of his sight, she reminded herself.

She felt that little tug at her heart again, pleased that he cared so much. He'd be mad when he woke up and found out she was gone. Furious, probably. But it was worth it, if she could figure out what it was that Dave was after. Because she had a feeling it was more than misguided morals and Keira felt just as protective of Calloway as he did of her. His story broke her heart. She couldn't help but wonder how much of *his* heart remained in pieces, as well. Every time he said his stepson's name, she heard the pain.

I want to fix that.

She knew justice wouldn't make Calloway whole immediately, but maybe it would start the healing process.

Keira slid her body free from Calloway's embrace, stood up and stepped to the closet. A stack of board games and her mother's rejects—the clothes she couldn't wear anymore but refused to part with—greeted her.

Keira snagged an oversize T-shirt and a pair of leggings, and reminded herself that she wasn't trying to impress Dave with her fashion sense anyway. That didn't stop her from cringing at her appearance as she caught sight of her reflection in the mirror on the back of the door.

Her hair was a disaster, and the wound on her thigh, though held together nicely by Graham's stitches, was still hideous.

She slid on the clothes and patted her hair. Now she looked as if she'd dressed up as her mother for Halloween.

"Nice," she muttered aloud before she remembered she was supposed to be keeping quiet.

Calloway stirred, letting out a noisy sigh, and Keira froze, her eyes fixed to his image in the mirror.

Do not wake up, she commanded silently.

He rolled to his side and stretched one arm up, and the bedsheet slid down, revealing a tantalizing amount of skin. Keira's eyes roamed the exposed flesh greedily for a second before she gave herself a mental kick in the butt and opened the door, cutting off her view.

She moved into the hall, wincing as the first telltale floorboard squeaked. But there was no sound from the bedroom, so she moved on to the stairs.

She went still when a loud knock on the back door reached her ears. Then she heard it squeal open.

What the heck?

With her heart in her throat, Keira tiptoed down the stairs and paused outside the kitchen. Part of her wanted to charge in and tackle whoever was in there. Part of her wanted to wake Calloway for protection.

She steeled herself not to do either.

After all, home invaders didn't usually knock before they let themselves in. Did they?

Her assumption was confirmed when a familiar voice called out, "Keira?"

Drew.

What was he doing here? He wasn't supposed to be back from his business trip yet.

She had to get rid of him before he figured out that Calloway was in the house.

Keira took a breath and stepped into the kitchen. She fixed what she hoped was a surprised—and not guilty—look on her face as she greeted him.

"Drew! Where did you come from? How did you even know I was here? You scared the heck out of me!"

He immediately wrapped his arms around her. "*I* scared *you*? Thank God you're okay!"

She extracted herself from his embrace, marveling at the fact that just a few days ago, she'd been considering pursuing a relationship with this man. She didn't feel the remotest bit of attraction toward him.

"Why wouldn't I be okay?" she asked.

Drew fixed her with a concerned gaze. "Your face is plastered all over the news, Keira."

"Is it?"

He raised a speculative eyebrow, and Keira told herself she needed to rein in the innocence a bit.

"They said you'd been in a horrible accident on the mountain. That your car went over the side of some cliff."

They'd identified her.

This is bad.

Did that mean that Dave Stark had given his official statement, or had his plan been circumvented?

Or is he the one that leaked her name?

Drew closed his hand on her elbow. "Hey. You still with me?"

Keira shook her head and moved away. "I'm fine. I just—I was about to sneak out for a quick cup of coffee. You want to come?"

Drew frowned as if he wanted to say no, and for a second she hoped he would. But then his eyes fixed on something just over her shoulder, and Keira followed his gaze to the spot where she and Calloway had abandoned their mugs earlier. Her pulse jumped.

"You sure you want coffee? Looks like you already had some tea for two," Drew observed.

She forced a laugh. "I guess I was a bit tired this morning when I got in. I made a cup, forgot about it, made another, then didn't drink either of them."

"So you didn't have company?"

"Company?" Keira echoed nervously.

Drew nudged her shoulder. "You know. A guest. Like me, but who doesn't know where your parents keep the extra key to the back door."

Keira shook her head. "No guests. Unless you're *actually* counting yourself. So…coffee?"

Drew nodded, and Keira breathed a big sigh of relief as he held the door open. She followed him out, careful not to let her eyes stray toward her bedroom window.

WHEN GRAHAM WOKE, he reached for Keira automatically. As though he'd been waking up beside her for years instead of days.

But a lot can happen in days, he thought drowsily. *You can lose a life. Start a new one. Fall in love. Become something you never thought you'd be.*

His hand slid across the bed, already anticipating the silky feel of her skin under his palm. When his expectation fell through, his eyes flew open. Her spot on the bed was decidedly empty.

Graham sat up and swung his bare legs to the floor.

"Keira?"

He waited about ten seconds for her to answer, and when she didn't, he grew irrationally worried.

"Keira!" he called a bit louder.

He snapped up his jeans and T-shirt from the floor, slipped them on without bothering to locate his discarded underwear, and moved toward the door. He cracked it open and paused. The house was ominously silent.

"Hey!"

He made his way downstairs, taking the steps two at a time. The sun was going down, and the main floor was nearly dark. Worse than that, there was no sign of Keira.

Where the hell had she gone?

He stepped from the bottom of the stairs to the kitchen and flicked on the lights. The two nearly full mugs of chamomile tea still sat where they'd left them.

Dread was pooling rather quickly in Graham's gut.

He walked around the kitchen slowly, trying to find a clue that would give him a hint as to where she'd disappeared to.

And whether or not it had been on purpose. Or for that matter...purposeful.

"She could've just needed something from the store," Graham told himself out loud.

The thought eased his mind for a tenth of a second. Then a little white card on the edge of the counter caught his eye.

He lifted it slowly.

"Sergeant David Stark," it read, followed by a phone number in bold.

"Well, that answers that," he muttered.

No wonder she'd dropped the whole ask-Dave issue so easily. She'd already made the decision to disobey Graham's request.

Did you really expect her to obey you?

She'd been nothing but a challenge since the second he pulled her from the wreck. Which he liked. Except right at that second. Graham gritted his teeth. Right that second, what he wished was that she was a complacent pushover waiting for him to make the decisions so he could keep her safe.

He paced the length of the kitchen, then out to the living room, then back again, trying—and failing—to find an outlet for his frustration.

He cursed himself for being played as much as he cursed her for playing him.

And play you she did. Like a damned drum.

Of course, his body had been more than happy to let her have her way with him. She fit in his arms so perfectly, it was as if she was made for him. And when she fixed those green eyes on him, her pupils dilated with need, her mouth parted slightly as she exhaled his name...

Graham shook his head. That kind of passion wasn't a ploy. That kind of chemistry couldn't be faked. So, yeah, she might've been manipulating him with sex, but she hadn't been immune to what was happening between them. He was sure of it.

Graham paused on his third run through the living room and ran his fingers through his hair. It really wasn't nearly as satisfying as it had been when it was still long.

He needed something to *do*. Something to occupy his mind and his hands. His eyes flicked around the room until they found the dimly lit computer in the corner.

It had been a very long time since Graham had used a computer. His brief search on the trucker's phone was the closest he'd come to that kind of technology since he went into hiding.

Keira looked you up. It's only fair that you look her up in return.

He smiled a self-satisfied smile. He was pretty damned sure she'd hate the thought of being checked up on.

DREW SET DOWN a paper cup in front of Keira. It was chocolate-and-coffee scented and topped with a generous dollop of whipped cream.

"Decaf mocha," he said. "I know it's your favorite."

"Thanks." Keira took a sip, grateful for the way the hot

liquid warmed her and for the extra second it gave her to gather her thoughts.

Drew waited patiently as she slurped off the whipped cream. He didn't deserve to be lied to the way she was going to have to lie to him. Another tickle of guilt rubbed at Keira's mind. She covered it with a second mouthful of mocha.

Guilt, fear and desire. Those three things seemed to have dominated her emotions since the second she laid eyes on Graham Calloway.

Drew finally broke the too-long silence. "You want to tell me what happened up there on the mountain?"

She met his gaze from across the table.

He really did know her well. Maybe better than anyone except her closest girlfriends. He'd been a shoulder for her on a few occasions, a great help to her parents on many more. And right that moment, she was selfishly tempted to tell him the truth, even if just to garner his opinion on what to do.

She opened her mouth and then closed it.

It's not your secret to tell.

And letting the metaphorical cat out of the bag would only ease the pressure of keeping it under wraps temporarily. It would expose Calloway in a way that Keira would never forgive herself for.

"I don't really remember what happened," Keira lied softly.

Drew frowned. "You don't remember?"

"I remember the crash. And the cop who drove me home. Everything between is kind of fuzzy."

"The cop who picked you up…did he say anything else about what happened up there?" Drew pushed.

"Like what?"

"Like the fact that when they were searching for you, they found some abandoned cabin that might've belonged to an accused murderer. That before that cop found you, they thought maybe the killer had got to you. They even issued some kind of manhunt just in case."

Keira's vision blurred for a dizzying second and she reached for the table to steady herself. She swallowed, her throat dry. She drank some more of the mocha. It did nothing to ease her parched mouth, and the rush of blood to her head wasn't letting up, either.

Was it a coincidence, or had Dave Stark taken his betrayal of Calloway a step further and exposed him to the press?

Oh, God. Are they still looking for him?

"Keira?"

"I'm okay," she managed to get out.

"You sure?"

"Yeah. I guess the thought of being that close to a suspected killer… What else did the news say about the alleged murder?"

"Alleged? This guy—Graham Calloway—has been on the run for years. If he was innocent, something would've turned up by now. You know, they never even found the kid's body? And apparently he stole some thirty-million-dollar painting from his wife before he killed her."

"He…" Keira trailed off, her thoughts suddenly a jumbled mess. "Did they say all of that on the news?"

"Online."

"I didn't read anything like that. He didn't—" Keira snapped her mouth shut.

"Who didn't do what?"

Dammit. She needed to get ahold of herself. Her tongue seemed to be working faster than her brain. She had to fix that.

"The cop," she said slowly. "He didn't say anything about any of that."

"What *did* he say?"

"To keep to myself. In fact, he'd probably be pretty annoyed with me if he knew I was out in public."

"I bet he would."

"What?"

"It's frustrating when you give someone instructions and they don't listen."

Keira sensed something ominous in his words, but she couldn't pinpoint her worry, so she lifted the mocha up and covered her concern with a gulp.

"I should take you home, I think. Wouldn't want to anger that cop," Drew stated.

Keira nodded, the bobbing motion making her head feel funny. Really funny. Weirder than it had since she'd first banged it in the car accident.

She stood up, bumping the table and sloshing around her mocha. She made a move to grab it, but Drew was quicker.

"You've probably had enough of that," he said.

That struck Keira as funny, and a tinny giggle escaped her lips. "Enough decaf mocha?"

"Mmm-hmm."

Drew slid an arm around her waist and clasped her elbow, then led her from the café to the street. It felt wrong to be in someone else's arms. But she didn't have the energy to pull away. Not even when she noted—rather vaguely—that they were heading in the wrong direction. They walked along in silence, Drew keeping Keira from stumbling, and Keira trying to grasp the elusive warning bells that kept sounding in her head.

They rang even louder as Drew paused in front of an older sedan.

"This isn't your car," she pointed out lamely.

"No," he agreed. "It's not. This car belongs to someone else."

"Who?" Keira wasn't even sure why she asked.

"Mike Ferguson."

A violent shiver wracked Keira's body.

Mike Ferguson. Calloway's *Mike Ferguson. The killer.*

"I don't think I know him," Keira lied.

"Don't worry. You're about to get to know him quite well, actually."

Keira met Drew's eyes, and they didn't look like his eyes at all.

In fact, the man she thought she knew—the one who'd been her parents' neighbor for nearly half a decade, who always had something nice to say about her clothes or her hair, and who mowed her dad's lawn *just so* when they were on vacation—was gone.

If Keira bumped into a man who looked like this in a dark alley, she'd run screaming in the other direction. She wanted to run screaming *now*. But when she moved her legs, they turned to jelly and the sidewalk wobbled. Drew caught her.

"I've thought a lot about what I would do if you ever fell into my arms, Keira," he said, his voice as dark as his expression. "It's unfortunate that it ended up being like *this*."

Keira flailed a little, but all she did was send herself into the side of the sedan. Her hips smacked the door handle hard enough to bring tears to her eyes. Drew's grip tightened.

"You should really be more careful."

"I'm careful," she said, her words slurred. "Usually."

"Not careful enough. Not today anyway." His voice dropped low as he went on. "If some killer *had* found you, and he *did* follow you here, he wouldn't have too much trouble getting in. What if that happened?"

"Alleged," Keira corrected, smacking her lips in an attempt to fend off the numbness that seemed to be overtaking her mouth.

"I'm not talking about Graham Calloway now, Keira."

"Who *are* you talking about?"

Drew smiled.

He smiled.

And it was a terrible smile that bared his teeth and turned his face hard. A smile that said, "Me."

Oh, God.

GRAHAM PULLED OUT the chair, straddled it and gave the mouse another click. In minutes, he'd had Keira's name plugged in. Except his search had been almost fruitless. Only two things popped up—a link to her social media and a brief mention in a local paper.

After a swift perusal of the first, and a read-through of the second, he felt as if a few hours with her had taught him more than the virtual world ever could.

So much for the magic of Google.

Then Graham frowned. Hadn't she said Dave told her that her accident was all over the news?

He tapped the keyboard again.

Keira Niles. Car accident.

Nothing.

Keira Niles. Rocky Mountains.

Even less than nothing.

Car crash, Rocky Mountain Resort.

Nope.

Maybe his search was too broad. Maybe her story hadn't reached anything national yet.

Graham racked his brain as he tried to recall the name of the local paper.

Derby Reach Gazette?

He typed it in and the computer autocorrected it to Derby Reach Post, and Graham added her name once more.

"Nothing," he muttered to the empty room. "What the hell is going on? I know she wasn't *lying*."

He was as sure of that as he was of the fact that her feelings for him weren't phony. So if she'd been telling the truth… Graham's fierce worry came back, stronger than before.

He pushed the chair back and, two seconds too late, realized he wasn't alone in the house anymore.

"Dave was the one lying to her," he said.

As if on cue, Dave's voice came from behind him. "I'll tell you what you want to know, Graham, if you agree to come with me.

Graham jumped to his feet two seconds too late and spun, prepared to throw a punch straight into his disloyal friend's face.

Unfortunately, the other man had a pistol levelled at his chest.

For a long moment, Graham stared at the weapon and seriously considered whether or not to jump him anyway. He took a step in the other man's direction, and Dave cocked the pistol.

"I wouldn't move again," Dave cautioned. "Not suddenly anyway."

"Are you really going to shoot me, Dave?" Graham demanded coolly.

"I'd prefer not to," the other man replied. "But I'll knee-cap you if I have to."

"What *do* you want, then?

"The same thing you do. To make sure Keira Niles is safe."

Graham shot Dave a disbelieving look. "You've got a funny way of showing it."

The policeman made an exasperated noise. "I've done everything I can. I took her off the mountain. I gave her strict instructions to stay home. I'm here now to—"

Graham cut him off. "Where is she?"

Surprise registered on Dave's face. "She's not here?"

"I thought she was with you."

"Me? Why would she be with me?"

"Because she wanted to ask you why you stopped helping me. Because she's stubborn as hell. Because I found *your* business card on the counter, and now she's gone."

"I wish she *had* called," Dave replied with a headshake. "She was supposed to, if you happened to walk through the front door."

"I didn't come through the front door," Graham muttered. "Where is she, Dave?"

The policeman lifted the gun and used it to scratch his forehead. "Motivation."

"What?"

"Mike Ferguson's guy…he must've followed us. Stupid of me, I guess. I took the man at his word."

Graham's blood ran cold. "You're actually working with him."

Dave didn't respond to the accusation.

"I'll take you to Keira," he offered instead. "But I'm going to need you to put on my cuffs."

Graham snorted derisively. "Like hell."

"We don't have time to fight about this."

"Then give me the gun." Graham shrugged. "Why would I even believe you know where she is?"

"What's the alternative here, Graham? You think I'm going to have you slap on the cuffs so I can drag you to *jail*? Think about that for just one second. Your rear end is *my* rear end. If I turn you in, it'll either come out that I've been helping you, and the justice system will take me down, or it *won't* come out, and Ferguson will take me

down instead. At least this way, we both stand a chance."
Dave paused and used his free hand to pull a set of handcuffs from his pocket. "I know that the second I let down my guard, you'll beat the hell out of me."

"I'll beat the hell out of you if I even *think* you're letting your guard down."

Dave sighed. "Cuffs, Graham?"

Graham grabbed them from the other man's outstretched hand. He held them for a second, feeling the rift between the importance of his past and the importance of his present widening. If he put them on, he might very well be sacrificing himself to the man who killed his wife and son. If he didn't put them on, he might never get a chance to save the woman whom he was undoubtedly falling in love with.

Already fallen in love with, corrected a voice in his head, and he gave the voice a mental nod.

Yes, he'd already found that crazy, can't-live-without-her feeling.

And he knew what it was like to have no chance at all to save someone he loved.

It wasn't really much of a choice at all. He slid the cuffs to his wrists and snapped them shut.

"Show me they're secure," Dave ordered.

Graham lifted his hands and tugged them apart hard enough to bite punishingly into his skin.

"They're secure," he replied coolly.

"Good." Dave tucked his gun into his belt and stripped off his jacket. "I'm going to hang my coat over the cuffs, and we're going to take a walk."

"A walk?"

Dave shook his head. "No questions, unless they're about the weather or the Derby Reach Cardinals. You're going to stay on my right side—my gun side—just a little bit in front of me, but not so far in front that it looks forced. Got it?"

"Baseball, gun side, best buddies strolling through the neighborhood. Got it," Graham agreed.

And as Dave led him through the house and out the front door, Graham realized he didn't even have to ask where they were walking to.

Chapter Twenty-Four

Keira didn't even know she'd passed out until she was already struggling to pull herself into consciousness.

And wakefulness was unpleasant enough to make her wish she was still asleep.

Her eyes burned when she fought to open them. Wherever she was, it was dark, but that did nothing to relieve the sharp stab behind her lids. In fact, the rest of her hurt just as badly. Her head throbbed. And her throat ached and her wrists were on fire.

She was seated, but the chair dug into her shoulder blades and into the backs of her legs, too. She tried to adjust her body to ease some of the pain—*any* of it—and failed miserably. She was completely immobilized. And starting to sweat.

Where was she? What had Drew done? And *why*? Dear God... What about Calloway?

She might've cried, if she'd had the energy to do so.

"Water?"

The unfamiliar voice cut through the panic building up in her system. Abruptly, consuming something liquid was more important than being free, and she croaked out an assent.

"Please."

A cool metal rim reached her lips, tipped up, then drizzled a stream of water down her throat. Keira sucked it back thirstily, and it was pulled away far too soon.

"It's the sedative," the voice told her. "It'll make you crazy thirsty like that. But you don't want to drink too much, either, or it'll just come back up again."

"A little more?" Keira pleaded.

The unseen man sighed, but he did lift the water to her mouth again, very briefly.

"Good enough," he said. "In a few minutes, I'll turn on the lights, but the sedative will have given you a wicked headache, too, and the light will exacerbate it, I'm sure. In the meantime…are you as comfortable as can be, considering the circumstances?"

Keira wasn't sure how to answer. The speaker's question was genuine sounding. Almost kindly. It was the voice of someone's grandfather offering a child a sweet treat. But he clearly wasn't there to rescue her.

"Ms. Niles?"

"I've been better," she whispered hoarsely.

She could hear the shrug in his reply. "I suppose you probably have. Maybe we *all* have."

"Are you going to cut to the chase, or just keep stringing her along?" snapped another angrier voice.

Drew.

"We can do things my way, or you can leave," the first voice answered him in a restrained tone, then turned its attention back to Keira. "Should we try the dimmer?"

He didn't wait for her to answer. There was a click, and the room was bathed in a low, almost tolerable light. Keira squinted against the watering of her eyes. She was in a formal dining room, pushed into a corner away from a heavy wood table. And two figures stood in front of her.

The first was the new Drew—his expression set in a cruel scowl.

The other was an older man whom she didn't know, but who looked vaguely familiar. Even in the dim light, Keira could tell that he was a cut above average and he suited his voice perfectly. His gray hair was thick and styled, his suit well tailored and his skin ruddy in a just-returned-from-the-Bahamas kind of way. He offered her a smile.

"Okay?" he asked.

"Okay," Keira agreed, her voice still burning like fire.

"You know Mr. Bryant," he said pleasantly. "But I don't think we've had the pleasure. I'm Councilman Henderson."

Councilman Henderson.

Keira's mind made the connection quickly. This was Calloway's father-in-law. The local politician with the wild-child daughter and the high ambitions and the reputation that needed protecting.

"You recognize my name, I see," he observed. "So that makes things a little bit easier. What I'm hoping is that we can make it *all* easy."

"Easy, how?" Keira wanted to know.

"Talking to her is a waste of time," Drew interrupted.

"If you weren't perpetually tired of wasting time," the older gentleman stated, "the painting would be in my hands and Holly would still be alive. I've told you before, there's doing things. And then there's doing things with finesse. Wouldn't you agree, Ms. Niles?"

"Finesse didn't bring you the girl," Drew retorted before Keira could answer. "I did."

"No," the other man argued, still sounding patient. "Whatever drugs you fed her brought her here. And I'm damned sure asking her nicely would have sufficed."

"You think *asking* her would have worked?"

"The girl is clearly in love with Graham and there's not much a girl won't do to protect the man she loves."

Keira opened her mouth to argue, but couldn't do it.

In love with him?

The realization made Keira's pulse race again, this time joyfully. Yes, she *did* love him, in that fast-and-hard, head-over-heels way that people wrote songs about. Everything about Calloway sang to her, made her thrum with life. The accident, the rescue…all of that had sped up the process, but there was no doubt in Keira's mind that the feelings

were genuine. The very real likelihood of death intensi-
fied it all the more. And it made denying it impossible.

"I do love him," Keira said, hearing the truth of the
statement in her voice. "And I'd lie to protect him. But I
don't know what you're talking about."

"You'd lie," Drew snarled. "But would you *die*?"

Keira's reply was defiant. "Yes."

"Good."

He lunged at her, his hand drawn back for a blow. Keira
braced herself, but he didn't make it close enough to hit
her. Henry Henderson's fist closed on the back of Drew's
collar, and he dragged the younger man back so forcefully
that he fell to the ground with a thud.

"You fail at *every* task I give you," Henderson said,
his voice betraying emotion for the first time. "You have
no patience, no fortitude, no redeeming qualities. None.
Now get out, guard the door and give Ms. Niles and me a
few minutes alone."

Remarkably, Drew didn't even argue. He just pulled
himself to his feet and slunk from the room. Henderson
waited until the French doors were closed, then pulled out
a chair from the table, seated himself and crossed his legs.
When he turned his attention back to Keira, he was completely calm once more.

"Sometimes my sons forget who works for whom. My
apologies," he said softly. "Now, where were we? Oh, right.
Asking first certainly wouldn't have hurt. Ms. Niles, Graham Calloway has something I want. The man has been
pouring his heart and soul out to you for days. He's either
told you what I want to know, or he'll come here to rescue
you and tell me himself. It's a win either way."

Keira barely heard what the man was saying. Her head
was too busy trying to wrap around his first sentence.

His son.

No, not his son. His sons. *Plural.*

And Keira had a sinking feeling she knew who the other one was.

She needed to warn Calloway.

She stole a glance at Henry Henderson. He'd snapped up a newspaper from the table and turned his attention to what appeared to be a crossword puzzle.

Good.

Keira's hands twisted behind her back in search of a vulnerability in the rope. And after just a few seconds of trying, she found a loose spot, no bigger than her pinky finger. She just barely managed to keep from letting out a relieved cry.

She looked at Henderson again. He face was placid, as if he had no care outside of what word fit into fifty-one down.

I've got one for you, Keira thought. *What's an eleven-letter word for "drawing one's attention away from something"?*

D-I-S-T-R-A-C-T-I-O-N.

Keira closed her eyes for one second, dug her pinky into the loop, then opened her eyes again and asked, "What makes you so sure Calloway will come for me?"

Henderson blinked at her as if he'd completely forgotten her presence. Which she was damned well sure he hadn't.

"Pardon me, Ms. Niles?" he said.

She was also damned well sure he'd heard her the first time.

"There's a chance he won't come."

Henderson gave her a considering look. "Does he love you?"

Keira's face warmed. "I don't know."

Henderson shrugged. "I guess it doesn't matter. I believe he'll come, love or not. He'll feel responsible for you and obligation is a huge part of Graham's makeup. But if I'm wrong—which *is* a rare occurrence—I do have another ace or two up my sleeve."

The loop widened under Keira's attention.

"Like what?" she asked.

Henderson shook his head. "I think that's enough divulgence for the moment."

He went back to his crossword.

Dammit.

She had to keep him talking.

"What makes you think he even has this painting that you want?" she persisted. "He might not have it at all."

An amused smile tipped up the corner of the older man's mouth. "He has it."

Henderson took another sip of his drink and scratched something else onto the newspaper.

Keira had worked her finger in up to her knuckle already, and on the other side, she'd found another loose piece.

"How do you know?" she persisted.

Henderson folded the crossword in half, set it on the table and placed the cup on top.

"He had thirty-two million reasons to keep it," he told her.

It was Kiera's turn to blink slowly, and she had to force her fingers to keep working.

"Dollars?" she asked.

"That's right."

"But…"

"But what? You thought he was nothing more than an everyday hero, motivated by a general care for the well-being of mankind?" Henderson shook his head. "I'm afraid not."

Keira wiggled her wrists. There was definitely some extra room now.

"If Calloway had a thirty-two-million-dollar painting, and he cared so much about the money, why was he living in a shack?" she asked. "Why wouldn't he sell it?"

"He's greedy, not stupid. The first thing I did when my daughter died was to report it missing."

"The papers didn't say a word about it," Keira pointed out.

A few more inches, and at least one hand would be free. Henderson smiled again. "They wouldn't."

"Why's that?"

"Because I didn't report it to the police."

Keira tugged a little harder on the rope and feigned confusion. "Why not the police? Wouldn't they be the best people to track it?"

"I'm afraid not." His tone was patronizing. "If a wanted criminal is going to sell a thirty-million-dollar painting, it's not going to be through the appropriate channels. The people I reported its theft to are the kind who monitor the darker side of things, Ms. Niles. People like your friend Drew."

"Drew?" she repeated.

One final little yank, and Keira felt the rope drop behind her. Quickly, she tucked her feet together under the chair to cover up the dangling evidence.

"The wannabe art thief," Henderson clarified.

"Well. That explains his wannabe expensive taste." Keira forced a laugh as she tried to take a casual look around.

The vase in the center of the table.

It was big and painted blue and probably worth more than a month's worth of rent. But it also looked breakable. Into small, sharp pieces, preferably.

She'd have to find out.

Chapter Twenty-Five

The house didn't just rest on top of its little hill. It loomed. Forbidding and hideous in its austerity.

It was the biggest one on the block—the one that all of the other houses in the neighborhood were modeled after. It wasn't that much older than its surrounding homes, but the lot was double the size. It was clearly designed not necessarily to stand out but to rule over.

Holly had told Graham that her mother had built the home, then given the rest of the property to her father to develop. A billion-dollar gift before the woman passed away and left everything else—the house, her fortune, her summer house overseas—to Holly herself.

Opulence.

It left a sour taste in Graham's mouth. It was one of the reasons the police believed he'd killed her. Killed *them.* Holly had spent the money—nearly every penny—and Graham, who had grown used to the *opulence*, was thrown into a rage.

The only thing left was the money in trust for Sam. The only way for Graham to get to that was to get rid of both of them.

Graham's jaw clenched involuntarily at the theory.

Money meant nothing to him. It never had, really. He'd gone into the medical field to help children who couldn't help themselves. He'd married Holly to help Sam.

But he'd wound up helpless, and the day he'd walked in and found Holly's body and Sam's blood…it was seared painfully into his memory.

The sirens had been close before Graham heard them. *Too close.*

He'd known he ought to get up, slip out of the house and pretend he hadn't been there at all. That he hadn't received the frantic phone call from Dave, hadn't come home from the motel and hadn't walked in on the devastating scene in the front hall of the home he'd shared with his wife and stepson.

Instead, he tore through the kitchen, bending down to open each low cupboard, calling out in a reassuring voice.

"Come out, come out, wherever you are!"

Where was the boy?

It was the only thing that stopped Graham from fleeing. He thought the boy had to be hiding somewhere, terrified. But where?

His heart had constricted as he moved past his wife's still form again, taking the stairs two at a time and forcing himself not to look back.

He might not have loved the woman the way he should, but in a million years, he would never have wished for something like that.

You tried to revive Holly, he'd reminded himself. *You really did. But you needed to find Sam.*

She'd been gone long before he got there. Blood loss. Or the fall down the stairs. Even with his medical expertise, Graham couldn't say what had ultimately killed her.

Sam.

A crushing anger pushed at the corners of Graham's mind at what his stepson had witnessed.

He *had* to be a witness.

Graham couldn't even begin to accept the idea that the boy might've met the same fate as Holly. He loved the boy too much. Like nothing else in the world.

"Sammy!" he'd called as he'd opened the boy's bedroom door.

The usual assortment of Transformers and Lego and art supplies were strewn throughout the room. Graham saw none of them. The only thing that held his eye was the bed and the dark circle in the center of it.

No. Oh, no.

Graham knew blood when he saw it. It covered his hands and chest now, just as it covered his vision.

"Dr. Graham Calloway!" The cold, commanding voice had come from the doorway. "Hands where I can see them."

Numb, Graham lifted his arms and placed his palms on his head and turned around slowly.

"They're dead," he'd said to the officer in blue. "Holly and Sam are dead. You're too late."

The later-damning statement was out before he could stop it. It was also the last thing he'd said in that house the last time he'd been inside.

Until now.

"Am I going to have to drag you in there?" Dave's question forced Graham back to the present.

"No," he replied, his voice betraying more than a hint of the overwhelming, emotional drainage he'd experienced on that day four years earlier.

"Let's move, then."

"Are you going to uncuff me first?"

"I can't do that."

"Level with me," Graham said tiredly. "Are you taking me inside *just* to hand me straight over to Mike Ferguson, or are you taking me inside with any hope at all of saving the girl I love?"

The hesitation in the reply betrayed the truth even before the words did. "It has to be both."

"That's not even possible."

Dave shot a worried glance up toward the house. "I didn't have much of a choice here, Graham."

"There's always a choice."

Dave's face clouded with anger. "I know you think the

past four years have been hard for you, and you only. But I lost something that day, too. Some *things*."

Graham rattled his cuffs emphatically. "What do you think *you* lost, Dave? *Your* freedom?"

"As a matter of fact, I did lose my freedom. Every person on the force knew about our friendship. I've never been promoted, never been given a second look for anything."

"You're blaming that on me?"

"My entire career was stalled when Holly died."

"Your entire career was stalled the second you started it, Dave," Graham snapped. "If I hadn't been there to bail you out of every bad thing you did, you'd be a two-bit criminal instead of a two-bit cop. Oh. Wait."

The other man narrowed his eyes. "I've made some bad choices, but I'm trying to make the right one now."

"By cuffing me?"

"If I don't cuff you, we don't get in. It's as simple as that."

"And what next? We get in there and you say you have to hand the keys to these cuffs to Ferguson because it's just that simple? Will you hand him the gun he uses to shoot me, too, and then blame *that* on simplicity?" The last question came out at a near yell, and Graham took a breath and tried to calm himself. "I thought you loved her, too."

"I did love her. Can we stop talking about this and go inside?"

Graham shook his head. "I don't think so. Not until you explain to me why you turned on me. Why you're helping the man who murdered Holly."

"He's not who you think he is."

"Now you're defending him? Dammit, Dave. You *loved* her. In a way that I couldn't. I never held that against you. I never even tried to stop it. So why do this?"

"It wasn't like that with Holly and me," Dave replied softly.

"You don't have to lie about it."

The other man exhaled loudly. "She was my sister."

It was the last thing Graham expected to hear. "Your what?"

"My sister."

"You don't have a damned sister."

"I don't anymore. But I did."

"Explain," Graham ordered.

"I don't think you really want to hear about it."

It was true. Part of him *didn't* want to hear. He didn't want to know what Dave was using to justify his actions. He didn't want to be asked to have any sympathetic feelings for anyone involved in Holly's and Sam's deaths. And he was sure that's where Dave was going with this.

He pushed past the desire to shut down.

"Explain," he repeated coldly.

Dave sighed again. "When my dad died, he left you cash for college. And even though you weren't his kid, I got it. You had a bond and I respected that. But he left me a different kind of legacy, Graham. He left a letter, confessing that he wasn't *my* real father at all, that my mother had an affair with a local politician. He didn't tell me his name. And I wasn't supposed to tell anyone that I knew. But it ate me up. Every waking moment, I thought about it. About who he might be. You remember how I was when my father died."

Graham *did* remember. He'd blamed the downward spiral on the senior Stark's death. It had made sense.

"How did you find out it was Henry?" he asked.

"Not long after you met Holly, you introduced us, and…I just knew it was him. Something in his eyes, his stance. It reminded me of myself. And he didn't even deny it when I confronted him."

"So you did what, blackmail him?"

"Not at first. I just threatened him with a lawsuit. He threatened me back. He said he knew people who would make me wish not only that I wasn't his biological son, but that I'd never been born at all. And I believed him. Completely."

"So Holly was a weaker target?"

"Not exactly."

Graham was growing impatient. "Stop being so taciturn, Dave. It's not helping either of us."

"Things got worse for me. The man I always thought of as my father was dead. The man who was my biological father threatened to kill *me*. So I did what I always did. I gambled away more money. I kept going until I owed my bookie tens of thousands. Until one of them—Mike Ferguson—sent someone after me."

Graham's anger reared its head again. "You knew him *before* he killed them? You—"

Dave cut him off. "I didn't *know* him, Graham. I never even saw him. I owed him money. And I told you that you didn't want to hear this."

Graham gritted his teeth. "Go on."

"The man he sent was named Drew Bryant, and he didn't even ask me for the money I owed Ferguson. Instead, he told me he was my brother. Mine and Holly's. Another affair, another son," Dave said bitterly. "Henry took the term 'sow your wild oats' to an extreme, I guess. Drew convinced me that Henry owed us something. He'd been working for him and knew of a better way for us to get some money."

Drew Bryant.

He couldn't be Keira's boyfriend-potential Drew.

But he has to be.

"No coincidences," Graham muttered, then said a little more loudly, "After that, you went to Holly."

"After that, we went to Holly," Dave agreed. "She didn't even hesitate. She started paying us right away. Took the cash out of the bank that same day."

"And you were more than happy to take it."

"I owed money, Graham. A lot of it."

"So you thought it was okay to blackmail Holly?"

"We didn't *have* to blackmail her. She gave me the money willingly. She was thrilled to have brothers."

"You bankrupted her!"

"No. I paid my debt, thanked her, then didn't take a cent more. I told Drew I was out, and he agreed. So I kept my nose to the ground and washed my hands clean of Mike Ferguson. I paid my own way for a year," Dave explained. "But Drew kept taking money from her. I had no idea. Not until he came to me and told me she'd run out, and that he was planning on stealing the painting. I wanted to warn her. I was too late."

Bile rose in the back of Graham's throat. "Always about the money."

Dave looked as though he was about to say something else, but the door to the house where Graham once lived swung open, and a well-dressed, furious-looking man stepped onto the front veranda. He motioned angrily at Dave and Graham.

"Do I need to drag you in *now*?" Dave asked, displeasure clear in his inquiry.

Graham stared at the man on the stoop.

"Is that him?" he asked roughly.

If it was—if that was the man responsible for Holly's death—Graham wouldn't have to be dragged in. Just the opposite. It took all of his self-restraint to not run at the man, knock him down and wrap his throat with the chain on the cuffs and demand answers. Under the coat, he flexed his hands.

"That's Drew Bryant," Dave said. "Holly's brother, and mine."

"Where's Mike Ferguson?"

"Inside."

They moved forward together, and when they reached the porch, Drew Bryant gave Graham a dismissive once-over.

"This is the husband?" he asked, his tone as derisive as his expression.

"You know it is," Dave replied.

"I expected you to be more…impressive," the other man said.

Likewise, Graham thought, but he made himself stay quiet, assessing in silence.

He wasn't tall, but he wasn't short, either. His clothes were nice and his hair was tidy, but there was nothing remarkable about him at all. Graham couldn't see whatever it was that made Keira consider him boyfriend material, and he didn't know if that was a relief or not.

"Ready?" Dave prodded.

"Let's go," Graham replied grimly.

He started to step to the door, but Dave put a hand on his shoulder and muttered darkly, "He's not Mike Ferguson. But I bet you're going to wish he was."

Chapter Twenty-Six

Keira waited until Henderson had immersed himself back in the crossword puzzle before she heaved herself to her feet and dove for the vase. Henderson reacted quickly, leaping up from his chair and pushing Keira away from her intended target. But her hand still managed to bump it, and she sent it rolling.

As the vase lumbered along, flashing blue on brown, Keira used the momentum given to her by Henderson's shove to propel herself under the table. When the older man bent down to grab her, she kicked out one bare foot, smacking him solidly in the forehead. He fell to his knees, but came at her again immediately. She struck him once more, this time in the chin. When he lunged a third time, Keira grabbed ahold of two chair legs and forced them together with as much strength as she could muster. They put a temporary barrier between her and the man hell-bent on getting to her. When he tried to shove the chairs out of his way, Keira gave one of them a push. It clipped Henderson in the eye, and he finally fell back, his hand on his brow.

"Drew!" he hollered.

And Keira thumped the chair forward again, harder than before. This time, the blow was hard enough to send him flying. He righted himself and shot her a furious glare.

"You little—"

Whatever he'd been about to say was lost in the sound of the vase hitting the hardwood floor and shattering.

Keira covered her eyes as the shards flew around her. She counted to three in her head, hoping that would give the porcelain enough time to settle, then opened her eyes in search of a big enough piece of vase to use as a weapon.

But Henderson was a step ahead of her. He already had a pointed chunk of porcelain gripped in one hand and was crawling toward Keira.

For a second, she was frozen to the spot, mesmerized by the gruesome sight in front of her.

Little pieces of blue flecked Henderson's face and around each of them was a dot of crimson. A bigger slice had jabbed into his shoulder, and from that, a steady stream of blood oozed.

He paused on the other side of the chairs.

Move!

It only took Keira a heartbeat to obey the command in her head. She scurried back, hit the wall behind her, then moved left, bringing herself closer to the door.

Bits of blue porcelain scraped underneath her as she slid along the floor, and she ignored the way they dug at her.

Three more feet.

But Henderson was nearly on his feet again and almost as close to her as she was to the exit.

Keira snapped up a piece of broken vase and held it out in front of her as she grabbed the door frame and pulled herself up.

"You might as well drop it. I'm bigger than you and stronger than you. I'm not afraid of hurting you. And I will," Henderson said, and Keira marveled that he somehow still managed to sound calm in spite of his threatening words. "I'm going to overpower you in seconds."

"And you're going to lose an eye in the process," Keira retorted.

"We'll see."

As he jumped toward her, the French doors flew open, and Henderson took advantage of Keira's momentary surprise. One of his arms closed around her, pinning her arms to her sides, and the other came up to press his own shard of sharp porcelain directly into her jugular.

GRAHAM STARED IN horror at the scene in front of him, the truth unfolding in his mind.

The gray-haired man—covered in abrasions and looking like a poorly aged thug—was absolutely someone he knew. Well. And he had Keira in a death grip and showed no signs of letting her go.

He's inches away from cutting her throat.

"Henry…"

"Mike," the man corrected. "Ferguson. At least as far as this little scenario is concerned."

Graham's stomach caved in; his head boomed with the revelation.

His father-in-law was a well-respected member of the community. A city councilman, with power and influence, and a reputation sullied only by Holly's exploits.

And a murderer.

Graham's mouth hung open, a dozen unable-to-be-articulated questions on the tip of his tongue.

Then he realized the answers didn't matter. Not right that second anyway.

Graham recovered from his momentary inability to move and strode forward, forgetting his cuffs, forgetting the two men on either side of him, forgetting everything except Keira and her safety.

"Stop!" his father-in-law commanded.

A little bead of blood formed under the point he had pressed to Keira's neck, and Graham paused. There was a responding shuffle from behind him, and he quickly found himself grasped by Drew on one side and Dave on the other. He made no attempt to throw them off. All of his attention was on the girl and the man who held her.

"Let her go," Graham said, not bothering to acknowledge his captured state.

"Unlikely," Henry replied.

His voice was full of the scorn that had characterized

him so well over the two years Graham had been married to the man's daughter. Graham paused, taking stock of the situation. He knew Keira was being used, not just as bait now, but also as leverage. He knew also that he was faster than the older man and he was sure he could incapacitate the two men who held him.

But can you do both things quickly enough and effectively enough to win?

Maybe, maybe not.

Henry probably wouldn't kill her, given a choice. It would take away that bit of leverage he had. But if he felt as though he didn't *have* a choice...

There was a click behind him and Graham knew he'd wasted too much time thinking about it. One of the two men holding him had cocked a gun.

"It's aimed at *her* head, not yours," Henry said. "Confirm that for me, Ms. Niles."

Keira's eyes lifted to a spot behind Graham, then she met his eyes and inclined her head. Just that slight nod was enough to draw more blood from her throat.

"Stop." Graham was pleading and he didn't care. "Don't hurt her."

Henry smiled. "Are you going to offer to take her place?"

"Yes," Graham replied right away.

Henry's smile widened. "I'd like to say I expected something less cliché from you, but it would be a lie. It's just the kind of bleeding heart offer I *would* expect from you."

"Because I care about something other than money and the public eye?"

"Because caring is your weakness. And that weakness is what got you in trouble in the first place. It's what made you marry my daughter when you should have stayed away and what got you accused of murder. It's what's going to make you give me what *I* want now."

Graham balked at the derogatory simplification of his personality. "I'm not giving you anything."

"Then I'll kill her," Henry replied with a shrug.

Graham forced himself to sound unmoved by the statement. "Like you killed Holly and Sam?"

His father-in-law sighed. "That was an unfortunate accident."

Graham's jaw clenched at the man's casual dismissal of the loss of life, as did his stomach. Before he could speak again, the man with the gun interjected.

"I'll shoot her," he offered. "Maybe in the hand, just to show you how serious we are."

"If you hurt her, I'll have no reason at all to help you," Graham snapped.

His father-in-law sighed. "Drew. I don't want you to shoot anyone at the moment. And, Graham, you should know by now that I never place all my bets on one number."

"You took every other thing from me," Graham countered.

Henry opened his mouth, but suddenly, Keira was alive in the older man's arms. She threw an elbow into his stomach and stomped down on his foot. Henry released her with a grunt and dropped the shard of porcelain to the ground. He reached for her, but Keira was too fast. She darted across the room and reached Graham just as Drew fired off a wild shot.

"I told you *not* to shoot in here," Henry snarled.

"You said not to shoot *anyone*," Drew corrected.

The older man strode toward the younger one, and Graham decided now was the only opportunity they might have to run. The one thing between him and the door was Dave. He met the police officer's eyes.

"Hit me," Dave instructed, just loud enough to be heard. Graham didn't have to be told twice. He pulled his still-bound hands together and rammed them into Dave's gut. As the smaller man fell to the floor, he dropped the keys to the cuffs and Graham snagged them.

Graham grabbed Keira's hand and dragged her through the French doors and out into the hall. He was glad to see nothing had been done to change the decor in the home. Everything was exactly as he remembered it. Including a large, heavy table positioned against the wall just outside the dining room. Swiftly, he got behind it and pushed— with considerable effort—so that it blocked the doors. Then he clasped Keira's hand once more and set off at a run without looking back.

Chapter Twenty-Seven

Keira raced to keep up with Calloway as he tore through the large home with easy familiarity. They hit the front door in moments, but once they were there, Calloway paused, glanced through the curtains and shook his head.

"Henry's got a man out there in his car," he told her. "I can see him from here."

"Out the back, then?" Keira breathed, her throat still raw.

"Probably just as risky."

Behind them, she could hear the thump of the three men as they fought through the small blockade.

"I've got an idea," Calloway said.

He yanked on her hand, and they moved from the entryway, through the family room, then paused at the bottom of the stairs.

"C'mon!" Calloway called loudly. "The master bedroom!" Then he put his hand on her shoulder and leaned in to whisper, "Wait here."

He thundered up the stairs, two at a time, his feet hitting the steps, loud and hard. When he reached the top, he turned around and tiptoed back down. Without asking permission, Calloway slid his arms around Keira and lifted her from the ground. In complete silence, he carried her into the kitchen.

Moments later, the bang of booted feet and deep voices carried through the house.

They're free.

But Calloway ignored them as he set Keira on the countertop.

"Just a sec," he murmured.

Keira watched in amazement as he crouched low, found a loose floorboard, lifted it, then reached into it. With a heave, he pulled on something inside and an old-fashioned trapdoor squeaked open. Calloway held it up.

"In," he commanded. "There's a railing on your right."

Keira didn't bother to argue. She stepped down into the darkness, her hand finding the railing immediately. She used it to guide her all the way to the bottom of the stairs. As she reached the floor, the light above her cut out, and the door clicked shut. In seconds, she felt Calloway reach her side. They stood there wordlessly, shoulder to shoulder, for a long minute.

"Wine cellar?" Keira finally whispered, just to break the silence.

"Man cave," Calloway corrected, just as softly.

He moved away briefly, then there was a click, and a blue-and-yellow neon sign came to life in one corner.

Vaguely, Keira was aware that her surroundings were similar to those of Calloway's hidden cabin. Wood panel walls and rustic decor.

Mostly, though, all she was aware of was Calloway.

It had only been two hours—maybe three—since she'd seen him. It seemed like a lifetime. She had to feel him. Touch him. Breathe him in and hold him there.

She slipped her hands around his shoulders, molded her body to his and tipped her face up expectantly. Calloway didn't disappoint her. He pressed his palms into the small of her back, pulling her impossibly closer, and tilted down to push his lips into hers.

Calloway's mouth was perfect. *He* was perfect. Perfectly imperfect. Perfectly *hers*.

For the duration of the kiss, the world disappeared. No crazy past haunting them, no violent men hunting them.

The men. The brothers, she remembered, and pulled away reluctantly.

"Dave Stark and Drew—the man I thought I was running to—they're *his* sons," Keira said in a rush. "And Holly's brothers."

He cupped her cheek. "I know. Dave explained it."

"So you were right," Keira added, "About there being no coincidences."

"Sometimes I wish I was wrong," Calloway replied grimly.

He kissed her once more, then moved across the room toward a raised, blank space on the far wall.

"That's just panel drywall," he said. "I sealed up a window, and it's still there on the other side. It comes out in the side yard."

"You want to break through?" Keira asked. "You don't think they'll hear it upstairs?"

"It's probably our only chance."

Calloway had already snagged a hammer from the tool chest. He angled the claw under the drywall and pulled at the points where the nails had been hammered in. It was a nearly silent endeavor, and in just a few minutes, he'd freed a quarter of the drywall. When he paused to tap the edges, several pieces of the chalky material crumbled away.

"Not too bad," he stated, sounding pleased.

The second half was even easier. The loose bits on the side Calloway had already pried off seemed to have compromised the structural integrity of the one he was taking apart now. It only took a few moments for the whole thing to come down.

The windowpane was covered in grime, and the latch squealed in protest as Calloway forced it back.

Keira sent up a hurried prayer that it would open in spite of its worse-for-wear appearance, then watched anxiously as Calloway put both hands on the glass and pushed. It resisted for only a second before it flew to the side, sending in a waft of fresh air.

Keira inhaled deeply.

"I'll go first," Calloway told her. "Then I'll help you through."

He grabbed the edge of the dirty sill, his biceps flexing as he pulled himself up. He went out quickly, then jabbed his hands back through.

Keira let his warm hands close on her wrists and drag her up. For a relieved moment, they stood toe-to-toe in the window well. It was short-lived.

Henderson's deep, calm voice carried through the air. "And here I was, thinking you might actually get away."

Keira looked up. All three men stood staring down at them. Drew's eyes were full of muted fury. Dave's were almost apologetic. And Henry's...they were bright with anticipation.

"This is it, isn't it?" he asked, sounding nearly gleeful.

Calloway didn't answer, and Keira though that was a bad sign for them. And Henderson seemed to take it as encouragement, too.

"Should we go back into the house?" His question was far too pleasant.

Calloway clearly thought so, too. "Are you giving us a choice?"

"Not even a little bit," Henderson told them. "Back the way you came."

They all slipped through the window—first Drew, then Keira and Graham, then Dave and finally Henry Henderson.

ONCE THEY WERE in the basement, Graham stood protectively in front of Keira. His father-in-law took a slow look around the dim room.

"Amazing," said Henry. "My wife *built* this house and I had no idea this room was down here."

"Maybe there was a good reason for that," Graham retorted.

Henderson shot him one of his usual impassive stares. "Yes. I'm sure there was. She probably planned on using it as a place to hide her wine. She was rather fond of it. Just like Holly."

"You have no right to say her name," Graham growled. "You lost that right when you took her life."

Henry sighed. "It was never my intention to harm her physically. It wouldn't have happened if Drew had taken care of incapacitating her properly in the first place."

Drew spoke up. "How was I supposed to know she had such a high tolerance for prescription drugs?"

"So you're blaming the murder on him?"

Henry shrugged. "Partially. I pulled the trigger because she got in the way. All I wanted was the painting. It was rightfully mine. But my wife somehow deemed Holly a better choice."

How the other man could be so blasé about the murders of his own daughter and his own grandson—murders the man had just admitted to committing himself—was completely beyond Graham.

"Speaking of the painting…" Drew piped up again.

Without bothering to think about the consequences, Graham turned and swung a fist. He hit Drew straight in the face and the other man collapsed to the floor, his eyes rolled back in his head and blood dripped from his nose.

His father-in-law took a quick step toward the unconscious body, but Graham was faster. His hand shot out and caught Henry straight in the throat. He backed the older man to the far wall.

"Are you going to *do* something, Stark?" Henry asked.

The policeman shook his head. "I'd rather not."

Graham smiled coldly. "Do you know what that is behind me?"

He watched as the man's brown eyes—so like Holly's, so like Sam's—traveled up and went wide as they found the framed piece of art, sandwiched between a Budweiser ad and a Rolling Stones poster.

"That's it," Graham said. "The thirty-plus million-dollar painting you killed them for, you sick son of—"

"Just her," Henderson corrected.

Graham went still. "What the hell does that mean?"

"I didn't kill Sam," Henry stated casually.

"That's a lie," Graham replied in a hoarse whisper. "I saw the blood."

"There was blood," Henry agreed. "Lots of blood."

"Sam is dead."

"He's not. If you let me get my phone from my pocket, I'd be happy to show you."

Graham wanted to tell the other man where he could shove his phone, but a small part of him filled with hope. He tried to fight the burgeoning emotion. He failed.

"Show me."

He loosened his grip just enough that the other man could reach into his coat. He pulled out a smartphone, held it up and punched in a pass code. In moments, a picture flooded the small screen.

A little boy with perfect blond curls and oh-so-familiar brown eyes. He was bigger, and not really smiling in the carefree way Graham had always remembered him. But...

"That's impossible," Graham breathed.

He couldn't take his eyes from the photograph.

"You know it's him," Henry said.

It was. Graham was sure.

"How?" he asked.

"The kid took a through and through," the older man explained. "Holly's second bullet. Went through her abdomen and nicked Sam in a pretty big artery. And you were right about the blood. Way more than I thought one small person could lose. Drew and I bandaged him up pretty tight, took him to a retired doctor I knew. Saved the kid's life."

"Why would you hold that back all these years?" Graham asked.

"What good would it do to tell anyone he was alive?" Henry countered. "Besides which, it made the police search for you that much harder. And I thought the guilt— or the desire for revenge—might get to you eventually. Bring you home."

"Where is he?"

"Close."

"Take me to him," Graham said.

"Let me have the painting, and I will."

"Sam first. We can come back for the painting."

Henry sighed. "Fine."

"Get Drew's gun, Keira," Graham ordered.

She'd been silent, letting the scene unfold, and now she shot an uncertain glance toward Dave.

"He's not going to stop you," Graham assured her.

Dave nodded, and Keira moved. But Graham had misjudged the other man's alertness, and as Keira's hand almost closed on the weapon, Drew sat straight up, twisted and pulled the girl forcefully into his lap.

"Put him down, Calloway. Or I'll shoot the girl," Drew announced coldly.

"He'll shoot me anyway," Keira stated.

Graham's heart squeezed. He couldn't lose her. He couldn't lose Sam again.

"I have to take the chance that he won't," he said. "I love you too much."

"I love you, too," she whispered back.

Drew snarled, "Enough!"

Graham's arms fell to his sides, and Henry shoved past him, his hands already reaching for the painting. But as he moved, Graham's foot shot out. The older man stumbled, straight into Keira and Drew. The gun flew from Drew's grasp. It discharged loudly, and a *riiiiiip* echoed through the basement.

"No," Henry gasped.

Graham's eyes followed his gaze, straight up to the painting. To the brand-new bullet-sized hole that adorned its center.

And Graham smiled.

Epilogue

Five Weeks Later

"Do you think the smoke has finally cleared?" Keira asked, unsure if she was hoping for a yes or for a no.

Graham seemed to sense the flip-flop nature of her question.

"Maybe," he replied. "Maybe not. We can wait here awhile longer. Your work said to take the time you need, and I'm not in a hurry, either."

He uncurled himself from the brand-new, built-for-two rocking chair on the front porch of the old log cabin. He stretched, wide shoulders flexing in a way that made Keira's blood heat up in spite of the chilly air.

"Is he asleep yet?" she wondered out loud.

Graham smiled, that same silly, dopey, love-filled grin that he always grinned whenever Sam was concerned.

"I was just going to check," he told her.

Keira watched his back as he retreated into the cabin, admiring the view.

My Mountain Man, she thought affectionately.

He was almost always at ease now that his father-in-law was behind bars. His own name had been officially cleared, too. Dave was let off with a slap on the wrist. And Sam… He'd spent four years shuffled between nannies, with—thankfully—little direct contact with his grandfather and the man's underhanded activities. He was as serious a kid as Keira had ever met, but he smiled a little more every day. And twice this week, Keira had heard him drop the word *Daddy* when referring to Calloway.

No, she decided. *I'm not in a huge hurry to get out of here.*

GRAHAM PEELED BACK the curtain to the closet-turned-tiny-bedroom and gazed down lovingly at his kid. His living, breathing kid. He'd never get tired of staring at that perfect little face. He was so glad that Sam had been spared the darker parts of Graham's father-in-law's life.

Graham's heart swelled, gratitude and awe nearly overwhelming him as it did almost every time he took stock of his life.

Accused murderer. Redeemed father. Loving husband.

Well, soon-to-be husband, if the ring in his pocket worked like he thought it would.

"Calloway?"

Keira's soft voice made him turn.

She'd stepped into the cabin, dropped her jacket and stood in front of the blissfully small bed they shared every night in nothing but one of his T-shirts. His favorite outfit.

"Sam's okay?" she asked.

"Perfect," he replied.

Keira smiled. "Like always."

"Like you," Graham teased, happy when she blushed.

He walked to her, wrapped her in his arms and kissed her thoroughly, just to make the pink in her cheeks brighten even more.

"Hey," he murmured when he pulled away. "Can I ask you something?"

"Anything."

He dug his hand into his pocket, yanked out the little box and balanced it on his palm. "On a sliding scale…how happy are you that you drove into a snowstorm, got rescued by a mountain man and almost got killed by a corrupt politician?"

Keira's eyes lit up. "Ten out of ten!"

Graham grinned and kissed her again, secure that fate was well in hand.

* * * * *

MILLS & BOON®

INTRIGUE
Romantic Suspense

A SEDUCTIVE COMBINATION OF DANGER AND DESIRE

A sneak peek at next month's titles...

In stores from 14th January 2016:

- **Scene of the Crime: Who Killed Shelly Sinclair?** – Carla Cassidy *and* **Blue Ridge Ricochet** – Paula Graves
- **Bulletproof Badge** – Angi Morgan *and* **Fully Committed** – Janie Crouch
- **Colorado Wildfire** – Cassie Miles *and* **Suspect Witness** – Ryshia Kennie

Romantic Suspense

- **A Secret in Conard County** – Rachel Lee
- **Colton's Surprise Heir** – Addison Fox

Available at WHSmith, Tesco, Asda, Eason, Amazon and Apple

Just can't wait?
Buy our books online a month before they hit the shops!
visit **www.millsandboon.co.uk**

These books are also available in eBook format!

5_MB517

'The perfect Christmas read!' - Julia Williams

Jewellery designer Skylar loves living London, but
when a surprise proposal goes wrong, she finds
herself fleeing home to remote Puffin Island.

Burned by a terrible divorce, TV historian Alec is
dazzled by Sky's beauty and so cynical that he
assumes that's a bad thing! Luckily she's on the
verge of getting engaged to someone else, so she
won't be a constant source of temptation... but this
Christmas, can Alec and Sky realise that they are
what each other was looking for all along?

Order yours today at
www.millsandboon.co.uk

MILLS & BOON®

Man of the Year

Our winning cover star will be revealed next month!

**Don't miss out on your copy
– order from millsandboon.co.uk**

Read more about Man of the Year 2016 at

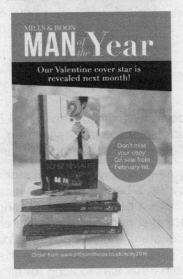

www.millsandboon.co.uk/moty2016

**Have you been following our
Man of the Year 2016 campaign?**
🐦 **#MOTY2016**